NO HAPPY

SHATTERED COLO

GUY HALLOWES

OMNE

National Library of Australia Cataloguing-in-Publication entry

Title: No happy valley: Shattered colonial dreams / Guy Hallowes.

ISBN: 9780994311658 (pbk.)

Series: Hallowes, Guy, 1941- author. Winds of change ; bk. 1.

Subjects: Life changing events--Fiction.
Man-woman relationships--Fiction.
Kenya--Fiction.
Kenya--History--Autonomy and independence movements--Fiction.

Dewey Number: A823.4

Cover design by Designerbility www.designerbility.com.au
Layout by OMNE www.omne.com.au

Published by OMNE www.omne.com.au

For
My Parents

Contents

Chapter 1

Kahinga Kinyore had been trained as a tractor driver but had left his last job to join Jomo Kenyatta and his Mau-Mau revolutionaries. He didn't know what he would be expected to do; he barely understood what the objectives of Kenyatta's organization were. What he did understand was that the white oppressors who had taken over his country would be chased out and he would clearly benefit from this event. He imagined himself in his last Bwana's house, drinking his beer and driving his motorcar. He might even inherit the man's wife or better still his daughter – or even better, both. He had been encouraged to return home, a village in the Fort Hall district of Kenya, by a "recruiter" who had been travelling round white-owned farms.

Apart from the immediate material benefits that would come with the demise of the white man, Kahinga had found it difficult to understand why the whites he had come across felt they were so superior to the local Africans; how they tended to trample unthinkingly on cherished African traditions, always assuming that anything the white man said or did was the 'right' way and making no attempt to understand the African point of view or even his language. Kahinga's native language was Kikuyu, but like most Africans he also spoke Swahili, a derivative of the language of the small coastal tribe of the same name, which was used throughout Kenya as a means of communication with the white community and between the various different tribes. It was a language of instruction and most people spoke it badly.

Kahinga could see that for himself and almost all his peers, unless things changed, life would consist of working for an M'zungu, a white man, on a farm where there was little or no prospect of advancement or obtaining an education and certainly no chance of actually owning a decent farm, since vast tracts of the best farmland had been reserved for white settlers, and the African reserves were already overcrowded.

At about five foot six Kahinga was average height for a member of his tribe; he had a sturdy build. His round open face and broad toothy smile were completed with a typically flat African nose and a pair of bright, brown, sparkling eyes. Kahinga was a natural leader: people tended to gravitate towards him and he had been selected as the leader of his age group at the tribal ceremonies for initiation into adulthood.

Although he could write his name Kahinga was virtually uneducated. He was intelligent and, like most of his tribe, hard working. His previous employer had selected him from the other labour on the farm and trained him to drive the tractors. He was a diligent worker and his employer had been sorry to lose him, and surprised too, since for obvious reasons he was unable to say precisely why he was leaving. Eventually his employer gave up trying to find out and dismissed the issue as being another incomprehensible African foible.

Kahinga was feeling uncomfortable. He had been sitting at home for six months waiting for the call. The call to what, he wasn't sure; he'd contacted the recruiter, who had told him to be patient.

So he waited. Then one day a toto, a small child, came. The child gave him a message to be at a village on the other side of Fort Hall at 6pm that night.

Kahinga found the village, which appeared to him like any other village in the area; there were almost twenty huts surrounded by a fence made of bushes piled one on top of the other. The cattle belonging to the people of the village were driven into this 'boma' at night. Traditionally this was done to protect them from wild animals, but the increase in the population since the advent of white settlement had driven most of the wild animals into the remoter regions; the main danger now was from two-legged predators.

Kahinga knocked on the door of the hut; the comfortably familiar smell of goats wafted through the doorway. As was customary the family's goats had just been driven into the hut for the night. Kahinga was re-directed by a suspicious looking woman.

He found the indicated hut. He rapped on the door – no answer. He rapped harder. It was dusk but he felt no concern.

Suddenly the door opened and he was grabbed by two people and dragged into the hut and flung on to the floor. His captors sat on him.

"Hey!" he cried, his voice muffled.

"Kahinga?" asked an old Kikuyu with a greying beard and a flywhisk in his right hand.

"Yes, Mzee (old man)." He was still lying face down with two people sitting on him.

"Let him go," instructed the old man.

Kahinga got up. The hut was circular, typical of the huts in Kikuyuland[1]. The walls were made of wattle poles daubed with mud for insulation, the floor was earth, beaten hard and treated with cow dung, the roof was thatched with grass and came to a point about 15 feet above the floor.

There were no windows and only one door. A small cooking fire had been built in the middle of the floor, and its smoke filled the upper part of the room. Only by squatting on their haunches could the occupants avoid the smoke, which eventually found its own way through the thatch. The advantage of the smoke was that all the insects that abounded in those parts were eliminated.

Kahinga's eyes slowly became accustomed to the gloom. Apart from the old man, Mzee, there were half a dozen or so others squatting on their haunches, all armed with an assortment of pangas[2] and knives. One man who appeared to be some sort of leader had a revolver stuck in his belt.

"Kahinga," said Mzee, speaking in his native Kikuyu, "you have been selected - he paused for effect. "You have been selected as a leader in our struggle against the Whites." Kahinga was of course aware of this. It was what he had been waiting six months for.

"Mzee, I humbly await your instructions."

Mzee made a brief gesture and an old, wizened man whom Kahinga had not noticed before came out of the dark recesses of the hut; he was clothed in monkey skins. Kahinga felt his gut tighten with fear. This was the witchdoctor. He was dragging a small kid goat with him.

"We need you to swear loyalty," growled Mzee.

Kahinga was too terrified to say anything. He was stripped naked and shoved towards the witchdoctor, who was now standing under an upright frame covered with creepers and some animal entrails, which had been brought into the centre of the hut.

Forced on to his knees, Kahinga felt a knife thrust into his hands and the kid goat was brought to him.

"Open the stomach," instructed the witchdoctor.

Kahinga was not in the least bit squeamish – he did as he was told and

1 Kikuyuland was the area reserved by the Government for the sole use of the Kikuyu and cousin tribes Embu and Meru.

2 Large bush knife about two feet long, normally very sharp

slit open the goat's stomach. The goat bleated wildly. The witchdoctor tore at the entrails and started to drag the warm, dripping innards all over Kahinga's head and shoulders.

"Cut the throat."

Again Kahinga did as he was told. The goat stopped its terrible bleating and the witchdoctor caught the animal's blood in the gourd he held.

Kahinga was manhandled towards the creeper-covered frame.

The witchdoctor shrieked, "Say after me!"

At this point Kahinga had almost gone into a trance; he was merely looking to survive the ordeal. He knew that one false move would result in instant death from two of the witchdoctor's assistants, who had been sitting round the hut earlier. Both had sharp pangas raised and they would need no second invitation to kill him. They were lusting for blood – any blood.

"If I am sent to bring in the head of an enemy or European and I fail to do so, may this oath kill me," chanted the witchdoctor.

"If I am sent to bring in the head of an enemy or European and I fail to do so, may this oath kill me," responded Kahinga.

He was then pushed through the frame and the witchdoctor made a fairly deep cut about one inch long on the flesh of his right upper arm. The gourd was shoved up to his face and he was made to drink some of the goat's still warm blood.

"If I fail to steal anything from a European, may this oath kill me."

"If I fail to steal anything from a European, may this oath kill me," repeated Kahinga.

Another cut on his arm, another drink of blood.

"If I fail to destroy the white man's farm and burn his house, may this oath kill me."

And so it went on, Kahinga repeating the witchdoctor's words hypnotically.

Another cut, another drink.

"If I know of any enemy to our organisation and fail to report it to my leader, may this oath kill me..."

"If I am ever sent by my leader to do something big for the House of Kikuyu, and I refuse, may this oath kill me..."

"If I refuse to help in driving the Europeans from this country, may this oath kill me..."

"If I worship any leader but Jomo Kenyatta, may this oath kill me..."

Then came the final cut and Kahinga finished the blood.

These were the seven deadly promises of the Mau-Mau oathing ceremony. Kahinga now had seven cuts on his upper right arm, bleeding profusely. The witchdoctor grabbed a handful of hot ash from the fire and rubbed it into the wounds, ensuring that there would be seven livid scars, which he would carry for the rest of his life – the insignia of the Mau-Mau. Like all Kikuyu, Kahinga was aware of the sacred nature of the number seven. The fact that he had made seven promises added greatly to the binding nature of the oath.

The oathing ceremony was now over. Kahinga started to remove the entrails that still adorned his head and shoulders. The witchdoctor grabbed them and draped them over the frame after removing one or two choice pieces for consumption. Kahinga was given his clothes back, which he hastily put on. He noticed that the others in the hut were smoking – from the sweetish smell he identified it as "bhang" (a local and very potent form of dagga or marijuana). He was offered a smoke, which he accepted. Although he felt the danger to himself was past, he had been badly frightened by the savagery of the ceremony.

One of the women had been called from outside and she was busy cooking the goat, which had already been skinned. Someone produced some traditionally brewed beer.

"Kahinga, you will go to Ol'Kalou."

"Yes, Mzee," he replied very shakily. He knew where that was. He had worked at Thomsons Falls, which was only about 30 miles away.

"You will find one Dibu," said Mzee, "who works on a farm there."

"Eh heh," Kahinga acknowledged casually. The bhang and the beer were beginning to have some effect. Someone had produced some ogalie (maize meal or posho cooked into a cake) and he was given some of the goat's meat, which had been half cooked on the fire.

"First we will find someone to go with you," stated Mzee. He nodded to the man with the revolver, and the woman was sent outside. A feeling of anticipation crept into the atmosphere of the hut.

Suddenly another man was dragged inside in much the same way as Kahinga had been. He was flung onto the floor and his two assailants sat on him. The witchdoctor, with his grisly, creeper-covered frame, had stepped back into the darkness of the hut, and the only bright light was from the fire.

The man was released, and Kahinga's eyes nearly popped out. It was his mother's sister's son, Njeroge. They had been brought up in the same village and were from the same age group. Kahinga was about to say something, but this had been anticipated and a restraining hand was placed on his arm. He kept silent.

The ceremony was started again. Kahinga felt apprehensive; Njeroge had always been a little squeamish and had not acquitted himself well at the initiation ceremonies that every Kikuyu boy went through at the age of fourteen. Njeroge had been the one who had cried when the witchdoctor cut his foreskin off.

"Open the stomach," growled the witchdoctor.

Njeroge hesitated, and then in his panic made a dash for the door. He managed to get about a yard. The savagery unleashed on him made Kahinga cringe in fright. The two assistants had no hesitation. High on bhang, they hacked Njeroge to pieces and most of the others round the hut joined in. The butchering went on long after poor Njeroge was dead and only stopped after an instruction from Mzee.

"Clear it up," ordered the old man.

The witchdoctor appeared with a sack and what was left of Njeroge was unceremoniously bundled into it. Someone made a half-hearted effort to clean up the blood on the floor.

Kahinga was now absolutely terrified. What was this? Who were these people? He knew of nothing in Kikuyu tradition that meted out this type of savage punishment. Getting rid of the white man was one thing, murdering fellow tribesmen - and his own relation at that - was another thing altogether. He began to regret bitterly his participation. However, he was committed – he had taken the oath. Right now he just had to survive.

While this occupied his thoughts another hapless victim had been brought in and was in the process of going through the ceremony, which was completed without too much incident.

The new recruit, Kinua, was given his clothes and sat next to Kahinga. Kahinga handed him the remaining half of the bhang cigarette he had been smoking and the gourd of beer. Kinua was shivering, Kahinga thought in absolute terror at what he had just experienced.

Through the haze of bhang and beer, Kahinga was aware that Mzee was talking.

"You will go to Ol' Kalou," the old man repeated.

"Yes, Mzee."

"Kinua will go with you and help you. You will meet up with one Dibu as instructed."

"Yes, Mzee."

"You will recruit more members, who must all be Kikuyu. Dibu has been instructed in the methods of recruitment and of swearing allegiance."

"Yes, Mzee."

"Any questions?"

"Where do we get money to travel?" Ol' Kalou was about 150 miles from Fort Hall.

Mzee laughed, as did all the people in the hut.

"The white man has in his wisdom provided trains – use them."

Kahinga knew what he meant. The trains travelled fairly slowly and it was possible, although risky, to jump on one outside a station and get off before the next. The main risk was the inspectors. They might have to jump off a train while it was moving at top speed between stations.

"Weapons?" said Kahinga.

Again they all laughed.

"The white man is careless with his goods," cackled Mzee. "He has too much to look after. You can take pangas, knives and even guns from him.

"Any other questions?" he asked.

"No, Mzee."

"Kinua will go with you; you will be contacted; you can go now," said Mzee, and waved them away.

Kahinga and Kinua got up and hesitantly made their own way out of the hut. Nobody else stirred. By this time, with all the excitements of the evening, it was after midnight as far as they could judge.

Kahinga knew that from then on his life would be transformed. He had made a choice; he had decided to fight the oppressor. He also knew, from the depths of his being, that what he had chosen to do might cost him his life. He expected to have to kill Europeans; he now understood that he would also have to kill his own tribesmen, even his own relations such as Njeroge. Despite his heavy greatcoat, he shivered in the misty night air as he and Kinua made their way back home.

※ ※ ※

Chapter 2

Peter Lawrence drove his extremely battered International one ton truck up the steep, dusty five mile track from the village of Ol' Kalou with mounting excitement.

He had never seen better farming country in Africa; the red oat grass was tall, the few cattle that were visible were sleek and fat and the country was well watered. He stopped the truck and got out.

From his vantage point the land fell away steeply and Peter could just make out the shape of the village below. The country then flattened out into a fertile, well watered plain. Lake Ol'Bolossat and the Wanjohe valley were visible in the distance and then the Aberdare mountains (Nyandarua in Kikuyu), the eastern boundary of the Great Rift Valley, rose steeply from the floor of the valley to about 13 000 feet. The plain had few trees and Peter could make out the dusty ribbon of road winding its way unobtrusively to the Wanjohe and the base of the Aberdares. The view was breathtaking. There was absolute peace; a few wisps of cloud floated above the mountains and beyond he could make out the majestic, snow-capped peak of Mount Kenya (Kirinyaga, the home of Ngai the Kikuyu God) towering above 17 000 feet. He felt as if he could almost reach out and touch it.

Peter was a big man, about 6'3" tall; he was well built and weighed just less than 200lbs. He had played provincial rugby in his native South Africa and was quite unsentimental and tough. The beauty of the view, however, almost brought a tear to his eye.

The steep slopes of the Aberdares were covered by unspoilt indigenous bush with a few animal tracks going through. The mountains teemed with wildlife: some elephant, leopard and plenty of forest dwelling antelope. An ideal refuge for the hunted.

Through the binoculars he scanned the flat plains below the mountain range. The land was all but empty, undeveloped, most of it nominally owned by someone but unused.

"Man, this is God's own country," he thought. He picked up a handful of soil near the road – fertile – much more fertile than the land of his birth, South Africa. "This looks as if it could grow anything," he mused.

He returned to the truck and tried the starter. Nothing doing. He always tried the starter first even though it seldom worked. That was why he'd parked the vehicle facing downhill.

Having got going again on the gears he continued on his journey. His brother Bill had bought a farm in the district a few months back in 1945 and the neighbouring place was now up for sale; they were thinking of running a partnership, pooling their very limited resources.

He loved this land – he would sign the papers today. There was 500 pounds in the bank and the Landbank would let him have the rest. Still, he'd better have a real look at the farm first. He'd also better enlist the support of his wife Jenny, since she'd have to help manage the farm.

There was one nagging doubt in the back of his mind. Since the war, the African population had appeared to be restless. Who was this bloke Kenyatta? What was all the talk?

Peter was an outstanding linguist, and apart from Swahili, the ungrammatical lingua franca of the region, he could speak and clearly understand Kikuyu. He had overheard some of the labour on the farm he was managing near Nairobi talking about Kenyatta. The word 'Uhuru', freedom, had been mentioned.

He had not discussed this with anyone else and now he tried to put the thought away. The British Government – the all-powerful British Government – was encouraging development of the region. He had heard that hundreds of soldiers were to be settled on vast tracts of crown land on the other side of the Rift Valley. The war had been won and there was a general mood of optimism about.

Peter had grown up on a mission station in Zululand, South Africa. Apart from his own family, his childhood companions had been the local Zulu children. His first language was Zulu, learned on the knee of his Zulu nanny. He had never really understood why the white people in Africa felt so superior to the local Africans. In his experience growing up, whilst he had held his own in the group that consisted of himself and twenty Zulu children, many of the group could outrun him and outjump him and he had, along with most of his companions, suffered some quite bad cuts to the head and shoulders when he took part in the stick fights indulged in by Zulu teenagers.

When he was sent away to a boarding school for white boys only, Peter had grown away from his boyhood companions. He had excelled at rugby, captaining his school team and later representing Natal, and had made friends among the all-white rugby fraternity.

He was in his early twenties when English relatives who had settled in Kenya suggested that he join them. He immediately fell in love with the country, and had no trouble finding work.

Before the war he managed a farm near Nairobi and the Kikuyu reserve and, since all of the labour on the farm were Kikuyu, quickly learnt the language. He knew that the Kikuyu, and indeed several of the Kenyan tribes had the same Bantu ethnic roots as the Zulu in South Africa and that some of the words, such as the word for water, and most of the grammatical construction in the myriad of Bantu languages down the centre part of Africa had similarities. The ethnic Bantu had formed a centuries old pattern of migration from the Middle East down through the heartland and the east coast of Africa and in some African countries formed the bulk of the black population.

The Second World War and Peter's service in the army created the opportunity for some formal lessons in the Kikuyu language. Although he was forced to speak Swahili some of the time, he found it an unsatisfactory experience because of the poor use of grammar in up-country Kenya and the limited vocabulary. Swahili was a language of master/servant communication and in Peter's view created barriers in human relations; he felt his knowledge of Kikuyu gave him insights into the community he lived in and the culture it represented.

Peter always prided himself that he understood the African as far as that was possible for a white man. His personal relationships were generally very good, based on mutual trust.

Now, as he looked out across the valley, Peter tried to put negative thoughts out of his mind. Why look for trouble? This was his opportunity to be completely independent; free from stupid employers who wouldn't let him do what he knew was right. He was young, he was a good farmer, and if the farm was suitable he'd buy it. Nevertheless, the doubt remained.

When he reached the farm, it was better than he expected. There were two major streams running through it and shallow gullies that were filled in the rainy season. There was little development – few fences, virtually no roads and some small, rather unkempt patches of pyrethrum. Peter was pleased to see that the small daisy like pyrethrum flower grew in the district. The flowers were picked, dried, and sold to manufacturers of insecticides who extracted pyrethrin from the flowers for their products. Although Peter's main interest was stock farming, regular income from a cash crop like pyrethrum would provide essential funds for the development of the farm. A few cows of dubious ancestry, reputed to be Ayrshires, wandered about, cared for by a ten-year-old boy. The land was steep; however, if contoured properly, it could be made arable, mainly for pastures.

There were also large areas of indigenous bush containing some small buck – bushbuck, duiker and other species – and several colonies of Colobus monkeys as well as dozens of bird species. Apart from the indigenous bush there were few trees.

The day was spent tramping over the farm. The climate was temperate, as it was over 8500 feet above sea level. On several occasions he disturbed a steinbuck and once a family of reedbuck. He whistled through his teeth and they stopped and looked at him. He carried no gun and would not have wanted to shoot one of them anyway. The reedbuck were on a fairly large swamp or vlei that also had a few geese and duck feeding on some of the wild grasses there. He would have to drain that swamp.

The commitment was building. It was what he wanted. He hadn't seen the house; Jenny would have to look at that.

The night was spent with a neighbour, Bob Halway, who owned the farm that Peter was about to buy as well as the farm on which he himself lived. Halway lived alone and was a cantankerous old man of about 55. As Peter was shortly to find out, he ruled his large labour force by fear and thorough bad temper, although he was always good to the Lawrences.

Peter arrived at about five in the afternoon, when Halway was weighing pyrethrum. He was a big man with a red face, an enormous stomach and wispy grey hair. A rhino hide whip, or sjambok, hung from his right wrist.

The labour were lining up with their sacks of pyrethrum, for which they were paid 50 cents for 10lbs.

This meant they were able to earn one or two shillings per day if they worked hard.

"Good afternoon, have a good day?" grunted Halway when he saw Peter.

"Wanjiru 20 pounds." The headman shouted the name of one of the pickers and the weight of pyrethrum she had picked that day. This was recorded by Halway in a book.

"Yes, fine thanks," answered Peter.

"Gichuru kidogo (small), 30 pounds." The headman called another name and weight.

All the labour for this type of work were women and children, the families of the men working on the farm, and almost all of them were Kikuyu.

Halway started to write down "30 pounds". Then he realised there was something wrong. Gichuru kidogo was only ten or eleven; Halway doubted if he could carry that weight. Moving very quickly for a man of his size, he tried to grab the boy, who slipped away and started running.

"Empty that sack!" shouted Halway. Sure enough, two large stones were in the bottom of the bag. Halway was beside himself with fury and started lashing out with his sjambok left and right. Fortunately the labour seemed to know his temper and he only managed to hit one or two; the rest scattered. Order was restored within about 20 minutes and the weighing was quickly completed with a very subdued group of labourers.

"Headman!"

"Ndio, Bwana."

"No rations for that family for a month," yelled Halway.

"Ndio, Bwana."

"Got to teach these bastards a lesson," said Halway, mainly to Peter.

Peter was appalled at the severity of the sentence. The family would not starve since they would get food from other labour and also from the small plot they were allowed to cultivate on the farm, but it would cause real hardship. Still, he could not interfere.

They went into the house.

"Drink?"

"Beer, please," said Peter.

Halway shouted instructions to the houseboy. "Well, what do you think?" asked Halway, referring to the farm.

"I must bring my wife up to look but I think we'll take it."

"Wise decision," said Halway. "I have a few other people interested but I'll keep it for you for a couple of weeks."

Peter knew this was merely an attempt to put pressure on him and it angered him somewhat. Halway had the reputation of being a hard businessman and he had made a considerable amount of money from buying and selling farms. He was well respected if not particularly well liked throughout the district.

Halway lived in some luxury by local standards and a sumptuous dinner was soon laid on, with two houseboys in attendance, dressed in long white kanzus as was the custom. There was a cook in the kitchen and two children, 'kitchen totos', to do the washing up. Peter was aware that Halway dined like this every night, mostly alone. All his kitchen staff were Kikuyu.

Peter went to bed after Halway had finished half a bottle of whisky and gone to sleep in his chair – the house servants would put him to bed.

During dinner, Peter had pumped Halway for details of the history of the district. The first settlers had arrived by ox-wagon around 1919 and had been given large tracts of land by the Government for a few shillings an acre. The settler community was mixed; there was obviously a large English community, a significant Afrikaans (South African Dutch) community, some German Jewish refugees from the holocaust in Europe, plus a smattering of others – Danes, Czechs and French. Peter would make a point of visiting some of the Afrikaners since he spoke their home language fluently, and he already knew one or two of the English families.

Peter bought the farm the following week, after Jenny had been to look at the house with him. It was a very small house, with a corrugated iron roof. There was one main room, with two small bedrooms on each side of it. A third door led to a back passage, which in turn led on one side into a room that was used for a kitchen and on the other to a bathroom. They had to walk through the bathroom to find the pantry.

The front of the house looked down on the Oleolondo River, about 500 yards away. The river only flowed during the rainy season and for most of the year consisted of a series of still, rush-filled pools. To the left of the house, about 100 yards away, stood the pyrethrum dryer, pyrethrum being one of the major crops of the farm. The pyrethrum dryer was built up against a cliff face. Further away a small stream flowed over the cliff, creating a beautiful waterfall which fell about fifteen metres into an area of impenetrable bush with some very tall, old cedar and other indigenous trees.

At the back of the house, up a short flight of steps cut into the natural granite that abounded throughout the area, was a shed with a shingle roof and an earthen floor. Instead of cement, mud had been used as mortar, as was usual in Kenya at the time, due to shortages caused by the war. The floor was earthen and had a natural channel, which acted as a drain. There was no door, only a doorway and two small windows.

The house was occupied by several Italian prisoners of war. Now that the war was over, they were about to go home. They were quite friendly. There was no cultivated garden, although the Italians grew some vegetables round the side of the house. Overall, the place had a seedy appearance. The rusty wrecks of several old tractors the Italians had cannibalised for parts were littered about the yard.

"It'll do," was Jenny's verdict on the house, "but it needs quite a bit of fixing up. When do the Italians leave?"

"Within a few months, according to Halway," said Peter.

Peter thought he had found what he was looking for. Both he and Jenny could see that with a great deal of hard work they could create their dream of personal freedom and independence and a future for their children. He put his worries about the political situation to the back of his mind. He was after all of Africa; it was all he knew despite his white skin. He'd deal with the black Africans in his own way as he always had.

CHAPTER 3

Kahinga and Kinua were very shaken by the experience of the oathing ceremony.

They made their way unsteadily back to Kahinga's village. Although they did not have much to do they had to wait there until they had been told the exact whereabouts of their contact, Dibu. With any luck they would be able to find work with the same employer.

Word came a couple of months later. Dibu had found work as the cook, 'mpishi', with one M'zungu called Lawrence. As far as they knew he was quite new to the district of Ol'Kalou.

Kahinga was impatient to start this new life. He had been hanging around in the Fort Hall district for too long. He hated being completely without money; he had paid the last of his funds as 'dues' to the recruiter who had arranged for him to be at the oathing ceremony, and his father kept asking him awkward questions which he could not answer. There was no way Kahinga could tell him that he had joined the Mau-Mau; instinctively he knew his father would want him to have nothing to do with the secret organisation.

They set off just as the dawn was breaking, having said farewell to their families. Kahinga took all his belongings with him. These consisted of the clothes he stood up in, an army greatcoat, a Kings African Rifles – KAR – hat and one decent pair of shoes, which he wore only on special occasions. He normally wore his car tyre sandals, made from cut up strips of rubber tyre. Kinua was similarly attired.

"We will go to Fort Hall station," said Kahinga, and they set off on foot. The station was some distance away and it took them until mid-morning to get there.

"I will find out what time the train is," said Kahinga.

"Stay here."

Kahinga went into the station, where a few people were wandering about. Eventually he found the Indian stationmaster.

"What time is the train to Nairobi?" he asked.

"What do you want to know for?" the Indian shouted at him in a very unpleasant manner. "You have no money. I suppose you are one of these train jumpers."

He hesitated, and then asked again.

"The train comes when the train comes, now get off my station." The Indian started to manhandle Kahinga.

Kahinga was furious by now and punched him in his ample paunch – then he ran. He could hear the Indian yelling, "Arrest the bloody man, I will have him arrested!" He found Kinua and together they raced a few hundred metres down the track in the direction of Nairobi and hid in a bush to wait for the train. Finally the pandemonium at the station died down. It was really too much effort to look for one troublemaker and the only thing that had been hurt was the stationmaster's dignity.

When the sun was high in the heavens the two men heard the noise of the train in the station, and after what seemed like an eternity, it eventually pulled out of the station and came up the track towards them, fairly slowly since it was uphill.

A couple of first and second class carriages went by with supercilious white and Indian people peering out of the windows. Kahinga was looking for third class, where the majority of the people travelled. He hopped on to the steps of a third class carriage as it passed, with Kinua close behind him. They opened the carriage door and squeezed inside amid the curious looks of the other passengers. The train was fairly full but somehow they found a seat and sat down on the hard, wooden benches.

The train lurched on and Kahinga went to sleep. He was woken with a start. Kinua was pulling at his arm. "Inspector," he whispered. The Indian inspector was at the other end of the carriage but slowly making his way in their direction. They both got up and moved as unobtrusively as possible down the aisle and into the next carriage where they found another seat.

Kahinga was certain that the inspector had seen them. There was only one more carriage and then the guard's van at the back of the train. He hoped that they reached Nairobi station before the inspector reached them. They would have to go into the station and chance their arm from there. In the smaller places they could probably get off before the station and escape detection that way, but that wasn't possible in the approaches to Nairobi.

The train stopped at various stations and in the ensuing chaos they headed toward the very last carriage. As they made their way to the back, a middle-aged Kikuyu woman looked at them intently and gave Kahinga a brief conspiratorial smile. She had a huge bundle with her and a baby on her back.

The inspector had now come into the last carriage and Kahinga and Kinua had positioned themselves at the very end. The man gave them a troubled look. He wanted no fuss. He was at the end of his shift and all he wanted was to get home to his wife and family. In any event, the train was now only a few minutes away from Nairobi station.

The middle-aged woman was now asked for her ticket. She smiled at him and then opened the bundle and made a huge play of looking for it, which in the end she produced from the depths of her ample bosom. By this time the train was slowly pulling into the station and both Kahinga and Kinua were on the steps of the carriage, with the door open. As the train slowed down they both jumped on to the platform and ran for the exit. Kahinga knew this was the time for bold action, and before the ticket collector at the gate knew what was happening, Kahinga had run straight into him, knocking him flying. He and Kinua then ran out into the street and mingled with the crowd. They heard a lot of whistle blowing at the station – to no effect.

Feeling exhilarated by their first successful adventure, they were anxious to try to catch another train going north, so they started walking out of Nairobi towards Dagoretti. It was late in the afternoon by this time and they had had nothing to eat or drink all day.

Kinua solved the problem by lifting a large parcel of groceries from an unlocked car outside an Indian shop. He was so quick that no one took any notice. The two men disappeared into some trees nearby to see what they had. Bread, butter, peanut butter, cornflakes, sardines, vegetables – no meat. They ate the bread and butter and were still hungry. With a great deal of effort the sardine can was opened.

"Ugh, Nyoka – snake!" gasped Kinua. "These Wazungu – the things they eat." He tossed the can away. They opened the cornflakes and tasted them.

"No taste," said Kahinga.

They opened the peanut butter and used the cornflakes and their fingers to scrape it out of the jar.

"No wonder the Wazungu have small pricks," muttered Kinua. "Eating stuff like this – ugh."

Nevertheless they polished off both the peanut butter and cornflakes. There were various other useless items like flour and baking powder which were tasted and rejected. They finished their meal and slept for a couple of hours, and then Kahinga woke up.

"We must catch the train before dawn," he said, shaking Kinua. "I know the place."

They walked and came to a sign: "Duke of York School for European Boys". Unable to read it, they continued up the driveway.

"Here," said Kahinga.

They clambered up an embankment and walked back into a cutting. Trains would travel very slowly past here because of the gradient. They sat down and waited. Soon enough they heard the chugging sound of the big Garrett engines and then saw the beam of light. The train moved very slowly and every few metres the engine made a desperate chu-chu-chu-chu sound as the wheels slipped on the rails. They clambered into a third class carriage. The other passengers took little notice of them since they were all asleep or half asleep. The train wound its tortuous way on.

The train was slow and Kahinga and Kinua managed some fitful sleep. Kahinga woke as the dawn light crept into the east. The train was just starting its winding descent down the escarpment into the Great Rift Valley. Looking out of the window on the way down the escarpment from Kijabe, he couldn't help noticing that the Kikuyu reserve here was even more overcrowded than in the Fort Hall area where his home was. He could see that the quality of the stock in the reserve contrasted sharply with that on the white owned farms. Here some of the cattle were not much larger than goats. Kahinga blamed this entirely on the frantic overcrowding in the Kikuyu reserve and he blamed the overcrowding on the Government. During his six month sojourn at his father's house waiting for the call to join the Mau-Mau he had witnessed and been subjected to some of the pressures that the people in the Kikuyu reserve had to deal with. Because of the overcrowding and overgrazing, soil erosion, mainly from washaways during heavy rainstorms, was degrading the land. The Government response to this was to try to force the population through appointed headmen to construct terraces across the land to prevent the washaways; all the labour for the terracing exercise came 'voluntarily' from the community and were mainly women, so Kahinga had seen his mother and sisters going off day after day to construct terraces all over the district for no pay; the headman was paid a bonus for the monthly yardage of terraces constructed in his area. Whilst Kahinga could see for himself that in the areas where terraces had been constructed the erosion had stopped, the forced labour for the construction caused deep resentment in the community. Also, because some of the plots were quite small, the effect of building a terrace across such a plot was to reduce its usage and value. This caused many inter-family squabbles.

Another problem had arisen because of the Kikuyu system of land tenure where fathers split up all the land they owned between all of their sons, with the result that many people owned several small pieces of land, often some distance apart. The Government had decided to enforce a land consolidation programme on the Kikuyu. Kahinga could see the sense of owning one piece of land instead of four or five; the problem was that the headmen gave the choice pieces of land to their own favourites and cronies and those out of favour ended up with rocky outcrops. Kahinga had himself spent a few nights moving Government survey pegs to try to redress some of the perceived injustices of the programme.

Kahinga also resented the way the Government had tried to interfere with local cattle breeding, persuading people like his father to sell cattle to the Meat Commission and reduce the number of head owned by each family. This really angered Kahinga: didn't they understand that the number of cattle a family owned determined the family's standing and status in the community? Who in his right mind under these circumstances would sell cattle? The crazy Government also introduced new breeds of cattle from Ulaya, England or overseas, which died unless they were given expensive injections and taken to the Government constructed dipping facility every week.

As the train slowly puffed and rattled its way down into the valley Kahinga's resentment grew. He woke Kinua and pointed to the well-ordered, white owned farms with plenty of space, sleek, contented looking cattle and pretty homesteads.

"Look," he said to Kinua, "these Wazungu have many acres for each family; of course their cattle are fat and there is plenty of grazing. We can't own any of this," he added. "It's all reserved for Wazungu."

Kinua, half asleep, looked bemused.

They looked out of the window of the train as it passed close by Mount Longonot. They saw several large herds of Thomsons Gazelle and a herd of Zebra; there were also some Giraffe in the distance.

During his stay at home with his father, there had been an attempt to conduct a census. The political activists, whether they understood the reason for the census or not, had told the population at large that this was another attempt to collect a poll-tax, which was a tax on each head of population. As far as Kahinga was concerned, the poll tax meant that the people had to go to the cities and the farms in order to earn enough money to pay the tax. Kahinga's father had also complained bitterly that with all the young people leaving their traditional homes, many of the normal tribal rituals were either being abused or ignored and he was concerned that the values within the tribe were being eroded. Kahinga himself was not particularly concerned about the tribal issues and he had enjoyed the money he had earned working on the white owned farms. Nevertheless he gleefully participated in persuading whole families together with their flocks and herds to disappear into the forest for a few days while the census was conducted by telling people that the Sirkali, government officials, were coming to collect poll tax. He hoped that whatever the Government were trying to do was completely wrecked as a result of his and others' actions.

The train had stopped at Limuru and Kijabe, where a few people got on and off. Kahinga and Kinua dozed through Naivasha, and a few miles before Gil-gil, Kahinga whispered to Kinua, "We must get off before the station."

They got up quietly and moved to one of the doors amid some curious glances from the other passengers. The train slowed down a mile or so before the station. They opened the door and jumped down an embankment. No one particularly noticed. They suffered a few scratches and bruises, but little the worse for wear, walked away from the track and crawled through a barbed wire fence. This was European owned farmland. They would try to find some fellow Kikuyu farm workers and avoid the owners.

As they ambled along a farm road in a fairly relaxed way they weren't really keeping a lookout for anything in particular when around the corner came a galloping horse with a red-faced white man in the saddle. He stopped the horse with some difficulty.

"Jambo," he said in an aggressive tone.

"Jambo sana bwana," Kahinga and Kinua chorused deferentially.

"Where are you going?" he said, still in Swahili.

"Ol' Kalou," replied Kahinga.

"This is not a public road," shouted the man, who was clearly the owner of the farm.

Kahinga and Kinua did not respond.

"Go back and go round the main road."

They turned around and proceeded to walk back the way they had come.

"And don't go and hide in a bush," yelled the man as he galloped off.

As soon as he was out of sight Kahinga and Kinua turned around again and continued on their way.

"Arsehole," muttered Kinua.

The farmer had achieved nothing except to further alienate the two men. They were much more alert now and leapt into the leleshwa – a local type of scrub bush – once when they heard the man returning on his horse. Towards evening they made their way to a small collection of huts, which they had seen earlier. They approached cautiously, hoping the people would be Kikuyu. If they were, it virtually guaranteed a meal and somewhere to sleep; if not, they would have to look elsewhere. As usual, several very thin, mangy dogs came rushing out at them, barking as they approached. Kinua aimed a kick at one of them. A tall man with longish plaited hair, a red blanket knotted over one shoulder and a pair of leather thong sandals on his feet emerged from a nearby hut to investigate the racket. He carried a spear.

"Shit!" hissed Kahinga. "Masai!"

The Masai saw them and asked them what they wanted. Kahinga politely enquired whether there were any Kikuyu in the vicinity. The Masai spat contemptuously and pointed vaguely north, pursing his lips and pointing his spear.

"How far?" asked Kahinga.

"Hapana mbale, not very far," was the surly reply. That could mean any distance from one to 20 miles.

They made off under the watchful eye of the Masai.

Half an hour later they saw some fires in the dark and came across what did turn out to be a small Kikuyu village. Both the Masai and the Kikuyu worked for the man on the horse. To avoid trouble they were always accommodated separately.

Once the two men had identified themselves they were made welcome and were given a huge meal of ogalie (maize meal cake), vegetables and mealies (corn on the cob). There was no meat. The white farmer only issued meat as a ration once a month and he wouldn't allow the labour to keep goats, although they were allowed five cattle per family.

The food was washed down with generous quantities of traditionally brewed beer made from crushed maize and sugar. Kahinga resented the fact that 'European' type liquor was forbidden to be sold or served to Africans; he personally preferred the traditional beer since in his experience the much stronger 'European' type liquor made people drunk and violent whereas the African beer had a lower alcohol content and therefore merely relaxed people and fuelled conversation. He would, however, have preferred to be allowed to make his own choice without Government interference. From his working experience on other farms he knew that the people in the village were supposed to have written permission from the farmer to brew and consume beer. As far as most people were concerned, to ask permission to do something that they had been doing for hundreds of years was ridiculous. Anyway, beer permits were normally only given out at weekends and everyone knew it took three or four days to brew the stuff. Most farmers had a good working relationship with the police, who warned the farmer if there was to be a liquor 'raid' or inspection. The farmer then in turn warned his labour and issued the appropriate permits. Kahinga knew that it wasn't worth working for an M'zungu who was at odds with the police, it was just too socially disruptive. His previous employer had also explained that from his point of view, he did not want half his labour force arrested on illicit liquor charges since he generally had to pay the bail and the fines as well in order to get them to return to work.

Very little was said during the meal, apart from a few belches of satisfaction. The women disappeared after serving the food; they had no business listening to men's talk. Mysteriously all the other members of the clan disappeared as well and Kahinga and Kinua were left with Zacharia[3], the headman on the farm and the acknowledged head of a clan of squatters living on the land. The farmer's name turned out to be Gibb.

Kahinga had determined quite quickly that Zacharia had the status of a squatter and that he and his clan had the right to till a certain amount of land on Gibb's farm as well as keeping some livestock. In turn the clan was expected to provide labour for the farm for nine to ten months of the year. The labour included all the able bodied men and when required the women and children as well for tasks such as picking pyrethrum. The labour was paid in the form of some cash plus rations for the time they worked; the accommodation, such as it was, was also provided by Gibb the farmer. Kahinga knew that the months that the labour did not work were unpaid and during that period the menfolk were expected to tend the crops and look after the cattle. If his experience was anything to go by, the women

3 Most Kenya tribes used biblical names as well as traditional names

looked after the land, the children looked after the stock and the men's unpaid leave generally became one long beer drink.

During the meal Kahinga had an opportunity to size up his host. He saw a short middle aged man with a few flecks of grey in his hair and his wispy beard. A pair of shrewd, bright eyes peeped out from underneath his KAR hat, which he rarely took off. An old pair of baggy khaki pants, a khaki shirt and a pair of car-tyre sandals made up his outfit. Zacharia talked about himself and his clan in a tone of pride and accomplishment; the clan gave off on air of modest wealth and contentment.

Zacharia was indeed content with his lot. He had more wives (three) and cattle than he could have expected had he stayed in the reserve and the clan brought in substantial amounts of cash – far more than they needed – both from selling labour and from selling produce. He and Gibb, the white farmer, had a modus operandi which Zacharia respected. He had no desire to emulate the worst of the white stupidities; for instance, he could not comprehend an apparently wealthy man like Gibb only having one wife. Gibb explained this particular stupidity by saying he was a Christian. Zacharia was also a Christian. However, he had married his three wives before he became one and was thus allowed to keep them. Even the Christians could not allow two wives and several children to be abandoned as a result of a man's conversion to the faith.

Soon Zacharia would have enough money to buy an old motorcar that he'd had his eye on for some time. The white man had showed him how to put the money into the bank and, stupidity of stupidities; they even paid him to keep it there.

The headman did not like the look of his two visitors and he made up his mind to find out what they were about. That was why he had got rid of the rest of the clan. He plied them with more beer.

Kinua described the incident earlier in the afternoon with the man on the horse – Gibb – and from his remarks Zacharia determined that his visitors were more than usually anti-white, so shrewdly he led the conversation in that direction. After a further hour or so and copious quantities of beer Zacharia more or less had the whole story.

"So who is this man Dibu?" he asked.

"He works for the Wazungu Lawrence," said Kahinga.

"There is an Indian trader, S.Shah, in Ol' Kalou who will show you where to go," said Zacharia. Kahinga made a mental note.

"I can arrange a lift for you in the milk truck to Ol' Kalou," offered

Zacharia, "tomorrow night on its way back from the KCC, Kenya Cooperative Creameries, at Naivasha."

Kahinga thanked him.

Kahinga and Kinua were allowed to sleep in the hut where they were, rolled up on the floor in a thin blanket. They woke up when the sun was in the heavens, with very thick heads. After a breakfast of oogie, a very liquid porridge made from maize meal, and sour milk they both felt much better. Kahinga reflected on the previous night and felt somewhat uncomfortable that he had perhaps said too much – still, Zacharia seemed harmless enough. Kahinga resolved to curb his tongue in the future.

Meanwhile Kinua had wandered off and found himself near a small stream. Further downstream he could hear the sounds of girls' laughter and some splashing. As he approached, one of them shrieked in mock panic and they all jumped into a nearby pool. There were three or four of them, unmarried maidens about 16 years old. They were all naked except for a small leather apron that covered the very bare essentials. The girls had been washing clothes and themselves when Kinua approached. They giggled but said very little. Kinua sat on a nearby rock and started to chaff them. Kinua was tall for a Kikuyu, at almost six foot; he was slim and athletic. He had high cheekbones and an aquiline look to his face, indicating some Masai blood in his background. The girls found him very handsome.

"Why don't you get on with your work?"

Shrieks of laughter. Eventually one of the bolder ones suggested playfully that he should join them. He stripped down to a very moth-eaten pair of shorts and was about to jump when the girls shouted: "No, no, no – everything off."

He hesitated. Maybe things were going too far. However after a moment he stripped off and jumped into the pool amid shrieks of admiration. After some more chaffing he found a piece of soap and started to wash. The girls needed no second invitation and within moments he was being expertly washed – all over. Things are definitely going too far, he thought happily. Without his really noticing, time passed and most of the girls disappeared with their washing – all except one. By this time he was thoroughly aroused and found himself fondling Sarah's small but exquisitely shaped breasts. He put his hand between her legs and there was an involuntary shudder from Sarah. She dragged him out of the water towards some trees on the edge of the stream. Her apron was torn off and she pulled him down on top of her. She was lying on a soft bed of leaves.

As he entered her there was a small cry as he broke her virginity – then she responded to him with a great deal of enthusiasm and he came hugely. She gave a small grunt of satisfaction and a grin. They lay on the leaves with the warm sun filtering through the trees, saying little. Within a short time her proximity and the warm sun made him stir again – and this time he was more gentle and she came beautifully and completely with a series of small cries. Kinua had never felt like this before. They stayed there most of the day, enjoying each other's bodies again and again.

"If I had known you were such a bull I would not have told my friends to go," joked Sarah. Kinua lay back in happy exhaustion.

They returned separately to the village. Kinua managed to avoid Kahinga and rolled himself up in his blanket in the hut and enjoyed what he considered to be a well-earned sleep.

After the evening meal they were encouraged to sleep for a couple of hours. Zacharia said he would wake them early enough to get to the main road where the milk truck was due to pick them up at 3am. Kinua did not see Sarah again and Kahinga, Kinua and Zacharia made their way to the road and waited for the truck, which after an unexplained delay turned up. The truck was on its way back from delivering the milk to the bulk depot at Naivasha and as soon as it stopped, the Indian driver and a labourer started unloading empty cans from the truck. Zacharia had a short, sharp argument with the driver and Kinua and Kahinga were allowed to climb into the cab. Kahinga wondered what Zacharia had on the driver; normally the favour would have cost something.

The journey to Ol' Kalou took a good two hours. The road was very rough indeed; in common with most roads in Kenya at the time, it was untarred. Kahinga and Kinua were oblivious to the apparent discomfort. They stopped every few miles to drop off empty milk cans and eventually arrived in Ol' Kalou just as the sky was showing a glimmer of light in the east.

The Indian driver had been quite uncommunicative at the start of the journey; Kahinga presumed he was sore about the way that he had been treated by Zacharia.

Once it was clear that Kahinga and Kinua were prepared to help unload the empty cans from the truck he opened up a bit.

No, he said, he did not know of the M'zungu Lawrence, but since the war ended there had been quite a few new Wazungu in the area. "It is good for business," he added, "for the shops in Ol'Kalou and for this business." He banged his hand on the steering wheel. "If this Lawrence is a dairy farmer then I expect we will transport his milk to Naivasha as well," he volunteered.

It turned out the driver was a part owner of the vehicle but that S.Shah, the store owner Zacharia had referred to, had put up the money to purchase the vehicle and had the majority share in the truck.

Kahinga considered all this information. He liked Indians even less than he liked the Europeans; if the Wazungu left their farms then the Indians would leave their shops and other businesses as well. "Then we will all be rich like the Wazungu and the Indians," he thought to himself.

Chapter 4

Ol'Kalou was an unremarkable place – it consisted of a small railway station run by an Indian station master, a police station, an African location which housed about 600 souls, a few shops catering for these people and then further away a garage that was virtually incapable of repairing anything and a doctors surgery. The surgery was run by a remarkable Frenchman who had spent the war in a concentration camp – he was fantastic in emergencies but day to day medicine bored him and a large part of the work was left to an untrained African dresser. Along the street (if it could be called that) were several Indian owned shops including a draper, a cobbler and a very good general store owned by one S.Shah who also owned stores in Ol'Joro Orok and Thomsons Falls. The major stores largely catered for the white farming community. The first of these had settled the area from about 1919, but the majority of settlers only arrived from the mid-thirties onwards and after the Second World War.

Kahinga and Kinua were unsure of where the M'zungu Lawrence's farm was, so they wandered aimlessly round the village and eventually settled on the steps of S.Shah's shop. It was still cold and they were glad of their greatcoats. From about seven o'clock people started moving about and Shah's shop eventually opened its doors at about half past. The Indian behind the counter was not especially pleased to see Kahinga when he entered the shop – however he grudgingly gave Kahinga directions to the Lawrences' farm. It took them a couple of hours to walk the five miles to the Lawrences – it was a very steep climb up a dusty, winding road. After making a few enquiries from people on the road and from the labour at the entrance to the farm they turned up at the back of the Lawrences' ramshackle house where they found both Dibu and the houseboy, Mwangi. Kahinga quickly made himself known – Dibu was already aware that Kahinga was due and told him and

Kinua to sit outside under a tree and wait for the bwana. Dibu gave them a mug of tea and half a loaf of bread each and they waited.

Peter Lawrence eventually turned up at about lunchtime and parked the truck absentmindedly in the front of the house. He spotted Kahinga and Kinua sitting under the tree and came over. "Jambo," he said neutrally.

"Jambo sana, bwana," chorused Kahinga and Kinua.

"What do you want?"

"Kazi (work)."

"What kind of work?"

"Tractor driver."

"What, both of you?" exclaimed Peter

"Ndio (yes) bwana," said Kahinga.

"We'll see, wait here."

Peter Lawrence went inside for lunch.

"What do those two want?" asked Jenny. Jenny was looking forward to moving into the stone cottage on their side of the farm. The Italians had left and they were now doing some minor repairs to make it habitable for themselves. They expected to move in within a few weeks.

"Tractor drivers," said Peter. "They look okay to me. I'll try them out after lunch."

"But you don't need two."

"I will, one of them can help me maintain the machinery when he's not driving and he can also plough at night."

"Better put that truck up the hill," Jenny changed the subject.

"Oh, damn, why did I leave it there?"

Peter finished his lunch and went outside and got into the truck. He tried the starter – nothing.

He opened the bonnet. There was something loose underneath and he crawled underneath; the exhaust pipe looked as if it was about to fall off. He pulled an adjustable spanner from his pocket and started to tinker. Suddenly he had an uneasy feeling.

"Cripes!" he yelled. "Bloody hell – siafu!"

He jumped out from under the truck, banging his head on the way. The ants were really biting – he had inadvertently lain down in a nest of them and his body was covered in a mass of red ants. Kahinga and Kinua saw what had happened and rushed over.

"Get these clothes off me!" yelled Peter.

They pulled his clothes off – within 30 seconds Peter was standing in front of the truck stark naked with the two Kikuyu pulling ants off him as fast as they could go. Jenny and the house servants rushed out and joined in. After about five minutes they had got most of the ants off him.

"Those things really bite," said Peter, slowly getting back into his clothes, making sure there were no ants left.

Kinua could not suppress a snicker.

"What's so funny?" growled Peter.

"Nothing Bwana." Kinua kept a straight face with difficulty.

Peter eventually regained his composure – he started to laugh and eventually they all laughed and laughed until their sides split.

"Keep those kids away, I'll fix the truck later," said Peter to Jenny. "Come let's go try out that tractor," he said to the two Kikuyu.

When Kahinga saw the tractor his heart sank into his boots. An ancient Farmall H. He prayed he would be able to start the thing – once it was going it should be all right. Peter left him to it. He turned on the petrol and the ignition.

"Come Kinua, help me," said Kahinga.

They both got hold of the crank and really gave it a turn. Miracles would never cease, the thing started first time. Kahinga beamed; when the engine had warmed up he switched to VOCO – power paraffin. No word from Peter.

"Where to?" asked Kahinga.

"You'll do," said Peter. "I'll pay you 80 shillings per month each which will increase after six months to 100 shillings. Each household also has half an acre of land for their own use and you can graze five head of cattle each. The land will be suitable for growing maize and vegetables."

"OK," said Kahinga. That was fair. It would be some time before they would have any cattle at all, and until they had a wife to look after their maize and vegetable crops they would probably not make use of the facility. It was good to know it was there though.

Having got the tractor started, they pulled the truck up the hill to a place safely out of the ants' nest where it could be started. Kinua fixed the exhaust.

"You have one week to build yourself a hut. It will have to be over the other side; we are moving to the other house soon. Kamau will show you where to get timber. You can stay with Dibu for the time being."

"Asante sana (thank you very much), bwana," said Kahinga.

※ ※ ※

Chapter 5

The Lawrences were still temporarily staying in Bill's house. Although Bill had bought the farm a few months back, he had not yet moved from Thika, where he was working. This house was on the neighbouring farm, about two miles away and consisted of two rooms made from cedar planks and a lean-to kitchen with an oil stove. Bread was baked in the bank behind the house by making two hollows one above the other. The dough was wrapped in newspaper and put in the top hole and a fire was lit in the bottom. The bread was delicious.

As was usual, the Lawrences had acquired two house servants, Dibu the cook and Mwangi the house boy. Both were Kikuyu and lived in nearby huts with a number of wives and hordes of small children. They were paid 80 shillings and 50 shillings per month respectively, with food and accommodation thrown in. They considered themselves fortunate compared to the vast majority of people who had no employment and to ordinary labourers who were paid 40 shillings per month. The elite were tractor drivers who received about 100 shillings per month, again all found.

During his sojourn in the Kikuyu populated districts near Nairobi, Peter had become acutely aware of what his fellow settlers called the "mess" in the Kikuyu reserve, some of which adjoined the northern boundaries of the city. He could see it was overcrowded, overstocked and overgrazed. He was dismayed by the low quality of the cattle and the fact that goats had been allowed to proliferate and were in the process of virtually destroying the landscape. He noticed the partially successful terrace building programme.

Through his own personal interest and through speaking to some of the older settlers he came to understand that because the British had stamped out inter-tribal fighting – Pax Britannica – the Kikuyu had emerged from the forests where they had often sought refuge from marauding gangs of

Masai. They had then been able to fully utilise their traditional lands and with their energy and ingenuity had prospered beyond all expectations. That together with the introduction of Western medicine had increased the survival rate and that in turn had led to the overcrowding in the Kikuyu reserve. The reserves might have been adequate when they were set up in the previous century but Peter could see that this was no longer so.

Peter, encouraged by his British relatives, had moved easily from South Africa to Kenya. There were no bureaucratic delays; as far as the British were concerned there was virtually free movement of white settlers within the Empire. Although Peter was born in South Africa he was not really certain whether he was British or South African. The distinction did not concern him greatly as for all practical purposes at that time it made very little difference. He spent the war years in the Northern Frontier District of Kenya and in Abyssinia – Ethiopia – which had been invaded and occupied by the Italians in 1936.

Kenya represented a dream for Peter Lawrence: the dream of personal independence. The acquisition of the farm in Ol'Kalou was a deliberate step in that direction. Very occasionally he felt a twinge of concern when he thought of the overcrowding in the Kikuyu and other reserves and he sometimes wondered how long the black Africans would tolerate white domination. He was comforted by the fact that successive British Governments of every political hue had encouraged white settlement, and even after the war, had continued to do so.

He also took some small comfort from the fact that Ol'Kalou – the place of Kalu, a Masai chief in days gone by – and many of the place names in the district, namely those with the prefix 'Ol', were Masai names. He understood that the district although claimed by the Masai had only been used as an emergency grazing ground in time of drought. This seemed rather a thin claim to Peter.

He also took comfort from his own being, his own knowledge of Africa, the fact that he spoke several African languages and that he generally had very good relationships with black Africans. He felt that whatever happened, whatever was thrown his way he would deal with it.

One evening shortly after Kahinga and Kinua's arrival, Peter and Jenny were sitting beside the fire, Peter asleep in his chair, Jenny knitting a garment for one of the children. The log fire had died down somewhat. The evenings were always chilly, the farm being between 8500 and 9000 feet above sea level and they had a fire, as much for the sense of security and comfort it gave as for the warmth, almost every evening of the year. Outside, they could hear the night noises of the bush.

Jenny got up to pump one of the paraffin pressure lamps. There was, of course, no electricity although a few of the farmers in later years were to install their own generating units.

Suddenly she became aware of a deathly hush – the tree hyrax that abounded had as always been making their awful, eerie noise and even they had fallen silent.

Jenny, who was not normally in the slightest bit nervous, felt a cold shiver go down her spine.

"Pete!"

"Yes, what is it?" – sleepily.

"There's… there's something."

"Just a hyrax probably." Peter shifted to get himself into a more comfortable position in his chair.

"No, there really is something."

A large herd of 100 head of recently acquired cattle started lowing and moving nervously around in a nearby makeshift boma - paddock. Peter was now fully awake and was also aware of the eerie silence. He grabbed the double barrelled 12 bore shotgun, loading it with SSG buckshot, put on his boots, whistled up his Alsatian dog and went out. Most of his spare cash was tied up in those cattle. He could not afford to lose them.

He shivered in spite of himself as he went down towards the boma. He shone the torch over the mob. There was something wrong – the cattle were all huddled together in one corner of the boma, all looking at something on the opposite side of the boma away from Peter.

A light breeze was blowing towards him, from the cattle to him. He knew there was leopard in the area. Their technique would be to get upwind of the cattle and cause a stampede and then pick off one of the calves.

Peter decided to go upwind as well; maybe if whatever it was picked up his scent it would decide that discretion was the better part of valour and disappear. If the cattle had not been there he would have fired a couple of shots into the bush in the hope of scaring the animal (he presumed it was an animal) off. Under the present circumstances this would merely have precipitated a stampede.

He kept the torch shining on the cattle and crept upwind. Suddenly he felt a chill, something was now stalking him. He couldn't see it or hear it but a sort of sixth sense told him that he was now the target instead of the cattle. Far from being intimidated by him, the "thing" (he was now almost certain it was a leopard) had maybe eaten human flesh before and regarded him, Peter, as a tasty morsel. The dog had also sensed what was happening and its hackles rose.

The dog really saved his life. It shot out from beside him and ran along the side of the boma. Peter saw a flash of something in pursuit of it, and then all hell broke loose. The flimsy boma broke and the 100 beasts came plunging towards him in a blind stampede. He tried to dive out of the way but a hoof accidentally caught him on the head, and he was trampled by several of the cattle in their rush.

He woke up minutes later, very battered and bruised but fundamentally none the worse for wear except for the damage to his dignity. "How could I be such a fool!" he swore to himself.

Then he heard Jenny frantically calling him from the house. She had obviously heard the commotion.

"Here I am."

"Are you okay?"

"Yes, I suppose so." He fumbled around in the dark and found his powerful torch and then the gun. By this time Jenny was with him.

"Dear God, look at you! You're covered with blood. What happened?"

He briefly explained. There was nothing he could do that night, but he had to get those cattle back. His dreams could be ended there and then if he lost many of them.

Jenny cleaned him up and bandaged a nasty gash in his head, which was where all the blood had come from. He had a few other bruises but nothing serious. His dressing gown and pyjamas, which he had been wearing (as was customary in Kenya after dark) were covered in mud.

The house servants appeared looking rather nervous, having heard the commotion. Peter explained what had happened and when it was clear there was nothing they could do, they retired to their nearby huts.

"What are we to do about the cattle?" Jenny asked, her voice full of anxiety. She was well aware of the financial consequences of losing them.

Jenny was a tall, slim woman of about 25, with blond hair. Her face was full of character. As the daughter of a Johannesburg businessman down south, she could probably have chosen a much easier row to hoe that following Peter Lawrence in his romantic quest for independence. However, now they were here she liked living here and nothing was going to put her off. Besides, giving up and leaving with their tails between their legs after such a short time, particularly after the pressure that had been put on them to return to South Africa by their relations, was not on.

"Can't do anything now," said Peter. "I'll get the boys and round up the cattle in the morning."

"What was it?" asked Jenny.

Peter shrugged. "We'll find out in the morning, I'm sure." He was thinking anxiously of the deep, heavily wooded ravines of which there were several only a mile or so from the house; if the cattle went in there he would never recover any of them.

About an hour later the dog returned, quite nervous and excited but unharmed.

"Chui (leopard)," pronounced Kamau the head stockman on examining the prints that they found near the boma the next morning. He and Peter had followed the prints which in turn followed the trail left by some of the cattle.

After some time Kamau said: "Old leopard, bwana."

"Oh," said Peter. "How do you know that?"

Kamau showed him various prints. One had a consistently lighter imprint than the others – he was limping. It was obvious that the leopard was unable to catch wild animals anymore and had therefore turned to domestic stock. Peter would have to get rid of this nuisance. But where were the cattle?

They found a place where the leopard had attacked and killed one of the larger calves, and not far away they found the half-eaten carcass wedged ten feet up in a tree. No sign of the leopard. He would not be very far away though. Worse still, there was no sign of the cattle.

That day Peter, Kamau and some other newly recruited labourers spent the day looking for the cattle. They found three.

"Three?" questioned Jenny later. "Three, out of a hundred head," she repeated, almost to herself. The news was devastating.

"What are you going to do about the leopard?" she asked.

"I've borrowed a rifle from Boschoff (a helpful neighbour) and I'll have to sit up with Kamau over the carcass when I've built a hide," he replied.

"If you are going to sit up all night and try to find runaway cattle all day you'll kill yourself. I'd better come and help tomorrow. The kids will be all right with Mwangi's wife here tomorrow."

The next day Jenny took the shotgun and went with one of the labourers in one direction and Peter and Kamau went in another direction. She took no food or water.

"Please be careful and don't get lost," Peter cautioned. "Always keep your eye on the sun and you'll know where you are."

Peter had a little more luck that day; he found ten head. He came back towards dusk expecting to find Jenny home, but there was no sign of her or the labourer who went with her.

"No need to panic," he thought. "I'm sure she'll turn up soon."

Jenny had gone off that morning quite confident and quite cheerful with a labourer whose name turned out to be PWD. He had apparently been born in a roadside camp belonging to the Public Works Department. They were following some promising tracks, now of course two days old. Jenny had lost all sense of time and distance and she and PWD had followed the tracks into some very thick bush where progress was perilously slow. At one stage they both got a terrible fright when they virtually stood on a waterbuck which leapt up from under their feet and dashed off through the bush. Late in the afternoon they had seen absolutely no sign of any cattle and Jenny decided they should head for home. They marched confidently off in the direction they thought was home.

After about an hour Jenny stopped. She had recognised no landmarks.

"PWD – are you sure this is the way home?" she asked in Swahili.

"Yes Memsahib," he answered and pointed in the direction they were going. They went on.

Just as night started to close in (being virtually on the equator the transformation between daylight and darkness took less than half an hour) they came to a small clearing. Jenny caught a glimpse of a leopard sitting on a dead animal, and then there was a yellow flash. She instinctively raised the shotgun to her shoulder and both barrels went off. Jenny was not very familiar with firearms and had held the gun away from her shoulder. The kick of both barrels going off together knocked her clean off her feet. This with the fright the gunshot gave the leopard probably saved her life; the leopard swerved off into the bushes and disappeared. Jenny picked herself up a few moments later, retrieved and reloaded the shotgun with great difficulty, she was trembling so much. There was no sign of PWD. She called and shouted. Deathly silence.

She sat down on a tree stump and wondered what to do. She was lost, there was a leopard nearby (possibly wounded), she was alone and it was almost dark. She very nearly panicked; her instinct was to start running. With a huge effort she pulled herself together; she had better climb up into a tree and make the best of it while she could see. She scratched herself rather badly on some thorns as she clambered up a tree and wedged herself in a fork about fifteen feet up. The shotgun had been left on the ground since she had needed both hands to climb the tree.

Peter in the meantime was becoming more and more anxious. By eight o'clock he had written half a dozen notes to various farmers – few farmers had telephones – and had dispatched the house servants with them. The notes explained his predicament and asked if the recipient and whatever labour was available could come to the Lawrences at dawn the next day so a search party could be organised. Peter personally went to the village and reported the matter to the police and also alerted the doctor, who he knew would assist in the search. He was already beginning to fear the worst.

Jenny spent the most terrifying and uncomfortable night that she had ever imagined. The bush was full of large and small noises. Sleep was of course nigh impossible; she almost fell out of the tree when a hyrax started its eerie racket in what appeared to her to be the next door tree. The dead animal of course attracted a number of predators - jackal, Jenny guessed from the excited "yip, yip" sounds they made calling to each other, and hyena, from the really evil sounding laugh they gave off when they discovered the carcass of the cow. One hyena obviously smelt Jenny in the tree and put its front paws up on the tree and laughed its eerie laugh. She shivered with cold and fright. Hyenas only attack vulnerable targets. She would certainly have qualified as vulnerable if she came out of the tree.

At one stage a colony of Colobus monkeys almost landed on her as they swung their way through the trees eating berries. She shouted to scare them off; if possible, they were even more terrified than she was.

During the night, which was moonless and pitch black anyway, heavy cloud rolled over and to add to her misery at about 4am it started to pour with rain. In her terror she had forgotten how hungry and thirsty she was – now the water just poured down and she was able to swallow a few mouthfuls. Within a minute she was drenched and cold. To add to her fright, it was a particularly violent thunderstorm and a cedar tree a few yards away exploded as a lightning bolt struck.

Peter woke with the thunderstorm. He felt so helpless; there was nothing he could do until dawn. Then his stomach gave a lurch as the thought struck him: the tracks - the tracks that he was relying on - would be completely wiped out by the rain. He almost wept. All thought of the cattle was gone – he must find Jenny.

The neighbours started to arrive well before dawn despite the rain. They were given breakfast. Peter was amazed at the turnout; their little cabin was crowded with about fifteen people. Obviously the neighbours he had written to had rallied round the district. One of the wives had come, who took the children in hand and also helped organise the kitchen staff. When the dawn broke the rain had slowed to a drizzle – Peter had briefed the group and described the country as best he could. The search party set off in various directions accompanied in most cases by half a dozen of their labour. All were well armed and had proper boots and raingear. To a man they all had food and water. Peter's hopes lifted; there was no way they would fail to find Jenny. The doctor had arrived and stayed at base. Kahinga and Kinua were now also asked to delay their hut building and join in the search.

Jenny, by now very stiff and sore, had somehow managed to clamber down the tree. Her shoulder where the gun had knocked her over was very bruised and she noticed that the scratches from the thorns were beginning to go septic. To add to her anxieties Jenny knew that septicaemia or blood poisoning set in very quickly if scratches were untreated, partly from the poison in the thorns and partly because of the climate. She had thought she would try to find a way out but since the sun was still obscured she had no idea in which direction to walk; besides she was very weak from lack of food and water and very stiff from her night in the tree. She shivered and decided to stay put. She was certain that Peter would have organised a search party – perhaps her best chance was to stay where she was. By about 10am the sun started to shine and Jenny managed to get most of her wet clothing off and hung it out on various bushes to dry. She had also had a chance to look at the dead animal, one of their prize cows. It had certainly not been killed by the leopard, but a great area had been trampled as if the beast had gone mad or died in pain from poison.

By midday her clothes were dry, the sun was shining and despite a certain light-headedness from lack of food she was in reasonable spirits – they had to find her soon, she thought. She went and sat in the shade and went to sleep.

By about 4pm the search parties started to return. Many of them brought cattle back with them. All in all some eighty head had been found by the end of the day, but there was no sign of Jenny. Peter, who had also been out was absolutely frantic with worry. He couldn't believe it; not a sign – not a single sign. Almost all the neighbours stayed on; they dossed down all over the little house, having been fed by the servants. At eight o'clock Peter heard Kamau calling from outside, "Bwana, bwana, come quick." He rushed outside. It was PWD who had somehow made his way back to the farm village that day. Peter took a deep breath; to get any information at all he would have to allay the man's fears that he was to be blamed for Jenny's disappearance. He must not show any sign of his own huge anxiety – this was their last chance of finding her alive. He sat down on a stone, having greeted PWD politely. PWD was shaking like a leaf; clearly he thought he was going to be punished. Peter spoke to him in Kikuyu quietly for almost an hour. In the end all he got out of him was a story of a leopard eating a dead cow and Jenny having shot at the leopard.

"When did this happen?" asked Peter.

"Yesterday, just at dark," was the response.

"Was the memsahib hurt?" asked Peter. PWD shook his head, he didn't know, he had just run frantically to get away. Peter told Dibu to take him back to his hut and make sure he was fed and kept warm, and he went inside to discuss what he had heard with the search parties.

"I saw an animal that had been half eaten," announced one farmer. "There was no sign of Jenny though."

"Can you get back there?" asked Peter anxiously.

"Not in the dark; in daylight, yes I think so," was the reply.

A brief discussion ensued. It would be foolhardy to go out there at night. There were deep, treacherous gullies to trap the unwary, as well as wild animals and snakes. No-one knew the country well enough to risk it. Peter put his head in his hands. He knew they were right. "Oh my poor, poor Jenny" he groaned to himself, suppressing the horrifying thought that for her the next day might be too late.

Jenny woke up at about 5pm with a start; she had been dreaming about being on the beach near Durban. It took her a moment or two to remember where she was, then absolute terror struck her. Could she survive another night up the tree? Could she get up the tree? She staggered to her feet and walked unsteadily into the clearing. Her mouth was absolutely dry, her tongue was beginning to swell, and she was dizzy. She kept seeing double. Then she stopped and screamed – she couldn't believe it. She got down on her hands and knees. Bootmarks, fresh bootmarks, all over the place. They had missed her while she was asleep. Her screams came out as a gurgle. "My God," she thought, "what now?"

A hyena moved into the clearing; he could see Jenny was done for and took little notice of her, her turn would come later. The hyena concentrated on the matter in hand which was filling himself full of the dead cow before any of the other predators could.

Jenny was terrified; she knew the shotgun was where she had left it the previous night and the hyena was between her and the weapon. She needed something to protect herself. She started to move round the clearing; the hyena looked warily at her, bared his teeth, let out his eerie laugh and started to move towards her. Jenny didn't know what to do. The shotgun was still twenty to thirty yards away and the hyena looked as if he meant business.

At that stage the vultures started to return to the carcass from which they had been displaced by the hyena, and the hyena then rushed back and chased the vultures away. Jenny used the distraction to stagger round and pick up the shotgun. As she did so, the hyena started to move towards her again. This time she remembered to hold the shotgun tighter and she quickly let fly with one barrel. Hyenas are not brave. The shot was wild and wide but no amount of food would keep him there. He had seen Jenny as a potential meal but she had now identified herself as a source of danger. The hyena shot off into the bush and kept going.

Through her dazed state Jenny now realised how much real trouble she was in. The predators were all around her, attracted in the first instance by the carcass of the cow. She fired a couple more shots into the air, though her shoulder hurt like hell. The only response was the empty echo of the shots all the way down the valley. She tried again. Same response. The vultures that by now were back on the carcass of the cow moved uneasily away. They didn't move far. They were experts in death; they knew when an animal or human was close to it.

Was this to be her fate? When the predators had finished with the cow would they then start on her?

Jenny staggered a few steps along the trail left by the men's feet. By this time she was almost delirious with hunger, thirst and anxiety, she had caught a severe chill in the rainstorm the previous night and the scratches from the thorns were becoming badly infected. She pulled herself together sufficiently to move back into the clearing.

The vultures had moved away again and another larger hyena had taken over. She was trying to gather some strength to climb back up the tree and while she did she watched the scene on the carcass. The predators took little notice of her now.

The scene was dominated by the large hyena; however some jackals had arrived and ripped into the carcass when they saw an opportunity for a mouthful. The hyena tried to keep them at bay and in fact spent most of his energy doing that. The vultures had moved away slightly; they were patient and in any event would rest in the trees at dark. There would be plenty left for them in the morning and there was also the promise of that other animal in the clearing that was making a lot of noise but appeared to be near death and posed no real danger. The vultures had a very distinct pecking order. The ones in the front were the smallest. Their dark red necks were sunk deep between their shoulder blades and they had deep seated fierce looking eyes. If any of the other vultures went near the carcass these vultures chased them away. There were then some larger ones which Jenny thought could have been Cape Vultures. The Maribou Storks had the lowest status, with their horrible looking jowls hanging below their beaks. Jenny thought they looked like a bunch of bankers all waiting over the dead carcass.

Jenny tried to contemplate her options. If she fell unconscious certainly the predators would attack her and eat her. Yet her best chance of rescue was to stay in the clearing. As she had already found out, moving twenty yards into the bush made her invisible. She could shoot at a couple of predators to keep them away but this didn't seem to scare them for long. Eventually she managed to wedge the shotgun in a branch of the tree and with the last of her strength she clambered into another fork in the tree on the edge of the clearing.

Although she was cold and frightened she knew she had to stay awake to survive. The cloud had blown away and by about 10pm a half moon appeared. To say Jenny had got used to the sounds in the bush would have been an exaggeration but she was at least able to identify the sounds more readily, the hyrax didn't frighten her anymore and she could see a couple of hyena and some jackals on the carcass from the light of the moon.

She must have dozed a little but sometime about 3am she was suddenly wide awake again. The hyenas and jackals were nowhere to be seen and at first she thought that the clearing was deserted but the moon was high in the sky now and she could just make out something on the carcass. She strained her eyes, her pulse beat faster and she must have moved slightly. The animal on the carcass turned around attracted by the sound. It was a leopard - she supposed the leopard that had caused all the trouble in the first place. It was only about twenty yards away. It would get her unless she could shoot it first - climbing a few feet up a tree would be no trouble for any leopard. The shotgun was loaded with SSG buckshot and would make a real mess of anything at twenty yards. She really had no option so she gathered what remained of her dwindling strength, carefully aimed the shotgun at the leopard trying to remember everything that Peter had taught her, held the gun tight, and took careful aim at the animal, then squeezed the trigger. The blast knocked her out of the tree; she was vaguely aware of the leopard leaping up and then staggering out of the clearing before she hit the ground.

PWD was given a meal and had started to tell Kahinga what had happened the previous day. He was clearly worried, not about himself but about Jenny and the fact that his behaviour in running away had put her life in danger. He hadn't been with Peter Lawrence for long but what he saw he liked. He spent most of the evening discussing with Kahinga what should be done. Eventually they all went to sleep. At about 1.00am Kahinga noticed PWD moving about.

"Where are you going?" he whispered.

"To find the memsahib. She will die if she is not found soon," replied PWD.

"You will also get lost and then the Wazungu will have to look for you also," Kahinga tried to reason with him.

"I can't sleep, I must go." PWD seemed determined.

Kahinga thought for a moment, and then he woke Kinua and explained the situation. The three of them crept out of the hut and stumbled off into the bush. Gradually their eyes became used to the dim moonlight and they made their way along the ill-defined paths that led into the bush.

After almost an hour Kahinga whispered to PWD, "Are you sure we are going in the right direction?"

"I think so," was the uncertain answer.

"If we find the memsahib, can you find your way back to the house?" asked Kahinga again.

"Oh, yes, I have been keeping a careful look out," was the more confident response from PWD.

They went on, stopping every few minutes to look and listen. At one stop, the bush was eerily quiet which was unusual.

Suddenly, not more than two hundred yards in front of them was the terrifying blast of a shotgun. All three of them nearly jumped out of their skins with fright and were frozen to the spot for a few seconds.

"It's the memsahib," yelled PWD and the three of them stumbled on through the dark until they came to the clearing. They found the dead cow and called loudly and repeatedly. Of course there was no response from Jenny. After searching the area for about ten minutes Kahinga found her, unconscious but still clutching the shotgun.

"Here she is," he called.

The others, who were nearby, came over.

"We must keep her warm," said Kahinga.

All three took their greatcoats off and draped them over Jenny.

"You, PWD, and Kinua; are you sure now you can find your way back to the house?" asked Kahinga.

PWD nodded vigorously. "Yes," was the answer.

"Then you two go back to the house quickly and bring Munyu (Peter's Kikuyu name) and the Doktari – doctor – and the other Wazungu. I will stay here and look after the memsahib."

PWD and Kinua did as they were bid.

Kahinga managed to disengage the shotgun from Jenny's grasp. He put it aside; he had no knowledge of guns and indeed was rather scared of them.

He tried to make Jenny as comfortable as he could. He could see she was badly injured and he hoped the rescue party would arrive soon. He collected a few stones from round about to throw at any animals that might appear. The pockets of all the greatcoats were searched; Kahinga eventually found some matches and was able to light a fire, both for warmth and to keep the animals away.

Peter was woken at about 4:30am by some banging on the back door and a voice calling.

"Bwana, come quick, come quick!"

He picked up his torch and found PWD and one of his newly acquired tractor drivers at the back door.

"Come quick, come quick, we have found the memsahib," PWD stammered.

"Where?" asked Peter.

PWD pointed.

"Is she by herself?" Peter asked.

"Kahinga is with her, she is hurt, please bring the Doktari," Kinua answered.

"Oh, yes, the other new tractor driver," thought Peter.

By this time the whole household was awake and within half an hour the search party was on its way.

Led by PWD, they found Kahinga and Jenny just after the dawn broke in the east. She was still unconscious. The doctor felt her pulse: it was weak, flickering. She had broken an arm in the fall. Kahinga's presence had undoubtedly saved her life.

"We must be quick," shouted the doctor. He gave her an injection and wrapped her up in warm blankets while a makeshift stretcher was made.

Kahinga showed them the shotgun with one spent shell still in the breech. They quickly put two and two together and decided that Jenny had shot at something, which act had caused her fall from the tree. One of the search party started to scout round the general area in search of whatever Jenny had shot at. The last thing anyone needed was a wounded animal running about especially if it was a leopard.

Boschoff, the neighbour who had leant Peter the rifle, suddenly called. He had been looking at the tracks round the cow's carcass.

"Leopard," he said. "She hit it badly, see the blood trail. Please be careful, it's probably wounded and close by."

He had plenty of hunting experience and gestured to one of the other farmers who was similarly experienced. Peter and the doctor were dealing with Jenny. Boschoff took charge.

"Please stay here," he said to the rest of the party. "We don't want any more casualties." "Come," he said and two of them slowly followed the trail of blood.

Boschoff had a high powered hunting rifle and his companion had a double barrelled shotgun loaded with SSG. They were following the blood trail and had gone about 100 yards when there was a flash of yellow and the leopard streaked out from a bush twenty yards in front of them. Both Boschoff and his companion fired simultaneously and the leopard was caught by both discharges in mid-air, crashing down to earth dead just in front of them.

Once they had caught their breath, they turned the animal over; one leg had obviously been caught in a trap some time before which had made the leopard lame and caused it to turn to domestic stock to live. Jenny's shot had badly wounded the animal in the chest and stomach; it wouldn't have survived more than a day or two at most. The leopard would almost certainly have got to the two farmers if it had not been wounded.

By this time most of the rest of the search party had arrived. Boschoff swore: "What a waste, what a beautiful animal." He pointed to the scars left by the trap. "If someone hadn't set the trap none of this would have happened."

Jenny was taken home on the makeshift stretcher, still unconscious, and with the doctor's help rushed to hospital in Nakuru about 25 miles away. Peter went with her, a neighbour having undertaken to look after the kids.

Apart from the broken arm and the effects of being without food and water for almost three days, she had pneumonia from her night in the rain and all her scratches were badly infected. She hovered between life and death for two days. When she did eventually gain consciousness, she was bewildered. She saw Peter.

"Where…what?"

"You're OK," said Peter. "You're in hospital. Everything's OK."

Recovery was quick, but her troubles were not yet over. A few days later Peter asked her, "Did you notice anything funny about that dead cow?" He was referring to the cow which the predators had been feeding off. She was still in hospital but due out within a day or so.

"As a matter of fact, yes," replied Jenny. "It looked as if it had gone mad or been poisoned or something.

"Rabies!" Peter was holding her hand. "The vet. labs. at Kabete have diagnosed rabies."

Jenny felt herself go all cold. What else could happen to her?

"Did you touch the animal?" asked Peter.

"Yes, probably – I don't know."

"You'll have to have injections then."

That meant fourteen injections (one per day with a large 8 inch needle) into the stomach. Still, even that was better than rabies, which was incurable. Her only fear was – had they diagnosed it in time? She wouldn't know for a month. The first symptom was a fear of water. Despite herself, a tear trickled down her face. She impatiently wiped it away.

Peter took her home a few days later and life gradually returned to normal. Jenny drank a lot of water in the days and weeks to come.

Peter had already thanked PWD, Kahinga and Kinua for what they had done. He didn't really understand why they had risked life and limb to do what they did. Especially the new tractor drivers who hadn't really even started work with them yet.

When Jenny recovered she went over to Kahinga and Kinua's newly constructed hut and was given a strong sweet cup of tea. She chatted to them for a while and told them they had undoubtedly saved her life. She found out they were from the Fort Hall district. After the visit all of them felt a growing bond. The Kikuyu were, of course, unable to explain the real reason they had come to Ol'Kalou.

The Lawrences found they had lost fifteen head out of the hundred that had been chased by the leopard. Several others aborted calves they were carrying. It was a hard blow in a hard country. Peter and Jenny discussed the whole episode at length over the next few weeks and months. The one thing they didn't discuss was giving up – it probably didn't occur to either of them.

Boshoff had the leopard skin cured for them and came over one day to present it to Jenny. He had had a leg amputated above the knee some years before after a rock fall in one of the gold mines in South Africa. His small farm was paid for out of the gratuity he received for his injuries. Farming, however, was much too dull for Boshoff; he was a great adventurer and had done just about everything including a great deal of hunting. The children absolutely adored him, mainly because of his many stories and anecdotes; they were a bit scared of his leg, though, which creaked horribly when he moved about. Jenny hated the thought of hanging the skin up in their sitting room – the whole idea gave her the creeps. Eventually she was persuaded and became used to having it around. Boshoff was always a good friend; if one needed help he was normally ready to lend a hand.

The rabies worry stayed with them for years with no apparent recurrence however. Some years later Peter had a visit from a friend at the veterinary laboratories at Kabete. They discussed the whole episode of the rabid cow.

"Sounds funny to me," said the vet. "Do you mind if I spend a few days looking around?"

Eventually, after about a week, he took away bundles of a number of plants. Weeks later, the answer came back: one of the plants, a member of the Cestrum family, was poisonous to cattle and the symptoms were similar to rabies.

Chapter 6

Zacharia had agonised for days, which turned into weeks, over the information that he had gleaned from Kahinga. This spelt trouble, which he did not need – he could see himself defending his position and possessions from a horde of Kahingas and Kinuas. He looked after his people; why couldn't they leave him alone and look after their own business. Eventually, as with most problems he had had since he had been on the farm with Gibb (which was quite some time) he decided to confide in the M'zungu. He would do it the next day.

Every day he and Gibb used to allocate the various tasks to the labour at seven in the morning, and on that morning when he went down to the yard he cursed. Gibb was all dressed up – jacket, tie - the works. "Must be going to Nairobi," he thought. Nevertheless after the jobs had been allocated Zacharia stood next to Gibb in a deferential way with his hat off. Gibb was about to leave but he knew his headman and he had a feeling that Zacharia had something on his mind. He knew it would not be a small thing; Zacharia had a great sense of perspective as to what was important.

"What is it, Zacharia?" asked Gibb.

"Shauri mkubwa sana (very big problem), bwana," was the response.

"Shauri gani (what problem)?" he was slightly impatient – he had to get to Nairobi by lunchtime.

Zacharia repeated himself.

"OK, come to the office," said Gibb resignedly.

Zacharia was given a large mug of tea. Gibb knew it was no good rushing him; the story would have to come out in its own good time.

"Shauri mkubwa sana," Zacharia said dejectedly.

"Tell me," said Gibb sympathetically.

"Those two you chased away," started Zacharia.

"Which ones?" He had a fetish of not allowing people to cross his farm.

"About one month ago – two Wakikuyu"

"Near the main road?" asked Gibb.

"Yes."

"You mean the bastards came back?" fumed Gibb.

"Yes."

"And you looked after them?" Gibb started to get angry.

"You know our customs – they are Kikuyu – we cannot turn them away," responded Zacharia.

"OK." Gibb calmed down; he was aware that his efforts to stop people crossing the farm were largely futile.

"They are very bad people," said Zacharia.

Gibb grunted.

Zacharia then went into fine detail about what he had learned from Kahinga including the oathing ceremony and the apparent objectives of the Mau-Mau organisation. Gibb listened intently. He wasn't too surprised to hear of an independence movement. The war had opened the Africans' eyes to what was going on in the outside world. It had also highlighted the fact that their colonial masters, the British, were not invincible. Gibb had no doubt that this was a serious problem, but he also felt that the trouble could be nipped in the bud. Gibb was an imperialist. The British had been on the winning side in the war; clearly it was in their interests to restore their colonies to their pre-war status as quickly as possible. The notion that the Africans could govern themselves did not occur to him; as far as he was concerned the things that the settlers had brought to Kenya - medicine, jobs, roads, railways, education etc. were of huge benefit to the indigenous population and there was no doubt in his mind that they needed the white man to administer all this for the general good of all. The whites were the masters; that fact was not questionable. He even wondered whether the blacks were capable of being educated, though he had been persuaded by his wife to erect a school on the farm where an African schoolmaster gave some basic instructions to the farm labourers' children.

Gibb asked Zacharia some questions. He was quite certain that he was being told the truth; there was no embellishment of the facts and Zacharia's demeanour indicated that he regarded the matter as serious. Zacharia finished his tea and left, confident that no questions would be raised by the other labour; from time to time he had a mug of tea in the bwana's office.

Gibb sat in his office and wondered what he should do. He decided that he'd better talk to the police. He knew a senior superintendent in Nairobi; that was where he'd go. The local "two year wonder"[4] wouldn't know what he was talking about or what to do.

Gibbs wife, Margaret, came bustling in. "I thought you were in such a hurry this morning," she said in her broad Scots burr. "My but you're looking very thoughtful; what did that old rogue want?" She was a devout Presbyterian and disapproved of Zacharia's three wives, with him professing to be a Christian.

"Nothing much," he replied. There was no sense in getting Margaret worked up; he would tell her in good time if there was anything to worry about.

"Come and have breakfast then."

Dave Gibb and his wife Margaret had come out to Kenya from the Scottish Highlands, with virtually nothing but the clothes they stood up in. With a great deal of hard work and some luck they now had a substantial farm of five thousand acres and were among the leading lights in the district. Of medium height, and slightly overweight, Dave was always prepared to listen to other settlers' woes and give them advice or help out if that was possible. He ran his farm labour in a kindly but strict way; they all knew he was boss and where they stood. Margaret was a small, mousy woman with grey hair and always had a pair of spectacles perched on the end of her nose. She'd had a strict Presbyterian upbringing and everything was judged against this background and often found wanting.

Gibb spent the two hour drive to Nairobi thinking about what Zacharia had told him. His thoughts also wandered back to his youth in Scotland, where his own father had slaved as a penniless crofter for his whole life. He shuddered. This country had been good to him; what he had was worth preserving. He had worked hard, brought up his two daughters in a decent, god-fearing way and given them a better life and better education than they could possibly have expected back home. He treated his labour well and they were substantially better off than their counterparts in the reserves.

As far as he was concerned any change in government structure would be to the detriment of all. However he couldn't help feeling anxious about the Labour Government in Britain, apparently about to abandon India. Could they possibly contemplate abandoning the rest of the empire? He was sure there was going to be a bloodbath in India. As far as he was concerned, the only reason the bloody savages hadn't been at each other's throats already

4 The settlers name for the police out on a two year contract from Great Britain.

was British control and without it the same would happen in Kenya. Still, he mused, if the British army withdrew from India, maybe there would be more troops available to send here. Comforted with this thought he drove into Nairobi. He went to the New Stanley hotel where he was to meet with a business acquaintance. He preferred Torrs himself, but he wasn't paying for the lunch. He was a little late but found a telephone.

"Superintendent Preston, if you please," he asked once the phone had been answered. He was put through without question.

"Preston here."

"Dick, this is Dave Gibb. I must see you. I'm in town today and going back tonight."

"Is this official or unofficial business?" asked Preston.

"I don't know, but I don't want any bloody eavesdroppers." Gibb wanted to avoid being invited to the Muthaiga club, which he disliked, being full of 'snotty-nosed Sassenachs'; it gave offence to his puritan Scots upbringing.

"When can you come?" asked Preston.

"Three o'clock," responded Gibb.

"OK. Three o'clock here; see you then," said Preston. He liked Dave Gibb; there was no nonsense there.

Gibb enjoyed his lunch although the business proposition was of little interest. He went to see Preston.

"Come in Dave, sit down. What can I do for you?"

"Dick, are you aware of an organisation called the Mau-Mau?" asked Gibb.

Preston was amazed and made a valiant effort not to show it. The police were aware of the fledgling organisation but they thought they had it buttoned up. Additionally, they had very clear, specific instructions from Whitehall to cover up the existence of the organisation from the public in Kenya. The reason for this was that the British Government had a major soldier settler scheme planned and any whiff of an independence or guerrilla organisation would put paid to that. To retain Kenya as part of the empire was current British Government policy, although Labour were in power, and to retain Kenya they had to ensure the settlers stayed.

"Well, yes," Preston had to admit. "It's a very minor operation and we are right on top of it. There's nothing to worry about, dear chap - nothing to worry about." Beads of sweat appeared on Preston's brow, which gave him a flustered look, despite his handsome face, immaculately groomed, silvery hair, neatly clipped moustache and beautifully pressed uniform.

"Crap," thought Gibb. "This bastard's covering something up, he's on the run."

"Well, let me tell you, this is no mickey mouse operation in my view" he said aloud.

"Nonsense my dear boy, nonsense," said Preston.

Gibb couldn't stand the English when they were like this; however, he managed to control himself. "Well, let me tell you the full story then," he growled and proceeded to tell Preston the detailed story that Zacharia had told him earlier that day.

Preston shifted uncomfortably in his chair, but as the story unfolded he became still; even he had not heard in quite such graphic detail the horrors of the oathing ceremony. At the end he was silent and Gibb knew he had made a huge impact on the man.

"Well?" enquired Gibb.

"Look, Dave," Preston said, recovering his urbanity, "we really appreciate your taking the time to come and report these matters, but I can assure you that we are fully aware of the situation and as I said we have our tabs on these people."

"Why don't you go and pick those two up from Lawrence's place," Dave volunteered. "I guarantee you they'll sing like birds given the right treatment."

This was the last thing that Preston had in mind. Start interfering with the farmers' labour and you had real trouble; this he knew from his thirty odd years' experience in the Kenya Police. Besides, they had very specific instructions from the mandarins in Whitehall and he wasn't going to rock the boat at this point. He had an outstanding record and was looking forward to his retirement in a few years' time in a cottage they had bought in Devon before the war.

"I don't think that will be necessary," said Preston coldly. "Thank you for this information anyway."

Gibb was tempted to really speak his mind, since he was absolutely seething. Somehow he managed to contain himself – he had known and respected this man since he had come to Kenya in his early twenties. "He must have his reasons for stonewalling me," he thought. He shook Preston's hand and left, a very worried man. He wondered what to do, and decided he should probably go and see Lawrence, whom he had not yet met. He liked to meet new arrivals anyway and had heard good reports of the man, although by the sound of things life was likely to be a financial struggle for the Lawrences for some years to come.

"Join the club" he mused, remembering that he had been even worse off when he arrived. He wondered what he was going to tell Zacharia.

Zacharia looked at him speculatively for the next few mornings and Gibb assiduously avoided his glances. About a week later Zacharia couldn't wait any longer and he stayed behind after the labour had been set their daily tasks.

"Come on," said Gibb resignedly.

Zacharia was given his mug of tea in the office and waited expectantly.

"I went to see the police in Nairobi and they have everything under control," said Gibb.

"Eh heh," said the old man.

Gibb tried again: "The police say they know about the Mau-Mau and know about all the leaders."

"They will then arrest Kahinga and Kinua?" It was as much a statement as a question.

"Well, maybe; they will watch them anyway."

Zacharia frowned; this did not sound like the Sirkali[5] of old. In the past, at the first sign of trouble the ringleaders were locked up. "Maybe the Sirkali are getting weak," thought Zacharia, "just like Kahinga said." Zacharia glared speculatively at Gibb. "This is not a small thing, bwana" he said respectfully. "These people must be stopped."

"I know," said Gibb. "The police say they have it under control." He sounded unconvincing.

"I will go with you to the police," offered Zacharia.

"I don't think that will be necessary," replied Gibb patiently. "I told them the full story."

They talked briefly of farm matters and Zacharia left.

Some weeks went by and Gibb was very busy; no plans were made to visit the Lawrences. However, fate was to intervene – in fact it had already intervened.

Once again Zacharia waited behind when the labour had been set their tasks.

"Yes Zacharia," said Gibb.

"Shauri, mkubwa mkubwa sana sana (very very big trouble)," wailed Zacharia.

Zacharia was given his usual mug of very sweet tea in the office.

"You know those people we talked about last time?" said Zacharia.

5 Swahili word for British officials.

"We've been through all that," said Gibb firmly.

Uncharacteristically Zacharia interrupted him. "No, no – that Kinua – he has made my daughter Sarah pregnant," Zacharia almost shouted at Gibb.

"OK, OK, calm down."

"She was promised to the son of the chief back in Fort Hall, and I was to get twenty of the best fat cattle for her," wailed Zacharia.

Gibb had never seen him in such a state.

"Maybe Kinua is the son of a chief."

"Kinua is the son of a rabid hyena," shouted Zacharia.

"OK, what can I do to help?"

"My daughter, very precious daughter violated and spoilt by that son of a mother-fucking baboon, now she's worth nothing," lamented Zacharia again.

"We will go to see Lawrence; Kinua will be made to pay. He will have to take her as his wife," said Gibb. "Maybe you'll get ten cattle."

Gibb knew that twenty cattle was exorbitant; the usual bride price was five or six cattle, a sheep for the feast and two hundred shillings in cash.

Zacharia recovered his composure a bit; maybe it wasn't so bad after all. "And to have a son-in-law who is one of these baboon Mau-Mau's," said Zacharia sadly as the thought hit him.

"Tomorrow we will go to Lawrence," said Gibb firmly. "Bring your daughter at seven."

Zacharia nodded and left.

The next day Zacharia duly arrived with his daughter, who was walking rather stiff-legged. Gibb surmised that she had been given a very sound thrashing. In his view she deserved no less – he was reminded briefly of his own eldest daughter training as a nurse in Nairobi; he hoped she had more sense.

They arrived at the Lawrences, who had by this time moved into the house now vacated by the Italian prisoners of war. At mid-morning Peter Lawrence had his head stuck under the bonnet of their one ton truck – this was a fairly frequent occurrence in view of the age and dilapidated nature of the vehicle. Lawrence approached and Gibb saw a tall, well-built man dressed in a bush jacket and trousers with an ancient and very battered army hat on his head. He was busy wiping his grease-covered hands on an old piece of cotton waste and then on his trousers. Gibb then noticed Lawrence's clear, bright blue eyes. He saw strength and determination; this man should be an asset to the district, he thought.

"Morning - Peter Lawrence." He shook Gibb by the hand.

"Dave Gibb."

Peter knew of the older man and wondered what had prompted the visit.

"Please come in and meet my wife."

Zacharia and Sarah were left with the truck.

Peter Lawrence introduced Gibb to Jenny and the usual cup of tea was produced. The conversation centred round the usual topics of the weather and the prospects for farming in general; then there was the story of Jenny's ordeal. After a while Jenny had a feeling that Gibb had something to discuss with Peter, so she cleared the tea things away and went out. Peter looked at Gibb expectantly.

Gibb had thought the matter over carefully and decided that unless Lawrence came up with anything negative he would not talk about Kahinga and Kinua's association with the Mau-Mau. He wanted to believe the police and he truly hoped that the whole thing would go away. He would speak only of Zacharia's problem with his daughter.

"My headman, Zacharia, has asked me to talk to you," be began.

Lawrence had seen Zacharia and the girl in the back of the truck and had shrewdly sized the situation up.

"Is the girl his daughter?" he asked. "Has one of my men been causing trouble?"

"Yes, it seems so; Zacharia told me that two men you took on a few months back passed through my place."

"Oh, you mean Kahinga and Kinua; they actually saved Jenny's life during the leopard episode. They are really good workers too - I think I'm very lucky to have them." Peter briefly explained Kahinga and Kinua's role in rescuing Jenny.

Gibb silently thanked the gods that he had kept his mouth shut. "Yes," he said, "Kinua apparently got his daughter pregnant."

"What do you want to do about it?" asked Peter.

"I'll have to let Zacharia sort things out with Kinua."

"Mwangi," Peter called to the house servant.

"Ndio bwana," was the cheerful reply.

"Find Kinua and tell him to come here,"

"Ndio bwana."

"This is going to be fun," thought Mwangi. From a brief conversation with Zacharia he had gathered the situation.

Kinua in the meanwhile had been doing his best to repair a small pump engine round the back of the tractor shed. He was unaware of Zacharia and Sarah's presence.

Mwangi came round the corner with a grin on his face which spelt mischief. "Munyu (Peter's Kikuyu name) wants to see you," he said.

"Eh heh; why?" asked Kinua.

"You've misbehaved yourself - a few months back perhaps," teased Mwangi.

Kinua took no notice but he went round the corner. He returned almost immediately a lot quicker. Mwangi almost split his sides laughing. Kinua aimed a kick at him. He was now terrified, firstly of Sarah and her father and then of his employer, whom he had learned to like and respect in the time he had been on the farm.

Flight was briefly considered, then he slowly composed himself. He made his way through some trees to the back of the house. Zacharia was called. He left his daughter in the truck.

"You abused my home," said Zacharia to Kinua, eyes blazing. "You violated my daughter."

Kinua kept his eyes averted and said nothing.

"Have you no tongue?" demanded Zacharia.

Silence.

"Son of a stinking, thieving jackal, answer me! Did you violate my daughter?"

Kinua nodded abjectly.

"I was promised twenty cattle as a bride price," thundered Zacharia. "Do you have twenty cattle?"

"No."

The discussion continued. Under normal circumstances Kinua's father would have been present; however he was miles away in the reserve somewhere and Kinua had to fend for himself as best he could. That he was obliged to marry Sarah was not in any way in dispute - the only debating point was the bride price. Sarah's feelings or point of view were not considered in any way by any of the parties. The one thing that Kinua could be certain of was that he would be in debt to Zacharia for many years to come; how long depended on whether he could persuade his father to help pay the price in the form of a few cattle.

Eventually the matter was settled. The bride price was agreed at six head of cattle, a sheep for the wedding feast plus 500 shillings, which Kinua hoped to borrow from Peter. The wedding day was fixed for a month hence at Zacharia's village. Peter and Dave Gibb emerged to find Zacharia back in the truck and Kinua at least able to look at him. Kinua knew he was pretty well ruined financially. He wondered what Kahinga would have to say about his marriage when he told him. A shiver went down his spine when he thought of the witchdoctor and the whole oathing process.

Gibb, Zacharia and Sarah left in the truck and Peter Lawrence went over to Kinua, who was looking decidedly dejected.

"Cheer up," he said. "You're getting married, you should be happy."

Kinua managed a smile. "Can I borrow 500 shillings?" he asked.

Peter blanched; he knew that would take Kinua months if not years to repay.

"And the rest of the bride price?" asked Peter.

"Six cattle and a sheep – can you help me with the sheep?"

"What about the cattle?" asked Peter.

"I will ask my father," replied Kinua.

So it was agreed Kinua was to borrow the 500 shillings, to be repaid at the rate of 30 shillings per month. Peter also agreed to provide a sheep from his own flock for the wedding feast.

Dibu wrote to Kinua's father to explain the predicament his son was now in and to ask for help in acquiring six head of cattle.

A month later the wedding went off without incident at Zacharia's village. However, it was preceded by some further bargaining when Kinua's father arrived a few days prior to the festivities. Secretly he was quite pleased with his prospective daughter-in-law; however, he was not about to let Zacharia know this. "Six cattle," he moaned, "for that old hag."

Zacharia remained unmoved.

"She has thin legs, sagging breasts and her hair is falling out."

No response.

"She has narrow hips," shouted Kinua's father. "She will not be able to produce healthy children."

"She has had no difficultly in starting one," countered Zacharia quickly.

"They will be sickly; they will die; she has no milk in her breasts," wailed Kinua's father.

This scene was repeated daily for the next day or two despite the fact that Kinua's father was an honoured guest in the village. Eventually the six cattle were agreed upon. Kinua's father would produce three immediately and Kinua would have to manage the other three as best he could over the next three or four years.

⨯ ⨯ ⨯

CHAPTER 7

The small cottage that the Lawrences now occupied had been cleaned up after the Italian prisoners of war had been sent home. All the money they had went into the farm so in order to make the house habitable they had to make do with what they could find.

They named the farm Naseby, which was the name of the place in England where Jenny thought her father had been born. Naseby was one of the famous battles of the civil war in 17th century England, the idea of which Jenny liked.

Bill had also decided to leave the management of both farms to Peter. This suited Peter; he was able to run the whole place as one unit. Bill was heavily involved in the Settlement Board, bringing to Kenya thousands of would be settlers from Britain.

The cottage had been thoroughly cleaned and the walls whitewashed. And since there were no ceilings, Jenny had gunny bags (grain sacks) cut up and then sewn together and put in as ceilings; they were also whitewashed. Jenny had found a way of adding red and green dye to the whitewash; the effect of this was sometimes rather garish but it did break the monotony of the harsh white.

The Lawrences had very little furniture; however Peter had hired a carpenter and he made chairs and a dining room table.

The bath was Peter's idea; he cut a 44-gallon oil drum down the middle lengthwise, then cut out two ends and welded the remaining two pieces together. The effect was like a boat with two blunt ends. The major difficulty was keeping the bath upright, which was achieved by placing a length of four by two timber against one side of the bath, the other being against the wall. The family managed this quite well, but visitors sometimes ended up on the floor with the contents of the bath.

The toilet was a "long drop" about 100 yards from the house. Running water was only available from the outside storage tank so flush toilets were unknown.

The house servants Dibu and Mwangi had moved from Bill's house and were now ensconced in the kitchen, which was a shed at the back of the house. Jenny had purchased an old wood-burning stove, on which somehow Dibu made the most wonderful meals. Jenny did almost no cooking but she employed at least two gardeners, so the household was amply supplied with vegetables and meat from the farm.

With the cattle he had bought, Peter had started a dairy business; within a year the same milk truck that had brought Kahinga and Kinua to Ol'Kalou now collecting the Lawrences' milk at 6pm every evening and dropping off the empty cans the next day. Initially the cows were milked by hand but once he could afford it Peter bought a milking machine.

The dairy was on Bills' side of the farm and Peter developed a piggery on that side as well. The head stockman Kamau and the labour involved in the dairy and the piggery lived on Bills side of the farm. Kahinga, Kinua and now Sarah and the house servants Dibu and Mwangi were in a village not far from the Lawrences' house. Peter also established a flock of sheep for the annual wool clip and he was able to sell lambs to the local butcher.

All in all the Lawrences had about 35 families on their 1500 acre property (their and Bill's farms together).

Their days started at 5am when the alarm went for the early morning milking and finished after dark with the evening milking. During the day Peter spent time building fences, making sure crops and pastures were planted correctly. Peter also hired equipment to dig boreholes, and laid pipes so that water could be piped around.

He built farm buildings, pigsties and a dairy shed. Either he or Jenny attended both the morning and evening milking. They planted pyrethrum, the daisy-like flowers of which when dried were sold as a base for insecticides; Jenny managed the picking and weighing of this crop. Most of the labour for this was provided by the women and the children on the farm.

Thirty of the 35 African families were Kikuyu.

The Lawrences also employed about 5 families of Luo people who came from near Kisumu on Lake Victoria. The Luo were accommodated in a separate village.

The Kikuyu were familiar with stock generally and also understood agriculture and machinery. The Luo were very reliable but had no knowledge at all of how to handle stock; in general they were afraid of them.

Within two or three years Peter and Jenny had the beginnings of a well ordered, well organised farm. They both worked from dawn until dusk seven days a week. None of this would have been possible without the labour of course.

Peter in particular managed his labour very well with a degree of sympathy unknown on most of the other farms. He always had people applying for jobs so he was able to pick and choose, and with Kahinga, Kinua and the head stockman Kamau providing a nucleus, within a very short time he had a stable, hardworking labour force. Jenny made it her business to know and understand the women on the farm and generally shared their trials and tribulations. She attended many births of children, acting as a midwife if she was unable to get the mother to the hospital in Nakuru (25 miles away) in time, which was frequently the case.

The Lawrences also participated in local affairs. Peter Lawrence became a member of the local council, which met monthly in Naivasha and Jenny joined the local women's league.

Both Jenny and Peter had a great love of horses and they had managed to acquire some half Arab thoroughbreds for themselves and ponies for the children, Robert and John, who were by that time seven and four respectively. Jenny absolutely adored the horses and rode whenever possible. Most of her chores on the farm were easily accessible on horseback and with the abundant labour there was always someone to hold the horse if she was busy doing something else. She also spent many hours teaching Robert and John how to ride, and also how to generally look after their ponies and the tack (saddles and bridles) associated with horses. Over the next year or two both Robert and John learnt to ride very well.

Jenny had done some competitive show jumping in her youth and whilst she was unable to even think about that while they were building up the farm, she had a few jumps erected in a paddock near the house and schooled both horses and ponies to jump. Her horse, Crest, stood at 16 hands and although he had been gelded had a great spirit and when the mood took her she really let him have his head. She was always exhilarated when she came back from a ride on her own with him. Peter spent a great deal of time either repairing fences or building new ones; to some extent this curbed Jenny's freedom to ride. She solved the problem by draping her jacket over any offending fence and then jumping the horse over it. Peter warned her to be careful doing this, as the fences were four and a half feet high and the ground sometimes rough. She took no notice. She loved that element of danger; besides, she had never felt so free in her life. They had their own place, they could more or less do whatever they liked despite the hardships imposed by their lifestyle; for them the Government barely existed and certainly made no attempt to control them or anything they wanted to do, and they lived by their own ethics and their own values. They could see that with a bit more hard work and some good seasons, they would own the farm outright and then they really would be free.

Robert had been enrolled at a small nursery school run by a local farmer's wife about twelve miles away. Because of the Lawrences' somewhat unreliable transport arrangements (the old International had given up the ghost, and all they had was a mule cart, until later they acquired an army surplus three ton Chevrolet lorry) Jenny arranged for Robert to board weekly with another family who also had children at the school. This involved Robert riding with Gugu the syce (groom) to the neighbour early on Monday mornings and staying the week, while Gugu brought the horses back to Naseby. Usually Gugu fetched him late Friday afternoon as well, but occasionally Jenny went to meet him and they rode home together.

Once they had been on Naseby for three or four years in order to provide more cash to develop the farm, the Lawrences decided to rent about 1000 acres of wheat growing country on the Ol'Kalou plains. During the ploughing and planting season and again during the harvest time Peter transferred his heavy equipment down there, for six weeks or so on each occasion, to get the job done. He, with Kahinga, Kinua and a few others including Dibu the cook, used to camp. Peter and his "boys" ran the equipment and Dibu kept camp and cooked all the meals. Jenny had to stay on Naseby and manage the home farm; occasionally if they felt they could leave the milking, Jenny and the boys would join Peter in the camp for a weekend. There was a wonderful trout stream nearby where they fished and tried to relax.

Peter always took his precious, newly acquired bolt action .416 Rigby hunting rifle, with a four shot magazine with him down to the Malewa (such was the name of the stream). He had recently taken an interest in photography and wanted to go to the NFD (Northern Frontier District) to photograph wild game. He would, of course, need someone to protect him while he attempted some of the more adventurous photographs he was planning, and whilst he thought he could persuade one of the neighbours to go with him, he decided to train Kahinga as a gun-bearer. This was the second season down on the Malewa; he had really started to trust his "boys". In order to do this he had to train Kahinga how to shoot and look after a rifle. So on one of the first Sundays on his own with his "boys" he told Kahinga of his plans and then told him he would teach him to look after a rifle and train him how to shoot. Peter vaguely noticed Kahinga's look of amazement when this plan was mooted; Kahinga couldn't believe his luck.

Peter was a hard taskmaster when it came to guns. He always felt that people were far too casual with them, so before Kahinga was allowed to fire a shot he was made to strip and re-assemble the Rigby in less than thirty seconds, blindfolded. Whenever he was handed the weapon he knew he had to point the gun away from the people around him and open the breech to see if there was a round of ammunition in it. He was taught never to move without making sure that there wasn't a round in the breech; if he ever went through a fence he had to open the breech; the safety catch always had to be on. At first he didn't really understand why all this was necessary but he was an apt pupil and eventually he really understood the power of the weapon and the responsibility that went with that power.

After two weeks of this training Peter eventually produced a largish piece of cardboard and marked a few circles on it. He then nailed it to a tree, making sure that any stray bullets would go harmlessly into a hill behind the tree.

He then showed Kahinga how to aim, to squeeze the trigger and not pull it and to hold the rifle tight into his shoulder to minimize the effect of the kick, which in a .416 is significant. Peter made Kahinga lie in the prone position about 100 yards from the target and told him to fire three shots at the target. When they went up to look at it, the target was unmarked. Kahinga's face fell. Peter then took the rifle and fired three shots himself; when they examined the target Peter had three bulls-eyes.

Two of Kahinga's next three shots were on the outer edge of the target. During the few weeks following Peter had Kahinga shooting at the target lying prone, sitting, kneeling and standing. He became completely familiar with the weapon. If he had had formal weapons training in the army he couldn't have been better drilled. Kinua always came along and learned how to clean the gun. He thought he could probably manage to shoot with it if he had to. Dibu too took a great interest in the proceedings. The "boys" couldn't believe their luck. In the early part of their sojourn in the Malewa Peter used to shoot a buck almost once a week to keep the camp in meat; after a couple of visits Kahinga took on this "chore" firstly with Peter and then on his own. He never did anything that betrayed Peter's trust; the time would come when he would have to, he knew that.

During the third year of operations in the Malewa there was an incident that brought them even closer together. The area had many snakes, the most dangerous of which were puffadders. Snakes generally move away when they hear footfalls but puffadders are slow to move and very quick to strike, and are deadly poisonous. Kahinga and Kinua had gone down to the river, which was about 100 yards from camp, to wash. It was approaching dusk on what had been a warm, sunny afternoon. Kahinga was leading the way down the narrow path that led to the river. He wasn't really looking where he was going; it had been a long day and he was really ready for a good meal and sleep. He stood right on a big, fat, six-foot monster of a puffadder, which immediately struck him right in the meat of his calf. He yelled.

Kinua saw exactly what had happened.

"Bwana, Bwana, nyoka (snake), come quick, Kahinga has been bitten," he called to Peter in Kikuyu.

Peter was having a quiet beer and chatting to Dibu whilst the latter prepared the evening meal.

He was ready for this; he always carried a tourniquet, a sharp knife and a vial of permanganate of potash for just this type of emergency. Dibu brought a bowl with some water in it and they rushed down the path to where Kahinga lay, already in agony.

Kinua had chopped the snake's head off with his panga and when Peter saw the size of the snake he said, "Shit, we're in real trouble; that thing will have injected a huge amount of poison into Kahinga."

He tore off Kahinga's shorts, turned him over and then tied the tourniquet as tight as he could around his right thigh.

He could see the puncture marks the snake's fangs had made in his calf; he made a deep cut through both marks and blood poured out. Dibu had mixed some permanganate into the water; Peter sucked the wound and spat, and then took a mouthful of the permanganate, which acted as a disinfectant. He did this for about 20 minutes, releasing the tourniquet every now and then to let the blood flow. Kahinga lapsed in and out of consciousness. Kinua had brought the three-ton lorry as near as he dared on Peter's instruction. It looked as though Kahinga was stable but they had to get him to the doctor in Ol'Kalou as quickly as possible.

They loaded Kahinga into the back of the truck, and Peter told Kinua to drive as fast as he could to the village. Dibu and Peter sat in the back, they kept the tourniquet on but as they came into the village it looked as if Kahinga was about done for. Luckily the doctor was still there and was equipped for this type of emergency. He gave Kahinga the maximum dose of the anti-snakebite serum when Peter told him the size of the snake. They struggled for about two hours and eventually the doctor said: "I can't do anymore; he'll have to make it on his own now."

There was one bed in the clinic and they put the now delirious Kahinga there.

"I'll be sleeping round the back tonight; if he gets worse call me," said the doctor.

With that he left them.

Peter, Kinua and Dibu took it in turns to nurse Kahinga; the two that were not on duty tried to sleep in the lorry.

By daybreak Kahinga seemed to be slightly more relaxed; he was still unconscious though and he remained that way for most of that day and into the night.

Sometime during the night Kahinga started to come to. Peter was with him at the time. Kahinga looked terrified.

"Nyoka (snake)" said Peter. "But you are OK now; you're in the clinic in Ol'Kalou."

Gradually Peter calmed him down and explained what had happened.

"Your quick action certainly saved Kahinga's life," the doctor told Peter the next day. "Even this new serum would not have helped him with the amount of poison he must have taken and with the amount of time it took to get him here."

The doctor wanted to make sure Kahinga and the others understood what he had said, so he repeated it in Swahili. Kahinga's brown eyes looked at Peter.

"How am I going to repay this debt? How can I hate this M'zungu when he saved my life?" he thought.

They eventually went back to camp and finished off what they were doing. Kahinga was back working full time within a week and was his normal cheerful self. They then returned to Naseby.

The incident with the snake shook Peter up; he had really started to rate his "boys" as companions, as people. Life seemed very fragile. "What if Kahinga had died?" he thought. He wondered what Kahinga's aspirations were. "Surely not to spend the rest of his life working for me, on Naseby," he mused. He never took the issue up with him though. He would have been mighty surprised had he done so.

※ ※ ※

CHAPTER 8

George Athill had just inherited his farm in the Wanjohe valley from a wealthy father who had for a time been part of the Kenya set, in the thirties. This Kenya set was known for high living and loose morals; one of its infamous activities were key parties where the men would put their car keys in a bowl in the living room, and the women would select a key and go home with whichever man owned it. The Wanjohe – known as the Happy Valley – was one of the reasons for the expression "Are you married or do you live in Kenya?"

Educated at Eton, George was not particularly bright, but it didn't seem to matter; for him privilege was what mattered and had earned him his position in society. He didn't really trust the colonials but when he saw the farm close to the foothills of the Aberdares he fell in love with the place. The farm had a manager on it and there really wasn't a great deal for George to do except enjoy himself. George was tall and good looking; he was independently wealthy, all inherited. The women loved him. Most of the men thought he was a drip, although he could be very charming and amusing when the mood took him. His family in England had persuaded him to go to Kenya and stay there; he was paid a handsome stipend not to return to England. Before the war George had joined Sir Oswald Moseley's 'brownshirts'. Their sympathies lay with the fascist policies of Hitler and Mussolini. The only reason that George had not been interned with his leader was because of family connections.

The Lawrences usually made a point of visiting newcomers to the district and after George had been there a couple of months the Lawrences popped in one mid-morning after they had done their chores in Ol'Kalou. The time passed pleasantly enough, though the parties had little in common. The Lawrences were tough, hardworking people who had to make it on their own and Athill had inherited everything he owned and had never done a stroke of work in his life. Peter had never even been to England, at that stage.

Just as they were about to leave George said to Peter, "Oh Lawrence, by the way, I hear you are into a spot of hunting up north; there wouldn't be a spare berth for me, would there?" Before Peter had time to think Jenny chimed in: "Yes, Pete, I'll be OK for a couple of weeks if you go in March; that's just before the short rains when the farm is at its quietest."

Peter couldn't think of anything to say; he didn't really fancy two weeks with George but without being overtly rude he couldn't turn him down.

"I'm mainly interested in photography," said Peter, "although I take out all the licences in case I have to shoot an animal."

"That's OK with me," answered George. He had never been hunting in Africa in his life. All he wanted was the adventure, he didn't think about what it would be like with Peter and his crew for two weeks in the bush.

Peter and Kinua spent about a week servicing the three ton lorry properly. By the time they had finished, it had never been in better shape. They set off from Ol'Kalou early one morning in March. They had agreed to meet at 3am outside S. Shah's store. George's manager had grumpily brought him from the valley. The morning was cold with a light frost on the ground.

Kahinga, Kinua and Dibu came with Peter; Dibu also insisted on bringing with him a ten year old boy who called himself Stanley (after Stanley Matthews the famous England soccer player) to do all the rough chores like washing up.

The Indian shopkeeper came out to see what all the noise was about, so they stocked up with a few extra provisions. Peter had all the camping gear that he considered necessary from his various sojourns down by the Malewa. They took potatoes and carrots and the like; soft vegetables such as tomatoes wouldn't last a day. Peter expected to shoot birds and small buck for the pot. He had his .416 Rigby with him and the twelve bore shotgun that Jenny had used in her episode with the leopard; they were clipped into a gun rack in the lorry cab above the seat. George had been told that Peter would bring most of the camping equipment, but he had a huge, new looking rucksack and four gun cases, all of which looked as if they had just came out of Purdy and Purdy's gun shop in Piccadilly. George had two double-barrelled elephant guns, a very new .350 Magnum Rigby and a twelve bore shotgun with silver inlay in the butt. On the pretext of admiring the armoury, Peter had a good look at all the guns. They had all recently been fired, none of them had been cleaned and all of them were loaded. Peter unobtrusively unloaded all the weapons before he returned them to their cases. He exchanged a look with Kahinga.

George also had a .38 revolver on his belt. Peter began to wonder about George and what the next two weeks would be like.

They drove through Ol'Joro Orok and Thomsons Falls to Nanyuki, where they spent the night on a farm with some old friends of the Lawrences. The evening passed without incident and the Kikuyu found accommodation with their fellow tribesmen. Nanyuki is at the base of Mount Kenya (Kirinyaga) and in the early morning they were able to admire the twin peaks of Batian and Lenana in the pink dawn. Peter in his enthusiasm took a couple of rolls of film. Kahinga and the Kikuyu paid their respects to the Kikuyu God Ngai who lived on Kirinyaga. The country from Thomsons Falls most of the way to Nanyuki was dry thorn scrub; Peter shuddered when he compared the land to his rolling hills and well watered farm at Ol'Kalou. Nanyuki was the dusty little administrative centre for the region. It served the white owned farms and was a tourist hub, being the base camp for expeditions to Mount Kenya and the Northern Frontier District.

Peter had arranged to pick up his hunting licenses from the Game Department there. He encouraged George to do the same. They also needed permits for themselves, the vehicle and the "boys". They told the police approximately where they intended to go.

The party went through Isiolo and then spent a few days at Archer's Post on the Uaso Nyiro River. They camped on the river and Peter and the Kikuyu erected the tents, such as they were - just a couple of awnings strung between the trees. George took his shotgun and wandered off.

"Don't go too far," warned Peter.

Five minutes later George came rushing back.

"Buffalo!" he shouted. "Hundreds of them."

Peter wondered and then grabbed his camera and Kahinga brought the Rigby; they went quietly down the path on the edge of the river.

"Wildebeest," whispered Peter.

Kahinga tried to hide his snicker. Peter took a few pictures.

By the time Peter and George got back, the camp was set up.

"Where are the tents?" asked George.

Peter pointed at the awnings. George looked troubled.

"I thought we were going to sleep in tents," he said. "What about the animals?"

"Animals won't trouble us here," said Peter. "We keep a log burning all night; they won't come within a hundred yards."

"Where can I wash?" asked George.

"River," answered Peter. "I may just have to put a couple of shots into the water to scare the crocs off. Keeps them away for about 30 minutes. We'll all go in and wash together with one of us keeping his eyes out on the bank."

George blanched. This wasn't quite what he had envisaged. He'd never bathed in the open before, let alone in front of the servants - and these were black servants!

"Say, old boy," said George. "I'm rather unused to this; do you think I could go upriver a bit?"

"Sure," said Peter. "I'll send Kahinga with you."

"Ah, no, could you come?"

Peter started to get the message.

"Ok," he said.

When George had finished Peter and the others washed in the shallows. Peter put a couple of shots into the river. George was nowhere to be seen.

Dibu in the meanwhile had prepared the supper. Ogalie and some meat they had brought with them plus a few vegetables for the Kikuyu and a roast and vegetables for Peter and George. Peter sat down near the fire and handed beers around.

"Beer?" he asked George.

"Say, old chap. Are you going to sit with the nigs?" George had never sat with a servant in all his life, and these were black people. There was no possibility that he could sit and have a beer and a meal with them.

Kahinga and Kinua watched. They understood no English but they could tell from the body language what was going on. Dibu pretended to be busy with the meal.

"Certainly," said Peter. "This is how we always operate."

George stormed off and lay on his camp bed under the awning. This was not what he had expected. For him camping was being waited on hand and foot, he expected a proper tent and he certainly wasn't going to hob-lob with Lawrence's black savages. He pulled a bottle of whisky out of his rucksack and drank heavily. Dibu brought him his meal, which he barely touched. He finished the whisky. Peter and the others talked in muted tones, mostly in Kikuyu; normally the first evening of a safari was full of good cheer and ribald jokes. Peter wondered what he was going to do about George.

When they all eventually went to bed Peter lay there and thought about George. He wondered what the Kikuyu thought of him. Kenya could do without this sort of bigot; life was difficult enough as it was. He went to sleep listening to all the familiar night sounds of the African bush: a crash here a hyena laugh there; somewhere in the distance a lion roared. Once when he got up during the night he shone his torch around and picked out the usual array of eyes around the camp; how he loved it all.

Early the next morning Peter and Kahinga went out early with the shotgun. They knew that at dawn the bush quail would be flying in from the desert on the early morning breeze to come to drink at the river.

George was still in a drunken state. Kinua had something to do on the truck; Dibu and Stanley busied themselves with the breakfast. Peter had the shotgun; Kahinga always brought the Rigby as a precaution.

The morning was cool, there was a hint of dew on the foot-high, brown grass and the bushes were slightly damp. The vegetation generally was sparse with small clumps of grass interspersed with bare red earth; most of the bushes were no more than ten feet high and were thinly distributed.

Peter savoured the morning; there was a hint of light in the east and he loved the smell of the damp bush. A little dik-dik skipped away; a francolin started its unearthly "karra karra karra" racket. Everywhere there was peace; the nocturnal animals were home or on their way there; the larger animals would be moving soon.

They found a likely spot and sure enough just as the dawn came up the quail started to fly. Peter picked his targets and fired left barrel, then right, reloaded and repeated the procedure. In a very short time he had ten quail in the bag. He gave the gun to Kahinga, who bagged another five.

They were just about to head back to camp when they heard four or five shots in succession. They ran back to camp. Kinua, Dibu and Stanley were hiding behind the truck. George was standing in the middle of the camp looking bewildered.

"Bloody snake," he growled.

"Where?" asked Peter.

"Gone."

It seemed fortunate that no-one had been hurt.

Peter asked the Kikuyu what had happened. They all shook their heads - they had seen nothing.

They had breakfast. George ate separately. After breakfast Peter decided he would have to make the most of things so he said to George:

"I suggest that we get Kinua to clean a couple of your rifles and then we can go out and see if we can spot some buffalo, which are plentiful in the area."

George grumpily handed Kinua one of his double-barrelled rifles and his .350. The gun was handed back to George, who growled aggressively at Kinua. "Boots," he said, "clean my fucking boots!"

Kinua completely ignored him.

George got up and screamed, "I said, clean my fucking boots!" He threw them at Kinua who managed to dodge the missiles. Peter had heard the commotion and came over.

The fury had completely overwhelmed George by now. He clenched his fist and took a wild swing at Kinua; he hadn't seen Peter approaching. George found his fist engulfed in one of Peter's large hands; he looked up briefly and saw the cold anger in Peter's hard blue eyes.

"Let me go, let me go you bastard!" yelled George.

Peter squeezed harder.

The agony was unbearable. George sat down heavily in the dust, Peter still squeezing his fist.

"You will never, never speak to my people like that again," Peter said harshly. "And if you attempt to strike anyone again I will have you charged. Now apologise."

George couldn't believe that a white man would take the part of an African in such a dispute; he rolled in the dust, clutching his hand in pain.

"Apologise," demanded Peter.

George was now bellowing in agony; his hand felt as if every bone had been broken.

"Apologise!"

"I apologise," squawked George.

Peter let George go and he got up and dusted himself off. He shot Peter a look of such hatred that Peter was shocked. He knew then that he had made a permanent, perhaps a dangerous enemy. He shivered despite himself.

An hour later the little party set off on foot, all rather shaken: Peter, George, Kahinga, Kinua and Stanley, who brought up the rear. Stanley proudly carried the lunch, which consisted of a few sandwiches for Peter and George and some ogalie for the Kikuyu. They all carried water bottles. They had decided to go out into the bush away from the river, join the river a few miles downstream and then make their way back to camp along the riverbank. Peter had his camera and telephoto lens. Kahinga carried the Rigby, George carried his Holland and Holland double-barrelled .450 express with Kinua reluctantly acting as his gun-bearer, carrying George's .350.

The day had started to warm up. The party moved fast and skilfully through the bush; the occasional antelope crashed out of the way. They stopped every now and then to listen and look. George started to sweat.

Kahinga pointed. "Nyani (monkeys)."

Peter saw the big male baboon just as it shouted its warning to the rest of the troop.

"Waugh," coughed the baboon.

Peter and Kahinga left the others in full view of the troop and crept round some bushes to approach the troop from the side nearest the river where the troop appeared to be heading.

They crept to within a few feet of the group. The big male was still making warning sounds; he was focused on Kinua, George and Stanley. Peter took roll after roll of film. There were mothers with young clinging to them, the juveniles were raking about playing games and a couple of males were strutting about keeping watch. The troop was moving along steadily eating grubs and berries. Suddenly one of the big males spotted Peter and Kahinga and rushed at them. Kahinga kept his head and fired a shot over the massive baboon's head. He stopped and bared his large yellow fangs, which would have given any unfortunate person a severely infected bite. Peter got many really good pictures. The baboons scattered.

The others joined Kahinga and Peter.

"Why didn't you shoot the thing?" inquired George aggressively.

"Not necessary," said Peter. "I came here for the photographs."

George grunted contemptuously.

The party went on and stopped under a thorn tree on a little hillock to eat lunch.

"Look for the vultures," suggested Peter.

"What's that?" asked George.

"Often the best way of spotting a lion kill, for example, is to see if one can spot vultures circling. They have wonderful eyesight, also they watch each other way up in the heavens and if birds in one area spot a dead animal - and they always do - then other vultures from miles around are attracted to the scene. It's one of the wonders of nature; even in death everything has a value."

George grunted; he couldn't have cared less about Lawrence's sentimental nonsense about nature. He would love to see a lion though. He started looking into the sky.

Shortly after that Stanley, who had taken the binoculars up a thorn tree, waved excitedly. The others were sitting in the shade.

"Nyati (buffalo)," he yelled.

"Quiet," said Kahinga. "You'll chase them away,"

Stanley came down the tree and pointed.

There in the middle distance was what appeared to be a huge herd of buffalo. They were moving slowly towards the river, grazing as they went.

"Come." Peter had quickly surveyed the scene; he could see the route the herd was to take on its way to the river. He tested the breeze. It was important that the wind was blowing from the herd of buffalo towards the humans, not the other way round.

They moved rapidly through the bush and within an hour had ensconced themselves in a large bush. Peter had calculated that the buffalo would pass within a few yards of where they were. He set his camera up. They waited patiently, even George.

The buffalo started to wander through the bush. It was a truly awesome sight. Peter had calculated that there were approximately 500 of them. They moved slowly with the cows and calves in the centre of the herd and a few large bulls guarding the fringes. Tick birds flapped around the herd. Most animals had two or three birds on their backs. Mostly they took no notice or were not aware of the humans; occasionally one of the bulls pawed the ground and glared furiously in their direction. Some of the tick birds squawked at the humans. Kahinga put the safety catch of the Rigby off just in case. Peter managed to take dozens of really good pictures.

George was getting restless. He just wanted to shoot one of the animals.

The last of the stragglers were passing by; there was a huge buffalo bull bringing up the rear. He had a massive pair of horns which came together in the centre of his head in two large bosses, and below that were a couple of malevolent, yellow-looking eyes. There were a number of tick birds on his back. From the scars on his hide he had obviously been through many battles to maintain his supremacy in the herd. He was old for a buffalo but was in good condition. The grazing had been good that year and despite his age he was the picture of unbridled power and health. He started pawing the ground.

Peter clicked away.

George knew that Peter did not want any shots fired.

"To hell with him," thought George. He'd never really taken orders from anyone, certainly not from an upstart colonial.

The buffalo bull was about 50 yards away in clear view. George quickly raised his rifle to his shoulder, took quick aim and pulled the trigger. He could hardly miss but the bullet went high; the buffalo bellowed in pain and anger and ran off into the bush. The herd scattered. If George had taken a little more care he could have dropped the animal on the spot.

"For Christ's sake, what did you do that for?" said Peter angrily. "Now we've got a badly wounded buffalo on our hands."

He'd heard the bullet slap into the animal. The shot had given him as well as every living thing in the vicinity a terrible fright.

"It looked like an easy shot," said George.

"Sure it was an easy shot, If you had said something, we could have made sure of it for you, now we'll probably have to follow this thing up for a couple of days."

"You and your bloody photographs," muttered George.

They picked up the blood spoor almost immediately. Peter knew that the animal would instinctively run away from the herd and into thick bush to protect himself; he was no use to the herd in this condition. Peter also knew that a wounded buffalo was the most tricky and dangerous animal in Africa. If the animal thought he was being followed he would double back on his tracks and try to surprise his pursuers by attacking them from behind.

They followed the blood for a couple of hours. Peter had hoped that if the animal was badly wounded, he might slow down and they would get him before dusk. No luck however. The buffalo might have been badly wounded - some of the blood was lighter in colour indicating a lung shot - but it was very strong and moving quickly. They stopped.

"I'm going back to camp," announced George. He was not under any circumstances going to spend a night out in the bush. He couldn't have cared less about the buffalo and as far as he was concerned one animal more or less, wounded or not, made no difference to him. He was not going to risk his precious life or his comfort for the sake of a wounded buffalo. He took no responsibility whatsoever for his actions. This was Lawrence's show - if he wanted to act the bloody hero that was his affair.

Peter sized the situation up. They would be better off without George. There was just enough daylight to return to camp.

"Stanley," he said.

"Ndio, bwana (yes sir)."

"You can find your way back to camp." This was a statement rather than a question. Stanley knew the way back, he just had to follow the river.

"Take bwana George back to camp as quickly as you can. We will follow the buffalo spoor until it gets dark, then we will camp. You must find us there in the morning; bring some food and ammunition."

Stanley's chest swelled with pride. The M'zungu trusted him.

George looked enquiringly at Peter.

"Stanley will go back to camp with you, you'll have enough time if you leave now," said Peter.

George was a little piqued; he really wanted everyone to return to camp, but he didn't say anything. He realised Peter thought he was a burden and half wished this wasn't so. Nevertheless he and Stanley set off.

"Oh George, lend me your double-barrelled, you'll be OK with the .350."

George handed it over together with the ammunition.

Peter, Kahinga and Kinua followed the buffalo spoor as quickly as they could, for about an hour.

Peter and Kinua then set about making camp. They cleared all the grass away from a smallish area and then collected firewood. They knew that snakes out of a sense of self-preservation try to avoid open spaces. So they wouldn't be troubled by them and the smell of wood-smoke would keep the other animals away.

Kahinga came back with a small impala, which they skinned and then roasted on the fire.

They only had the clothes they stood up in, but it was a warm night and they all managed some sleep on the ground round the fire.

Stanley woke them up just as the dawn was breaking. He had brought food and ammunition.

Peter looked at him.

"Everything OK?" he enquired. "You got bwana George back to camp OK?"

"Ndio." Stanley avoided Peter's eyes. He had got George back to camp, but George had immediately hit the bottle and until he fell asleep on his bed had made a thorough nuisance of himself. Twice Dibu had to fetch him when he walked off by himself. Stanley felt he was better off here. Dibu would have to cope by himself.

Peter didn't enquire further. They had a wounded buffalo on their hands and they needed to deal with that first. He would worry about George later.

They quickly had some breakfast, took some of the impala in case they had to spend another night in the bush, and covered up the fire. They left the rest of the impala on the ground near the camp. The scavengers would find it soon enough.

They quickly picked up the spoor; Kahinga and Kinua were good trackers so they took it in turn to lead. The blood had dried but it was still quite clear; the buffalo was badly wounded. Stanley was intrigued and he followed his elder's actions with obvious interest; he'd never been involved in anything so exciting in all his young life. Peter kept a careful watch out both in front and behind. He had the double-barrelled express, Kahinga had the .416. Peter knew that if the buffalo charged it would probably be from a very short distance and at best he would get two shots off, so they would have to be accurate.

As expected, within an hour the wounded animal had gone into very thick bush down near the river. Progress was painfully slow with their clothing being ripped by "wait-a-bit thorns".

They came across a place where the animal had rested a while. There was a pool of blood there. Kahinga looked at Peter.

"One hour old, maybe," he said.

Kinua nodded.

They had better be careful now, as the buffalo bull would be aware that he was being followed and would be on the alert. The bush was really thick; they could see only 20 to 30 yards. It was very hot; there was no breeze in the thick bush. A black mamba – snake – hissed at them and slithered away quickly.

Peter was unhooking himself from yet another "wait-a-bit". He would call a halt and they would then decide what to do.

Suddenly as if from nowhere, slightly behind them and to the left came the buffalo. It had obviously circled them and had got downwind of them. It made no sound, except for the sound of the hooves on the ground and the noise of crashing through the bush. To start it had its head up, but when it got closer it put its head down; the buffalo had summoned up the very last of its energy to do the maximum damage to the humans. He was really, really angry and sore; his eyes, normally tinged with yellow, were now blood red.

Kahinga acted like a veteran; he knelt on one knee and quickly got three shots off. The heavy solid steel tipped bullets slapped into the ferocious animal and it fell a few feet short of Peter and Kahinga. Peter lowered George's double, unused.

The buffalo was huge, about 5 feet at the shoulder, and weighed probably 1200lbs. The horns were the biggest Peter had ever seen, 50 inches from tip to tip. The hide was scarred from the animal's long life.

Peter took a few pictures with Kahinga, Kinua and Stanley standing next to the dead buffalo. They were holding the guns.

They cut the horns out; maybe George would want the trophy. He had after all drawn first blood. They left the rest of the carcass. The hide was useless; the scavengers would clean it up.

They then all trudged back to camp. Kinua carried the horns most of the way. They arrived back in camp well after dark.

George was sitting in splendid isolation at the campfire; there was half a bottle of Scotch sitting on the table in front of him. From his demeanour the rest of the bottle was sitting inside him; he was awfully drunk. Dibu appeared from the shadows looking disconsolate.

Peter took the still bloody horns from Kinua and dumped them none too gently in George Athills lap.

"Your buffalo, George," he said.

George fell over backwards in his deck chair.

"Shteady on, old chap," he said getting up drunkenly. "Wash all thish about now?"

"You got first blood, so it's your trophy. Normally the person who gets first blood does follow up his wounded animal though," said Peter. "Lucky none of us was hurt – it came pretty close though."

Peter and the Kikuyu went down to the river for a wash; they couldn't go far in because of the crocodiles.

Dibu had prepared a delicious dinner with the quail from the previous day. George had already gone to bed.

The next day they took a track from Archer's Post to Garba Tula, which was a dusty little trading outpost serving the local community. On the way they had seen some vultures circling a couple of miles off the road and they bumped their way through the bush and quietly came up to a pride of lions sitting over a zebra kill. George's first instinct was to grab for his gun. Peter had anticipated this and restrained him.

"Not this time, George," he said.

"Damn you Lawrence," growled George but he made no further moves. He would have his revenge on this bloody upstart colonial.

They sat and watched the lions for an hour or more. Peter took several rolls of film.

The lions lazed about; they took very little notice of the lorry. The Kikuyu in the back kept very still. There was little danger, the lions had had their fill and weren't looking for another meal.

There was one big male with a large brown mane. He kept a watchful eye on the proceedings; the three lionesses were still eating. Although the lionesses normally catch and kill the prey, when it comes to eating they defer to the male. Now it was their turn. There were a few cubs about, who collected a cuff round the head if they came too close. Their turn would come when the lionesses had had their fill. The vultures had started to gather; any of them who came too close was chased away. There were also a couple of hyena pacing about impatiently, but they kept well away. The lions would have no compunction but to kill them if they came too close.

After a while even George started to watch the scene with fascination. At first he just took in the scene, then with a few judicious words from Peter he started to understand the pecking order, the basic orderliness of how nature disposed of this zebra the lions had killed. First the lion, then his family, then the vultures during the day and the jackals and hyenas at night (the hyenas had jaws strong enough to crack all the bones) and finally the ants. All that would be left within a week would be parts of the skull and maybe a bone or two.

"Nothing in nature kills for pleasure, they kill to eat or to survive - so different to the human condition," mused Peter aloud.

Peter had arranged for a couple of canoes at a village at Bahadale which was a good two hours driving from Garba Tula. Bahadale was a village belonging to the Rendille, a small tribe who lived on the Tana River and survived on their cattle and with a bit of fishing. The river was part of their lives and they knew its every twist and turn, its every sandbank and its every mood.

The group camped by the side of the river on the edge of the village. Whilst the Kikuyu pitched camp, Peter went to see the chief with whom he had had dealings once before during his time in the army.

The chief greeted Peter warmly. They spoke in Swahili; Peter did not speak the chief's language and although the chief could speak Kikuyu he wouldn't do so unless he was forced to. Relations between the two tribes were poor and had been for generations. Before Pax Britannica there had been many clashes of small gangs, both tribes used to steal cattle and women from each other. Most of this had now been stopped by the British; the animosity, however, remained.

Peter agreed to return later for the traditional beer drink with the chief and his council of elders. George was invited; the Kikuyu were not. Peter eventually persuaded George to join him, after he had had his solitary dinner as had now become the custom. He only agreed to come because Peter said it was a great honour and George was therefore able to attach some status to the event.

The Kikuyu understood perfectly well that Peter was obliged to pay homage to the chief. It would make their trip down the river much more pleasant and they could expect help from any of the few villages down river should they need it. The chief held sway right down as far as Garissa. Nevertheless during dinner they ribbed him about his new found friends and made all sorts of ribald remarks about getting off with nubile Rendille maidens.

"You should be so lucky," muttered Peter. He knew the Kikuyu well enough to know that that was exactly what they had in mind.

The chief was a good host and the beer, made from crushed maize, sorghum and sugar was plentiful. This beer relied on airborne yeasts and was unfiltered so it tasted like a very thin gruel. Peter was used to it and knew it was basically nutritious, and the alcohol content quite low. The beer was poured into a large gourd, tasted by the chief and then passed round, first to Peter, who took a sip, then to George. George hesitated.

Peter said, "It's OK, you can't possibly come to any harm."

George said in a strangled voice, "But they're all going to drink out of this."

Peter then said, "Look, our honour depends on this; screw this up and we may have trouble on the river."

Put this way, George took a small sip. He was a great believer in honour, when it suited him. The conversation went from the weather to the state of the crops; how the tribe was faring; the state of the mother river. Peter translated for George. Peter had a great facility for putting himself in the shoes of his African brothers; he had lived among them all his life and really understood what was important to them. He told them a little of the farm at Ol'Kalou.

"The river is very low this year, we are waiting for the rains," the chief volunteered.

This was important information. The Tana rose on Mount Kenya and if the rains failed up there, there would be trouble for the Rendille. Peter also knew that if the river was low, logs and sandbanks would tend to make the journey more treacherous.

Peter and George wandered somewhat unsteadily back to their camp. Peter hoped that George was gaining a little understanding of the country. Little did he know George had only revenge in his heart. As far as he was concerned, Peter had made a fool of him in front of Peter's black servants; he thirsted for retribution and his only interest from now on was just that. He was determined to bring this bloody little colonial upstart down.

Peter said to George as they turned in, "Kinua is taking the truck to Garissa after we leave tomorrow. You can either go with him and stay with the District Commissioner – DC, or come with us in the boats. The boats will take about three days to Garissa. We will camp rough by the side of the river."

George said, "I'll come with you in the boats."

On their way back to bed Peter checked on the Kikuyu. Dibu and Stanley were asleep, but there was no sign of Kahinga and Kinua. Peter knew perfectly well where they were; he just hoped that they wouldn't get into trouble with the people in the village.

In the morning, Peter had to wake Kahinga and Kinua; they had obviously crept into their beds at a very late hour. The glamour and apparent sophistication of the "out of towners" had won over the hearts of a couple of the local maidens with their stories of buffalo hunts and the like. Compared to what they considered to be their rather dull, unglamorous lives with the prospect of eventually being married off to a Rendille fisherman, they considered Kahinga and Kinua almost to have "film star" status. Both the Kikuyu had had a very pleasant, very active evening.

The boats Peter had arranged were two canoes roped together. The party had two complete boats like this. Peter, George and Kahinga were in one boat and Dibu and Stanley were in the other with all the camping and kitchen equipment. Each double boat had two boatmen. The canoes were almost 18 feet long and were made by hollowing out logs.

Kinua was to take the truck to Garissa with the equipment they couldn't fit into the boats plus four other boatmen. The boats would be split up into individual canoes at Garissa and would need two paddlers in each to bring them back to Bahadale.

Peter said to George, "I suggest you bring just one of your doubles; we don't really have room for the other. Besides, they might get spoilt if the canoe gets flooded for any reason."

George could see the sense of this but said, "You mean I should trust that bloody savage with my guns?"

Peter just looked at him. The spare guns were put into the truck.

Most of the village came out to see them off. Peter could see there were a couple of the older looking teenage girls who were more than a little excited; he guessed they were the lovers that Kahinga and Kinua had found the previous night.

The Tana flows from the slopes of Mount Kenya to an outflow to the sea between Lamu and Malindi. From Bahadale to Garissa the river was often over to 200 yards wide, but it was quite low at this time of year just before the rains on Mount Kenya and it flowed quietly on its way to the sea. The river was always brown from the silt, even at the time when it was quite clean and unpolluted. Recently, with the increase in population, there was more erosion on the banks adding to the silt and an increase in human pollutants being added to the river. Peter wondered how many years longer this idyllic scene would last.

They paddled their way down stream. There was very little sign of human habitation, just an occasional village with a few moth eaten cows. Once they saw a herd of camels. The river was full of crocodiles and hippo. The hippos were curious creatures and often followed the canoes for a few hundred yards, bobbing up unexpectedly behind the boats. They didn't follow far, never really straying out of their territory. They saw crocodiles of every size and shape, mainly lying on sandbanks enjoying the warmth of the sun. If they were on a straight stretch of river they kept paddling; when they came to a bend in the river they let the current take them to make sure they didn't disturb whatever was round the next corner. Peter got the most fabulous shots of crocodiles sunbathing, of large herds of zebra, wildebeest and antelope coming down to drink. There were also on several occasions herds of sixty or more elephants and they saw a large herd of buffalo. The place was teeming with game; most of the time they just allowed the boats to drift down past the current attraction. When the animals became aware of the boats they normally just wandered back into the surrounding bush. On the edge of the river because of the proximity of the water there was thick bush and many large trees; in most places the green bush vegetation gave way to desert scrub within 100 yards or so of the river.

The river was a great magnet for animal and human alike. Once when they were drifting round a corner there was a herd of impala at the water's edge drinking. Suddenly there was a big splash and a momentary bleating, and the impala scattered. A crocodile had quickly taken one of the impala. Within minutes the tranquillity of the scene was re-established, the impala had returned nervously to drink, and there was no sign of the crocodile or its unfortunate victim. The impala knew that the crocodile had taken what it needed; none of the rest of them would be victims that day.

Peter took hundreds of pictures. Even George remained interested; this was truly wild Africa. They were wholly dependent on their own resources. There were no radios, or telephones - no communication of any sort. If they got into trouble they themselves would be the only people they could depend on for help. It would take days for help to come from Garissa once the people there became aware of any problem and in any case, how would they know if the party got into difficulties? He shivered despite himself. He looked at Lawrence busy taking pictures; he almost envied him. Despite Lawrence's white skin he fitted into this scene perfectly: he spoke many of the languages; he seemed to understand what these black savages were all about. He even understood the animals; Lawrence was really in his element. George really started to hate him. He wondered to himself how Lawrence would get on in his, George's, home environment in England. The women of course would fall at his feet - he was tall, suntanned, good looking and of course very much his own man and dependent on no-one but himself, God how George hated him.

George was woken out of his reverie; they had eased their way round a bend in the river and there in the stream was the most enormous elephant splashing himself, spraying water over his back and generally enjoying himself. The elephant was still some way off and was not aware of the boats; Dibu and Stanley's boat was several hundred yards behind the lead boat.

Kahinga tapped Peter on the arm.

"Very steep bank on the left hand side; the elephant will have to leave the river on the right; we should stay left and try to scare him off."

Peter nodded. The elephant was in the main stream on the left side of the river; the boat was drifting down towards it. Kahinga pulled a round into the breach of the Rigby and put a shot over the top of the elephant.

The elephant obviously got a terrific fright and ran as best he could through the water to the right hand bank of the river. When it turned round Peter saw it had a handsome pair of tusks on it. The animal was not very old and was obviously in its prime. Peter guessed that it may have been ousted from its herd by an old bull; there was no sign of any other elephant.

As the boat carrying Peter, George, Kahinga and the boatmen drifted down opposite the now fleeing elephant, suddenly before the beast left the river it turned and charged the boat. Peter was busy taking pictures. The elephant was trumpeting, and had his trunk high in the air.

"It will back off, put a couple of shots over its head," said Peter.

Kahinga obliged with three shots from the .416 in quick succession. Kahinga quickly reloaded

This seemed to further enrage the elephant. George nervously fingered his double. Peter continued to take photographs. The elephant came on; then all at once the boatmen dropped their paddles and jumped into the river, crocodiles or not. George hesitated, then he dropped his gun and followed suit.

The elephant was now closing in.

Peter dropped the camera; luckily it was on a strap round his neck. He grabbed George's abandoned double.

"We'll have to shoot," Peter said to Kahinga.

Kahinga pumped three shots from the .416 Rigby into the elephant. He might as well have used a peashooter for all the effect it had. The elephant now had his trunk well tucked in and was pressing home his charge.

Peter raised the double. He prayed that it was loaded. The elephant was now looming; he aimed at the base of the trunk and fired. The animal staggered but came on. Peter knew that if he wanted to stop it he would have to get a brain shot; because of the angle, any shot into the animal's skull would just skid off the massive head. His second shot was from only about ten yards, and he again aimed at the base of the trunk. This time the animal screamed and then just crashed down into the river. The trunk flopped into the boat and the wave caused by the elephant crashing down almost swamped the boat - water streamed in.

Peter was stunned by the primeval scene. After the noise and thunder of the previous few seconds there was now a deathly hush, no noise at all. The birds were quiet, the monkeys in the trees sat stock still, it was as if the whole world was in awe of the clash of two primeval forces. Peter was transfixed for a few seconds; he looked at the dead elephant, its eyes now glazed over in death. Peter looked at Kahinga who grinned wanly.

"Close," was all he could say.

The boat with Dibu and Stanley in it now came alongside; they had had a grandstand seat. Stanley helped Peter and Kahinga bale the boat out. Peter looked around and saw George and the two boatmen standing on the river bank. They managed to guide the two boats over to the bank. There they finished off the bailing.

Nobody said much. They were all struck with the power and the might of the clash which might easily have resulted in the boat being smashed and Kahinga and Peter being killed.

"Nice pair of tusks," said George eventually.

"We'll be lucky to get them though," said Peter. "You just watch."

Within an hour order had been restored: the birds sang, the monkeys played. The great bulk of the elephant lay in the river. Because the river was so low it stuck out like a large grey rock; also the elephant lay in the shallows. The main channel of the river was deeper. The crocodiles had now started to appear, attracted by the smell of blood, and a couple of them were tearing at the carcass. The vultures had started to circle; one or two of them were perched in nearby trees.

"Within a few hours that carcass will be covered with crocs. We won't be able to get near it," said Peter.

George shuddered.

Nothing was said about George jumping off the boat. His resentment against Peter increased.

They had already spent one night on the banks of the river. After a couple more hours they decided to call it a day and camped again. Everything appeared to get back to normal but the adrenalin was still flowing through everyone's veins and the feeling of excitement in the camp was palpable.

Peter persuaded George to go out and see if he could find some meat for the evening meal. Peter played around with his camera, which luckily had come to no harm during the episode with the elephant. The growing bond between Peter and Kahinga was strengthened even further. They had saved each other's lives.

Kahinga and George came back with a small impala. George was very pleased with himself since he had shot it. He seemed to have altogether put out of his mind the incident with the elephant.

Late in the afternoon of the third day after they had left Bahadale they drifted into the small pier at Garissa. Kinua was there with the lorry and the rest of their gear. He had set up camp a little way outside the town. He handed Peter a note.

"The D.C has invited us to dinner," Peter told George. "He has also suggested that we should go up there for a bath and a cleanup."

So they left the Kikuyu to themselves and went over to see the D.C, who had a largish bungalow in the small town of Garissa overlooking the river.

※ ※ ※

Chapter 9

Peter and George were dropped off at the D.C's house. The D.C's name was Mike Nicklin.

George used the washing facilities first and Peter sat on the veranda sipping a cold beer. He had managed to get a message to Jenny to phone him at the D.C's house; she would have to use the neighbour's phone as they had no phone at Naseby.

The D.C had been called away back to his office to deal with some urgent matter.

There was an African girl sitting on the steps; her job was to keep an eye on the two Nicklin children who were seven and eight. Peter couldn't quite identify her tribal roots so he addressed her in Swahili; he soon realised, however, that she spoke Kikuyu, so he switched to that.

Rafiki, for that was her name, turned out to have a Kikuyu father and a Masai mother; she appeared to be nineteen or twenty years old. She was tall (about 5'10"), she had a few beads in her fairly long, frizzed-out hair. Peter noticed her high cheekbones and slightly elongated face; she had an almost aristocratic air about her. She had a small nose, full lips and very white, even teeth, and some small beads in her ears. Even through the rather shapeless dress she wore he could see a pair of large, firm breasts and that she was slim; she had long, lithe limbs and was barefoot. Her skin was brown. Despite himself, Peter thought that he had never seen such beauty. The Masai in her gave her many of her physical attributes, including her bright smile and the look of her face. She was obviously intelligent and he found out that she had done a couple of years in a mission school in Kikuyuland near Thika. Peter gathered that the Nicklin children were to go to boarding school in England in September and that Rafiki would then return to Thika.

The conversation flowed easily; she told him a little of how hard it had been growing up in the crowded Kikuyu reserve, and how she wished to continue her very limited education. She was really uncertain about her future; she had enjoyed the job with the Nicklins and wondered what life could offer her, other than becoming the wife of some minor chief and being treated as a chattel, like her mother before her.

Peter was non-committal. He perfectly well understood the social arrangements of the Kikuyu and indeed most of the people in Africa; he didn't see it changing for centuries. He told her a little about the trip and the farm. It was extraordinary how easy it was to talk to her; he'd never in all his life had a conversation like this with a black African woman. It was almost as if they were soulmates.

One of the children had run down the garden. Rafiki scrambled after her. They were always careful about allowing the children too near the river bank, for fear of crocodiles. Peter strolled down after her. Once she had rescued the child she came back to Peter and pointed.

There was a small herd of elephant drinking on the other side of the river. They sat and watched quietly, the large bull keeping watch, the female elephants disciplining their children. In Peter's experience most Africans took the wildlife for granted. Clearly Rafiki was as interested as he, Peter, was.

The D.C returned and Rafiki went off to deal with the children.

"Extraordinary girl," said Peter.

"Oh, yes, Rafiki," said Mike Nicklin absently. He'd never really taken much notice of her; that was his wife Sue's department.

"I gather the kids are going to boarding school and her job more or less ends there," said Peter.

"Say, you are well informed," observed Mike disinterestedly.

Peter was disturbed by his meeting with Rafiki. He also felt guilty. He couldn't get her out of his head. "Come on, pull yourself together man, you'll never see her again anyway," he thought to himself.

Mike Nicklin had been in Kenya about ten years, all that time in the administration. He and his wife really adored Kenya. Although they were both from English stock, Kenya had given them almost everything they had. They had had many different postings and apart from speaking Swahili he had picked up a smattering of the other languages. As a family they spent most of their holidays exploring this wonderful country. He really wondered at the wisdom of sending his children to boarding school in England, but this was part of his contract and it seemed a pity not to give them the opportunity. He was aware that the local schools for whites were of a high standard. Nicklin, like many others in the administration, didn't have a lot to do with the settler community. His current posting at Garissa was mostly concerned with the indigenous population and their welfare and with border incursions from the Somali Republic to the east and independent Ethiopia to the North. He administered his vast territory with competence and sensitivity. There was no settler community in his territory. He only had contact with the occasional "safari" like the one Peter was now on. He was of course aware that Kenya was administered in what was considered the interests of Great Britain and the great British Commonwealth. Some of the policies didn't make sense in the context of the local settler community.

He also knew something about the Mau-Mau; fortunately they were not in his present area of operations. He wondered why so little was being done about the organisation. Mike Nicklin had heard Peter talking to Rafiki in what he had determined was Kikuyu, and he was intrigued. Peter and he chatted; Peter told him where they had been on their safari, and about the incidents with the buffalo and the elephant. Peter didn't deal with George's behaviour in any way. Nicklin knew enough about human nature to pick up the fact that George had not exactly covered himself with glory. He felt sure he would get the full story in due course via the servants and he didn't want to further upset an already delicate situation by asking direct questions.

George emerged from his long sojourn in the bath and Peter then left Mike Nicklin and George together.

George immediately established that they had some mutual acquaintances in England and armed with this reassurance started to try to undermine Peter.

"Strange one this Lawrence," said George. "Sits with the nigs in his campsite - almost shares it with them on an equal basis. Even washes with them."

Nicklin didn't find any of this surprising. It was how he operated when he was on safari. He didn't know how else you found out what the locals were thinking unless you shared things with them.

He was also offended by George's use of the word "nigs" which was a shortened form of "nigger".

He just said, "Hm, that's very much how I operate."

George was silent for a minute and then said, "All his staff seem to be really familiar with firearms; Lawrence seems to have trained them very well."

"Saved your life," said Mike Nicklin. "Why should you be complaining?"

They didn't discuss the Mau-Mau; Nicklin thought that George probably knew nothing about it. Nevertheless he had a point. Lawrence's people were all Kikuyu and this was the tribe involved in the Mau-Mau - the only tribe. Mike Nicklin wondered what he should do. Lawrence had done nothing illegal but if one were to take the threat of the Mau -Mau seriously, it was clearly a mistake to train the Kikuyu in the use of firearms. He would have a word with his friend Dick Preston who was Superintendent of Police in Nairobi when he was next there, sometime in the next three or four months.

Peter returned; he had just spoken briefly to Jenny. Everything on the farm was fine and they had had some light rain - the beginning of the short rains. He needed to get back.

They had a very pleasant dinner. Mike and his wife Sue shared Peter Lawrence's real love of Kenya and the bush and they swapped anecdotes all evening. George was a little bit out of the conversation but he was happy being waited on hand and foot by two servants wearing the long, white kanzu, a white cotton robe of Arabic origin, red fez on the head, red cummerbund and of course barefoot. Peter and the Nicklins thought nothing of this outfit; it was quite usual throughout Kenya for servants to be dressed like this. George wondered about the bare feet.

"We must go and get those tusks," announced Nicklin at the end of the evening. "I have a plan - you do have your licences, don't you Peter?" he enquired.

"Oh yes," said Peter.

The next day Nicklin produced a powerful motorboat and with Peter, Kahinga, Kinua and a few police askaris – African constables – they made their way rapidly up river. George did not accompany them; he had no desire to revisit the scene of his shame. An amazing sight met their eyes: there was what seemed like hundreds of crocodiles all over the place, still gnawing at what remained of the poor elephant. The place literally crawled with the reptiles; however a few shots were fired and that together with the noise of the boat sent the crocodiles scooting away for cover.

It took the men a couple of hours to dislodge the tusks. They had to keep chasing the emboldened crocodiles away, but by lunchtime they had loaded the two large tusks into the boat and were on their way back to Garissa.

Peter popped into the Game Department in Garissa to fill out the appropriate forms for the animals he had shot. George had already found a lift with the police back to Nairobi so Peter and the Kikuyu cleaned up all the equipment and packed everything ready for an early departure in the morning.

Kahinga already knew about Rafiki and sought her out that evening. As if by accident he brushed up her right sleeve: sure enough there were the seven scars. So she had been through the oathing ceremony as well, which was really unusual for a woman. The women normally were expected to play a passive role, providing food and looking after domestic issues; this generally would have applied to Mau-Mau operations as well.

They talked awhile. Neither of them really understood what was expected of them by the hierarchy of the Mau-Mau. Kahinga told her of the safari with Peter and their various adventures. Truly this M'zungu Lawrence seems to be different, she thought. Her interest had been sparked by the easy conversation she had had with Peter the previous evening - she had wanted it to continue. She liked the Nicklins but this somehow was different.

The Kikuyu were now staying in the Nicklin compound along with all the other people employed personally by the D.C.

Kinua was surprised when Kahinga returned early.

"What's the matter with you?" he grinned knowingly. "Your charm is now failing you?"

Kahinga looked at his friend. "She's one of us, she's taken the oath," said Kahinga.

Kinua had almost forgotten the seven scars on his arm.

"So?" he said.

Kahinga looked a bit sheepish.

"I tried hard to get under her dress," he said. "She wouldn't have any of it."

Kinua pretended to look serious. "You must be getting old, maybe you should get married," he said. "Soon all the young maidens will think you are too old to get it up."

Kahinga gave his friend a playful clip round the head.

"She asked many questions about Munyu, about the farm and all our people there. She spoke to Munyu yesterday; she said he seemed to be different from the other Wazungu."

Kinua had a very uncomplicated view of life, taking everything much as it came. Sure, Peter was a good M'zungu; it didn't go any further than that though. They went to sleep.

Peter spent another happy evening with the Nicklins. Mike managed to get the whole story of out of him on the subject of the buffalo and the elephant and George's behaviour. He had already heard from the servants that Peter had prevented George assaulting Kinua. Peter was somewhat reticent, not wanting to make more of it than was necessary, however.

Peter and the Kikuyu left early the next morning. He had made real friends of the Nicklins, and hoped they would accept an invitation to the farm.

They dropped Kahinga at Thika on the way into Nairobi; he would see them in a couple of days at Kikuyu just outside Nairobi, where Peter was staying with friends. Peter had some chores to do in Nairobi and he wanted to see how his photos had turned out. He also thought he could sell the tusks. He dropped dozens of spools of film into a specialist photographer that he had been in touch with before.

He sold the tusks for a thousand pounds, did a few chores round town and then in the late afternoon went round to see how the photographs had turned out. The photographer Jay Firmin greeted him with excitement.

"Where did you get this stuff?" he said, "It's magnificent; I very rarely get anything this good and I've only developed half of it!"

"Have you got the elephant shots?" asked Peter.

"Yes, here they are, how did you do this?"

Peter explained.

"Well you're a cool customer, you really deserve these shots. Fantastic!" said Jay.

They went through the rest of them.

"Look, I'll tell you what," said Jay. "I can sell stuff like this to all sorts of magazines round the world. Make me your agent and I'll do that."

Jay at first demanded 50% of the sale price. Peter bargained him down to 25%, which he still thought was steep. This was a real windfall; it would certainly help with the development of the farm.

"When are you going again?" asked Jay.

"Dunno, I have a farm to run," answered Peter.

"Farm - what the hell are you doing with a farm when you can produce stuff like this? You could be world famous," said Jay aggressively.

"That's not the point," said Peter.

Jay just shook his head, "Don't worry, you produce the stuff and I will sell it."

Kahinga went to see his father, Kinyore.

"You must get married," he was told.

"To whom? I must first find a woman," said Kahinga.

"I have found one Wanjiru for you to marry."

Kahinga knew of no Wanjiru.

"Who will pay the bride price?"

"It has already been arranged," said Kinyore. "Six cattle, which I will provide, and one sheep for the wedding feast, which I think your M'zungu can provide. You will have to find 200 shillings in cash; maybe your M'zungu will also give you that; you say you helped him hunt the elephant."

Kahinga met Wanjiru the same day. She seemed fine. She had good strong legs to work in the fields and looked as if she could bear him many fine children. So it was decided. Love did not enter into the matter; it was a concept that was really not considered when marriage was the point at issue. Marriage was much too important to let a silly concept like love enter into consideration. Certainly it was hoped that the bride and groom would come to like each other. Kahinga knew he could rely on his father to have done his homework. He would have checked out Wanjiru's family in detail for any mental and physical defects in the family background. Kahinga considered he had a bargain, a wife virtually for nothing; the bride price would be paid for by his father and Munyu. He was delighted. The wedding would be at Kinyore's village in about one month.

Kahinga was also called to the village in the Fort Hall district to see the Mzee.

"The fight will start," said Mzee. "You will kill Halway."

This wasn't quite such good news. He didn't really yet know what the objectives and strategy of the Mau-Mau were.

"When?" asked Kahinga.

"We will send word," replied the Mzee.

"I understand that Munyu has taught you how to use guns," said the Mzee enquiringly.

"Yes, I have been hunting with him."

"I know."

"Where did you hear this from?" Kahinga was quite nervous; the hunting trip was barely over.

The Mzee smiled.

"We have our sources," was all he would say. "You will take all Halway's guns," instructed Mzee.

Kahinga was dismissed. He was quite worried; he was about to get married but he was committed to this crazy organisation. What was he going to do? Before he left he had another conversation with his father.

"You are far enough away from here not to be involved with these Mau-Mau baboons." It was a statement not a question.

Kahinga looked away.

"Be warned, stay away from them. You know your mother's sister's son, Njeroge, disappeared a few years back. Mau-Mau we think."

Kinyore sensed danger but said nothing more. He just wanted peace, and grandchildren.

Kahinga then made his way to Peter's friends near Kikuyu. Peter had had a few chores to do for the farm in Nairobi that day. Peter told Kahinga that he had sold the tusks well and that he, Kahinga, would get 1000 shillings (50 pounds) as his share. For Kahinga that was really good news; he told Peter about his impending wedding plans. Peter agreed to provide the sheep for the wedding feast. Dibu and Kinua were also given a small 200 shilling (10 pounds) share of the booty from selling the tusks. They made arrangements to leave early in the morning to go back to Naseby. The two weeks away had really cemented the relationship between Peter and the three Kikuyu; they had all had a great time. Peter had made some money from selling the tusks and he had the prospect of another windfall from the photographs. They all looked forward to going home.

Peter was woken about midnight; there was an urgent telephone call.

"It's Dave Gibb here, Peter."

Why was Dave phoning him here at this time of night? How did Dave know he was here? His heart beat faster; there must be something wrong.

"There's been an accident," said Dave. "It's Jenny, you need to get back here quickly."

"Jenny?" Peter's gut tightened. "Is she hurt?" he asked.

"Yes," said Dave.

"Is she OK?"

"No, just get back here, it's really serious."

The line went dead. Peter couldn't tell whether Dave didn't want to speak to him anymore or whether the rather primitive telephone service in Kenya at the time had cut them off. He thought of trying to phone back, but wasn't sure where Dave had phoned from.

He roused the Kikuyu, said a rushed farewell to his friends and they set off. They arrived back at the farm in the pitch black hours before the dawn. They all felt awful, expecting the worst.

Chapter 10

Jenny was coping with running the farm and enjoying it.

She went to the milking in the early morning and the evening on the new Ferguson tractor they had just bought. It had a self-starter and needed no cranking so she could manage it easily.

The children, who were on holiday from school, were left in the care of Kinua's wife Sarah who by now had one healthy boy of her own, with another one on the way. Sarah was very happy with the arrangement; it meant a little extra money and she liked being in the Wazungu's house. She'd never really seen anything like it in her life and she admired all the Lawrence's belongings; glasses, china plates, pictures on the wall, beds with sheets on them. She wasn't really envious, just interested.

When Jenny came back after eight in the morning she would have breakfast with the kids, provided by Mwangi the houseboy, since Dibu was away with Peter. Mwangi wasn't much of a cook but between him and Jenny they managed well enough. Jenny and the kids would then ride out to the pyrethrum picking which was in full swing. It was important to pick as much as possible and get it into the pyrethrum dryer before the short rains came in April.

She thought Peter would be pleased with her ministrations on the farm. The milk yield was up and they were now sending 20 cans (200 gallons) of milk on the truck to Naivasha every day. She had coped with all the minor ailments of the cows in the dairy. She had managed to weigh the pigs and had sent a load off to the Uplands bacon factory at Kijabe. Most of the pyrethrum had been picked and was being dried in the pyrethrum dryer and put into sacks ready to go to KFA (Kenya Farmers Association) in Nakuru. Peter could take a load in with the lorry when he returned. They had lost a couple of lambs to the jackals, but that was normal. She really felt on top of the world. The labour had really behaved, there had been no fighting or drunkenness and the weekend milking, when there was sometimes trouble, had gone off without a hitch.

As she and the children rode out to the pyrethrum she said to them, "Dad is coming home tomorrow." They knew. They both had a little gift that they had made for the occasion.

Robert was now at a government boarding school in Nakuru about 25 miles away and John made the weekly pilgrimage on horseback to the neighbouring farm, where he stayed the week and was taken to the local school further up the road from there.

Everything at the pyrethrum picking was fine and under control. They decided to ride on a little; it was such a beautiful day, with the sun shining and a few wispy clouds overhead. The Aberdares stood out in the blue distance and a tablecloth of cloud enveloped the summit of Sattimma, the highest point in the range. Mount Kenya had disappeared into the haze.

Jenny decided to do one of her jumps; she draped a sack over the barbed wire, took the horse, Crest back thirty yards and set him at the fence. She had done this dozens of times before and the pyrethrum pickers and the children just watched without any anxiety but with admiration. The horse trusted Jenny completely and she increased the pressure in her legs and lifted him for the jump. The ground was slightly damp from the previous night's rain and just as Crest took off he slipped slightly on the wet ground. He still tried bravely with Jenny's help, to clear the fence but his front legs caught the top of the fence and his momentum with his front legs caught made him do a cartwheel. Jenny was flung off; she landed on her head and then the horse - all 800lbs of horse - came thumping down right on top of her. The horse staggered up and stood there. Jenny lay absolutely still, her body and pretty face crushed.

For a split second everyone stood stock still, shocked. Then Robert jumped off his horse, dropped the reins, climbed through the fence and ran to his mother.

"Mum, Mum!" he said.

He tried to get her to respond.

John and the pyrethrum pickers crowded round.

Robert, who was then nine, took charge. "Bring some sacks, coats, blankets and keep her warm. John, stay here with her I'll go and fetch the doctor."

Robert's childhood really disappeared; at that moment he suddenly became an adult with adult responsibilities. He understood the country and the nature of the life they had. Along with the very real freedoms came the hardships, the dangers and the sudden elimination of life. In his heart of hearts he knew that Jenny was dead. He had seen the horse crash on top of her; he didn't see how she could survive. He remounted his horse, a dapple grey mare he called Ripple, went through the gate and then flew down the farm track, made a great splash through the drift and then raced up the other side. Ripple seemed to sense the urgency. They rounded the water tank and went flying down the main road and into the neighbour's driveway. Then clattered along the driveway and came to a dead stop as Robert jumped off and raced inside the house.

The neighbours' name was Marks; they were survivors of the holocaust in Europe and some of their fortune had been restored to them by the German authorities. They had built a new house and were among the few people in the district able to afford a telephone. Robert and John often rode over there and were given orange juice and Mrs. Marks' special vanilla biscuits, which somehow she always had handy.

"Whoa, whoa, young fella," said a gruff German voice. "Not so fast, what's the matter?"

"It's Mum," said Robert. "She fell off her horse, I think she's dead, please call the doctor!"

"OK, OK, we get the doctor." He made the call.

"He's on his way. Young fella, just sit down for a minute and catch your breath; tell me what happened."

Mrs. Marks appeared looking really concerned with the orange juice and the vanilla biscuits.

Robert told them what had happened.

"Ok, we go in the car, yes, you leave the horse here," said Mr. Marks.

"OK," said Robert.

They met the doctor at the entrance to Naseby and then went to the scene of the accident.

It was much as they had left it. Jenny was covered in blankets, she hadn't stirred. John was sitting beside her holding her hand; he just looked stunned. One of the pyrethrum pickers was holding the horses. Crest was covered in blood; he had been badly cut by the barbed wire fence.

The doctor brought his bag and crouched down next to Jenny. He tried her pulse - nothing. He tried in several places to find a pulse, but there wasn't a flicker. He then examined her injuries in detail. He shook his head.

He took the boys aside; they knew the worst by now. "I'm afraid she's dead," he said in as kind a voice as was possible.

They nodded.

"She had no chance with those injuries. What actually happened?"

Robert told him.

John started to cry.

Robert held him.

They got the body back to the house; Sarah and a couple of the women from the farm washed and dressed Jenny and put her on the bed. The horses were looked after and the vet called to deal with the injuries to Crest. There was a sort of disbelieving silence round the farm. Neighbours popped in and out. Somehow the normal farm chores got done. The pyrethrum picking had been abandoned, but the milking was done and all the stock looked after.

Dave Gibb and his wife Margaret stayed the night and tried to comfort the children.

"I've phoned your father," Dave said, "he's on his way; I expect him before morning."

Peter and the four Kikuyu came into the house and woke everyone up. The boys rushed to him. They took him to see Jenny; it was almost as if she was asleep. Peter took her now cold hand and kissed her crushed forehead. He wept; they all wept. Kahinga, Kinua, Dibu and Stanley all came in to pay their respects. They had a very early breakfast. Peter was devastated. He had such a lot to share with Jenny: the trip, the sale of the tusks, and his success with the camera. All this had now turned to dust. What was it all for? With whom was he going to share this rough piece of Africa that he was turning into an orderly, productive, beautiful farm? He tried to comfort his children. They all staggered through the day in a daze.

The funeral a few days later was an enormous affair. It was held in the little Anglican Church in Ol'Kalou which the Lawrences had helped raise money for and had helped to design and build. The church was full and there were people outside. The Lawrences had known many people in the district and beyond and most of them were there. All the farm workers from Naseby had come, some on the lorry, some on bicycles, and some had walked the five miles into the village of Ol'Kalou.

As they lowered the simple coffin into the ground Peter noticed this was the first grave in the little churchyard. Was that a sign of permanence? Was this how communities became part of the landscape? Peter hugged his boys closer.

Everyone went back to the club, which was a mile out of the village. The club consisted of a largish club house, a tennis court and a polo field.

As with the church, the whites were admitted into the clubhouse and the Africans stayed outside.

"Is black sorrow somehow worth less than white sorrow?" Peter thought.

He spent some time with his farm workers. He hoped they understood; this was neither the time nor the place for thoughts or conversation of that sort. They were here to remember Jenny.

The Nicklins had come all the way from Garissa for the funeral. They stayed with Peter and his children afterwards for a day or two. It was a relief to come into the Highlands, to escape the heat of Garissa and the NFD.

"How will you look after the boys?" asked Sue.

"This is just a thought," she said, "but we are going to put our children into boarding school in England in September. We're all going on home leave in June on the boat and we're going to settle the boys in with relatives in England, where they will go for their short holidays. Rafiki, who has been wonderful, might be happy to come and work here. She is half Kikuyu, so she would get on with your people."

Peter had almost forgotten about Rafiki. How long ago their meeting seemed now. "I don't know… maybe. Thank you, anyway," he said non-committally.

Jenny's parents had come up for the funeral from Johannesburg. They wept bitterly for their daughter but they had understood her. They knew how happy she had been with Peter, building up Naseby. They also knew she had had a wild streak. After the funeral they stayed a few days in the uncomfortable little house and eventually suggested that Louise, Jenny's younger sister, should come and stay at least for a few months.

Although Jenny's father was well off and had provided a modest amount of finance to help purchase Naseby, he recognised Peter's need to 'make it on his own.' He thought Peter was doing a fine job on the farm and he never sought to further involve himself in the place.

Jenny and Louise had both been brought up in what in those days was considered to be the lap of luxury. Either of them would have been very comfortable in the salons of the wealthy gold millionaires in Johannesburg or the drawing rooms of the aristocracy in England. Jenny, however, had chosen to follow Peter and between them they had started to create a beautiful, productive farm.

Louise had no such aspirations. In looks she was very much like her sister:

tall and slim with straight, naturally blonde hair. She was very pretty and turned many male heads. Louise kept all the men at a distance, however. She had no intention of spending her life in a backwater like Kenya, and looked forward to returning to the fancy tennis parties in Johannesburg at which she shone and the hunt meetings and cocktail parties in England in the summer. She had promised her family to help Peter out for a while but beyond that she did not wish to be committed.

Peter had already built a small room onto the house at one end of the veranda. It was made of stone, cut on the farm; the mortar was just mud since cement was unavailable and the window was a wooden shutter since glass was difficult to get even so long after the war. The only door opened onto the veranda.

Louise was shown the room and gasped in horror. To live in this hell hole instead of her light, breezy room with its ensuite bathroom in Johannesburg. And the bathing arrangements - her eyes popped out on stalks when she saw the tin bath. "Dear God," she thought, "I'll turn into a frumpy old country bumpkin in six months in this place."

There and then she made Peter promise that every few months she would be taken to Nairobi to stay with friends so that she could at least enjoy some of the benefits of civilisation. Not that Nairobi really compared with London or Johannesburg; still it was better than nothing.

The boys needed some discipline as well. She wondered what Jenny had done; the children more or less ran wild round the farm when they weren't at school.

"Just like the black kids," she thought. She made them wear shoes.

The conversation at meal times made her stomach turn. Louise was used to discussing politics or the latest hunt ball, or someone or other's promotion in some big corporation or even sometimes a good gold share to buy on the Johannesburg stock exchange. She considered herself sophisticated and smart. Here the conversation was very down to earth; almost invariably they had to discuss worms. Peter seemed obsessed with them; if he wasn't worming the sheep, it was the cattle or the dogs. Then there was that ghastly knife he always carried with him that he used to castrate pigs with in the morning, clean out abscesses on sheep in the afternoon and then he'd gaily peel an orange or apple with it at mealtimes.

The laundry arrangements nearly drove her demented. She was used to having clean clothes every single day. Here the rule was Mondays and Thursdays only. Inevitably Peter managed to get mud or cow dung or some sort of filth on his clothes every day. Certainly by Wednesday and Sunday nights Peter's clothes and the boy's clothes more or less stood up by themselves. If they wanted to live like that they could, decided Louise; she would continue to have clean clothes every day.

She also noticed that the boys wore no underpants. Everything was fine when they were standing up but when they sat down in a chair their genitals tended to fall about all over the place. She shuddered; she'd had her fair share of boyfriends but she did not want to be reminded of the shape and form of male genitals on a daily basis. Dear God, this was an uncivilised country. She bought them underpants.

She also found the servants a trial; they certainly were not up to the standard of the very polite blacks her parents employed in Johannesburg. Mind you the state of the kitchen was something else. That old broken down stove. It was surprising that they didn't get food poisoning at every meal. When she raised this with Peter he gave her a lecture on the benefits of clean dirt.

"How else do people get appropriate antibodies in them to fight real disease?" he said.

They could keep their antibodies, she thought. She preferred cleanliness.

One day she was standing on the veranda and she saw the boys galloping about wildly in the paddock below the house. The boys were riding bareback and the game was to put a handkerchief on a bush and gallop past and pick it off the bush. The handkerchief was at first placed at about the same height as the horse but as the game progressed it was put lower and lower down the bush. Whoever failed to pick up the handkerchief when it was their turn or fell off the horse, lost. This game really improved their riding skills; they had to know how the horse would behave and almost be a part of the horse to manage.

This particular day was some months after Jenny died, when the boys were home from school. The boys were completely absorbed in the game as she approached. The game was getting to its climax; John had just picked up the handkerchief and had almost come off. Robert was determined to win; in order to pick the handkerchief up he had to lean right over virtually parallel to the ground. Just as he made a grab for the handkerchief the horse caught a glimpse of Louise round the far side of the bush. It shied and Robert came tumbling off, almost landing at Louise's feet on the soft grass. She shrieked. Robert jumped up unhurt. John caught the horse.

"Haven't you got any sense?" she yelled at them. "Your mother just died doing daredevil things off the back of a horse and now look at you!"

"It would have been OK if you hadn't frightened the horse," Robert said.

She insisted that they stop the game. If she had anything to do with it, they would stop it altogether.

When they had finished with the horses and were on their way back to the house Robert picked up a dry cowpat.

John looked at him.

"What's that for?" he asked.

"You'll see."

During the day he managed to put the offending article in Louise's bed. "That'll fix her," he thought.

Louise got a terrible fright when she got into bed that night. When she had calmed down she thought, "Two can play at this game."

Instead of running to Peter she had another plan.

Sometimes at lunchtime she made the boys sandwiches and they sat outside with a glass of lemonade. She had put part of the cowpat in Robert's sandwich.

Robert had wondered why nothing had been said to him and as he took a bite of his sandwich they were both looking at each other. Robert took a large bite of cowpat. He realised quickly what had happened; instead of spitting it out there and then he quietly got up and went round the side of the house and got rid of the sandwich. Even the dog wouldn't touch it. He washed his mouth out and went back to the others. Louise had a look of triumph on her face; Robert said nothing. One up to you, he thought, but I'll fix you.

"Did you enjoy your lunch, darling?" said Louise innocently.

"Yes, thank you," muttered Robert.

They looked at each other; both had a half smile on their faces; they each knew the game was on.

Peter had no inkling of any of this and neither of them was going to tell him anything.

Peter had always thought that Louise was an attractive woman. That is, if he'd been asked he would have said, "Sure, certainly, she's pretty," or something to that effect.

Louise would have given a similar answer if anyone had asked about Peter.

She had wondered what he would be like in bed. Although he was good looking he somehow didn't appeal to her. She giggled to herself, "He'd probably smell of cow dung or something worse."

She had never understood why Jenny had come up here to marry Peter. Although she could see there was much in him to admire, for Louise he was just too rural and Kenya had made him more so.

Half the district was expecting that possibly Peter would marry Louise. It seemed to make sense; she was family and fairly like Jenny in looks.

One of the bolder young farmers suggested it to him at the club.

"You must be joking. Louise - my sister-in-law - forget it," he said. "It would be like sleeping with a perfumed wet fish," he thought to himself.

Peter liked having Louise about, though. She had managed to help him with the pyrethrum picking and did the odd shift at the dairy. She and Peter were always welcome at dinner parties.

Various people in the district were famous for their New Year parties as well, and it was at one of these parties, about 18 months after Jenny died, that Louise met her match. The usual crowd was there, most of whom she knew and liked though none of them interested her as a mate. Then she was introduced to Giles Dingley-Ferris. When he shook her hand there was almost a spark; her loins went all liquid.

Giles was very tall, even taller than Peter, but sparely built. He was good looking and always well turned out Most of the time he looked as if butter wouldn't melt in his mouth. He was in Kenya to advise the Government on some investment prospects and had taken the opportunity to visit some relatives.

"Come on, behave yourself," she thought. "You'll probably never see him again."

"Stockbroking, company directorship, all that sort of thing," was how he responded when Peter asked him what he did.

That evening Peter really wanted to go home. It was after midnight, they had seen the New Year in and he, Peter, had to get up to the early morning milking. He couldn't find Louise anywhere. Eventually she emerged from an upstairs room on Giles' arm looking like the cat that had just finished off the cream. She was radiant and couldn't have cared less what anyone thought. Peter shook his head; what Louise did wasn't his business.

All the way home Louise was raving on about Giles this and Giles that. Peter couldn't get a word in edgeways.

"Well, he'd better come over for lunch or something," said Peter eventually.

"Lunch?" she had the grace to blush. "I've asked him for the whole week."

"Oh, all right we'll put the kids on the floor in my room; he can have theirs."

"Don't worry," she said, "he's sharing my bed."

Peter was amazed at her directness.

"Are you in love or something?" he asked after a short silence.

"Yes, most definitely... yes, of course... I've never felt like this ever before," she stammered.

Giles stayed ten days. He really loved the farm and tramped all over it with Peter. One day they were on the top of a hill overlooking the cottage.

"Say, old chap, this would be a marvellous site for a house, wouldn't it?" said Giles.

"Yes – the best. Jenny and I did have some plans drawn up but with one thing and another it hasn't been built."

Before Giles went home, he and Louise decided to get married in the summer in England.

In the meanwhile, Louise carried on with her duties on the farm. She and Robert continued to spar, in a fairly friendly way, when he was home from school.

He put a frog in her bed one night; the next day he found the frog in one of his gumboots.

Then one day Robert found a young, two-foot long, harmless grass snake, when he was out with his airgun. He put it in Louise's bed and went to his own bed full of anticipation. He was just snuggling down when he felt something wriggling in his bed. He jumped up and the grass snake bit him right on his penis. He yelled blue murder. Peter and Louise came rushing into the room with a light to the sight of Robert hopping up and down with a small snake attached. The snake let go and slithered under the bed. Robert was patched up and his dignity more or less restored.

Louise couldn't contain herself; she burst out laughing.

"What's so funny?" asked Peter.

"He put the thing in my bed in the first place. I saw him come out of my room this afternoon; I knew what he was up to and just did a quick transfer. Serves you right, eh Robert?"

Robert looked shamefaced. It looked as though Louise had won.

She put her arms around him.

"She isn't so bad," he thought.

Now she was leaving them forever.

Bill persuaded Peter to take the boys with him to England for a holiday, so they could go to the wedding. "I'll take care of the farm," he said. "You need a good break."

Giles turned out to be Sir Giles with a large estate in Oxfordshire – Dingley House – and a house in London. Peter and the boys stayed on the estate while James and Louise went to the south of France for a week's honeymoon.

"Is there anything you really want to see while you are here?" Giles asked Peter when they returned.

"Sheep dog trials," said Peter.

"Sheep dog trials it will be," said Giles. It seemed a strange request, but he liked his brother-in-law and wasn't going to question any of his tastes.

Peter and the boys were royally entertained. They went to a cricket match at Lords – England vs. Australia. They went to Wimbledon and they went to the theatre in London.

Giles was a member of the local hunt so they went fox hunting a couple of times. Peter and his sons rode very well and had a great deal of enjoyment out of it.

As George had predicted, the ladies absolutely loved Peter and couldn't get enough of him. On a couple of occasions one of them crept into his bed in the middle of the night and left before dawn; he made sure they were not disappointed.

Robert was in his element. "I could really get used to this," he thought.

Peter had gone north to see a well-known breeder of Ayrshire bulls. Peter thought he might import one to improve his herd. While he was gone Robert and John had been staying with Louise and Giles in their London home.

Louise said, "How do you like it here, Robert?" She could see Robert was mesmerised.

"It's great, it's really opened my eyes," he said.

"You might like to think about coming to university here or to do some sort of training," suggested Giles. "You could stay here, at least for a while."

"That sounds fantastic," said Robert. "I still have a few years left at school in Kenya though,"

He would not forget this offer; he certainly wanted to spend a few years here and it gave him a great goal.

Peter and his sons left England somewhat reluctantly. Their journey home was, by the standards of the day, relatively painless.

They flew on B.O.A.C (British Overseas Airways Corporation) to Rome, then Khartoum in Sudan, Entebbe in Uganda and then Nairobi. Three days it took altogether.

Bill, who had been looking after the farm while they were away, met them at the airport.

"Everything's fine," he said when asked. "Rafiki is now established in the room that Louise had. She's a bit of a come down after Louise though."

Peter had written to the Nicklins when Louise had announced her intentions and had made arrangements for Rafiki to take her place. He was conscious of the fact that Louise had actually done a great job with the boys. She had tamed them a little and had really become their friend. They were both at boarding school in Nakuru now and Rafiki would only be needed during the holidays. Maybe she could also be trained to help on the farm.

Louise had got used to Naseby in the two years she was there. She still missed some of the little luxuries of her life in Johannesburg but was able to recognise that maybe all of them were not necessary.

"You can only sleep in one bed," was how she thought about it.

She had partially tamed the boys and the servants had done her bidding without question.

Louise truly admired what Peter was doing with the farm: creating something of great value from an untamed piece of African bush. She was glad to see the back of it though. She really loved Giles and was looking forward to being the mistress of his various houses. She hoped some day she could produce children like Robert and John; she would certainly miss them.

Chapter 11

Life on Naseby settled down to something approaching normal. Peter missed Louise very much and he was also frantically busy. John seemed to have accepted the situation and he liked Rafiki. Peter was more concerned about Robert's attitude, which was not hostile - he just took absolutely no notice of Rafiki. Instinctively, Robert felt that somehow Rafiki would usurp his rightful place beside Peter.

When the boys were home Rafiki was busy from morning until night, but during the week she had time on her hands. Peter knew he would need her at least until the children went to secondary school, so he wondered what he should do about the girl.

During the evenings Peter normally read books on all sorts of subjects. He kept up with developments in the farming and stock breeding business, which was of vital interest to him. He also read history books, particularly on Kenya, and the occasional novel.

Rafiki had never known anyone to read books like Peter did. She knew a little about schoolbooks but her education was limited. One evening they got into conversation on the subject. They always spoke in Kikuyu, which both of them were comfortable with.

"Why do you read all the time," asked Rafiki. "What is so interesting in the books?"

All the Kikuyu men she had known just sat round the fire in the hut and smoked and drank tea or traditional beer and talked. Certainly they told stories; there is a great oral tradition throughout Africa and Rafiki had listened to hundreds of their stories. Also in most huts the only real light was from the fire, so reading was not practical, and the printed word was almost unknown in most parts of sub-Saharan Africa before the advent of the whites.

This conversation gave Peter an idea. He found out that Rafiki had two years of education at a mission school but that for various reasons she had dropped out after that. She could read a little and write her name. So the next time he was in Nakuru he went to see the Rift Valley Correspondence School.

He wondered before he arrived whether he should tell the principal the whole story. Most education resources were directed to the white population and he wasn't sure whether this school dealt with black kids at all. He was also worried about Rafiki's age, which turned out to be nineteen (she looked older than that). Rafiki would have to start with school work normally set for eight or nine year olds. When he met the principal, a Mrs. Robinson, he decided to tell everything: Jenny's death, his children and Rafiki. She didn't turn a hair.

"I really wish we had a few more of the older and younger blacks enlisted with us. The problem is supervision; they need a parent or someone to supervise and guide them. If you undertake to do that then I'll take her on."

"Fine," said Peter.

He hadn't known what to expect. He thought he could deal with the supervision in the evenings; during the day he would be busy with the farm.

The arrangement was that work was sent by post on a weekly basis.

Rafiki was enthralled. She was enrolled in a Grade 3 course, which would normally be done by an eight year old. The way it worked was that Peter would spend an hour or two each evening reading the instructions from the correspondence school and then making sure that Rafiki understood. Rafiki then worked through everything herself.

If Peter were around at lunchtime he would answer any questions. Rafiki had to fit in her other chores in between time but with Robert and John away at boarding school these were not onerous. The house servants did all the housework and each week Dibu and Rafiki concocted between them a list of groceries for Peter to buy at the Indian duka (store) in Ol'Kalou. There was a gardener, who continued to look after the vegetables. The flower garden deteriorated somewhat, although the gardener kept the lawn mowed.

Far from this additional burden being a chore, Peter was amazed at the progress that Rafiki made and the real interest she showed. Despite the fact that the material was for children much younger than she was, she devoured it hungrily. She did grades three, four and five in the first year. Peter could hardly keep up. Peter found himself more and more looking forward to the evenings. He always worked hard on the farm; in fact he lost himself in it. He hardly had time to think of Jenny and what she had meant to him. Occasionally he went to the little churchyard in Ol'Kalou and sat by Jenny's grave and tried to talk to her, wherever she was.

When the boys were at school all this worked very well. Theoretically the correspondence school went on holiday at the same time as the boys, but Rafiki was keen to continue with her studies, so although she had much more to do during the holidays she still tried to continue with the course and needed Peter to help her in the evenings. At first the boys didn't seem to mind, but then when Peter and Rafiki were together every evening at the dining room table after supper, Robert in particular started to notice.

In the past when Jenny was still alive they had all sat in front of the fire in the little living room and either Peter or Jenny had read the boys a story. Even Louise had been part of this ritual. Now they were left to their own devices. Without realising it Peter was almost becoming a stranger to his own children. Peter always went to the early morning and the evening milking, which was important to the farm since it brought in monthly income; there was always one or other of the animals that needed attention and Peter really liked to keep his eye on the details. Peter saw everyone at breakfast and then went out on the farm again, seeing to the numerous little chores. All the cattle were dipped once a week. This involved driving the cattle into a narrow walkway, at the end of which was a narrow concrete bath about twenty feet long filled with disinfectant; the bath (or dip) was about eight feet deep so that when even the largest animal plunged into the very murky water that held the disinfectant, they went in over their heads and then swam to the other end. This process kept the ticks, which were numerous in Kenya, off the animals. He also had to inject the whole herd periodically for Foot and Mouth disease, East Coast Fever and Blackwater Fever; most of this was done on dipping day.

Twice a week he went into Ol'Kalou for supplies and to pick items up from the railway station. He sent pigs to the bacon factory twice a month and the sheep required constant attention. He had fortunately given up the Malewa lands the previous year but all in all he was very busy.

He had completely forgotten that he had promised to teach Robert how to drive the tractor. Robert did not remind him. A rift had appeared between the two; all that Robert could see was that Peter was spending more and more of his time with "that black bitch" as he was now thinking of her.

Robert and John usually spent the morning riding. John had taken over Ripple, the dapple grey mare, and Robert was now riding Jenny's horse,

Crest, who had completely recovered from the accident. They always took the dogs. One day they went over to the Powers, a neighbour about five miles away, to see their children. Robert then decided on a plan to really shock his father. They just stayed on and were invited to supper and to stay the night. Robert told their hosts that they had told Peter that they might stay the night, so no-one even tried to inform Peter. John was worried but Robert told him just to shut up. They stayed the night.

Peter came home at lunchtime, noticed that the boys were not there but didn't worry.

When they were still not home after the afternoon milking both he and Rafiki really started to worry.

"Where the hell are they?" he shouted at Rafiki. "You're supposed to be looking after them."

"They always go for a morning ride. I have never been with them; you know I don't ride. They've always come back before," she said evenly.

"Kahinga said he saw them going over towards the Powers." Peter was about to get into the truck and drive over there when it started to really pour with rain. He would just get bogged down if he went now. At about midnight they noticed that the dogs had returned and were in their kennels; they were soaking wet. Peter spent a miserable night hoping that the boys were all right; he barely slept.

Robert and John had breakfast, said goodbye to their hosts, saddled up their horses and rode home. They wondered about the dogs but presumed that they had had enough sense to go home. Robert knew there would be a row and he really relished the thought; John shrank from the idea - he hated seeing his father angry.

They got home about mid-morning and started to unsaddle the horses in front of the house. Peter and Rafiki came out; Peter was relieved but furious.

"Where the hell have you been?" he yelled.

"Powers," said Robert. "Anyway, what do you care?"

Peter was taken aback and his fury increased.

The boys had unsaddled the horses and put the saddles away on their racks. Robert ignored Peter and started to rub Crest down and brush him. John started to do the same with Ripple.

Peter had almost never laid a hand on either of the boys but he was by now absolutely livid; he made a grab for Robert. Rafiki stepped in between them but Robert pushed her violently away.

"I'll fight my own battles," he growled.

The situation might have got out of hand but Crest saved the day; he reared up in fright with all the sudden movement. Robert still had hold of the reins and was pulled off his feet. Peter backed away and everyone stood still. Robert got up and calmed the horse down. He continued with what he was doing and ignored Peter.

Peter was absolutely fuming, but he began to get an inkling of what the problem was. Robert finished brushing Crest, cleaned out his feet, handed the reins to John and then went and collected the feed for the two horses. They always fed them after a ride. Peter glowered but said very little; he was having trouble controlling himself. John was nervously looking from Peter to Robert. Robert was outwardly calm but inwardly elated. He'd won; he'd made his point. Maybe his father would notice him now. The horses finished their feed, the boys hopped up on their backs without saddles and cantered them slowly back to their paddock. They slipped the bridles and the horses cantered away and joined the others with a lot of whinnying. Robert and John sauntered back to the house.

After the boys had gone, Rafiki said to Peter, "Maybe he's missing his father; he only has another ten days of holiday left and then you will see almost nothing of him for three months. Because you are so busy you have almost ignored him since he came home from school. You have not been riding, shooting or anything. John told me that Robert was expecting to be taught how to drive the tractor these holidays."

Peter was absolutely mortified. His son, his precious son, what would Jenny have thought of him? He held his head in his hands.

The boys came back. Robert looked at Peter speculatively; Peter did not know what to say.

Rafiki asked, "Did you have a nice time at the Power's house?" Robert just glowered at her.

John said nervously, "Oh yes, they showed us how to shoot their air-gun and Mr. Powers showed Robert how to drive the tractor."

Peter's face fell even further. He was really ashamed of himself, but he was a proud man; what was he to do.

"I have to go into Ol'Kalou for a few things; do you want to come?" he said.

John said, "Oh yes."

Robert hesitated; he wasn't going to roll over that easily. "No," he said. "I think I'll take the dogs shooting."

So it went for the rest of the holiday. Peter and Rafiki agreed to suspend the correspondence course until the school term started again.

Peter read to the boys again in the evening but always John's books; Robert never brought him anything to read and when Peter was reading to John, Robert read or pretended to read his own book.

Rafiki tried to intervene and said to Robert, "Your father understands, he's trying to be with you but…"

"You just keep out of this," interrupted Robert. "Just keep out of it, he's my father." He stormed off.

They had one attempt to teach Robert how to drive the tractor. This was interrupted – a cow was sick.

Robert went back to school. In secret he was actually quite pleased; his father was now taking more notice of him. Instinctively he resisted, just in order to reinforce the guilt. In his heart of hearts he really wanted to be very close to his father; he really admired him. He really had to get rid of "the black bitch". He could see she was about to usurp his dead mother's place and for him this really threatened what he considered to be his rightful place beside his father. At his age he was absolutely unable to think of his father as having any needs and wants of his own.

Rafiki was absolutely shocked when she opened up her correspondence course after the new school term had started. Every lesson had already been completed, every essay written. She thought, "It must be Robert; he's just trying to tell me that we're doing the same work and I'm supposed to look after him." She wept; she wondered what to do. She wasn't going to tell Peter but at that moment he walked in unexpectedly and said, "Oh, I see, you've finished all that."

"No," she said. "I didn't do it."

"What do you mean?" he asked.

"Someone else did it, probably Robert," she said and a tear rolled down her cheek.

Peter looked through the work. It was well done, but he was furious. He didn't need to be told why Robert had done what he had done. They would replace the papers and carry on with the course. What should he do about Robert though?

Life went on; the weekly letters from Robert were a bit skimpy but still came. They mainly dealt with soccer, cricket and his new passion, rugby.

The correspondence course resumed. Peter decided that Rafiki could do more to help around the farm so he started to teach her to drive. Besides the three ton lorry Peter had now bought a pickup truck.

The house servants had watched Rafiki's progress in the Lawrence household with interest. Rafiki and Dibu were of course both aware that the other belonged to the Mau-Mau. To all intents and purposes the Mau-Mau was dormant as far as either of them or the others were concerned. They had almost no communication and certainly no instructions from the central authority. Dibu in any event encouraged Rafiki to learn whatever Peter Lawrence was willing to teach her.

Rafiki was a very good pupil and for Peter it was a joy to teach her. As far as driving the car went, there was no history of the use of machinery of any description in Africa so fundamentally it was an alien experience. Peter was a very good, very patient teacher; Rafiki had trouble steering straight and to start with, every time she tried to change gear there was a terrible grinding sound in the gearbox.

"Half a pound of iron filings in the gearbox," was all he would say and they both laughed and then he showed her again. Eventually she became a reasonable driver and Peter was able to let her drive round the farm on her own. She was eventually able to do some of the supervision at the milking, which involved weighing and recording what each animal gave at each milking, as well as feeding the calves and just seeing to it that all was well. Rafiki learned how to milk with the machine. Milking was easy; she had been around cattle all her life. She eventually managed the machine. Recording was an important part of maintaining a complete record of each animal; by now Peter had a very respectable herd of Ayrshire cattle and, because of his meticulous records, was able to sell them well in the district and beyond. If an animal's milk yield was down substantially on the day before, it was also the first reliable sign that the animal was sick.

Peter used artificial insemination to upgrade the quality of the herd. With the proceeds of the sale of the tusks he had been able to import a pure-bred Ayrshire bull from Scotland who gloried in the name of Shiehallion Knight Errant. Shiehallion, Peter knew was a mountain in Scotland, presumably in Ayrshire; where the rest of the name came from he wasn't sure. The Africans made many attempts at pronouncing Knight Errant. If there was any doubt they just called him "Ndume Kali" which means fierce bull in Swahili. And he was terrifyingly fierce; he had an oversupply of testosterone in his blood stream. The mere sight or smell of a human sent him into paroxysms of blood red rage, especially if they came near any of "his" cows. Knight Errant was huge, weighing well over 1000lbs and he had a set of very sharp, fierce looking horns. His progeny improved the average milk yield by leaps and bounds. Everyone except Kamau the head stockman, who personally looked after him, and Peter was terrified of him. He was a great asset.

Rafiki was also able to look after the pyrethrum, a job that Peter had done since Jenny died.

Once or twice during the correspondence course lessons and particularly when he was teaching Rafiki how to drive he touched her by accident. There was no mistaking the electric shock that both of them felt; when Rafiki looked at him with those liquid eyes he felt his mouth go dry. Rafiki had never worn any kind of underwear; her breasts didn't really need much help, they were firm and upright. Peter couldn't take his eyes off them without a great deal of effort.

Peter was aware of his feelings and thought, "This is all I need, to fall in love with a black woman. I'd be drummed out of the district."

The next time he was in Nakuru he brought a few pairs of pants and a couple of brassieres. He had to rein her in somehow. When he returned, he gave them to her. She opened the packet and looked puzzled; what was all this? Peter was embarrassed; he tried to explain. The children were both away. The servants had served the supper and had gone. Rafiki was still puzzled by this gift and Peter's rather self-conscious and garbled explanation of what the garments were for. She struggled into the pants; to say that they fitted snugly was an understatement. Still, she quite liked the idea; she'd taken her dress off and paraded about the room admiring her stunningly beautiful body in the small mirror in her room. Then she picked up and examined one of the brassieres. The way Peter had explained it somehow this garment was to fit over her breasts. She tried and tried; either there was something wrong with what she was doing or the garment was far too small. She only had one person to talk to, Peter, so unthinkingly she picked up a bra and went into the living room.

Peter was reading a magazine. He had just bathed and was sitting there in his customary dressing gown and slippers. When she came in the front door his eyes nearly stood out on stalks. He'd never seen anything like it before: there in his living room was this goddess like creature. She was tall, with long legs, and all she was wearing was a pair of the pants he had bought her, white pants which contrasted spectacularly with her flawless brown skin. Her beautiful large breasts came erect under his stare; the nipples puckered. She was holding a bra in one hand and had a puzzled smile on her face.

"This thing, I don't understand how it fits."

To start with she had no idea of the effect she was having on Peter.

The magazine dropped from his hand, he stood up and moved towards her. When he touched her hand he was amazed at the intensity of his feelings. He stroked a breast, and she moaned. They didn't kiss; she didn't know what kissing was and had never seen a movie. The bra dropped from her hand and she started to tug at Peter's clothes, which all came off in a rush. He ripped off and tore her newly acquired pants. Somehow they had now moved outside and were lying on the grass. She took him inside her and they made the most beautiful love. It was a warm moonlit night. Peter had never experienced anything like this in all his life and if anything, her feelings were even more intense. Neither of them understood or tried to understand what had happened to them; what the implications of their relationship could be on themselves, their respective communities or those close to them.

They lay there on the lawn for a while, then went into Rafiki's room and made love again. This time it was less hurried and if anything more intense.

Eventually Peter laughed and said, "Let me now help you with the bra."

What he had bought was far too small. She giggled and with their new-found intimacy said, "You think I have small little mangoes, look I have the best big ripe melons," and she thrust one of her big breasts into his face. They made love again.

Rafiki had been told that Wazungu had small penises but that wasn't true of Peter. She loved his strong hard body. During the initiation ceremonies of puberty she had had unrivalled views of her age group's respective members, but she had seen nothing like this. She began to wonder if all the rumours about the Wazungu were just that - rumours.

Chapter 12

Before Jenny died the Lawrences had decided to build a schoolhouse on Naseby to educate the children of the farm workers. As had been done in other districts, they had planned to enlist the support of the four or five neighbouring farmers whose labour would benefit.

After Jenny's death Peter continued his efforts to persuade his neighbours and other local people that a school was a good idea. He knew that while some local Africans went to mission schools, the missions provided for a very small fraction of the need. The Government had started to provide educational facilities for Africans in many parts of Kenya but these again only provided for a small proportion of the population and it was only through good fortune and determination that many Africans obtained school leaving certificates. There was no university in Kenya until just prior to independence.

Peter realised that in his district, unless he and the other farmers provided a schoolhouse and a teacher, the children, like their parents, would receive no education. The other farmers could see that this was so, but were not all willing to participate in the exercise. They worked hard enough to provide for their own needs and those of their children and the education of African farm workers was not a priority.

A number of arguments were put forward. One argument suggested that since the British Government ruled directly from Britain, they provided the legitimacy for Government. They should provide for black education if that was what they wanted. Peter argued that no Government could do everything for everyone and that it was up to them, the settlers, to do something.

Another argument was that almost all the taxes were paid by the whites. If the blacks wanted education they should be taxed accordingly. Peter argued that that would take years because of the low income of the Africans and surely it was in the farmers' own interests to do something now.

Others were hostile to the very concept of educating 'a bunch of black savages'. Many of these people had had what they considered to be bad experiences with the partly detribalised Africans in the urban areas who they considered had 'got above themselves.' Peter saw little sense in arguments for trying to keep the whole of the black population ignorant. After all, one of the supposed benefits of white settlement was the 'civilisation' of the blacks. He didn't see how that was possible without education.

After many months of discussion, Peter persuaded his neighbours to help him erect a schoolhouse on the corner of Naseby near the main road, to make it accessible. It was a simple, one roomed building with rough, wooden walls and a thatched roof; it was built on a concrete base.

James Waichagga was appointed as teacher. His modest salary was paid by the Government and they also provided some basic materials. His housing and keep were provided by Peter and four or five neighbouring farmers whom Peter had persuaded to join the scheme.

Housing James was a bit of a problem. He was educated (almost up to school leaving standard) so he regarded himself as a cut above the almost wholly uneducated farm workers. He did not really want to live with his family, in the type of hut village that Peter had on his farm. He also expected the whites to recognise his status and treat him more as an equal. Most whites would not have even considered this. Some were openly hostile and treated James with absolute contempt; they regarded educated or semi-educated Africans as upstarts, to be put down at every possible occasion. The question of accommodation was eventually solved; James moved into the little cabin that Peter and Jenny had occupied on Bill's side of the property before the stone cottage on Naseby had been vacated by the Italians. This set him apart from everyone in the community. The whites did not accept him as anything approaching an equal and the Africans on the farms thought he looked down on them, which he did.

James had an impossible job. He had about fifty children from the ages of six to seventeen with varying abilities all in one room. Some had had a smattering of education. Nevertheless he did a creditable job. He concentrated on the basics: reading, writing and arithmetic. The language of instruction was Swahili; the school was supposed to be for all the tribal groups on the farms, but in practice most of the attendees were Kikuyu.

Many of the parents of the children at the school were also suspicious of the school. Few of them had any education and all of them had seen the effects of people drifting to the towns and cities and the loss of their traditions and cultural roots that resulted. They also were uncomfortable with James' attitude and they thought that if these attitudes were what education provided, then they wondered what the benefits were. The result of this was that attendance at the school was somewhat desultory. If there was, for example, some money to be earned picking pyrethrum, or the family vegetable patch needed tending or a younger child in the family needed looking after, then this took priority for most parents. Education was a sort of optional extra. Nevertheless, despite its deficiencies, Peter and indeed the neighbours who were a part of the foundation of the school and who paid most of the expenses, modest as they were, felt that it was all worthwhile and that over the years the farm workers would learn to value education more than they currently did.

There were also some people in the district who were hostile to the concept of education for Africans and hostile to this symbol of African advancement in their midst. George Athill was one of these. He saw his position in society as a right; he did not support the concept of universal education even in Britain. Here in Kenya, applying that concept to what he considered were a bunch of black savages was an abomination. George applauded the fact that there was a ruling class in Britain; he really believed that everyone in society had their own predetermined place.

Apart from the fact that he was an embarrassment to his family, one of the reasons why George had decided to come to his inherited farm in Kenya was the advent of the Labour Government in Britain. As far as he was concerned, they had given India away, and he was quite determined that the same was not going to happen in Kenya. Educating the Africans was one sure way, he felt, to generate discontent in the local population. "Keep them in their place," he thought. "We, the British, know what's good for them." In his eyes the local population were so much better off under the British yoke; they had almost stopped fighting each other, and some medical care was being provided. The concept that Kenya could be granted independence and that what George thought of as "this bunch of bloody black savages" could govern themselves, was completely absurd. George didn't think the lower classes in Britain could govern themselves, and he used the current Labour government as an example of this. The fact that the school was on Peter's farm was an added irritant.

George was really enjoying himself in Kenya; because of his connections he was a welcome dinner guest with the top people in the administration in Nairobi and he had even been to dinner at Government House once. He had also been on what he considered to be a real safari, where he had his own tent, all meals were served by deferential black servants in white Kanzus and a fez; the guests dressed for dinner whatever the weather and champagne was served. He had wounded a couple of antelopes but none of the Lawrence style fuss was made of that; the hunter and gun bearer, as far as he knew, dealt with them. George couldn't have cared less. He was treated in the way that he thought he deserved; none of this scrubbling about, hob-nobbing with a few ignorant savages like he was expected to do with Lawrence. After this safari he felt more bitter than ever towards Peter; he'd show that bloody upstart colonial.

Now that Rafiki was able to manage the milking on her own, Peter was able to take the occasional Saturday afternoon off. Gugu the syce would ride the horses, Ripple and Crest down to the club and he would enjoy a few chukkas of Polo. The standard was quite high; in fact Ol'Kalou was one of the leading clubs in the country. Peter's limitation was that he only had two horses; he really needed four or five to be fully competitive, since the horses needed adequate rest between chukkas. Sometimes he was able to borrow an extra horse. These inadequacies never really bothered Peter; he was a very good horseman and a very good athlete, and when he was on the field he always acquitted himself well.

George, in contrast, had no less than eight of the very best polo ponies available. He was popular in the club and lent his ponies out to other members, but never, of course, to Peter. Peter was a much better player and if they were on opposite sides took great delight in riding George off the ball and if possible into the nearby mealie (maize) field. This infuriated George even further.

One Saturday afternoon after all the games had finished, the players were all sitting around having a beer. Peter had been encouraged to bring a selection of his photographs taken on various hunting trips down to show people. Peter rarely talked about them but one or two of them had appeared in international magazines and Peter had a sort of minor celebrity status in the district. There was much admiration as the photos were passed around. Included in the pack was the photo of Kahinga, Kinua and Stanley holding rifles over the dead buffalo - George's buffalo. In the confusion, some instinct made George slip the photo into his pocket. It was after all his buffalo. No-one noticed, least of all Peter, who, despite his natural modesty, was enjoying being the centre of attention.

George had had by his standards a wonderful afternoon; he had scored a couple of goals and had lent his ponies out judiciously to other people, which tended to make him popular.

Now this bloody upstart Lawrence was hogging all the attention. It was childish he knew, but George longed for the natural authority that Peter generated and that he felt should rightfully be his by virtue of his birth, and his place in society.

Peter collected the photos and was about to leave when George said unpleasantly, "And how's my little Kaffir Boetie[6]."

Peter didn't really want to say anything. He knew that not everyone in the district thought that the school was a good idea, but hoped they would all see the benefit of it in time. There was a hush. Most people were aware of some tension between Peter and George but weren't really aware of all the reasons for it. This was delicious; they wondered how Peter would respond.

He looked at George quizzically and smiled. "Had any swimming lessons recently, George?"

They all laughed. George went bright red; he was absolutely furious. Most of the people in the room knew a version of the story of the trip down the river, when George had jumped out of the boat in the face of the elephant charge and had left his gun in the boat. Peter had said very little about the incident; most of the information had come through the bush telegraph and had probably started with Kahinga, Dibu and Stanley.

"Damn you, Lawrence," growled George as he stormed out. "I'll get you one day."

There was silence. The group broke up and most people went home.

Dave Gibb said to Peter, "Be careful of him Peter; he has connections in high places, including the Governor I'm told."

"That counts for very little here," Peter said. "The Government does very little for us and we like it like that."

"You may be right," said Dave, "Just be careful, that fellow is like a wounded hyena, I would put nothing past him."

Peter and Dave went home.

George was seething; he had no sooner started to build some credibility in the district than Lawrence made a fool of him again. The fact that he, George, was really the cause of his own problems never occurred to him.

---

6 Kaffir Boetie - An Afrikaans slang expression meaning literally Kaffir Brother. Kaffir was a derogatory word for Africans.

A few days later George had occasion to meet with a few of his cronies. They had a bit to drink and the conversation was steered round to Lawrence.

"Don't really like the idea of that school," volunteered one.

There was a chorus of assent.

"Bloody black savages, what would they do with an education anyway," remarked another.

"Ah ham han heducated hafrican," mimicked another.

They all roared with laughter.

"Tell you what," said George. "We should burn the bloody place down."

There was silence.

"No-one will know. The place is right on the main road. A couple of gallons of petrol, one match and whoosh, it will be gone in minutes. It'll take three months to rebuild it if they ever do," volunteered George.

So it was agreed. A few nights later George and three of his friends chose a dark moonless night; they went up to the school, splashed some petrol over the building and set fire to it.

George was mighty pleased; they waited for a few minutes to admire their handiwork. The school was completely destroyed in minutes. George and his friends went on their way.

Peter went past at 5:30am on his way to the milking. He was shocked by what he saw. The school building was completely destroyed. He stopped and could smell the petrol.

"Damn," he said to himself. "Who would do such a thing?"

He knew there was opposition to the school in the district. There had been disagreement in the district before, but this was not the way they solved their differences.

When Peter arrived at the dairy he spoke to Kamau the headman and told him what had happened. Peter wrote notes to the neighbours involved, suggesting a meeting at the school site that morning. He would see the police after the milking. Stanley was dispatched with the notes and James was called to the dairy.

Peter met with the neighbours. They were all shocked. Still, they were tough people and were not going to be intimidated.

"We'll rebuild it straight away," said Peter.

They all agreed.

The materials were all collected that day and within four days they had a brand new schoolhouse.

George came past a few days later, mainly to admire his handiwork, and was so amazed by the sight of the new school house that he nearly drove off the road.

He found his friends and told them. "Look, we can't give up now; we'll just go and do it again. No-one has any idea who did it," said George convincingly. "I think we should give that bloody jumped up savage who pretends to be a schoolteacher a bit of a workout as well, maybe scare him off," said George.

"What do you have in mind?" asked one of the others.

"I know where he lives; it's the old house near the dairy on Lawrence's place," said George. They all knew that Peter lived a couple of miles away and would not be able to intervene.

A week later, when there was half-moon, all four of them drove up to a point within one hundred yards of Bill's house, crept out and from about fifty yards poured a volley of shots into the roof of the little cottage. They ran back to the car and drove off hurriedly. The school building was not far away; they would burn it down again. No-one would be any the wiser.

Gert Boschoff was one of Peter's neighbours and he had helped fund the school. He wasn't really sure of the value of educating the Africans; he himself had virtually no education and he wasn't sure of its value to anyone. Still, he trusted Peter Lawrence; Peter was a very good neighbour and was always ready to lend a hand when asked. Gert had committed himself to the school and he was dammed if he was going to run away from this situation. If the school was to open or close he was going to be part of the decision and he was not going to let some unknown coward dictate to him just by burning the thing down.

Gert's house was not far from the school and he had found a vantage point sixty or seventy yards away behind a large rock. He thought the people who had burnt the school down might try again, so he had sat up for a couple of nights behind the rock, to no avail of course.

Just after midnight on this particular night, he was relieving himself outside and he was certain he heard a volley of gunfire wafting in on the breeze. He went inside and grabbed his rifle, telling his wife what he was doing. Because of his wooden leg he was quite slow in getting to his vantage point and he arrived there just in time to see a pickup truck stop on the main road near the school. Four men jumped out carrying a can.

Gert wasted no time; he was a very good shot and he shot out the tyres of the truck that were visible to him. When the first shot went off, the four men dropped the can and ran back to the truck. Gert put a couple of shots into the engine, he put another one into the fuel tank, and the truck burst into flames. The men backed off; they appeared to be unarmed. It seemed that they had left their firearms in the vehicle whilst they set fire to the school. They then started running down the road. Gert fired one shot over their heads and yelled at them to stop. They continued running.

"Ok, have it your own way," he thought. "I'll wing one of them; that should be enough."

He took careful aim and fired. One of the men fell clutching his leg, the others made no attempt to stop and kept running.

His wife by now was yelling in Afrikaans. "Is everything OK? Gert, are you hurt?"

"I'm OK; bring the car,"

He limped slowly up to the man in the road, who was yelling blue murder. The man was George.

"Don't shoot, don't shoot," he cried. "I can explain everything."

"I want to hear no explanation, I'm sure however the police might want a few," said Gert curtly in his thick Afrikaans accent. Gert's wife Cora had by then brought their little car along.

They tied up George's leg with some strips from his trousers. The wound was bleeding profusely; he had taken the shot in the right thigh.

"The doctor first, then the police," said Gert.

"No, no - no police," blabbered George. "I'll give you five thousand pounds."

Five thousand pounds would mean a lot to Gert - the different between his current impecunious state and being able to afford to develop his farm.

Gert was incensed.

He gave George a very hard backhand slap. George's head snapped back; blood dribbled from a cut on his mouth.

"Shut up, you verdomde[7] blerry[8] yellow belly rooinek[9], I'll finish you off right now if you say another word."

He made a threatening gesture with his rifle.

George cowered.

He really was in trouble now. What would his family back in England think if he was charged with arson? He'd forgotten about shooting up the

---

7 Cursed - Afrikaans.

8 Colloquial Afrikaans pronunciation of bloody.

9 Afrikaans word for Englishman. Boer war origins meaning redneck; the English troops were badly burnt by the sun

teacher's house. Gert and Cora took George to the doctor.

"Who shot him?" asked the doctor.

"I did," said Gert. "The rooinek bastard was trying to burn down the school on the Lawrence's place, again." He looked at George. George said nothing.

George was taken to the police station. The African sergeant had no idea what to do; he had never had a white man in trouble here before.

"Just give me keys, I'll lock the bastard up myself," said Gert. "You go find the inspector."

So it was done.

Gert made a detailed statement.

In the meantime Peter had as usual gone past the school in the early morning and had seen the burnt out vehicle and the can. He left everything alone. When he arrived at the dairy a very shaken James was there to greet him. Peter started the milking off and then took James to the police. He bumped into Gert just as he was leaving.

"What's going on?" he asked. "I saw the burnt out vehicle on the side of the road near the school."

Gert explained.

Peter explained why James was there.

"Ah yes," said Gert. "I thought I heard some shots, that's what made me sit in my hide near the school."

"What time did you get shot at?" Gert asked James.

"About midnight, maybe just after," was the reply.

They all went back into the police station. George told them nothing.

The Criminal Investigation Department – C.I.D – were called in from Nairobi. Within a few days they had matched the tyres of the burnt out car with tyre tracks near where the shooting up of James' house had taken place. They had fingerprints from the can.

George's lawyer told him to make a full statement as a state witness and implicate all the others.

"You may get off with seven years," he was told. "If you mess them around they could double that."

It was a clear cut case; no evidence was in dispute; it only had to be presented to a court.

George and his friends were out on bail but they fully expected to be prosecuted and jailed within months if not weeks.

Superintendent Preston had been impressed by the way his men had handled the case. It was open and shut and would go to court shortly. He regularly went to see the Governor on routine matters. One day the Governor was unduly agitated.

"This Athill case," he said.

"Yes," Preston was unconcerned.

"Drop it."

Preston's jaw almost hit the table. "They're as guilty as hell."

"Drop it, orders from the highest possible authority," reaffirmed the Governor.

Preston was flabbergasted. "Look sir, the whole district will be up in arms; do you want them to take the law into their own hands?" remonstrated Preston.

The Governor looked up at him coldly. "If you value your career, your pensions, and everything you have worked the past thirty years for, drop it," he barked.

"What about the newspapers?" asked Preston.

"They've been taken care of," replied the Governor.

"And the English ones?" asked Preston.

"We have ways of looking after them," said the Governor.

Preston shook his head, it was beyond him. There was this sordid little case, albeit involving a man with now obvious connections in high places. He wondered why the British Government would risk all for a pipsqueak like George Athill.

Preston took his leave.

The case was dropped. Nothing was said.

After a few months Peter became concerned. There were these four men who had significant evidence against them still running about the district scot free.

He bumped into Dave Gibb one day in Nakuru.

"Look Dave," said Peter. "This lot are as guilty as hell, they've almost admitted it. You know Preston; maybe he will tell you what's going on. I phoned the editor of the newspaper a few days ago, but he was very cagey."

Dave was due in Nairobi early the following week. He went to see Preston.

"I've come about the Athill case," he said. "People are getting agitated; they don't have much time for Government in any case and now they smell a rat. They know that Athill is well connected."

Preston was evasive.

"We still have evidence to collect," he said lamely.

"Crap," said Dave. "We all know Athill turned state witness; what's going on?"

Preston was embarrassed; he was under pressure and he wasn't used to being addressed like this. "Out," he said. "Out."

Dave got up and went to the door. He looked at Preston and said evenly, "This is clearly a cover up. People in the district have no confidence in Government as it is. They will see this as an invitation to take the law into their own hands."

Preston just glowered. Dave left.

He reported the conversation to Peter when he next saw him.

"What do you think we should do?" Peter asked.

"Don't know," said Dave.

George was blackballed by the members of the Ol'Kalou club. He didn't really care; he had his Nairobi friends who didn't know much about the incident. It further reinforced his belief in the class system and his privileged place in it.

Chapter 13

Peter went to the early morning milking the night after he and Rafiki had first made love. The children were away at boarding school.

Peter knew that his life would be very different as a result of his new relationship with Rafiki. On the one hand he was elated, he felt absolutely marvellous and he was deeply in love. On the other hand, he knew that this relationship would not be accepted in any shape or form by the white farming community. A part of him said, "This is absolutely crazy. I really do not need this complication in my life; I wish that Rafiki did not exist." He knew that this was impossible; the die was cast and he, Peter, would have to cope with whatever came his way as a result. He would never walk away from the relationship, however difficult things became.

Rafiki woke up as Peter left her bed to go to the milking. For a split second she couldn't understand why she felt so happy. Then it all came back to her. She giggled to herself when she thought of Peter's clumsy attempt to buy her some underwear. She delighted in the memory of their lovemaking. She couldn't believe how she felt. She had made love to a few of her fellow Kikuyu age group, some of whom she had liked very much, but there was nothing like this. She just lay there for a few minutes and savoured it. Then almost by accident she brushed the seven scars on her right arm.

"The Mau-Mau," she thought. "What am I now going to do?"

She put the thought out of her head; she would cope with that when it came. For the moment this development in her life was too rich to throw away; she was going to walk down this path whatever the consequences. She was in love.

For a few days nothing much in the household changed. The servants noticed nothing. Peter and Rafiki were very discreet during the day but at night they made wild love all over the house - in the bath, in every room in the house; even in the middle of a heavy rainstorm in the garden. They had never known such joy. In their heart of hearts they knew it couldn't possibly last but they didn't care. They just enjoyed each other.

Then Robert and John came home for the school holidays. Everything seemed quite normal to Robert at first. He and John enjoyed their regular riding and Peter taught him how to drive the Ferguson tractor. He used to take it out after Kahinga or one of the other tractor drivers had finished for the afternoon and do a couple of hour's ploughing.

Then Robert began to notice a subtle change in his father's relationship with Rafiki. Most of the time he ignored her. Nothing had been said about the homework he had done "on her behalf" but he knew that this was now kept under lock and key in her room. It was just the odd glance, the odd smile that he noticed and once when they thought he wasn't looking he thought he saw them holding hands. More than that though, it was the body language that told him something was going on.

One night when he woke up; he thought he heard his father going out of the front door. He thought nothing of it; maybe he was just going outside to relieve himself.

For some reason Robert was unable to go back to sleep and he noticed that his father had not returned more than half an hour later. Robert then got up; he saw that the front door was open and so was the door to Rafiki's room. He heard voices coming from the room. He had his torch with him, and he went into the room and switched it on. Peter and Rafiki were caught like rabbits in the headlights of the car. They blinked and Peter said, "What the hell are you doing in here?"

Robert responded quickly, "I could ask you the same question." He then left quickly and locked himself in the little room that he and John shared.

Rafiki tried to stop Peter following, but to no avail. Peter tried to open the door but couldn't and rapped on the door.

"Open up Robert, I will explain."

"Go away," yelled Robert.

By this time John was also wide awake. "What's up, what's up?" he said.

He got no response from either party.

Peter eventually went back to Rafiki's bed; the damage had been done. At least it was now out in the open. He would talk to the boys in the morning.

Rafiki said nothing, she just cuddled him. Peter intended to speak to his sons the next day after breakfast, but they had gone riding. John was about during the day but Robert made himself scarce. Robert was wondering what he should do; he had hoped that Rafiki would somehow go away and then he, Robert, could take his rightful place by his father's side. This development meant she would be an almost permanent fixture of their existence. He had spent all his life on the farm and knew well enough what his father and Rafiki did in bed; the whole idea of it disgusted him.

It was a few days before Peter managed to get both boys together. John was curious; Robert had explained roughly what was going on but he was so embarrassed by the whole episode that he was only able to tell John that their father and Rafiki now shared a bed. Robert was surly and uncooperative.

Peter began, "Look, Rafiki and I are in love with each other."

John was intrigued; he'd always liked Rafiki.

Robert was contemptuous.

Peter tried to explain again, "You may not understand now, but we are really in love and may want to spend the rest of our lives together."

Robert looked away.

John looked at him and said, "What does that mean?"

Before Peter could answer Robert said, "He's like the bull Knight Errant and the cows, he's servicing her in the same way."

John went bright red.

Peter was exasperated. This was not going well; how could be explain? He tried again a few times but without much success.

"What are the Gibbs, the Powers, Gert Boschoff and all the other people in the district going to say? Will you take her to the club? Will you be invited to dinner anywhere?" Robert yelled. Robert was tall for his age with a shock of unruly blond hair; in appearance and character he was very like Peter and just as determined.

Before Peter could answer he yelled again, "What are all my school friends going to say? Is Rafiki going to come to speech-day and shake hands with the headmaster?"

Peter knew all that was correct. The schools that the boys attended were for white children; blacks were only there as servants.

Peter said, "Please try to understand and help me. We're really in love; I can do nothing about that. Judging a person by the colour of their skin is really stupid and unacceptable and will get this country into a great deal of trouble."

This cut no ice with Robert; the way the whole society was organised was based on skin colour. Robert was not able to articulate this but he could see himself getting into endless fights defending his father. For him it was a disaster.

John was a bit slower; he was still intrigued by what Peter and Rafiki did in bed. "Does this mean we will have a little baby brother or sister soon?" he asked innocently.

Robert blanched. The thought of this was even worse. The fact that he, Robert Lawrence, the hero of the school rugby team, probable head of school within a couple of years, might have a sibling who was in the local parlance a "Nusu-Nusu" meaning half-half (i.e. half white, half black) was unbearable.

"The child won't be able to go to your school, John, or mine," he yelled. "What are you going to do, send it to James' school?" He referred to the farm school.

"There is no child," said Peter evenly.

Everyone calmed down. Peter began to understand what he had taken on. There was no possibility that he could back out though.

Robert was furious; there must be something he could do to get rid of this woman. She was in his eyes now the monster that was about to destroy his life. He'd cried bitterly when his mother died but nothing had prepared him for this.

He eventually decided to write to his uncle Bill; maybe he could talk some sense into this stranger, the man he so admired, his father.

John was still thinking about what his father and Rafiki did in bed. He liked Rafiki; he didn't really care about the rest of it.

So Robert wrote to his uncle; he rode into Ol'Kalou himself one day and posted it. Peter had no idea.

Life on the farm went on. Robert had little to say to Peter and nothing to say to Rafiki. From time to time he had noticed Stanley hanging around; eventually he invited Stanley to play a game of impromptu soccer on the lawn. Stanley ran rings around Robert and John. Although Stanley was a couple of years older than Robert he was fascinated by the skill and determined to learn from him. Eventually the daily soccer game became a feature of the day.

John suggested that they should teach Stanley how to ride. Everyone thought that was a good idea, including Stanley, although he was terrified. He'd never been on a horse before. The teaching was somewhat rudimentary; John and Robert just put him on Flicker the pony and for the first couple of rides on Peter's suggestion Robert led Stanley's horse on a leading rein, so if Stanley lost control, the pony couldn't run away. Stanley fell off a couple of times but when they established that he was unhurt, John and Robert just bundled him back on the pony and they went on their way. Before the end of the school holidays, the daily soccer game had been transferred to the Kikuyu village, which was a few hundred metres from the Lawrence's house. There they could at least find four or five a side to play with. They spent a fair amount of time there and their Kikuyu language skills improved greatly. Stanley also learned to ride reasonably well.

Robert had put the issue of his father's relationship with Rafiki to the back of his mind. Rafiki had now moved into Peter's bedroom; as far as they both were concerned the time for pretence had passed. Robert consoled himself that he would be returning to school soon so he wouldn't have to worry about the issue. He was also certain that Bill would be able to talk sense into Peter.

The house servants were horrified when they found out. When Peter was away Dibu found Rafiki alone and remonstrated with her.

"This is against all Kikuyu tradition."

"What will the Mzee say when he hears this?"

"How will the children look?"

"Where will the children go to school?"

"How can your father greet you with this M'zungu in tow?"

So it went on.

Rafiki just said, "I don't understand it, but I have never felt like this before in my life. I must follow it through. It must be the same for Munyu; he will lose his place in the community here when they all find out. He says he can't understand it either but says he must follow it through to the end."

"What about your commitments to the Mzee?" asked Dibu.

Rafiki shrugged. She really didn't want to think about that.

"This thing will end in disaster for all of us," warned Dibu. "The time will come for the Wazungu to leave and then where will you be?"

"Munyu has been good to you too," hissed Rafiki. "Will you kill him, when the time comes?" she asked.

Dibu looked uncomfortable.

"See, it's the same for you," she said.

Bill Lawrence had received Robert's letter and was horrified. He wondered what he should do. Several years older than Peter, he was nevertheless somewhat in awe of him. When they were boys, Peter had always been a shining light whereas Bill had always had to work hard for relatively minor successes. He also knew how obstinate Peter could be once his mind was set on a course. Eventually Bill drove all the way to Naseby to see Peter.

What he found turned him cold. There was Peter sharing his bed and apparently his life with this black girl. The three of them sat down to dinner together, as equals. Bill had never sat down to dinner with a black girl before. The girl, he admitted, was very beautiful, well dressed and had good table manners. Her conversation was sensible when she had something to say and she kept her mouth shut when she didn't. Despite this Bill was horrified. He confronted Peter when they were alone the next day.

"Peter, come to your senses man; this so called relationship will offer you nothing but trouble. The relationship is in its early stages; cut your losses and run," advised Bill urgently.

Peter looked at him.

"Bill, you simply don't understand," said Peter. "Even if I wanted to, which I don't, I simply can't walk away from this, whatever the consequences. You have to understand; she means more to me than you can imagine."

"More than Jenny?" said Bill quietly.

"That's different," Peter felt guilty enough as it was.

"Why is it different?" asked Bill.

Peter put his head in his hands.

"I'm in love with her," he said. "I think of her every waking moment; I can't wait to get back here every evening. In many ways I wish it were not so, but it is. I can't give her up."

Bill scratched his thin, greying hair, wondering what to say. He couldn't fathom any of this; he was a fairly unromantic man himself, comfortably married. He was quite glad he had never experienced anything like this himself – especially if it was likely to get him into the hot water that in his eyes Peter was in.

He brought up all the potential problems: about Peter being ostracised by the local community; about the interests of his children; about the education and upbringing of any children that Peter and Rafiki might produce. Eventually Bill gave up. Before he left he said, "I simply don't understand, and I think you are crazy but you are the brother I have always admired all my life. You will need help; if I can do anything please let me know."

The rumours started to spread round the district.

Dave Gibb came to see Peter and had a conversation similar to the one he had had with Bill.

Gert Boschoff came.

The Nicklins came from Garissa and remonstrated with both Peter and Rafiki.

Half the district came, all with the same result.

Peter had been really popular in the district; most people just shook their heads and blamed Jenny's death for the whole thing.

Peter was blackballed from the club.

Some people made snide remarks in the village.

For Peter life just went on. He was deliriously happy; the relationship with Rafiki grew and grew. Rafiki became almost indispensable on the farm.

Peter had taught Rafiki how to drive the pick-up truck. She was fine driving around the farm and needed no licence there. To be able to drive to Ol'Kalou to do the chores, however, she would need a licence. Peter taught her the Highway Code, such as it was. He then booked a driving test in Nakuru and they went in together.

When Rafiki turned up for the driving test the driving inspector was non-plussed. Still, she had a booking; it was his job to test her. She drove impeccably as Peter knew she would. The inspector was amazed; he'd expected to fail her. He went to his superior.

"This test," he started lamely.

"Yes, yes, what is it?"

"It's a woman."

"So?"

"A black woman."

"Fail her; find a reason to fail her."

The inspector then went over the pick-up with a fine tooth comb; all he could find was a cracked rear-view mirror. That was enough; they failed her.

"It's Lawrences black whore," he told his boss.

"Another reason for the failure."

Peter knew what was going on, and he was not going to give in. Eventually on the third attempt they could find absolutely no reason to fail Rafiki, so she was grudgingly given a licence. Peter realised what he was up against.

All the dinner invitations dried up.

They were not completely isolated though. The Marks next door had escaped the holocaust in Germany by the skin of their teeth; they understood discrimination. They were constant visitors, far more so than before; they didn't particularly like Rafiki but they knew Peter needed the support.

The other surprising supporter was Gert Boshoff. Gert with his Afrikaner background could have been expected to be strongly opposed to Peter's liaison with Rafiki.

"I had a black girlfriend once," he said regretfully. "I gave her up for all the wrong reasons; still you have chosen a very stormy path my friend." He came over for morning tea quite frequently and got quite used to Rafiki.

Robert was affected much as he had thought he would be. As the rumours spread, his school friends abandoned him. He was dropped as captain of the rugby team at school; they couldn't afford to drop him altogether though, he was too good a player. He got into fights when people made cheap remarks about Peter, but since he was big and tough, most of the boys, even those who were older than he was, steered clear.

The children were no longer invited to neighbour's farms, and did not get an invitation to the next Christmas Party at the club. Ironically this forced them to depend more and more on Stanley and his friends in the village. Both boys rode like cowboys; however, they couldn't go to pony club meetings in the district. They already spoke Swahili; they became absolutely fluent in Kikuyu as well. Robert bitterly resented his exclusion from the white society. He blamed Peter for it all; just about everything that he had predicted had happened. Nothing that Peter could do mollified him in any way. He made his friends in the village and he was strong enough to play and work hard at school. He developed a very tough shell. John reacted differently; he'd always liked Rafiki and they stayed friends. John couldn't have cared less about the neighbours or neighbour's kids; he loved living with his strong elder brother and he developed great friends among the black kids in the village.

Rafiki became pregnant.

She was beaming one day when Peter came home. "I've been to the doctor in Ol'Kalou," she said. "I'm expecting a baby, your baby."

He held her; he was pleased but wondered what other pressures this would bring, and he wondered what sort of a world the child would come into.

Robert just looked up at the ceiling when the boys were told.

"Nusu-Nusu," he thought to himself.

John was thrilled and couldn't wait for the child to appear.

Once it became clear to everyone in the district that the relationship between Peter and Rafiki was permanent, Peter and his family were almost entirely cut off from all the social and recreational activities in the district. Instead Peter and Rafiki spent their free time going for long walks round Naseby, often on a Sunday. Peter always took his camera. After a few weeks of this the walks began to have a real purpose: Peter used his well-developed hunting skills to stalk and get very close to many of the species of buck on the farm and he was able to take brilliant pictures of the bush and the

Colobus monkeys in the forest. Rafiki became fascinated with the exercise and was soon better than Peter in tracking animals and getting close to them.

Within a year, between them they developed a catalogue of much of the wildlife on the farm and many of the bird species. Peter also acquired some flash photographic equipment so together they spent many nights in hides around the property and got good pictures of the nocturnal animals as well. They captured jackal and hyena, and once even got a magnificent picture of a leopard on a dead goat, after many nights of sitting and waiting. Rafiki took great pleasure in preparing the catalogue.

Especially on warm days after a successful 'stalk' and in the remoter parts of the farm they often ended up making love - in the tall grass, next to the river, in the forest, once with a group of curious Colobus monkeys looking on.

Before Rafiki became pregnant they had only skirted round the very sensitive subject of the future political developments in Kenya. Once Rafiki knew she was going to have a baby she became bolder and on one of their walks after they had made the most passionate love and were lying naked in the warm sun she said, "This child of ours, how can it be properly educated?"

Peter looked away. "Well we both know that he or she can't go to the schools that Robert and John go to."

"No, not yet. Maybe that should change," said Rafiki.

"The child can do the correspondence course like you."

"O.K, but it's not quite the same," said Rafiki.

"You could go to Ulaya, England; Giles and Louise would help you out and see to it that the child was well educated. The education in Ulaya is... (He was going to say very good).

Rafiki jumped up, furious. "You want to send me away to Ulaya?" she yelled.

She stood over him, magnificently naked in her blackness, her breasts beautifully erect. Peter in his imagination thought he could see a hint of the baby, their baby, in the slight swelling of her belly. He stood up and pulled her towards him. They made love again.

"You don't have to go Ulaya," he said quietly. "This country will have to change; I don't know how quick that will be but I am sure we will find a way of educating and looking after our child."

Rafiki didn't say much more. She wondered about the scars on her arm and whether this would lead to bloodshed and what her role would be.

"It will have to change," was all Rafiki would say.

Rafiki was reticent about entering into a full-blooded discussion with Peter on the subject of the political future of Kenya. She did not want to think about what her role in the Mau-Mau might be or how this would affect her relationship with Peter. What would his role be, she wondered. Would he be expected to be part of the police?

Peter knew in his heart of hearts that the system would have to change. He wondered if the change would come quickly enough. His experience in trying to find support for the school suggested that change would be resisted to the bitter end.

They never really had a satisfactory conversation on the subject of political change. It was just too difficult. Peter was now isolated from his community and Rafiki did not want to discuss, or even think too deeply about, her involvement with the Mau-Mau.

Chapter 14

Although Dibu had committed himself to the Mau-Mau and was authorised to conduct oathing ceremonies, this was all some time ago. He had settled down at Naseby, liked Peter Lawrence and half hoped that the whole issue would go away or at least if there was to be any fighting he could be left out of it. He had two wives and many small children, some of whom went to the school on Naseby at which James taught. His senior wife was bullying him to acquire another wife.

"There is far too much work," she would say. "I am getting too old to look after all these children and need help to look after the fields. Another young wife could also pick pyrethrum faster and we would have some more money."

She was hoping to save enough money to send her eldest son away to high school. Most of the other Kikuyu in the villages on Naseby were quite content with their lot. They were certainly better off than their relatives in the Kikuyu reserve. They liked Peter Lawrence and felt that he treated them well. They were aware, of course, that the people working on other farms were not as well treated and in some cases badly abused, such as those on the farm on Peter Lawrence's boundary: Bob Halway's place.

Notwithstanding that, they recognised that conditions had always varied. Some people lived in villages in Kikuyuland where the chief was relatively benign and others lived under virtual tyrants. Such was life.

One evening when Dibu was on his way home after serving dinner to Peter, Rafiki and the children, a figure came out from the shadows, stuck a revolver in his face and said, "Come with me, we must talk."

He was taken to an area of scrub bush not far from the village and there he and this shadowy stranger met with a group of seven or eight others. All were armed. Dibu was frightened; he couldn't see any features of the people who had abducted him. They eventually came to a small clearing where there was a very small fire burning. Dibu recognised the man with the revolver as one who had been at his own oathing ceremony. His gut turned over.

"So it is all about to start," he thought.

"How many Kikuyu on this place?" asked the man with the revolver.

"About thirty families," Dibu answered.

"How many have taken the oath?"

"Well, there's Kahinga, Kinua, Mwangi, Rafiki - that's four," said Dibu.

The man with the revolver came over to him and kicked him hard in the stomach, Dibu doubled up. Two of them grabbed his ears and pulled him upright.

"Those oaths were done years ago; I was there," he hissed. "How many Kikuyu have you recruited into the Mau-Mau?

The man had his face right up against Dibu's; he could smell the sweet smell of bhang. Dibu was now really scared, so he said nothing. "Listen, you pig-fucking shit heap, we will be back in six months. By then all the Kikuyu on this farm had better be part of the Mau-Mau or you are dead - do you understand?"

Dibu nodded miserably.

They then beat him with fists and clubs and when he fell down they kicked him within a inch of his life.

"Stop," hissed the man.

The fire was put out and the gang slipped away into the forest. Dibu lay there for a while and when he was certain he was alone, he gradually sat up and felt himself all over; nothing appeared to be broken. He staggered to his feet and made his way very unsteadily back home.

It was well after midnight when he arrived home. His senior wife, Phyllis, opened the door. She had been running around all the huts in the village looking for him to no avail. She had been on the verge of going to seek help from Peter when Dibu came in.

She couldn't believe her eyes. There was her gentle Dibu looking very ragged, bleeding from several cuts, his eyes all puffed out, looking as if he had had a fight with a gorilla.

Phyllis opened her eyes in terror and almost screamed. Dibu stopped her.

"Get Mwangi, quick," he whispered. "No one else."

She went.

His second wife collected some water, helped Dibu remove most of his clothing and bathed the cuts.

Mwangi and Phyllis came in, Mwangi looking sleepy. He had to get up before six to set up the kitchen for the day.

He took one look at Dibu's battered body and suddenly became very wide awake.

"What happened?" asked Mwangi; he could guess though.

Dibu briefly explained, after having got rid of the women.

"So the time has come," said Mwangi.

He didn't mind; he'd quite fancied that Rafiki until Peter Lawrence got in there first. Although he had two wives himself, he used to pursue all the unattached Kikuyu females on the farm and beyond.

They discussed the situation for an hour or two and then Mwangi went back to bed.

Dibu's wives returned.

Phyllis looked at him.

"So?" she questioned.

"We must kill the white people," said Dibu lamely.

"White people did this to you?"

"No, no," said Dibu.

"Then what are you talking about?"

Dibu shook his head.

"Go to sleep," she said. "In the morning we will talk."

Dibu was not able to go to work for a few days.

Rafiki had taken over the duties of nursemaid to farm workers and she went out to see Dibu.

She was shocked by what she saw and was really frightened when he told her the reason. She put her hand to her already distended belly, and wondered what lay in the future. It seemed these people were serious; where did that leave her? She had crossed the colour divide. She went home frightened and worried. Worried for her unborn child, scared of the future.

Dibu eventually told Phyllis the whole story of the Mau-Mau. He told her what he understood of its objectives, how people were recruited, and the oathing ceremony. He told her the men would be expected to join the gangs, live in the forest and conduct raids on white owned homesteads. He told her how the women would be expected to carry food into the forests for the gangs to live on; he called the women the "passive wing".

Phyllis was intrigued. Dibu was very surprised at her reaction; he was expecting some resistance to the idea and remonstrations. That couldn't have been further from the truth. Phyllis felt that her life was hard, too hard.

She had very little time for any white people and was ready, very ready to do anything to help get rid of them.

Most of the women, it turned out, felt much as Phyllis did. The men were reasonably content; they had their wives and families, some cattle, the occasional beer drink, a place in the community. Life was much as it had always been; they had to work but that wasn't all hard, especially if the person they had to work for was like Peter Lawrence. Some of the women's discontent was caused by their place in society; as far as they were concerned they were merely treated as chattels, and had no real rights. Their husbands often beat them, and expected them to do all the hard work: looking after the children, washing clothes in the river, cooking, tending the fields, carrying water from the river to the village plus picking pyrethrum for the Wazungu. Anything would be better than the lifestyle they presently had. Their motivations might have been somewhat mixed if anyone had cared to examine them. Nevertheless they tended to be very eager supporters of the Mau-Mau.

Once Dibu had recovered and discussed the situation with Mwangi, Kahinga and Kinua, they decided to have oathing ceremonies every Friday and Saturday nights. They needed plenty of bhang and beer. They were already growing bhang in the forest; Peter was surprised about the number of beer permits he was asked to sign over the next few weeks. Rafiki was left out of it; her position was somewhat ambiguous and they weren't really sure how to deal with it.

The way they operated was to invite all the adults of one or two families to a beer drink in Dibu's main hut; so at least two adult males and a number of women were always present. This was not unusual and so no-one's suspicions were aroused. To start with they chose the families who they thought would offer the least resistance or would be most enthusiastic about the aims of the Mau-Mau.

The way they ran the ceremonies was, having brought the family (without any children) into the hut; they would ply the men with beer and perhaps provide some food. Dibu would then start by leading the conversation in the direction of 'Uhuru' or self-government. He never rushed things; once he had his audience sufficiently mellowed he would then explain the aims of the Mau-Mau. Once this was done, Phyllis would take the women back to their own hut and explain what their role would be. It was not considered worth asking women to take the oath; they were mere chattels anyway and would do what they were told, as they had always done. They collected oathing funds of sixty shillings per adult male; Dibu always religiously handed the money over to the man with the revolver during his periodic visits.

Dibu would then make the men take the oath. They didn't have goats on the farm, so they had no kid goats to kill. Instead of blood they drank beer. Dibu and the others knew all the people on the farm very well. If there was the slightest resistance, a small threat of violence from Mwangi always convinced the victim that it was in his best interests to cooperate. They always put the seven cuts in the upper right arm but they made small cuts. They didn't want Peter Lawrence or any other Wazungu to see the cuts and become suspicious.

When, after a few weeks, all the male farmworkers had taken the oath on Peter Lawrence's side of Naseby, Dibu and Kahinga then went to see Kamau, the head stockman on what was Bill's side of the farm near the dairy.

They explained the situation to Kamau, who was cooperative if not enthusiastic. Kamau's family were dealt with first, then all the other Kikuyu farmworkers and their families went through the oathing ceremony over several weekends. There were no hitches.

Then came the question of James Waichagga, the teacher at the little farm school, and his family. After much discussion they all decided that the best way to tackle James was to talk to him on his own and then ask him to deal with his wife. The problem with James was that he had made no attempt to become part of the Kikuyu community on the farm. He really saw himself as superior to the mere farm workers. In a place like Ol'Kalou he had few friends. He was certainly not welcome in the white community, although Peter Lawrence and Rafiki tried to make his family welcome, with little success. Peter found James a cold fish who was almost hostile to him, Peter, and treated Rafiki with disdain like he did all the other farm workers. Whilst the workers tolerated the school and on balance thought it did some good, they had really began to dislike James, mainly became of his supercilious attitude.

One Saturday afternoon, Dibu, Kahinga, Kinua and Mwangi were sitting around in Kamau's hut waiting for James to come past on his bicycle, as he often did one he had tidied up the school. James was a bit later than usual and it was almost dusk. Dibu stopped him and asked him politely if he would join them for a few minutes. James declined, so Mwangi and Kahinga, who were nearby, pushed him off his bike and after a brief struggle dragged him into Kamau's hut. Kamau was at the milking.

James had actually joined the Mau-Mau some months before and his brother was a self-styled general in the organisation, who gloried in the name of General 'Black Mamba' Waichagga; the name came from the general's absolute disregard for human life; he was ruthless.

Dibu and the three other Kikuyu were fairly high on bhang and traditional beer. They had been waiting a couple of hours for James so their judgement may have been impaired by the wait. They were impatient and slightly nervous because they wondered what James' reaction to the oathing ceremony might be. They were, in short, not prepared to tolerate any nonsense or resistance from James, whom they saw, mistakenly, as aspiring to a 'white' lifestyle and who they knew looked down on them.

Once they had James inside Kamau's hut, they dragged him to the floor. Mwangi and Kahinga sat on top of him holding him down. James continued to struggle. Dibu said to him, "We want you to take the oath."

James was still; he didn't know what Dibu was talking about. Dibu did not mention the Mau-Mau.

"What oath? Let me up!" came the muffled yell from James.

They eventually let James sit up.

"What are you talking about?" James was disdainful. He also noticed that all his assailants were less than sober.

"Let me go, you drunken fools, what do you want?" he yelled.

"We want you to take the oath, I have explained that already," shouted Dibu.

Dibu and his assistants were now very nervous and wanted the ceremony to be completed as quickly as possible.

James had started to have an inkling of what they were talking about, but he was not about to give up what he thought was some sort of an advantage. He had no idea of the danger he was in; he was just determined to put these peasants back in their place.

"What oath? What sort of oath can you possibly have the authority to make me, James Waichagga, take?" he sneered.

"Will you take the oath?" yelled Dibu.

The matter was now rapidly moving out of control.

"What oath? I know no oath," persisted James.

"Will you take the oath?" yelled Dibu again.

"No, you naked bab..."

He was going to say baboon but he didn't get that far. Kinua, who had been hovering in the background with a panga in his hand, just stepped forward and swung his panga. The first blow half severed James' neck;

Mwangi and Kahinga let a very surprised looking James go. The second blow finished the job off and James' head rolled away from his body. Blood pumped out all over the floor of the hut.

The four Kikuyu stopped and stared speechless at what had transpired. They certainly had not intended to go that far. After a minute or two Kahinga said, "Quick, we will have to clear this up and bury him."

"Where?" said Mwangi.

"Here, take this sack," said Kahinga. "We will take him to the Wazungu's lavatory near the house where James lives, and tie some heavy rocks on his feet. The lavatory is more than thirty feet deep; no one will find him there."

"Here, Mwangi, you help me. Kinua, you clean up this hut - make sure there is no sign of blood anywhere - and you, Dibu, take the bicycle down the main road and into another M'zungu's place. Throw it in the bush there; make sure no-one will ever find it."

Kahinga had effortlessly taken the lead. The others did not question him in any way; there was no need to.

Kahinga and Mwangi struggled through the bush and eventually managed to get James' body and head to the back of the lavatory. They tied a couple of stones to his legs and then managed to force the body through the wooden lavatory seat. The body dropped with a loud plop into the mess below.

"They'll never find him there," said Kahinga.

They looked around to see if there were any traces of blood. This was difficult since they had no torch; they had only the light of the moon to see by. They went back to Kamau's hut; Kinua and Dibu had gone and Kamau greeted them with some surprise.

"The others have gone; I thought you were with them," he said.

"We will go now," said Kahinga. They left quickly.

Kamau wondered what had been going on. He had noticed a smell of blood when he returned to his hut; perhaps an oathing ceremony had been conducted. He asked no questions. Sometimes it was better not to know.

James' wife came knocking at Kamau's door an hour or two later. She hated dealing with the farm workers in the village.

"Have you seen James?" she asked haughtily.

"No," said Kamau, which was the truth.

"He hasn't come home yet from the school."

Kamau said nothing; normally James' wife would have been invited in but because of her attitude she was left outside. Eventually she went away.

When James failed to show up at school on Monday Peter called the police.

It had rained heavily in the intervening two days so any tracks that Kahinga and Mwangi might have made while they were disposing of the body were largely washed away. The police were not particularly interested. James and the school had already been the subject of one fruitless case, involving hours of police time with no result. The police inspector wondered if George Athill was responsible for this latest problem; he certainly was not going down that path again if he could help it.

"If I spent a lot of time looking for every missing wog[10] I would never do anything else," he said to Peter unpleasantly. "Why it's necessary to have the bloody school in any case I don't know. It's caused nothing but trouble since you started it," he continued.

Peter didn't try to argue; he didn't have any idea of what had happened to James; for all he knew James might have decided to walk out.

James' wife had noticed a couple of smears of what could have been dried blood in the lavatory and the seat had a few strands of string torn from the sack clinging it. She did not in any way connect this with the disappearance of James.

Two or three months went by. A now very pregnant Rafiki had temporarily taken up James' responsibilities as the teacher. This was not a particularly satisfactory arrangement since her own education was only a year or two ahead of the elder children in the class. The children liked her well enough and were curious about what the baby would look like. "Nusu-Nusu" was what they called it.

Dibu was severely shaken by the killing of James, but he was gradually beginning to relax. The police had shown no interest and James' wife had now returned to her family in Nairobi. She was convinced that James had actually walked out on her; neither of them had been particularly happy at Ol'Kalou. They didn't fit into either community in the district and she eventually decided there was no point in waiting for him. She might as well go back to her smart friends in Nairobi.

Dibu was waiting for the visit of the man with the revolver who had beaten him up so badly and had promised to return to see what progress had been made with recruiting other Kikuyu to the cause. He was always very careful when he returned home in the evening and tried not to leave his hut after dark.

One night quite late there was a knock on the door.

"Who is it?" asked Dibu.

10 Wily oriental gentleman. British slang for Africans and Indians at the time.

"Waichagga," said a voice.

"Waichagga who?" asked Dibu

"General Waichagga; I came to see you six months ago; open up."

Dibu was alarmed; Waichagga was James' surname. He wondered what was to come.

"Open up or we will burn this place down," said Waichagga.

Dibu eventually opened up.

The man with the revolver and two others entered the hut.

"No noise - send the women out," ordered Waichagga.

Dibu did as he was ordered.

"We want to hear your report," Waichagga was quite calm.

Dibu told him what they had done. He also handed over the fees collected at the oathing ceremonies. The General appeared to be impressed.

"My brother was teaching here on this farm and his name was James," said Waichagga.

Dibu's stomach turned over. He now realised how much real trouble he was in. He tried to remain calm.

"He disappeared a few months ago," said Dibu, trying to keep the nervousness out of his voice. "He left before we were able to ask him to take the oath," he continued.

Waichagga watched him.

"He's lying," he thought. "He's already said too much."

Waichagga watched and waited; one of his attendants was about to speak; Waichagga put a hand on his arm. "Silence."

Dibu became very nervous. Beads of sweat appeared on his brow.

"Tell me about the ceremonies," said Waichagga. He could not have cared less about the ceremonies; he certainly believed that Dibu had done what he claimed he had done; he just wanted Dibu to talk.

Dibu was relieved, so in great detail he told Waichagga about all the ceremonies. Eventually Waichagga had had enough. He put up his hand. Dibu stopped and looked enquiringly at him.

"Got you, you bastard," thought Waichagga. "I'll get you but not today."

"We must go now," he said, "I must be in Thomsons Falls by morning." Actually he was going in the other direction, but he always tried to cover his tracks.

Waichagga and his henchmen got up to go; as they left the hut he pinched Dibu's neck and said, "Remember General Waichagga - General 'Black Mamba' Waichagga."

They slipped off into the night. Dibu was by this time shaking like a leaf and he suddenly had to sit down. He knew he was in deep trouble, the deepest possible trouble there was.

Stanley had been watching the goings on in the village for some six months now. He had heard some stories about oath taking. He had also seen Waichagga slip into Dibu's hut and had heard most of the conversation from outside the hut. He didn't understand yet what the organisation called the Mau-Mau was, but he could see it was going to affect his life. He wondered how and when. He wasn't unhappy with his life but he felt that his white friends Robert and John had more scope than he had.

Stanley could see that his own prospects were basically limited to working on the farm. Robert was already talking about secondary school. Stanley decided to talk to his friends next time they played soccer.

Chapter 15

Rafiki gave birth to a very large, very vociferous boy.

There was no time to take her to the hospital; Sarah and two other women from the Kikuyu village were called. Peter was bundled out of the room - this was no place for a man - and within three hours the baby was born.

They weighed him on the kitchen scale. Almost 9lbs.

Peter did call the doctor, but when he arrived there was almost nothing left for him to do.

"Should we take her to the hospital?" Peter asked.

The doctor shook his head.

"No need; she'll be up and about today and she needs no attention," was the reply. "Bring them to the clinic within a week or so, and I will examine them; they're fine, nothing to worry about," he added.

The doctor had adopted a neutral stance with regard to Peter's relationship with Rafiki, at least on the face of things. Privately he thought Peter had made a fool of himself and he thought that there was no possibility that the relationship would last. Still it wasn't his business, and they had produced the most magnificent baby.

"We will call him Kamau," said Rafiki happily.

"Kamau Lawrence," thought Peter; that sounds really odd.

They had many discussions about the name but Kamau Lawrence was what was registered.

Robert took one look at his new brother and whispered under his breath, "Nusu-Nusu." That was how he would always think of him; he wanted nothing to do with him or his mother.

John was much more supportive and he helped Rafiki as much as he could.

Robert and John had continued their various games with the children in the village. At times the talk came around to the new baby Lawrence.

'Nusu-Nusu' was what Robert called him. In time all the children and all the farm workers adopted the name.

The reaction of the farm workers to start with was one of curiosity then some of them started to discuss the long term future of the child. All the Kikuyu had taken the oath and were now wondering what would follow. They had all been told that the Wazungu would leave and that that they would be given some land of their own.

"Rafiki, the mother is a Kikuyu, she belongs to us," said Dibu.

"Nusu-Nusu does not look like a Kikuyu," said another. "He cannot stay with us."

The debate raged on over the months. Many of the farm workers were openly hostile to the idea of a mixed race child living among them. Others were more tolerant.

The white community in general were horrified. Margaret Gibb more or less forbade her husband to visit the Lawrences.

"They're breaking all God's laws," she said. "They're not married and yet they have a child. It's against the laws of nature for the black and white races to mix. The wrath of God will visit them in the not too distant future and they will deserve every ounce of pain and grief that they get," she continued.

Dave grunted. He was disappointed in Peter; he thought the man had gone crazy. Losing one's wife was tragic but it had happened to others and it seemed unnecessary to go off the rails like Peter had.

Peter and Rafiki were still really happy. Peter ignored the fact that he was persona nongrata throughout the district. The farm was developing well and he was getting reasonable prices for all his produce.

Gert Boschoff and the Marks were the only people who continued to visit.

Peter and Rafiki enjoyed watching little Kamau grow up. He was a very strong baby and very determined; he learnt to crawl and had taken his first few steps by the time he was ten months old.

The Italians who had lived in Peter's house all those years ago had for some reason left a 7.65mm Beretta automatic pistol behind, together with some ammunition. Peter had greased it and stored it without doing anything with it. One day he decided to take it out; he cleaned it and fired a few practice shots at a tin can on top of a fence post; it was deadly accurate. Rafiki had wandered over and he showed her the basics of handling the weapon; she fired a few shots but was not particularly interested. The weapon was kept accessible but out of reach of the children, especially little Kamau.

Robert had been at the government primary school in Nakuru for some years; John was a more recent arrival. They both suffered horribly from the other children teasing them and bullying them. They all knew about Peter's relationship with Rafiki. Robert was big and strong; he was also one of the older boys now so few of his fellow pupils had the courage to take him on. John, although no weakling, was younger and susceptible to some of the older boys picking on him and bullying him.

Robert watched the situation; most of the time John was well able to look after himself. Peter had given both the boys boxing lessons. One day Robert had been busy and came out from classes to find a huge crowd of boys cheering something on, on the playing field. He decided to investigate and found John being beaten up by two of the older boys who were both in Robert's class. The whole crowd were baying for blood and yelling "Kaffir[11] boetie[12], wog lover". When Robert appeared they all fell silent. Robert handed his bag to one of the smaller boys and went up to the larger bully, who was in the same rugby team as Robert.

"Visagie, what's all this?"

Koos Visagie was a very big boy for his age. He wasn't very brave, but his adrenalin was up and he pushed at Robert.

Robert stepped aside and hit him with a left in the stomach and a right to the chin. He went down. Robert pulled him to his feet and hissed, "You stay away from my brother."

John in the meantime had recovered and his other assailant was backing off rapidly.

At that moment the headmaster appeared. What he thought he saw was the two Lawrence boys beating up two other boys. He personally was disgusted with Peter Lawrence and what he thought of as his black mistress. His negative feelings were transferred to the boys.

"What's going on here?" he asked.

"Lawrence boys attacking those other boys," he was told. "Unprovoked attack, no reason."

The headmaster was furious.

"Stop that," he yelled. "Both of you Lawrences come to my office."

The crowd broke up. The head knew that there were fights among the boys, and he rarely interfered, but this appeared to be different. When they arrived at the office he asked, "What's the meaning of this?" Before

11 Derogatory word for African

12 Brother

either Robert or John could answer he said, "I'm going to have to expel you as bullies." He was already under pressure from parents to get rid of the Lawrence boys; this seemed a good excuse.

Robert blanched. "Please let me explain sir," he said.

"There's nothing to explain, I saw everything with my own eyes," was the reply.

At that moment there was a knock on the door. It was the small boy to whom Robert had handed his bag.

"Yes Christiansen," said the head.

"Can I see you for a minute, sir?"

"Not now, can't you see I'm busy," he growled.

"I was there sir, I saw everything, please, let me explain," he pleaded.

The head made Robert and John go out.

"Yes," he said impatiently.

Christiansen then explained everything; how the fight had started and Robert's intervention. The head listened. His shoulders hunched; he was not an unjust man and he had almost made a decision to expel two kids unjustly.

He dismissed Robert and John, and made a few more enquiries from boys he trusted. They all confirmed Christiansen's story. He felt ashamed.

A few days later Robert went to see him.

"Yes," the head said shortly.

"Are we still going to be expelled?" asked Robert.

The head looked down. "No," he said. "I've made some enquiries and it appears you were not to blame for what happened."

Robert looked at him enquiringly, but he said nothing more.

"What about Visagie and the other boy. If I hadn't come along, my brother would have been badly beaten up." Robert was truculent.

The headmaster looked at him. "Don't push me, Lawrence," he growled. "You got off this time; you may not be so lucky next time."

Robert's eyes narrowed but he said no more. He left the office.

The headmaster felt even more ashamed. It was his job to protect these kids, not to victimise them.

As it happened, it was just as well he didn't expel the Lawrences.

A few weeks later the headmaster's wife Marjorie went hiking with a friend on Menengai, an extinct volcano just behind the school. There were a few tracks and paths but access by car was difficult. The walking was magnificent and the whole area was accessible from paths behind the school. She had been up there a few times before, so knew her way around. Sometime during the day, when they were walking across a narrow ledge of lava rock from the volcano, a large snake slithered across Marjorie's path. She started in fright, then and fell about five feet, breaking her right leg. Her companion, Helen, who was visiting from England, was distraught. They were alone; her companion was injured, there was no one about, and she didn't know the way home. Marjorie was in agony. After an hour or so two African children appeared; when they saw Helen they started to run away.

"No, no," cried Helen. Something in her voice made them stop.

They came over reluctantly and Helen was able to point to Marjorie's leg by sign language she and Marjorie were able to make the kids understand what the problem was. They tried to get the kids to report the matter to the school so help could come.

"Sculu, Sculu," was all they got out of the kids. They ran off in the direction of the school.

"Hope they understood," Helen muttered.

Sometime during the afternoon the two raggedy looking kids came into the school. The first reaction of the teachers was to chase them away; there had been some thefts at the school and these kids looked like trouble. The children wouldn't be budged, however, and kept pointing up the mountain.

One of the teachers tried questioning the kids in Swahili, but they were Kikuyu and hadn't yet learned to speak Swahili. The teacher wondered how he could communicate with them; it was mid-afternoon and the African staff were off duty. Eventually he had a brainwave. "Go and fetch one of those Lawrence kids, quick," he said to a pupil. "They're on the sports field. I'm sure they will be able to help; they speak some of these languages."

There was a nervous fifteen minute wait, with the Kikuyu kids continuing to point urgently up the mountain.

Robert appeared. He greeted the kids in Kikuyu. Very quickly he had the whole story.

"There are two white women up the mountain," he reported, "one of them at least is badly hurt; they think she has a broken leg; anyway she is unable to walk." He spoke to the kids again and established that only one of the women was hurt.

The teacher and Robert collected a stretcher and some blankets and a first aid kit from the sanatorium. The school, being a boarding school, had a small sanatorium looked after by a nursing sister.

The master, Robert, John, Visagie and a couple of others followed the kids up the mountainside. By this time it was after 4 o'clock in the afternoon.

"Hope these kids can find the place again," said the master.

John spoke to the kids.

"They seem very certain," he replied. Within an hour they had found Helen and the injured Marjorie. Marjorie was in great pain and was now getting cold as the sun went down; she was shivering.

The master, who had some first aid training, gave her an injection. They put her on the stretcher and set off down the mountain. Within a couple of hours they were back at the school sanatorium. There was a doctor there and within a few minutes he had arranged to transfer her to the local (whites only) hospital. The headmaster was at the school; he came over to Robert.

"I understand I have to thank you for all this," he said evenly.

"Oh, not really," said Robert. "It's these kids; if they hadn't come down from the mountain we'd be in real trouble."

"The kids - they're still here," said the surprised headmaster. "What do they want?" he asked.

"Probably a reward," said Robert. "They come from a Kikuyu village round the back of the mountain. It will take them a long time to get home, but if you drive them in your car it should only take half an hour or so."

The head hesitated. He was worried about his wife. Robert looked at him.

"Your wife is in good hands; I'll come with you if you like," he said.

So they set off, the head and Robert in the front, John and the two Kikuyu kids in the back. The kids chattered away excitedly.

"They've never been in a car before," John told him.

"They come from a family of ten children, their father has two wives and many cattle," John translated. "Their father is the headman on a white owned farm."

So it went on. About forty minutes later after they had turned down a very rough track they came to the village. They all jumped out.

Shadrack was the boys' father's name. He was amazed to see his children climbing out of a very fancy looking M'zungu's car.

Robert greeted him respectfully in Kikuyu and explained the situation. Shadrack beamed. He invited them into his hut.

The headmaster hesitated; he had never been inside an African hut in his twenty years in Kenya.

Robert said quickly, "Please accept, sir, it will make a great deal of difference to them. I have explained who you are and it will give Shadrack much honour; if you don't accept I think they will be upset."

The headmaster saw the good sense in that.

They went into Shadrack's hut and sat on a few stones round the fire. The men in the village all made their way into the hut; the women and children went out. One of the women brought in a gourd of traditional beer. Shadrack took the first sip and then passed it to the headmaster.

"It's OK," said Robert.

He took a sip and passed it on; eventually it came to Robert and John.

"You're not supposed to drink," said the head somewhat light-heartedly.

"They treat me like an adult because I'm white," replied John. "I promise I will only take a small sip," he added grinning.

The conversation was conducted wholly in Kikuyu, with both John and Robert translating.

The head was fascinated. He noticed that once you sat below the smoke level, it was quite warm and comfortable. There were no mosquitoes. The hut was sparsely furnished, although there were two rickety looking iron bedsteads with rather ancient looking mattresses on them. There were a number of skins and blankets about; a bicycle and a radio were the only concessions to a Western lifestyle. The only light was from the small fire; when his eyes got used to the gloom he noticed two dogs lying in the corner, in amongst the myriad of cooking pots and pans.

The conversation went round the history of the Kikuyu in the area; Shadrack's grandfather had come there fifty or so years before. They talked about education and the prospects Shadrack's children had of ever having any. They asked about the headmaster's family. He was then reminded of the reason they were here in the first place and caught Robert's eye.

Robert said his thankyou's to Shadrack, and suggested to the headmaster that he should give five shillings each to the two kids. That was a very small sum to the whites, but riches indeed for the two children. They took their leave.

"You seem to understand these people," said the head eventually to both Robert and John.

"We've been brought up with them," said Robert. "We have a couple of very similar villages on my father's farm; we know the people and their customs there very well. Besides the last couple of years we haven't had many white friends, because of our father's troubles and all that."

The head was amazed at the mature and simple way that Robert had presented all this. The last few years must have been agony for both of these kids, firstly losing their mother and then heaving to deal with a hostile white population even at school. His respect for the two boys increased.

They called at the hospital. Marjorie had had her leg set but was still very sleepy from the anaesthetic. The staff nurse said she would be fine, and he could come back in the morning. She wondered where the headmaster had been; firstly he smelt of wood-smoke and some sort of beer and secondly she was used to spouses worriedly pacing up and down. This person seemed to be taking it all rather casually. From what she had heard Marjorie was lucky to be in the hospital and not still up the mountain freezing.

The head drove the boys back to their dormitories.

He gave them a brief update on Marjorie's condition in the few minutes it took to return to the school. He thanked them again.

The head had had what for him was an extraordinary experience. In all his years in Kenya his contact with the local population had been confined to the black servants at the school and in his house on the school property. He was very excited when he returned home and related his experiences to Helen. She was displeased and thought he should be worrying about poor Marjorie.

He dined out on the experience for some years to come and was instrumental in encouraging white farmers in the area to set up schools on their farms. He even encouraged some of the teachers on his staff to visit the schools and help out where they could.

Robert and John's lives became a little easier at the school. The head now had a certain understanding of what they had been through and communicated that to the other members of the staff. The attitude eventually percolated down to the pupils in the school. The Lawrences were after all regular sorts of people, much like most of the others at the school; they were both good at sport and quite competent in the classroom.

Robert was often asked advice by the head after the rescue and Marjorie always greeted both the Lawrences warmly whenever they met.

When he was at home, Robert had established a modus operandi whereby he completely ignored Rafiki; he had a rather distant relationship with his father. Both he and John did some work on the farm. They drove the tractors, helped with the ploughing and had been shown how to run the milking operation, so they were on occasion able to drive the tractor over to the dairy and make sure all the chores were done. They still played some soccer with Stanley and his friends and still rode every day when they had time.

Robert saved all his pocket money and the small sums that Peter gave him for work done on the farm. When he was eleven he had persuaded Peter to buy him a Slazenger single shot .22 rifle. Peter had hesitated but rationalised the situation by saying that at eleven he had a hope of the boy listening to all his safety instructions regarding firearms. He also hoped it would bring them closer together; he was still conscious of the fact that Robert couldn't really understand his relationship with Rafiki. He had also heard some reports from the school headmaster, who was now rather more sympathetic than he had been before.

Peter gave Robert a gruelling training program for the .22, as he had done for Kahinga a few years earlier. Robert very quickly became a good shot and shot pigeons and small buck found on the farm.

One lunch time Robert and John were returning with a few pigeons they had shot earlier. They came round the side of the house and there was little Kamau playing on the front lawn. Nothing strange about that. Robert was just about to go into the kitchen to try to persuade Dibu to pluck and cook the pigeons for him when John said urgently, "Hey Robert, look, there's a big snake just near Nusu-Nusu." They always called little Kamau Nusu-Nusu.

Robert looked up. There was little Kamau walking unsteadily forward with his arms outstretched towards a huge cobra, which had now reared up with its hood out. It was just about to strike.

Robert lifted the rifle, aimed quickly and carefully and squeezed the trigger. Thoughts flashed through his brain: "Maybe my troubles with this bloody little half-caste will be over. I only have one shot in this rifle - what happens if I miss?"

The shot just about took the snake's head off. Robert and John went rushing over; John grabbed little Kamau. Robert beat the now very dead snake with his rifle butt just to make sure.

Rafiki had heard the shot and came out onto the veranda. Her heart almost stopped when she took in the scene. There was John clutching little Kamau, who was looking bewildered and had started to cry although he was completely unhurt. Robert had finished with the snake and had picked it up; it was a good six feet long.

"What happened?" she asked anxiously.

John explained.

Rafiki paled and took little Kamau from John.

She just looked at Robert and nodded. She wished, she really wished that she could find a way of getting closer to this boy. He was so like his father; she really didn't understand why he hated her so.

※ ※ ※

Chapter 16

After one of their soccer games Robert and Stanley had gone down to the ford in the river to skim stones across the top of the water. Robert often went down there just to sit. There was an old cedar tree nearby, which housed a huge nest made up of what appeared to be a jumble of sticks. A hammerhead stork family had made its nest there for years; the storks took little notice of the boys. Peter had given Robert a list of what he termed 'Royal' game that under no circumstances were to be shot, and the brown 'Teguan' (Peter used the Zulu name for the bird) was definitely on the list. The storks lived on frogs and snails in the river.

The river also housed a few reedbuck and often some ducks. It was a nice peaceful spot.

After the game, which they decided was even, they sat down by the river and Stanley said, of course in Kikuyu, "There will be a big meeting tomorrow night."

"Oh," said Robert. "So what?" he thought.

"General Waichagga will come," volunteered Stanley.

Robert's interest perked up a fraction. He was watching some Wydah birds doing their mating dance. "Who is General Waichagga? Hey! Wasn't that James the teacher's name?"

"The same," said Stanley.

"Who is General Waichagga then?" asked Robert. He had forgotten about the Wydahs.

"He is the big general from the Mau-Mau."

"Who are the Mau-Mau?"

"The Mau-Mau is a secret organisation; they will kill all the whites and chase them away," replied Stanley. He did not think twice about what he had said. As far as Stanley was concerned, Robert was not a white, he was just his friend, and he wanted to impart this vital information to his very best friend. Since the general's previous visit Stanley had kept his eyes and ears open; he'd heard about the meeting when he'd overheard a conversation that Dibu and Kahinga had had.

"Where is the meeting?" asked Robert.

"Dibu's hut," was the reply.

They threw a few more stones and then they went to their respective homes.

Robert had the .22 and he walked up the river bank on the way home. There were a few old cedars on the banks of the river. He saw some duck ahead and stalked them. He shot one of them and the dog was sent to fetch it.

He thought about Stanley's remarks and wondered if he would ever see the day when he might inherit the farm. He knew the blacks had a raw deal; the fact that such an organisation as the Mau-Mau existed didn't really surprise him. As with most people of his age he thought he was immortal and didn't really worry about the future. It made him think though.

When he got home Robert was just in time to intercept Peter before he went into the house after he had returned from the milking. Peter always tried to be sensitive to his son's moods, but he wanted to see little Kamau before he was put to bed.

"What's the problem?" he asked hurriedly.

"You know John and I play a lot with Stanley and his friends," said Robert.

"Yes, I think that's a good thing," said Peter.

"Yes, yes that's not the point," Robert interrupted him.

"Then what is the point?" Peter was getting impatient.

"There's to be a meeting of the Mau-Mau in Dibu's hut tomorrow night late; General Waichagga will be there," said Robert.

Peter was shaken. He'd heard about the shadowy organisation, but who was this General Waichagga? "James' name was Waichagga," said Peter questioningly.

"The general is James' brother," said Robert.

They went on chatting for a while. Eventually Peter said," I had better see if I can hear what is said at the meeting; I will listen outside the hut."

"I will come too," said Robert.

"No, absolutely not; one of us in trouble will be enough. You stay out of it, and Robert, please don't breathe a word to anyone else - no one - not John, not Stanley, not Rafiki," said Peter firmly.

Well, thought Robert, he never said much to Rafiki anyway; he'd have to watch what he said to John and Stanley.

Peter had been asked for a few beer permits for the next night, which was a Saturday. He guessed the beer was for the meeting.

On the Saturday they all went to bed as usual. Peter muttered to Rafiki something about making sure the bull was OK. She thought nothing of it; he'd spent a lot of money on that bull and occasionally went out at night to see if he was OK, especially if he thought he was anything but fully fit.

Peter left the house at 11:30; he took his army surplus greatcoat and the little Beretta pistol. He took some charcoal from the now dead fire and blacked his face and hands.

The dogs were chained up. He checked the chains. He certainly didn't want any dogs running around attracting attention.

It took Peter fifteen minutes to walk to the village. Luckily they had locked all their dogs up since they were expecting the general and all the Kikuyu from the other village on Naseby. Peter sat on a little hillock overlooking the collection of huts and just watched for ten minutes. He could see Dibu's hut and women were scurrying backwards and forwards to and from the hut carrying what looked like beer gourds and food. The women and children were supposed to be in one hut. The meeting was for men in Dibu's hut. Suddenly he saw a figure move around in the shadows and creep up to the wall in Dibu's hut. He wondered who that would be; he would just have to listen on the other side.

Robert had heard his father get up and go out. He was damned if he was going to be left out of this; anyway what would happen if Peter was discovered? He took his precious .22 and followed Peter; he thought about taking one of the dogs but decided he would be better off without either of them.

Robert watched Peter sit on the hillock and decided that would be a good vantage point. When he saw Peter disappear he crept up to the hillock and took in the scene.

Peter moved quietly down into the village and took up a position on the opposite side of the hut from the other shadowy figure. There was obviously much interest in the goings on in the hut. Peter could hear muffled voices; he took a knife out of his pocket and chipped a small hole in the mud wall of the hut; after a few minutes he had made quite a largish hole and he could see into the hut. Apart from the fire there were a couple of paraffin lamps hanging up in the hut. Peter was looking straight at the person he assumed to be General Waichagga.

The general was speaking in measured, authoritative tones. All thirty adult Kikuyu men from Naseby were in the hut; Peter could see Dibu, Kahinga, Kinua, and Mwangi - all his trusted Kikuyu. His heart sank right into his boots; he couldn't believe his eyes.

The general went on to spell out what was expected.

"Kill the cattle," he said.

"With what, how?" came a question.

"Cut the tendons in the back legs, with pangas; the cows are then useless; the Wazungu will have to shoot them."

Heads nodded in assent. That was smart.

"The same with sheep and pigs," said Waichagga.

"You can set fire to crops and grass and buildings," he added.

He told them how to organise themselves into small gangs of five or six, firstly to operate from the farms and if that became too difficult then to move into the forest.

As Robert was watching from the hillock, he saw two men come out of the hut and creep round the corner. His heart leapt into his mouth. Had they seen Peter? Suddenly there was a muffled cry and a figure was grabbed by both men and dragged into the hut. He wondered if it were Stanley.

Peter had seen the two men leave the hut and then return moments later with Stanley.

Waichagga's eyes glinted. "Who is this boy?" he asked.

"Stanley; he is the son of Njeroge over there," said Dibu.

Njeroge, come here," ordered Waichagga.

He gave Njeroge a stick.

"Beat him," he ordered.

Stanley was lying on the floor, held down.

Njeroge gave him a few half-hearted whacks.

Waichagga jumped up, snatched the stuck from Njeroge and gave him a few very hearty whacks. "Like that," he said. "If you don't beat him properly I will, and I'll beat you too."

Njeroge gave Stanley twenty very hard hits on his back and buttocks.

Waichagga grunted.

"What will we do with him?" he asked.

Nobody said anything.

Dibu then said, "He should take the oath; that will keep him quiet."

There was a chorus of assent; they were all afraid of Waichagga and what he might do.

Waichagga nodded.

So Dibu made Stanley take the oath.

Waichagga watched. He was not totally happy with the ceremony - there was not enough fear in it - but he let it go. He had much to do.

Peter watched. He was horrified that they would make a youth take such an oath. They made seven cuts in Stanley's upper right arm. Peter suddenly thought, "My God!"

He'd always noticed the seven cuts on Rafiki's upper arm. She'd given him no real explanation for them. Had she been through this ceremony?

If she had this was trouble indeed. Peter knew enough about Kikuyu culture to understand that Rafiki must be considered something special by the hierarchy of the Mau-Mau to be considered worthy of being made to go through the ceremony. Women in general were just considered chattels, possessions for the convenience of men.

Peter had seen and heard enough. He knew then that he was in real trouble. These people whom he had trusted, all of them - Kahinga, Kinua, Dibu, Mwangi, now even young Stanley and his precious, precious Rafiki - were all involved in an organisation that was dedicated to getting rid of all white people. That probably included him, he didn't know. What was he supposed to think now? He gathered himself; he'd better be careful. If he were found here, heaven knew what would happen to him; it didn't bear thinking about.

He looked about, and having made sure that the coast was clear crept away from the little cluster of huts. He walked slowly back to the house.

Robert had wondered why Peter stayed outside the hut for so long; he became very cold. Eventually he saw him cautiously move away; he noticed that he walked back to the house with stooped shoulders and a rather depressed looking gait. Robert wanted to go to him but he couldn't. His relationship with his father was now quite distant and he wasn't sure what the reaction would be, especially as he had been told that he was not to accompany Peter to the meeting.

Peter crawled into bed next to Rafiki at four o'clock in the morning.

"How is the bull?" she asked.

He'd almost forgotten.

"He's okay now," he said.

Peter didn't sleep a wink; he got up again at the usual five thirty and went over to the dairy. There were a lot of thick heads apparent among the milkers that morning, but they all seemed quite cheerful and greeted Peter in the normal way. It was as if nothing had happened.

General Waichagga had stayed with Dibu that night.

In the morning he said, "Three months – you will receive instructions, then the action will start."

As he left he gave Dibu a look of such malevolence with his horrid, snake-like eyes that Dibu visibly wilted.

"Your time will also come," thought Waichagga. He would get to the bottom of his brother's disappearance. If Dibu was involved he would pay; he would pay heavily.

Robert watched Peter for a day or two, then one day got him on his own and asked, "Did you go to the meeting, Dad?"

Peter nodded.

"Anything interesting?"

Peter looked grim. He wasn't ready to talk about it. "Nothing you need to worry about," was the reply.

A few days later when the boys were playing with Stanley, he showed Robert his seven cuts. He was very proud. Stanley explained that he had listened outside the hut where the meeting was held and had been caught, beaten by his father (he showed Robert the marks on his back) and then made to take the oath. Stanley explained to Robert the seven promises of the oath. Stanley felt like an adult. He had already been through the initiation ceremony that boys went through at puberty but this felt more important. He was after all the only one of his age group to have taken the Mau-Mau oath.

Robert was quite taken aback with Stanley's explanation. Stanley didn't think of Robert as white, just as his friend. Robert did not tell him that he had watched from his vantage point and Peter had listened in to the meeting.

When Robert got home he again managed to corner Peter. He told Peter what Stanley had told him and shown him.

"Did you see any of that?" asked Robert.

Peter hesitated. Eventually he replied, "Yes, I saw it all and a lot more besides. I'm going to the police in Nairobi next week. It's really very serious; please don't say anything to anyone."

The boys went back to school. Everything on the farm went back to normal. Rafiki spent most of her time looking after little Kamau. They had found another teacher some time before to take James' place; he lived on another farm with the ordinary farm workers, so much of the emotion connected with the school calmed down.

Rafiki occasionally looked after the milking for Peter and continued to supervise the picking and weighing of the pyrethrum. She made no attempt to do anything for Robert and John was really beyond looking after now. She was still close with John though and shared many confidences.

Peter went to Nairobi a few days after the boys had returned to school. Rafiki never went with him on these trips. She knew that because she was black she would be refused admission to the hotels or restaurants there and Peter's friends with whom he often stayed were an unknown quantity as far as she was concerned. Anyway she was needed on the farm; she felt very much part of it. Peter shared everything with her, the state of the finances included. She never really understood this part, the amount of money seemed huge to her, certainly compared to the wages of the farm workers. Peter assured her that he didn't consider them (that is the Lawrence family) to be very well off. She was aware that most of the money that the farm earned went straight back into development.

Although he treated Rafiki as a partner on the farm, they never did anything about that in a formal sense, much as they never bothered to actually get married. It was unlikely that Rafiki could have been included legally as a partner in the farm, as the whole of the area of which Ol'Kalou was part, and in fact great tracts of the Rift Valley, were reserved exclusively for European or white ownership. The Africans were restricted to the areas set aside for them as reservations. There was no legal reason why Peter and Rafiki were never married; they just never bothered.

Peter had made an appointment in advance with Superintendent Preston. He had some other chores to do in Nairobi, mainly connected with the farm. He also needed to see Jay Firmin. He had over the years taken many more photographs, mainly of things in and around Ol'Kalou, all of which he had sent to Jay and many of which Jay had been able to sell around the world to various magazines. He also showed him the photos he and Rafiki were now taking of the wildlife round the farm, some of which they were also able to sell. All the money from the photos went straight into developing the farm. He used none of it for himself or his family.

Peter had never met Preston before but had generally heard good things of him. Preston had some concerns about Peter; he'd heard that he had gone off the rails since his wife had been killed in that horse riding accident. There was some talk of him taking up with an African woman and that they had had a child. He also vaguely remembered some report by Nicklin, the D.C. at Garissa, about Peter having trained a Kikuyu to be proficient in the use of firearms.

Peter was ushered into Preston's office. They shook hands and sized each other up. Peter saw a tall, silvery haired man, slim with a now silvery military moustache. Preston's uniform was immaculate, as was his office. Preston saw a tall, well built, blond man, with clear bright blue eyes, very tanned from the hours he spent outdoors. Peter always gave off an impression of inner strength; now Preston had a sense of worry as well, as if the cares of the world had descended on to Peter.

They exchanged a few pleasantries. Preston had always encouraged the farmers to make contact with him; they were a great source of information and indeed inspiration. These were the people who really had a stake in the country and were helping to build it up. Eventually he said, "So you have some information for us?"

"Yes, indeed," said Peter. Peter then told the Superintendent the complete story of his "attendance" at the meeting of General Waichagga and the oathing ceremony he had watched. He told the policeman that it was clear that all his Kikuyu labour were involved in the Mau-Mau and that he expected violence against property and the white community to start within two or three months.

"Two or three months?" asked Preston.

"I heard Waichagga tell my people that they would be contacted within three months, and that they would have to destroy stock and burn farm buildings as well as kill farmers when they were able."

Preston had heard similar things from a few different sources. This was very clear and very specific; Lawrence had after all attended this meeting.

Preston said nothing.

"There are a couple of other things," said Peter.

Preston raised his eyebrows.

"I have a tractor driver, Kahinga, who has been with me some years now."

"Go on," encouraged Preston.

"I have done a bit of hunting, really associated with my photography," Peter went on. "I trained Kahinga as a gun bearer, so he's totally familiar with firearms; in fact I almost gave him an army drill."

"You've done nothing illegal," said Preston.

"I know, but this fellow has leadership ability; he knows something about firearms; he's potentially dangerous. You should pick him up, along with all the others on the place."

"Maybe; at present we are sitting tight; we have the whole thing under control. If we pick up your Kahinga then the whole leadership will be alerted and they will go underground. At present we have our tabs on all of them," Preston responded.

Peter nodded. "Is there anything I can do?" he asked.

The last thing the police needed was the local farmers taking the law into their own hands.

"Not at the moment. If this thing blows up we may need volunteers for the Police Reserve, but not yet," he replied.

Preston thought the interview was over and started to get up.

"There's one other thing," said Peter.

"O.K," said Preston somewhat impatiently.

"You'll have to bear with me," said Peter. "This is very difficult for me, but I think it's important."

Preston leant back in his chair.

"It's about Rafiki," Peter started to explain.

Preston's face was expressionless. He could see when someone was about to spill their guts, and he hoped the information was relevant.

"She lives with me on the farm; we have a small child."

Preston nodded.

"She has seven scars on her right upper arm; I suspect she has been through the oathing process as well," continued Peter.

"She won't say anything about it though; she wasn't at the meeting, but it is most unusual for a woman to be involved in something like this. I know the Kikuyu quite well and the women are just expected to do the men's bidding. In almost every case no male Kikuyu would go to the trouble of making a woman take the oath."

This was becoming interesting. Preston asked," What did you say her name was?"

"Rafiki; her father lives in the Fort Hall area."

Preston made a note.

"The women on the farm have apparently been told that they will have to carry food to the people in the forests if and when they take refuge there," Peter said.

"Yes, I've heard that," said Preston. Preston thought, "My God, this fellow is in a real mess, all of his own making." He was tempted to feel sorry for him, but then he saw Peter's eyes. Feeling sorry for him was not going to help; he had a feeling that Peter was more than capable of looking after himself.

"Are you going to do anything then?" asked Peter.

Preston said impatiently, "This is one part of a large jigsaw; please now leave it to us."

They shook hands and Peter left.

On his way back to Ol'Kalou he decided to call on Dave Gibb. He arrived about teatime. The Gibbs were surprised to see him. After some perfunctory greetings Margaret Gibb said to him in her broad Scots accent, "I suppose you'll be wanting a cup of tea then?"

"If you don't think I will defile your crockery," replied Peter, smiling. He knew how Margaret Gibb felt about his relationship with Rafiki.

"Och, you, Peter Lawrence, God's wrath will descend upon you very shortly if I'm not mistaken. Fathering a child out of wedlock and the mother a black woman. You're just as bad as the blacks. We should be setting an example." She was very angry, which accentuated her broad Scottish burr.

Dave interrupted, "Now, now Margaret, enough said." Margaret stamped her foot, glared at Peter and went out. The tea arrived a few minutes later carried by a black servant. Peter exchanged a few pleasantries with her in Kikuyu. She beamed.

"You've provoked certain passions in the district," said Dave.

Peter nodded. That wasn't what he had come to talk about.

"Dave, I went to see Preston today," he guessed that his friend would also know Dick Preston.

Gibb nodded.

Peter told him the whole story. Dave's demeanour became more and more sombre.

"I told Preston about your Kahinga and another fellow that was with him years ago," he said.

"What?" said Peter in exasperation, "You mean that you knew about Kahinga and the Mau-Mau? When was this and why didn't you tell me?"

Dave explained his conversation with his headman Zacharia and his visit to the police.

"I was going to tell you on that first visit I made to your place," Dave explained. "Something stopped me. I guess I was hoping that the police were right and that it would all blow over."

"It looks as if I have been targeted deliberately."

"Maybe," said Dave, "but it could all be a coincidence, they could have all found jobs elsewhere."

"I wonder what I should do."

"Please don't do anything rash," said Dave. "Maybe the police are right and they do have it all under control."

"O.K," said Peter. He left without seeing Margaret again.

Superintendent Preston was now very worried. There had been increasing evidence that the Mau-Mau was growing in strength and that they were about to start a campaign of violence. Lawrence had told him that they were going to start activities within three months. "Three months," he thought; he should be retiring in three months' time. "What God-awful timing." He'd have to stay on, he supposed.

He made careful notes of the interview with Peter and then went to see the Governor. He'd been briefing the Governor on the security situation on a regular basis.

He gave the Governor a detailed account of his interview with Peter Lawrence.

"Sir, I think we should pick the leadership up now and lock them up."

The Governor nodded.

"Is Lodwar ready?" he asked.

"Yes, completely," said Preston. "The staff and everything is in place. They have nothing to do."

The Government had already constructed a prison camp at Lodwar in the semi-desert to the west of Lake Rudolf in northern Kenya for this very purpose.

"O.K, I'll have to contact Whitehall."

Preston nodded. He hoped the decision would come quickly.

He hoped in vain. In late 1951 the British Government was in election mode, and nobody was making any decisions, least of all about Kenya where nothing had actually happened yet. Since the war the British Government had had to cope with the partition of India, the Palestine crisis, which had led to the creation of Israel, and Korea; hot spots were emerging in Cyprus and Malaya. Kenya could wait a few months.

Kenya couldn't wait at all.

※ ※ ※

Chapter 17

On some mornings, when Peter did not go to the milking, he allocated the various farm workers the myriad jobs round the farm.

On the particular morning in question, Rafiki had gone to the milking and Peter rang the farm bell, which consisted of an old plough disc hanging from a tree. There was an old piece of scrap iron to beat it with.

The previous night he had heard on the radio that the King of England had died. He thought that he should say something about it, but he really wasn't sure if it meant anything at all to the farm workers; it ought to mean something to him personally; he felt positive about the Royal Family although he had only been to England once in his life. Many of the settlers called England home; Peter even did so, though he was born in South Africa and felt most at home in Kenya.

"Bwana Kingi na kufa," (the King has died) he announced to all the labour in Swahili. Since there were people of tribes other than Kikuyu, he had to speak in Swahili not Kikuyu.

There were oos and ahs from the assembled labour; this reaction was what they supposed was required of them.

In point of fact they had no real idea of who the King was or what he meant to them. They thought of him as a sort of shadowy chieftain who lived in Ulaya (England/Europe) where most of the Wazungu came from. What effect his death might have on them and their lives they couldn't imagine. Anyway it seemed important to Munyu, and he was their boss, so they expressed their sympathy. They were even more amazed when Peter told them that the dead King's daughter would succeed him as monarch and so would become their ultimate chief.

Kahinga and Kinua were spending the morning repairing a tractor.

"Who is this Kingi?" asked Kinua.

Kahinga felt he had to make some sort of a reply, although he really had no idea either.

"Kingi Georgi," was the reply.

Kinua had heard of him but really only in the context of the Kenya prisons, which were known as 'Hoteli ya Kingi Georgi' (King George's Hotel).

This was even more puzzling: the notion that the big chief would lock up his erring citizens and then feed them made no sense. A solid beating or a spear into the heart for serious offences he could understand. And why on earth would such an important person be involved in such mundane detail?

He shook his head. "The Sirkali must be getting soft," he said. "They can't find a man to be the chief so they now have a woman," he continued.

"Yes, Risbet," said Kahinga. That was the best he could do with the name of Elizabeth the new monarch.

"Will she live in Nairobi?" asked Kinua.

"No, no, same as before, she lives in Ulaya," was the answer.

This had never made sense to Kinua. At least his own chief was visible; you could go and see him. It might take several days of waiting to get an audience, but then you put your case to him, he made a decision and that was that. How would he ever go to Ulaya to see this chief? He had a very vague notion of where Ulaya was. If it was further than Nairobi, this would present great difficulties.

"Ulaya is over the sea," volunteered Kahinga as if reading Kinua's thoughts.

Kinua had never seen the sea, but if it was bigger than Lake Naivasha, then indeed it was big. "Maybe it is time for a change in the chief," said Kinua.

It was not unknown for hereditary chiefs to be deposed if they were deemed to be no good. The quickest and easiest way was to kill them.

Kahinga nodded.

General 'Black Mamba' Waichagga had sent one of his henchmen to them a couple of days before. They had been told to destroy Halway's property and kill him. This was to be the start of the campaign to rid Kenya of the white settlers.

The following Friday night Dibu, Mwangi, Kahinga and Kinua held a council of war. They knew what they had to do but had no idea how to go about murdering Peter Lawrence's neighbour. They didn't know his personal habits - whether he carried a gun or anything else about him. The only weapons they had were the pangas that Peter supplied to all his farm workers. They would have to make sure that the pangas were sharp. After much discussion they eventually decided that one of them should go over to Halway's farm and try to find out something about Halway's movements. They eventually selected Stanley.

Stanley had only the vaguest idea of what was expected of him. He went over to Halway's place about mid-morning and hung about the kitchen. All Halway's servants were Kikuyu, so he was greeted civilly and he just chatted.

About lunchtime Halway came in. He hated the blacks. When he saw Stanley he asked his house servants aggressively, "Who is that toto (boy)? What does he want? Send him away."

They explained to him that Stanley's mother was sick and he had come to tell her sister who lived on Halway's farm.

Halway had no sympathy or understanding of his labour and had no way of knowing whether this was true or not.

"Well, what's he doing here? Has he delivered the message? If he has, send him away."

The cook then made a big play of picking up a stick and chasing Stanley away.

Stanley by then had very little information; however on a subsequent visit he learnt that Halway always had dinner about 7pm. He had no other useful information except that Halway employed a cook, two house servants and two kitchen totos to do the washing up.

Kahinga and Dibu eventually decided that a Friday night would be the best. They had decided that not only would they have to kill Halway but that there should be no witnesses so any house servants that were about would have be dealt with as well.

Eventually a group crept out just after dusk, led by Kahinga. The group included Dibu, Mwangi, Kinua and six others. All had very sharp pangas but no other weapons.

They waded the river that separated the two properties and arrived at the back door of the kitchen in Halway's place a few minutes before seven o'clock. All ten of them nervously crowded into the kitchen; the house servants were absolutely terrified.

"Chakula," (food) yelled Halway from the house. "Come on, hurry up! What are you waiting for, you idle black savages."

He had a nephew out from England staying with him and thought he would give him a few lessons on how to deal with the blacks.

Kahinga was very calm; he said to the house servants, who had placed two plates of soup on a tray, "You throw the soup in their faces, we will do the rest."

"Come on, hurry up," came a further yell.

One of the servants, dressed in his white kanzu and fez, very nervously picked up the tray and carried it into the dining room followed by the other servant, similarly dressed.

Halway was sitting at the head of the table with his back to the door but the nephew was sitting in a position facing the door. His eyes nearly popped out of his head when he saw the servants being closely followed by three black men brandishing pangas.

Halway turned around to see what the problem was. The servant carrying the tray was so nervous that he tripped and the soup went straight into Halway's face and all over his dinner jacket.

"What the… " Halway got no further. Kahinga swung his panga and Halway's bald pate opened up like a melon; blood poured out. Kahinga gave him another couple of blows to finish him off. The nephew tried to run upstairs, but Kinua caught up with him and aimed a savage blow at his legs. He fell over, screaming in absolute terror, and Kinua eventually killed him with a blow to the head.

Mwangi had killed one of the house servants but the other one escaped with Mwangi in hot pursuit. He killed him as he was trying to get through a fence about one hundred yards from the house.

As soon as Dibu heard the noise from the house, he and the other six members of the gang set about killing the cook and the two kitchen totos. Just as the mayhem had started another teenage boy had arrived on some errand or another, and he was dispatched with the rest of them. "Guns," yelled Kahinga. "We must get the guns."

They ransacked the house and eventually found a good hunting rifle, a twelve bore shotgun and a couple of ex-army .303's. There was also more than one thousand rounds of ammunition. They found a couple of canvas bags for the ammunition, took all the money they could find and left with the guns.

Just as they were leaving Kahinga kicked two of the paraffin lamps over, which burst into flames. One of them was near a curtain, which caught fire.

Halway had a few mangy dogs around the place. They were used to numbers of black visitors and had taken no notice of Kahinga and his gang. When the violence started they ran away to hiding places in the garden.

Kahinga looked about; two dead whites, six Kikuyu. He wondered, whether it was always going to be like this.

Instead of running back to Naseby, the gang set off with their booty in the opposite direction. They had planned to run into a village on Halway's boundary on the opposite side of the property to Naseby. This village was occupied by Kipsigis people who had no involvement with the Mau-Mau and who generally were suspicious of the Kikuyu.

They came to the village at about nine o'clock in the evening; all was quiet. They did their best to wipe down two of the bloodstained pangas and then left them separately propped up against two of the huts. The gang then separated in the village and arranged to meet down by the river a few hours later. They assumed, successfully, that the police would follow their tracks to Kipsigis village; hopefully by then some of the Kipsigis would have picked up the pangas they had left and put their fingerprints all over them. The police would then blame the Kipsigis for Halway's murder.

The gang found their way to the river a few hours later. Kahinga then insisted that they walk up the river back to Naseby. No dogs, if they were available, could possibly track them now. They washed themselves and their weapons in the river, any bloodstained clothing was burnt and buried in the forest and they wrapped the guns and ammunition they had stolen in a canvas tarpaulin and buried them also in the forest.

They crept back to their huts just before dawn.

Peter was standing on his veranda at about 10pm just before he was going to turn in when he noticed a glow coming from the direction of Halway's house. Just then there was a commotion; the dogs started barking. He told them to be quiet.

"Bwana, bwana, come quick," a young man who was completely out of breath came into the lamplight.

The dogs' hackles rose and they growled.

"Quiet," he said to the dogs.

"Yes, what's the problem?" asked Peter quickly.

"Watu na uua Bwana Halway." (Someone has killed Halway.)

What had happened was that, when the servants had failed to return home, one of the wives had gone up to see what the problem was and had found the house blazing and the carnage. Halway's labour force was now trying to bring the fire under control.

Peter briefly explained to Rafiki what had happened. He would take the young man with him, call the police and then go over to Halway's farm.

Rafiki had a deep, sinking feeling in the pit of her stomach. "So this was the start of it," she thought. She knew she would be forced to participate. She wondered what it held for her and Peter. It could not possibly be good.

Peter went to the neighbours to use the telephone.

"Halway murdered, you say?" said Mr. Marks.

"Yes - according to this fellow. I could see the glow of a fire from my veranda."

Peter rang the police and spoke to the duty sergeant in Swahili.

"What did you say?" said Peter angrily. "You'll come in the morning? Halway and a number of Kikuyu have been murdered and you say you'll come in the morning! Get me the inspector."

He was given a phone number.

The police eventually arrived at 3am. They were not used to dealing with emergencies like this, especially in a sleepy little place like Ol'Kalou where the police station was manned by a white inspector and six African askaris. They did have a dog with them.

Peter drove back to Halway's place with the messenger. He was almost sick when he saw the carnage. The fire had done some damage but had been put out before it completely destroyed the place.

They found Halway and his nephew and one of the house servants butchered in the dining room, they found the four people in the kitchen and eventually the one house servant caught in the fence. Peter knew that this was the beginning of the insurrection; he had a very shrewd idea of who was responsible.

When the police arrived he left them to it, after suggesting that they came over to Naseby when they had finished since he thought he knew who had committed the murder.

The next day was Saturday. It was only a half-day of work but he was anxious to see at first-hand what his farm workers looked like. He got home and persuaded Rafiki to do the milking. He went out as usual at 7am and rang the bell. When all the farm workers assembled he told them that Halway had been murdered in the night. The response was a lot of "Oo's" and "Ahs". He looked at them closely; Kahinga and Kinua looked ashen and he noticed a few others who didn't look so good either. He'd already seen Dibu and Mwangi in the kitchen; they looked exhausted. There was no doubt in his mind. His people had done it; he'd have to turn them in to the police.

He waited a couple of days, but he had no visit from the police. Eventually he went down to the station.

The young inspector was very ebullient.

"Got the bastards," he told Peter. "Six Kipsigis arrested this morning."

Peter was aghast.

"Yes," he said, "we followed their tracks to the Kipsigis village on the next door farm, found a couple of pangas, covered in blood, and we've matched fingerprints to some of the men in the village. Open and shut case. The bastards will hang."

Peter said, "Look, hold on, maybe you've got it wrong. I can tell you that the Kipsigis would not have hacked the people to pieces like that. They have spears and simis[13]; they would have run them through with a spear more likely."

The inspector was not in the slightest bit interested. As far as he was concerned one bunch of blacks was much like another and anyway, wasn't this Lawrence fellow the one who had taken up with a black woman? He'd heard all sorts of stories from the members of the club, particularly George who had told him that Peter even sat and drank with his blacks while they were on safari. He wasn't about to listen to rubbish from such a source.

Peter tried again, "Have you found the guns they stole?"

"No, not yet, but we will," was the reply.

"Look," said Peter. "I know these people well." He explained about his clandestine attendance at the meeting on the farm. "I would bet the farm on the fact that my people were involved. I could name my suspects now; why don't you at least pick them up and interrogate them."

The inspector was even more piqued when Peter told him that he had gone straight to Nairobi with the story of the meeting.

"You should have reported it here first," he said.

Peter was silent. That wasn't the point. Peter tried to persuade him to at least come to the farm, and perhaps search for the missing guns. If Kahinga and company had murdered Halway, they would have buried the guns somewhere reasonably accessible. He was certain that they would find them with a thorough search.

Eventually the inspector arrogantly dismissed him.

"Look Lawrence, we've got our suspects all safely locked up. As I told you, it's an open and shut case. Now I'm busy."

As Peter left he said, "I wish you were right, but you are not. This murder had nothing to do with a bunch of Kipsigis. It's the start of the Mau-Mau uprising. We're in deep trouble."

The inspector looked blankly at him. He'd never heard of the Mau-Mau.

The story of Peter's visit to the police of course went round the club. It suited the local whites to believe that it was an isolated case.

13 Thin, long bladed bush knife.

"Bloody wog-loving lunatic," said George. He couldn't have cared less who murdered Halway but was happy to further denigrate Peter. If the police had arrested some people, that was good enough for him.

Peter eventually managed after trying for some days to phone Superintendent Preston.

"Look Superintendent, I know you are busy but your people up here really need to look further than the Kipsigis. I am certain that the people on my place whom I told you about are involved. They've set the Kipsigis up."

It suited Preston's book to believe the evidence that had been presented in this case. The police knew that the situation with the Kikuyu was getting more serious but they had been told to keep a lid on the situation, at least until after the British Election.

"Look, Mr Lawrence, I appreciate your concern, but I have been through all the evidence myself, and it is an open and shut case. The Kipsigis will hang," he said.

The conversation continued. Preston had a nasty feeling that Peter was probably right. He'd liked Lawrence; it was pity that he had taken up with a black woman though.

Anyway, it was his job to let justice take its course; he shouldn't interfere personally with murder cases, even one with a high profile like this one.

Peter also spoke to Dave Gibb and his neighbour Gert Boschoff. They believed Peter.

Dave Gibb also phoned Preston.

"Look Dick," he said, "I know Lawrence has blotted his copy book with this black woman and all that, but I can tell you he knows these people like the back of his hand. It's hardly in his interests to go running about suggesting that you arrest most of his labour force. He's spent years training them. If he is suspicious then he has good reason to be. The people he's talking about are the same ones I told you about years ago now; you really should take this further."

Preston could see the good sense in what he was being told but he had his instructions. He really began to worry though. He was basically a just man and the thought of sending innocent men to the gallows, even if they were black, horrified him. He was even more worried about the security situation; he could see the whole thing was about to blow up in their faces.

And it did.

※ ※ ※

Chapter 18

Since Halway's murder Peter had known that he would have to talk to Rafiki about her involvement in the Mau-Mau and also what the future held.

He put it off and put it off. The boys had come home for the holidays and it had been a particularly happy time. Little Kamau was growing up; the two big boys played with him, even Robert, and seemed to accept him. Everything on the farm had settled down.

During the school term Robert had received a letter from Peter telling him that Halway had been murdered. It was also reported in the newspaper. Robert and John barely knew Halway; they had been over to his place on the odd occasion delivering messages. When the wind was blowing in the right direction they could sometimes hear him bellowing at his labour force.

Peter had talked to Robert about the incident during the holidays and told him that he suspected Kahinga and the people on Naseby of the murder and why. Robert thought it all made good sense.

When Robert went back to school he happened a few days into the term to bump into the headmaster, who was now much more sympathetic to the Lawrences.

"Nasty business that Halway murder," he volunteered. "He lived in your district, didn't he?" he further inquired.

"He was our neighbour, actually," replied Robert.

"Oh, really; they seem to have found the murderers though, don't they?" said the head.

"Maybe," said Robert.

Robert then went on to explain Peter's suspicions and the police reactions.

"My father says this is the beginning of a major rebellion, called the Mau-Mau," said Robert.

The head had never heard the Mau-Mau mentioned before. He wondered how vulnerable the school was; luckily most of the black people working there were not Kikuyu.

The story gradually spread. Eventually the newspapers started mentioning the Mau-Mau. The white settler community were split into those who were happy to believe the police version of the Halway murder and those who thought it was likely to have been Kikuyu who perpetrated the crime. The latter generally were the people who were closer to their farm workers and at least tried to have some understanding of the black population.

It was early one Sunday afternoon, and Peter and Rafiki were having tea on the front lawn. Little Kamau was running about happily in the garden. The sun was shining, there was a faint breeze – there was almost nothing to spoil the day. Peter would go to the milking in an hour or so.

Peter looked at Rafiki; she was stunningly beautiful. She had on a short sleeved shirt and a skirt. When they were alone she never bothered with underwear; she really found it too constraining. She had however taken to putting it on when they had guests or when she was out anywhere. He looked at her.

"My love," he said gently.

She looked up. She knew what was coming and had dreaded this moment for weeks.

"Those scars on your right arm," he continued.

She nodded, fingering the scars.

"I now know they are from the oathing ceremony of the Mau-Mau."

She looked up surprised. This was the first time she had heard the organisation mentioned in the household.

"You remember when I went out the other night a few months ago to look after the bull?"

She nodded.

"There was nothing wrong with the bull."

Rafiki looked up. She wondered what was coming.

Peter then held her hand and explained his clandestine attendance at the meeting where Stanley had been given the oath. He explained General 'Black Mamba' Waichagga's attendance.

She shuddered. She remembered 'Black Mamba' from her own oathing ceremony. He'd tried to rape her afterwards.

"Why didn't you tell me about this before?" she asked.

"I don't know, I didn't know what to think," he answered.

Peter then explained that he was almost certain that Kahinga and company had murdered Halway and not the Kipsigis as the police thought.

He also explained that he thought this was the beginning of the Mau-Mau rebellion and the quest for independence.

She looked at him. She supposed he was right but she had not been approached by anyone, she supposed because of her relationship with Peter.

Peter went on. "It's very unusual for a woman to be made to take the oath."

She looked at him.

"They must have had something special in mind for you when it was done," he continued.

She didn't know what to say.

"Come on, tell me," he insisted. "All this is going to be very difficult for both of us; we had better try to understand exactly where we each stand."

Eventually she said, "There were five or six of us, young girls, especially selected by the leadership to take the oath."

"Go on," said Peter.

"They told us that when the fighting starts our people will go into the forest."

"Yes," said Peter.

"It will be difficult for them to find food."

Peter nodded.

"It will be our job to collect food and organise other women to carry it into the forests for them."

"My God," thought Peter, "they have been planning this for years." "Will you go?" he asked.

She looked at him. "I have no choice," she whispered. A tear trickled down her face. "If I don't go they will kill my people."

Peter knew this was true.

"And you?" she said, then she added, "you could take little Kamau and go to Ulaya, until all this is over."

Peter looked at her and then said vehemently, "And leave all this to go back to the bush - just leave all my hard work to go to waste. I could never do that."

She put her hand on his arm. "I know, please don't be upset."

Privately she knew that shortage of land for the burgeoning African population was a major political issue. This area was ideal for settlement. She thought that the land would in the end have to be given back to the Africans; that was, after all, her understanding of what the fight was all about.

They were silent for a few minutes and just held hands.

Eventually Rafiki got up and took little Kamau and dumped him on Mwangi's lap. Mwangi didn't mind; Kamau shrieked for a few moments and then settled down. He liked Mwangi; Mwangi was great with little children.

She went back to Peter.

"Life may not be very easy for us now," said Peter.

"No," Rafiki agreed.

"You will have to go back to your people," said Peter.

"And you to yours," said Rafiki.

They both knew what this meant. Whatever their relationship, and whatever the justice or injustice of their own communities' positions, in the final analysis each would have to return to his own. Neither of them could really conceive being part of or working with the other community.

Rafiki was not in any way bitter. She really valued her relationship with Peter and loved him as she had never loved anyone. It was clear, however, that she could never be part of the white community as it was presently structured. Her child could not go to a white school; she could not even be a legal partner in the farm. Her legal status in her own country was that of a second or third class citizen. She was not welcome in any of the white institutions such as the local club or the hotels in the main cities. She could see that all that would have to change.

Peter, too, knew that change was inevitable. He hated the fact that Rafiki could not be taken anywhere - to the club or the hotels. Their child could not go to any of the recognised schools, either Government or private. The only solution was to send him to England for education where, although he would be regarded as a curiosity, as far as Peter knew he would be admitted to both the government and private school systems. Having said that Peter knew of no African who could possibly have done what he had accomplished on Naseby. He thought that the local people would also need a great deal of help and understanding from people such as himself if they were ever to run a Government. Besides, if they thought they were going to toss him off this farm by force they had another think coming. He also reflected on the true richness of his relationship with Rafiki; they were both really African, one white, one black. They both felt the same way about the land, the country. He also appreciated her gentleness, her humour; they had almost never had a cross word to say to each other.

They kissed. He'd had to teach her that; generally Africans would have thought kissing was a very unhygienic and quite unattractive pastime.

The dairy was forgotten; Rafiki dragged him into their bedroom. He removed the few clothes she had on. He could never get enough of her beauty. They made love all afternoon.

At seven o'clock Mwangi banged on the door. "Hodi," he said.

"My God, what time is it?" asked Peter. It was seven o'clock.

He'd forgotten the dairy, everything. He could never have replaced those moments, that special afternoon. He felt enriched and very sad. He knew it could not last.

Little Kamau came running into the room.

They got up and had dinner. Little Kamau was put to bed.

"Whatever happens," said Peter, "we must not forget what we have here; it's precious to both of us."

She held his hand. She would not, could not forget.

CHAPTER 19

When Peter was out during the next week Rafiki confronted Dibu and Mwangi together in the kitchen.

After the usual talk of the weather, the crops, their children and their wives she said, "Munyu says that you killed Halway."

She had decided on the direct approach and watched them both carefully as she said it.

The eyes said it all. They quickly glanced uneasily at each other and then all too quickly tried to respond.

"The police…" started Mwangi, and faltered; normally he left all the major speeches to Dibu.

"The police," continued Dibu, "the police have charged those stinking Kipsigis with the murder."

Rafiki was contemptuous.

"The police know nothing; that little, wet-behind-the-ears inspector down there at the station, he barely knows whether his prick is standing up or lying down." Privately she thought, "It probably makes no difference anyway," and giggled to herself.

They chuckled. They let their guards down a bit.

"Come on, I'm part of the Mau-Mau too, you know." She lifted the sleeve on her right arm, showing the scars. "You know as well as I do the Kipsigis had no reason to kill Halway. The instruction must have come from 'Black Mamba'."

They looked at each other again. The mention of General Waichagga surprised them both. Nobody as far as they knew had told Rafiki of his visits.

She knew she had them then. "He came when Stanley was made to take the oath. He talked about killing Halway then."

They looked really puzzled. How on earth did she know all of this? If that little bugger Stanley had opened his mouth he'd get the beating of his life: they thought as one.

"What do you know about Waichagga?" asked Dibu

"What do I know about Waichagga?" responded Rafiki. "He was there when I took the oath," she said noncommittally. "I know he was in charge of the Ol'Kalou area. I'm sure he is the one who gives you instructions. I know he was here. He must have told you to kill Halway."

By this time they had recovered their composure.

"No, no it was those dirty Kipsigis," Dibu muttered.

He needed time: this was a serious development. He must discuss this with Kahinga. Rafiki knew she would get nothing further out of them today. She also knew that Peter was right.

As if reading their minds, as she was going out she said, "Munyu has already told the police what he thinks: they are not listening to him. They think the Kipsigis did it."

The relief on Dibu's and Mwangi's faces was palpable.

Rafiki smiled and went out.

The security situation in the district and in the rest of the White Highlands where the Kikuyu had any influence deteriorated rapidly. There were several more murders. The white population responded by arming themselves; there was a run on the gun shops in Nairobi and Nakuru.

Eventually the Government declared a State of Emergency. The leadership of the Mau-Mau, including Jomo Kenyatta, were first imprisoned at Kapenguria and then after a lengthy show trial were found guilty and were incarcerated in the prison already prepared for them in Lodwar. Some British conscript troops were sent to Kenya.

Dibu had discussed with Kahinga the conversation he had had with Rafiki.

They decided to let sleeping dogs lie unless she raised the issue again. If she did they would have to tell her. They knew she would be expected to play a major role in the campaign ahead; no one would have considered it worthwhile making her take the oath otherwise.

All the Kikuyu were concerned about Rafiki's relationship with Peter, and this was made even more complicated by the advent of the child. They all liked and respected Peter but he was an M'zungu and all the Wazungu would have to leave.

Rafiki tackled them a few weeks later again in the kitchen.

After the usual greetings she said to them, "Well, are you going to tell me more about Halway. You've had plenty of time to discuss it with Kahinga."

They hesitated.

"Come on," she said. "I'm in this too."

They then all sat down in the kitchen and Dibu explained everything. How he had been sent to the district, and that Kahinga and Kinua had been sent to join him. The oathing ceremonies, General Waichagga's visits and Halway's murder. He left out the details of James' murder; she didn't need to know that. Dibu knew that whatever else happened he would be called to account for that at some stage.

Rafiki was astounded by the story and the preparations that had gone into the insurrection. She felt a little piqued that she had been left out of it all. She understood the reasons though.

"What are you now expected to do?" she asked anxiously.

"We are waiting for 'Black Mamba'," replied Dibu.

They knew the General had been busy with all the goings on in the district.

They all hoped that nothing further would be expected of them. They had got away with one murder; they wondered if they would be so lucky next time. Obviously this was unrealistic. General Waichagga had his hooks into them and was unlikely to let them go.

Rafiki felt completely trapped. On the one hand she was still in love with Peter and was really happy in the relationship. She had a fine healthy baby.

On the other hand she could see that the present situation had to change to give that very relationship a chance to be accepted as part of the mainstream of society in Kenya and to give that child a chance to be properly educated.

She really hated the idea that she might be forced to leave Peter and Naseby. She wished they would just leave her be, to look after Peter and nurture their child and when it was all over she could benefit from the changes that would have to come in the society. Rafiki knew that was completely unrealistic. She had given her word, she had taken the oath; she was committed. She didn't know what to think; at one point she thought that if she had to go she could leave little Kamau with Peter. She really hated that idea that he would grow up separate from her, probably with a whole lot of "white" attitudes.

She often cried herself to sleep at nights. Peter often noticed her wet cheeks as they snuggled up. He tried to get her to tell him what the trouble was, but in his heart of hearts he knew.

"What a mess," he thought. "Maybe it would have been better if I had never set eyes on her," he thought. "What about little Kamau, what about the richness that has surrounded me these last few years," his thoughts continued. He didn't know either.

In the end the issue was taken out of their hands.

Dibu and company had another visit from "Black Mamba".

"You will kill Lawrence and his two white brats," they were told.

There was a deathly hush around the hut; Dibu and Kahinga looked at each other. They could have rushed Waichagga there and then and killed him. The General even felt a little nervous; he fingered the revolver in his belt, and his two henchmen fingered the triggers on their sten-guns. It was useless; they all relaxed. The general couldn't wait to get out of there; he'd never felt so uncomfortable in all his life. They now had their instructions; woe betide them if they failed to follow them.

The general also had another bone to pick with Dibu and company. He had questioned his sister-in-law at length about his brother James' disappearance. The only thing she could think of was the few possible blood spots and traces of sacking in the long drop near the house on Bill's side of Naseby. He and his henchmen had gone to investigate and had eventually pulled a headless body from the revolting mess. He was able to identify that the badly decomposed body was indeed James by a copper bracelet on his right wrist. The body was allowed to sink back into the mess. He would certainly exact his revenge on Dibu; he smiled evilly at the thought, his little snake-like eyes darting about.

When "Black Mamba" had left, Dibu and Kahinga looked at each other.

They couldn't possibly attempt to kill Lawrence; in the first place he had saved Kahinga's life and they liked and respected him. Besides, they thought that he would probably kill three or four of them before they got him.

Along with all the other whites Peter had been asked to join the police reserve and he now sported a .45 Webley revolver and a sten gun. The farm workers had witnessed Peter firing his revolver at night. Flames about a foot long came from the barrel. It needed no imagination to understand what that would do to one of them at close quarters.

After a few days they came to the only possible conclusion: they would leave Naseby and return to their homes in the reserve. They would have to deal with "Black Mamba" but they thought they could do that better from the reserve than from Naseby. The men in any case would be expected to join the gangs in the forest so the women would probably have had to leave anyway.

So Kahinga and Dibu made elaborate plans for the move. All thirty Kikuyu families were to move. They pooled all their fairly limited resources and arranged to hire a number of lorries from various Indian traders in Ol'Kalou and Thomsons Falls. They then bided their time.

Peter along with all the other police reservists were obliged to man the police station on a roster basis. Dibu and Kahinga found out when Peter was next on duty and planned to leave that night.

For the few days before the planned departure date, Peter was pleasantly surprised to find everything done in exactly the way he had asked them to do it. The tractors were properly serviced, the tools were put back in the right place, the feed was properly stacked, the dairy was scrubbed clean and so on. He half believed that at last his admonitions were sinking in and that the farm workers had really started to listen to him. On the day they planned to leave there was nothing out of place; the milking was finished early. It was almost as if they were trying to say, "Thank you, we respected you, you must go your way and we must now go ours."

Peter went home, had supper and left early for his shift at the police station. He said goodbye to Rafiki.

"I'll go straight to the dairy in the morning and see you after breakfast."

The house servants had also left everything in the best order possible. Rafiki was also pleasantly surprised; she had been told nothing and suspected nothing.

As soon as the Kikuyu saw Peter leave the farm, the lorries drove in, half to the village near the dairy and half to the village near the main house. Everything was ready to be packed onto the vehicles. Each family's possessions were loaded up and then all the women and children. As each truck completed loading it left.

At the beginning of the loading one of the Indian lorry drivers started to demand more money. Kahinga had recovered and cleaned the guns taken from Halway's house. He didn't speak; he just levered a shell into the breach of the high-powered hunting rifle that he had adopted as his own. He fired it at the Indian's feet.

"Just joking, just joking," yelled the Indian in terror.

Kahinga said nothing; the loading was completed. They checked all the huts; they had left nothing - not a chicken, not a cooking pot - nothing.

Kahinga nodded to Dibu. They would now have to fetch Rafiki. They went up to the house; the dogs went crazy. They called out; it was after midnight. After a while Rafiki came out sleepily and quieted the dogs.

She then called out and the two men appeared; she was amazed to see Kahinga carrying a gun.

"What's happening?" she asked as she let them into the house.

"We're going," said Kahinga. "You too. Waichagga told us to kill Munyu; we can't do that so we are going back to the reserve," he continued.

"You will come too; Waichagga will kill you if you stay here. Anyway you are needed for the struggle," added Dibu.

"Bring Nusu-Nusu, he belongs to us," said Kahinga brusquely.

"Come, hurry, we haven't got time to waste," yelled Dibu.

"I need a few minutes; I need to pack a few things."

"O.K, but hurry." Dibu and Kahinga sat down on the arm-chairs in front of the ashes of the fire.

Kahinga had never been in this room before. He looked about him: pictures on the walls; nice furniture; windows letting in plenty of light. He had no real aspirations to live like this, he thought.

Rafiki kept her head. She knew she had to go. Peter had been testing the little Beretta pistol left behind by the Italians. It was hanging in its holster and belt on the back of a chair. Some days earlier she had tried it on for size; it fitted her perfectly under her dress next to the skin. She fancied she would need it in the days ahead; there was no need for any of the menfolk to know she had it. She quickly packed a canvas bag for herself and one for little Kamau. She was just finishing writing a note to Peter when Dibu came in.

"No, no note," he snatched it away and tore it up into little pieces. "We must go now;" he snatched up the bags.

Kahinga picked little Kamau up. He was pleased; he thought it was all a nice new game.

Rafiki grabbed a greatcoat off the peg, thinking that she might need it, and within fifteen minutes the last three years of her life had been snatched away from her.

She didn't have time for a backward glance or to even shed a tear. She and little Kamau were bundled into the front of the lorry and they set off. All the other vehicles had gone.

Peter left the police station at 5am in a light-hearted mood. He'd managed some sleep and there hadn't been much going on at the station. He'd got great plans for the day; there were a couple of fences that needed repairing and he'd have to spend a bit of time on the borehole.

When he arrived at the dairy it was eerily silent. Normally at this time the cows would be being driven in to the paddock next to the dairy ready for the milking. He checked his watch - just after 5:30am. He'd better check the village. He drove the few hundred yards to the village and got out. Again there was no movement; he shone the headlights of the pick-up on the huts. A door swung idly on the breeze. He went cold. "They can't have gone," he thought. "They can't have just disappeared." But they had.

He went round the huts, calling names and shining his torch. Not a sound. They had left nothing, not a dog, not a chicken, not a rickety old bedstead, nothing. The place was completely deserted.

Peter sat down on a tree stump. He then got a terrible fright; the alarm clock that he had given to the farm workers had started to ring in the hut next to him. He went in and turned it off. They had taken nothing that didn't belong to them. It was as if all these people that he had known, that he had nurtured, never existed; they had just disappeared into thin air.

Then his gut gave another wrench. Rafiki! What about his precious Rafiki and their child? Peter leapt into the pick-up and raced back to the little cottage on Naseby.

He kept the car running and ran down the path; he turned the corner. The dogs greeted him like a long lost friend. The door to the house was open; then he knew, he knew she was gone. He rushed into the bedroom; the dawn was now breaking so he could see the rumpled bed. He felt it - cold. They were long gone.

He slumped down on the bed and noticed the little scraps of paper on the floor. He tried to piece them together. He thought of chasing them, but realised that even if they had left as late as 2am they would be past Nairobi now and well into the reserve. He'd never find them. He put his head in his hands; he'd never felt so alone in his life. Rafiki gone, the farm workers gone. The house was deathly quiet. There would be no Dibu or Mwangi there today, he knew that. He sat for a few minutes.

One of the dogs whined and woke him from his reverie. The cows; he'd better find a way of getting them milked otherwise they would get sick. He got up, shut the door of the little cottage, whistled up the dogs and drove the pick-up to the Kikuyu village on his side of Naseby. He knew what he would find. It was completely deserted. He noticed they had left all their own livestock. Each family was allowed five head of cattle: that was about one hundred and fifty head. About enough to pay off all the various loans he had made to the people.

He drove to the small collection of huts some way away, which housed the five families of Luo people on the farm. He explained to them what had happened and asked the senior man O'Kongo if they had heard anything.

"We heard some trucks and a gunshot; we kept inside; there was nothing we could do."

The five Luo and a few of their older children went with Peter to the dairy and they milked the cows. The Luo were not really stockmen and were rather apprehensive. It took most of the morning to complete the early morning milking. Peter's main concern was to make sure each cow was fully milked out; otherwise he would have to contend with infected udders. He also knew he had to start the afternoon milking early to get it done before dark. Milk production was down; cows do not like being messed around; their routine was disrupted and they were being handled by strangers.

Peter managed to phone Bill, who came to his rescue with two of his sons. Within a couple of weeks the routine at the dairy had returned to some sort of normality. Work on everything else on the farm had come to a grinding halt, although Peter saw to it that all the stock were fed.

Bill agreed that he could hold the fort for a couple of weeks while Peter went to recruit more labour. There was no point in recruiting Kikuyu again. He headed south of Nairobi to Machakos, the home of the Wakamba, whom Peter had worked with in his very early days in Kenya. They were not involved in any Mau-Mau business.

First, however, he would go to Thika to see if he could find Rafiki. Although he had been busy keeping the farm going and he'd had Bill and his sons to keep him company, he'd really missed her. Sometimes at night he mistakenly reached out in his sleep, hoping to feel the warmth of her; he often woke with a start, feeling the empty cold bed next to him. He was seldom able to go back to sleep afterwards.

Before he went to Machakos, Peter spent a few days at Thika. First he went to the D.C., who was not very sympathetic, especially when he found out who Peter was and who he was looking for. He had no sympathy with whites who "strayed" across the colour line. Peter then spent fruitless hours going from village to village and being sent on various wild goose chases. He had a feeling that people knew where Rafiki was but they certainly weren't going to tell him.

Eventually after three days of fruitless search, a toto (small child) thrust a piece of paper into his hand and ran off. There was a scrawled note to tell him to be at a certain place at eleven the next morning. His heart lifted; this had to be Rafiki.

He went to the appointed place; there was a middle-aged man, upright with a severe look on his face. Rafiki's father. After a very perfunctory greeting Wainaina said to Peter in Kikuyu, "You have abused my daughter. You did not ask my permission to marry her. She had your child. You paid no bride price. You, like all Wazungu, have come here and abused every Kikuyu custom. You are trying to destroy us."

He was furious; Peter could not get a word in. Eventually Peter said that he loved Rafiki and wanted to look after her. Love was not a concept that Wainaina even remotely understood and he was certainly in no mood for a philosophical discussion on what was for him an obscene western concept.

He spat contemptuously. "It is because of people like you that these baboon Mau -Mau are running about, also destroying our people, our culture. Soon we will all have to go and live in the forest."

Peter tried to say something.

"You will never see Rafiki again. If you come here again I will kill you myself. The child, even with his stinking half-white skin, will be brought up as a Kikuyu in Kikuyu tradition and speaking only Kikuyu. I will see to it. Now go." Wainaina pointed aggressively to Peter's pick-up.

Peter was shaking with the injustice of it all. He was just about to grab Wainaina by the shirt front when six men emerged from the side of the hut. They were all armed with pangas; one had a gun.

"Go," said Wainaina and went into his hut.

Peter beat a hasty retreat.

He wondered what he should do now. He needed to think about what Wainaina had said. It seemed to Peter that, with the best will in the world, he had alienated himself from his own people and he certainly seemed to have upset the Kikuyu.

Peter got into the pick-up and went on his weary way to Machakos. He had had very cordial dealings with a chief in the district when he worked at Athi River before the war, and he went back to see him. After long discussions, eventually the chief agreed to help him recruit farm workers for his farm.

Peter knew this would require patience; nothing in Africa could be done in a hurry. He spoke some Kamba but not fluently. After a day or so people started to turn up and within ten days he had thirty families of Wakamba all signed up. He arranged transport and a couple of weeks after he had left Naseby he returned with a full complement of labour. It all seemed so easy. Was it just? He no longer knew. Would these people desert him just like the Kikuyu had? He didn't know. Was his dream of owning his own farm here, just a dream? He couldn't answer that anymore.

Within six months the whole place was back to normal. In terms of general competence, the new labour force was much the same as the old. The Wakamba women, however, refused to have anything to do with the pyrethrum. Peter ploughed it all out. Milk production was up, the sheep were doing fine, pig prices were up and there had been plenty of rain.

Peter was still very lonely. The boys were at school most of the year, Robert now at secondary school in Nairobi, John still in Nakuru. There was no word from Rafiki or any of the others. The local community still shunned him.

Peter never got as close to his new labour force as he had been to the old one. He felt he couldn't go through all that again; he just kept his distance. He improved security around the farm: the security situation through the country continued to deteriorate. More British troops were brought in.

'Black Mamba' hadn't forgotten. If Dibu and Kahinga were unable to kill Lawrence, then he supposed to he would have to do it himself.

Chapter 20

Peter was still running the farm alone. He had looked for some managerial assistance but had no luck. Bill sometimes came to help; it was in his interests to do so as he still had a half share in the operation. Bill had little interest in running the farm; he was busy bringing new settlers by the boatload into Kenya. He also thought Peter was doing a great job.

Peter was standing on the veranda one night, at about ten o'clock. There was a quarter moon, and the night was quite clear. A nightjar, a type of nocturnal bird, called. A cow mooed. It was the picture of rural peace. He was just about to go to bed, when another nightjar called. Peter's instincts sensed something amiss; he waited. The first two calls were from up river; within a minute a third night jar call came from down river, then a fourth.

Nightjars are solitary birds and Peter knew that it was unusual to hear more than a single call at a time. Four calls in the space of five minutes meant something sinister – such as humans imitating the call. He was sure it was the Mau-Mau and wondered whether they were planning to attack him. The possibility that this might happen had worried him ever since the night his Kikuyu labour left. He had explained his fears to the boys on various occasions and discussed a plan of defence with them.

Now, he woke his sons, who had been home for school holidays for only a few days. They were immediately wide awake. Peter thought, "Well, the Mau-Mau had better understand that I know what they're up to." He took the Rigby out and levered a round into the breach. He fired one shot up-river and one down. The night jar calls ceased and for about twenty minutes there was silence. During that time Peter, Robert and John prepared themselves for an attack.

General 'Black Mamba' Waichagga had been frustrated by the fact that

Lawrence's Kikuyu farm workers had left the farm without attacking Lawrence. He knew that Lawrence would put up a fierce resistance and that there might be some casualties. If those casualties were Dibu and Kahinga so much the better; it would save him having to do something about them. He had not forgotten that they had murdered his brother and he was just waiting for a good opportunity to exact retribution. He also realised that the thirty or so farm workers on Naseby might not have been enough to deal with Lawrence properly. He believed in 'overwhelming force'.

So the General had collected sixty of his best fighters. Some had already been in the forests in the Aberdares (Nyandarua) for a few months. Most were armed with sharp pangas but some among them had guns. He had his revolver, there were a few armed with service rifles stolen from the army and two had shotguns; then there was his pride and joy - a Bren-gun, a light machine gun, which they had acquired. He had no idea how Lawrence was armed but he certainly felt, with some justification, that overwhelming force was on his side. He did know that Lawrence had no telephone so unless someone escaped, once his men got inside the house they could finish the Lawrences off at their leisure. The idea of calling to each other with nightjar calls was his. He was certain that the average M'zungu would have trouble recognising the call at all and would not be the least suspicious of multiple calls. He was therefore a little disturbed when, no sooner had they started calling each other, than Lawrence fired one shot up river and one down. This Lawrence was clearly going to be a tough nut to crack; now it seemed that the element of surprise had been lost. Waichagga's strategy was simple. Twenty men would attack through the forest from up-river, twenty from down river and twenty from the back. The twenty at the back would also be able to cut off any chance of escape.

Part of Peter's plan was that if there was a chance John, now eleven, would leave by the back door and escape on one of the horses to raise the alarm. He would have to ride bareback, as there wouldn't be time to saddle the horse, but this was no problem.

John had a much lighter build than Robert. Many children of his age would have been intimidated by Robert's character and athletic ability. None of this bothered John in any way. He was a very good horseman and he knew that for the family to survive he had to alert the neighbours. He brushed his brown hair out of his eyes. He wore dark clothes and no shoes.

John crept out of the back door with Ripple's bridle in one hand and Robert's .22 in the other. He went up the steps to the deserted kitchen; he listened. He nipped past the kitchen and crouched down near the boiler. There was no shadow, no movement. He ran past the wash line and stopped by the honeysuckle hedge. He crept along the fence line stopping every ten or fifteen yards. The cows in the paddock just above him mooed nervously. He came to a gate and then ran along another fence line that went at right angles. He crept through the fence. The stables were just twenty yards away, slightly up the hill. The cows in the next paddock were now mooing nervously; he thought he saw shadows.

Then all hell broke loose; what John thought was a machine gun opened up in front of the house and he could see shadowy figures, dozens of them, running towards the house from all directions. He heard constant gunfire from the house. Quickly he ran to Ripple's stable and put the bridle on. He led her quietly from the stable. There seemed to be figures among the cows, all moving towards the house. There was a track from the stables with the cow paddock on the left. There was a fence between the track and the cow paddock and another fence on the right of the track, which was about twenty yards wide. If he could get down the track and past the barn he would be in the clear. He could get caught going down the track; he shivered.

He could now see figures in the paddock; they looked as if they would cut him off. He was leading Ripple; she seemed to understand the need for stealth. Then there was a yell; they had seen him. He leapt on the back of the horse and galloped down the track; the shadows were racing towards the fence to cut him off. He had the .22 in his right hand, loaded and cocked. Suddenly there was a bellow and he heard the thunder of hooves and a few startled yells. The bull Knight Errant was in the paddock with the cows and had charged a group of the attackers. From the noise he had obviously done some damage.

The bull's timely diversion gave John just the few seconds he needed. He dug his heels in and Ripple responded beautifully and thundered down the track. John thought that he had just about made it into the clear when a black man swinging a panga loomed up on his left. John swung the gun over and at almost point blank range shot the man in the face. He disappeared and the horse put its head forward and literally flew the last few yards down the track and into the clear. There was a huge explosion from the house. He galloped on; he would be at the neighbours within twenty minutes or so.

Back at the house, Peter and Robert had prepared themselves well. "Smash all the glass in the windows," said Peter. "There's no need to have flying glass as well as bullets coming at us."

All the lights were turned off. It was pitch black inside the house. There was some light from the moon outside. They had jammed the dining room table up against the front door and as much of the other furniture from the living room as possible had been stacked in the back passage. All the doors were bolted.

Peter had his .416 Rigby and his .45 revolver; he also had a hand grenade that had been issued by the police reserve. He made sure it was properly primed; it hung on his belt. Robert had the twelve bore shotgun and plenty of SSG buckshot. Peter had also trained him to use the Sten gun. They waited; Peter hoped that John had got away.

Suddenly from about one hundred yards away a Bren gun opened up and spattered the house with bullets.

"I wonder where the hell they got the Bren from," Peter thought. He recognised the slow rat-tat-tat from his army days. "I'd better fix that."

"I hope we'll be able to see the flashes," he said to Robert. A skilled operator might be able to hide the flashes; he hoped the operator was unskilled. The Bren hammered away. Sure enough, there in the middle of the paddock the flashes were clearly visible. Peter took careful aim and fired but the flashes continued. He aimed fractionally to the left. The Bren stopped.

"Got him," he said.

By this time shadows started to appear on the lawn; Robert aimed, fired, aimed, fired. There were a couple of yells. At one point he thought he saw a shadow fall down.

All was not going well for 'Black Mamba'. He'd lost the element of surprise. He'd been in the cow paddock thinking that the animals would provide ideal cover. He hadn't reckoned on the damned bull. He'd seen the horse gallop away, so he knew he had an hour at the very most to get into the house, kill Lawrence and get away. Two of his men had been badly hurt by the bull and he thought another had been shot by the person on the horse. And now after a couple of bursts the Bren, his key weapon of attack, had fallen silent. There was sporadic gunfire from the front of the house. He'd better try the back. He led ten of his men to the back door and in double quick time they had smashed the door down.

"This is better," he thought. "We'll be in there in no time."

Five of his men were in the little passage trying to move furniture so they could get into the living room and the rest were crowded just outside. Waichagga saw a figure open the door into the living room, hesitate for two or three seconds and then flick something the shape of a potato into the back passage. The door slammed. Peter had tossed the grenade and then pulled Robert against the back wall. There was a huge explosion in the confined space of the tiny passage. The door from the passage to the living room came off its hinges and came flying across the room. Robert put his head round the doorway and emptied a magazine from the Sten gun into the void. The gun jammed. The whole passage was a bloody mess of body parts and blood and broken furniture.

Waichagga had been just to one side when the grenade blew-up. The five men in the passage had no chance, he knew, and the blast had also caught the other five who were waiting at the entrance to the passage. They were all lying about on the kitchen steps either dead or badly wounded. He was just moving past the carnage when a vicious burst of fire came from the inside of the house. One bullet hit him in the upper arm and knocked the revolver out of his hand. He clutched his arm and ran to the side of the house; he yelled for his men. One of them helped tie the wound up. He wasn't giving up yet. About thirty of his men had gathered, and he wondered where the others were; surely not all of them were casualties.

"Go and fetch the Bren gun," he instructed one of his people. They would try again shortly. This time maybe through the front door.

Peter and Robert caught their breath. They managed to jam one of the beds into the back passage.

"That should stop them, said Peter.

The dogs were chained up inside the house. Both had become almost hysterical when the attack began. They were large Alsatians; Peter would let them out only as a last resort. During the lull they looked to their weapons; Peter managed to get the sten-gun working again.

"Do you think they've gone?" asked Robert anxiously.

"I wouldn't bet on it," said Peter. "There are too many of them to give up that quickly."

As if to answer the question the Bren opened up from much closer. The first burst caught Peter in the right shoulder and right arm. He was smashed against the back wall of the little living room. Blood poured out, bits of bone stuck out at all angles.

"Shit, this is it," thought Peter.

Robert rushed over. Peter was in agony but kept his head.

"Quick, let the dogs out, and pass me my revolver. You must get the bastard with the Bren, otherwise we're done for."

Robert did as he was told.

In the minute or so since Peter had been wounded the man with the Bren had approached to within thirty yards. He was walking forward spraying the house with bullets, some of which were screaming into the little cottage.

Robert took the Sten gun and from the corner of one of the window frames, emptied half the magazine into the approaching figure. The man was lifted into the air; the Bren kept firing as he fell with the contents of the magazine spraying in a wide arc. The sten jammed again. Robert threw it down in disgust. He picked up the shotgun.

Peter had managed one-handed to tie a bandage that he had ready round the wound. Robert helped him tie it up. The wound was still bleeding profusely. They could expect to be rushed at any moment now. Peter was sitting by the back wall with the revolver in his left hand.

"Six shots," he thought. "That means six of the bastards."

Robert crouched down against the back wall.

The dogs had squeezed out through the back. Robert and Peter waited.

Meanwhile, John had galloped his horse as fast as he could to the Marks.

"What is it, what is it?" asked Mr. Marks.

"Attack. Mau-Mau attack," yelled John.

They called the police.

John hesitated.

"Call the doctor too please," he said. "There was a huge explosion in the house just as I got away - that was the grenade going off. They were only going to use it if the attackers got inside."

Mr. Marks called the doctor.

After a very brief respite, suddenly there was a great shout and the front door buckled. Robert discharged both barrels of the shotgun through the flimsy wood. Several hands came through the window frame and started pulling it out. Robert fired again.

"How long can we hold out?" Robert thought. "Dad?"

No response.

"Dad!" He shook Peter.

No response. Peter was unconscious. Then all hell broke out at the front of the house.

"Yaah, umbwa (dogs)," was the yell.

The dogs had come round the side of the house and were viciously biting everyone in their path. Then Robert saw the beam of the headlights from a car. The noise from the front of the house ceased.

Robert could hear a few more yells as the dogs chased the attackers down river.

Waichagga saw the lights. He'd seen the dogs biting his people. He called the men off, knowing it was too late. Now they would have to get away before the police caught them. The plan was to disappear down the river and then split up into gangs of four or five. He would have to get into Nakuru to have his arm attended to.

The police were now much better prepared than at the time of Halway's murder and within half an hour of being called were at Naseby.

Jan van der Westhuizen was six foot six of bone and muscle; he had been on duty when the call came in. The six askaris he had with him were slightly scared of him but he was a natural leader. As they approached the cottage at Naseby they saw figures running from the house. They piled out of the truck and approached. They called out, "Police!"

"In here," yelled Robert. "My father's been shot, he's unconscious."

They managed to get one of the Dietz paraffin lamps going and then one of the pressure lamps.

Peter was lying in a pool of blood, he was unconscious.

Van der Westhuizen felt Peter's pulse. Still strong, but he had lost a lot of blood. He tried to tie the wound up better, but at least three rounds had gone into Peter's shoulder, smashing it to pieces.

The doctor arrived, shortly followed by John and Mr. Marks.

The doctor examined Peter.

"I will take him to Nakuru now," he said authoritatively. "It's the only chance he has."

Robert looked at John. They were both dry-eyed.

"John, you go with Dad. I'll stay here and see what I can do to clear up the mess and keep things going."

Van der Westhuizen came over and put his hand around John's shoulder.

"Vragtig (truly) you did real good man, you must have got out of here just in time."

John briefly described the escape and the bull's part in it.

They got Peter onto a stretcher and into the doctor's car. John went with the stable but still unconscious Peter.

Van der Westhuizen and the askaris had now taken a look around. "How many of them were there?" he asked Robert.

Robert shook his head. He didn't really know.

"Dozens," he said. "They came at us from all sides."

"Well we've got fourteen dead, two hurt by the bull and two with shrapnel wounds from the grenade."

"There may be one in the paddock," said Robert. "Did you find the Bren gun?"

"Bren, did you say they had a Bren?" asked Van der Westhuizen.

"Look in the front garden."

They looked.

"No Bren; a couple more bodies though."

At dawn the farm workers arrived from the nearby village. They had heard the attack and had firmly locked themselves up until it was over. They had no weapons. When it was all over they had run to a few of the neighbouring farms. The neighbours started to arrive just after dawn.

The house was a complete mess. The roof over the back passage had been blown off and all the external doors were smashed. Most of the furniture was smashed or had bullet holes in it. There was broken glass everywhere.

Robert looked about him; he couldn't believe the carnage. He had to put one of the dogs down, it had been so badly cut up by the attackers.

Gert Boschoff came to the rescue. "I'll help them sort this mess out," he said. "Won't take long."

Van der Westhuizen came over. "Must have been about fifty or sixty of them," he said. "We've got about twenty here, dead and wounded; quite a few escaped down river."

Robert looked at him.

"You'll have to come down to the station later," said Van der Westhuizen.

"O.K. you go, I'll look after this," said Boschoff. "I'll get started on some repairs for you. Perhaps you can stop in at Shah's for some wood, corrugated iron and glass."

The police left.

Robert called the dog and went to the pickup. It was untouched. He was a competent driver but had no licence. Licences were only available from age 17.

He called in at the dairy where the milking was in full swing. He briefly explained what had happened and said he would be back for the afternoon milking. He drove into Ol'Kalou and went to S.Shah's store to order the basic items to repair the cottage. It was still a bit early and there were few people about. The Indian storekeeper had heard the story already though. He looked at Robert thoughtfully.

"Sorry about your father, I hope he's going to be O.K.," he said.

Robert shrugged. Despite himself a tear slid out from one eye. He wiped it away impatiently. "He's in good hands," was all Robert could say.

"If you need anything please let me know."

Robert nodded. "Thanks, I'll remember that."

Robert picked up the supplies and drove to the police station.

Van der Westhuizen was just finalising his report with the inspector.

Robert walked in.

The inspector looked at him slyly.

"How did you get down here?" he asked.

"In the pick-up," said Robert unthinkingly.

"Can I see your driving licence please?" asked the inspector.

Robert looked at him blankly and then he looked at Van der Westhuizen for support. The inspector came round the desk, "I want to see your driving licence now, you little kaffir boe… (He was going to say boetie).

For Jan van der Westhuizen this was the last straw. It had been a long night, there was a severely wounded man on his way to hospital and this fool was worrying about driving licences.

He stood up, picked up the inspector by the lapels of his starched khaki uniform and pushed him against the wall of the office.

All the breath went out of the inspector.

Van der Westhuizen dropped him; the inspector fell.

"Listen you little two year fucking wonder; this is what you are going to do. One - as I have already suggested, you will organise five patrols from the Lawrence's place this morning. Two - if I ever hear you calling anyone a kaffir boetie again I'll break your fucking neck. Three - you will issue this man (he yelled the word man) with a fucking driving licence now. Now get up."

He toed him with his huge boot in the way he would have moved a dead snake or a piece of dung.

The inspector got up unsteadily.

Just then Dave Gibb walked in. He'd heard of the attack and just come to the police station to confirm the situation.

"What's up?"

Van der Westhuizen explained everything.

"O.K. let's get the patrols set up." He took charge. The inspector just did as he was told.

Within an hour twenty five of the local farmers had been contacted. They were now all rushing to Naseby to follow-up.

Dave Gibb had found five WaNderobo trackers from various sources in the district. He said he would co-ordinate the patrols himself.

Robert was issued with a driving licence.

"What age should I put in here?" asked the inspector nervously.

Gibb looked at him.

He wrote down seventeen.

Robert and Van der Westhuizen left. Gibb looked at the inspector. He had considered phoning Preston in Nairobi but had decided that this fellow wasn't all bad. He just needed a little conditioning.

"You realise what a damned fool you've just made of yourself don't you?" he said to Inspector David Evans.

The inspector opened his mouth and started to swallow almost like a fish out of water.

"Look Mr. Evans, you've spent too much time in the company of idiots like George Athill. Lawrence is actually O.K., maybe just a bit misguided, and you (he pointed a finger) don't understand the history. If I hear one more piece of nonsense like I heard from you today I will make sure you'll be on your way back to Blighty – England – before you can say Jack Robinson."

Evans looked stunned. He'd never been spoken to like this before in his life. He knew of Gibb's long time residence in the district and his connections with the police hierarchy. He kept his mouth shut.

Gibb went on more quietly now. "If you need any help, any history of people in the district, just call. I've been here many years. Now let's get on with these patrols."

After leaving the Lawrences' farm, Waichagga's group had split up.

"Go to the road," Waichagga instructed those who were with him. "We will stop a car."

They made their way to the road; it was just about daybreak. They cut some branches from a nearby tree and placed them across the road.

The first car just accelerated and crashed through the barrier

The second car slowed and stopped.

Waichagga's men leapt out of the bushes, opened the car door and pulled the driver out. They butchered her on the spot. She was the wife of one of the Indian shopkeepers in Ol'Kalou, going into Nakuru for supplies. Her five year old son who was with her was similarly dispatched, without thought, without compunction.

"Clear the road," ordered Waichagga. "Dump the bodies in the bush."

The road was cleared and the bodies dumped as instructed. The bushes from the road were dumped over the bodies.

They all piled into the car. One of Waichagga's men had some rudimentary knowledge as to how to drive a car. Twenty hair-raising miles later they drove past the K.A.R (Kings African Rifles) barracks at Lanet and joined the tarred road into Nakuru. All Waichagga's considerable survival instincts now came into play. The last thing he wanted to do was to attract any attention.

"Make sure you keep to the speed limit."

He had to point to the needle on the dial and the position on the dial. The driver was unable to read.

They turned off the main road, went round the back of the abattoir and found their way into the African location. Waichagga had had some dealings with a Kikuyu nurse in the past and knew where she lived with her husband and three children. They stopped outside a small but neat little house made from concrete blocks. They all got out. Waichagga knocked. That day he was in luck; the husband had already gone to work. Grace Wamboi was only due at the hospital at 2pm and there was one small child too young to go to school.

Grace's eyes widened in terror at the sight of the five men. They pushed themselves into the little house and shut the door. Grace started to protest.

"Shut up and listen," said Waichagga. He explained the situation and showed Grace the wound. His upper arm was now very swollen and had gone a livid purple colour; the bullet was still in there.

"You need a doctor," said Grace. "There is no equipment here."

"Doctor, doctor," hissed Waichagga. "There are no Kikuyu doctors. Anyone else will report me to the police."

"Indian, there is an Indian who is sympathetic," she replied.

"No, we can't trust them, you do it," said Waichagga.

There was much discussion.

Eventually Grace persuaded them that the Indian doctor was their best bet.

"O.K., but he must not know to which house he comes, so blindfold him. He must not be able to recognise any of us, so we will all wear balaclavas or masks. I and one other will stay here with the child. You three and Grace will fetch the doctor. If you are not back by 2pm we will leave with the child. If that happens you will not see the child again. Go." Waichagga glared at Grace.

Peter had been taken to the hospital in Nakuru and had been examined by the best orthopaedic surgeon in the place.

"I'll see if I can save the arm," he said. "How much blood was lost?"

"Quite a lot I think," said John.

The G.P had already returned to Ol'Kalou. He supposed he would be dealing with the other wounded from the attack during the rest of the day.

Peter was given a blood transfusion and they stabilised him. He came to and saw John.

"Where am I?" he asked.

"Hospital, you're badly wounded." John hugged him.

"I remember being shot; what else happened?" His shoulder throbbed.

"I called the police and the doctor; the attackers all ran away. Robert is fine, he had to shoot one of the dogs," John replied.

"The dogs - I guess they saved our lives."

"And Knight Errant." John explained how he had got away.

Peter tried to smile.

The surgeon came in.

"I'm afraid they made a bit of a mess of your shoulder," he said evenly. "You certainly won't be able to use it for a long time. The worst that can happen is amputation."

"Should I get myself to England?" asked Peter shakily.

"No, no point, there's nothing we can't do here," said the surgeon.

"O.K."

Peter was eight hours in the operating theatre.

"I think I've saved the arm," the surgeon told Peter the next day. "You'll have to spend a week or so in here and then you'll have to keep the arm immobilised for another six weeks; after that we'll see. You'll never have full use of it again; how much use probably depends on you. You were hit by four slugs and the whole shoulder, collar bone and upper arm were smashed to bits."

Peter nodded numbly. He knew he was lucky to be alive.

John spent two more days staying with friends near the hospital. He then arranged a lift back home.

Waichagga was becoming anxious. It was already 1:30pm, only half an hour to the deadline, and there was no sign of Grace or the doctor. At five minutes to two the party arrived. They had a blind-folded Indian with them. Waichagga and all his henchmen had balaclavas on. The blindfold was removed.

The doctor examined the wound. "I need 500 shillings for this, up front," he said.

This was not unexpected.

Waichagga nodded. 500shs was produced.

The doctor gave him a shot of morphine.

"This is going to hurt," he said.

"How long will this take?" asked Waichagga.

"Forty minutes maybe, but you cannot move for at least two hours," was the response.

"Just leave us for a minute," Waichagga said to the doctor.

He beckoned to the others. "Kigoro, take the car down to the lake, set fire to it, and then come back here."

"Go to this place," he told another man, giving him an address. "Tell the people there to find transport to take us to Fort Hall."

He spoke to the nurse: "You, Grace, your husband and children will not come back here until I have gone. Wacheera will go with you to make sure that happens. You, Waithiru, stay here, keep this child here."

Everyone went out. Dr. Chetty came back. He had heard that there had been an attack on a farm in the Ol'Kalou area on the lunchtime news. He supposed this was part of the after-math. The news had been very sketchy. He knew better than to say anything.

He gave the man in the balaclava a local anaesthetic in his arm. He was already groggy from the morphine.

"God, when did these people last have a bath," he thought. "I suppose they've been in the bush for months."

He got to work.

The bullet was in the fleshy part of the upper arm and quite close to the surface. He made a cut, squeezed the wound and out came a slug.

"Lucky it did not touch a bone," he said.

Waichagga had barely moved, although there must have been some pain. The doctor washed and disinfected the area as well as possible. He gave Waichagga some additional dressings and disinfectant and gave him strict instructions about washing the wound and changing the dressings.

Dr. Chetty was quite unnerved by the whole process. Although he was unable to see Waichagga's face, he would never ever forget his snake-like eyes. They were truly evil, and watched his every movement.

Grace and Wacheera came back.

Waichagga was still a bit drowsy.

"Blindfold him. Is there a back way?" he asked Grace. "You, Waithiru, go with Grace and this doctor; make sure he will not be able to find his way back here, then let him go." He nodded to Waithiru. Waithiru came closer.

"You will do nothing to these people, we will need them again. Make sure they are safe."

They went out.

Waichagga and Wacheera smoked a cigarette. They had taken their balaclavas off.

"I'm going to fuck her," volunteered Wacheera.

'Black Mamba' looked at him with those evil, snake-like eyes.

Wacheera knew that look. He knew he was in trouble; he started to shake.

"You stupid little fucker, didn't you hear what I said," growled Waichagga. "We will need these people again. Do them harm and they'll go to the police, but if they gain something from it we can count on them again."

Waichagga was not averse to the occasional rape; he'd raped a few women himself. He wasn't stupid however.

Wacheera considered himself lucky to have got off so lightly. If Waichagga hadn't been so groggy he would have been beaten or worse.

They took Dr. Chetty through a few little laneways in the African location. When they were certain that there was no way he could find his way back they took off the blindfold. They had had a few curious glances on their way through but most people were sensible enough not to notice. Waithiru had carelessly taken his balaclava off. Chetty made sure that he would recognise him again if he needed to.

Grace looked at Chetty knowingly. He got the message, and slipped Grace 50 shillings without Waithiru noticing.

When they got back to the house there was a small pick-up outside with one of the original gang plus another person driving.

Waichagga was being helped by Wacheera into the front seat.

"Aren't we going to wait for Kigoro?" asked Waithiru.

"No," said Waichagga. "He has been too long with the car; maybe the police have picked him up. There have been reports on the radio about our attack on the Lawrence place." He then said more quietly so Grace couldn't hear, "They have also found the bodies of the Indian woman and her child; we'd better get out of here."

He was right. Dave Gibb had co-ordinated the patrols out of Naseby and then taken one out himself.

All the Nderobo[14] trackers had gone out with the first patrol. They knew that the gang would split up at a certain point. Sure enough; two miles

14 WaNderobo – Forest dwelling tribe. Extensively used by the security forces as trackers. Related to the Kikuyu.

downriver they split up into five groups. The trackers made doubly certain which groups had gone in which direction. They then waited for the individual patrols to come along and each tracker was allocated to a patrol.

Dave and four others brought up the rear. They had managed to find horses for all five of them so they were much quicker.

"Boots," said the tracker. "Must be the leader," said Dave. It also made following the tracks easy.

Dave lifted the little Nderobo on to the front of his horse and they cantered after the tracks.

"They're making their way to the road," observed Dave. He instructed one of the members of the patrol to return to Naseby and bring his pick-up. He suggested they meet on the road.

Within an hour they had found the grisly remains of the Indian woman and her child.

Dave stopped the first car that came along. It was the wife of one of the farmers in the district. She had not heard about the attack. It didn't require much imagination for her to put herself in the position of the Indian woman.

He asked a member of the patrol to accompany her into Nakuru as an escort.

"Please go straight to the police in Nakuru," he told them. "Give them all the details."

They left.

The other member of the patrol arrived in his pick-up.

They loaded the bodies into the truck.

"We'll go to the police station and get that idiotic inspector to get someone in the Indian community to identify the people and then hopefully we can get a description of the car phoned through to Nakuru."

They left together with the tracker.

The remaining two members of the patrol returned the horses to Naseby, each riding one horse and leading another.

Within an hour they had identified the woman as a Mrs. Chetty and her son. The description of the car was radioed to the police in Nakuru.

Inspector Ian Davies had the afternoon off and he had taken his girlfriend Vanessa down to the lake to admire the flamingos; his own personal interest in flamingos was somewhat limited but the park at the lake was normally deserted during weekday afternoons and he was hoping that he might persuade Vanessa to let him be the person to deprive her of her virginity. It was not to be.

When they arrived there, there was an African behaving rather strangely. It looked as though he had splashed something on a car and had unsuccessfully struck a couple of matches.

"Hey, he's trying to set fire to the thing," said Ian.

He rapidly drove up, and jumped out of the car. The man started to run. Ian pulled his service revolver and fired over his head.

The man stopped, with his hands up.

Ian beckoned.

"What are you trying to do?" asked Ian.

The man looked blankly at him. Ian always carried his handcuffs with him. He quickly cuffed the man.

"Vanessa, I'll keep this fellow covered in the back. Can you drive us to the police station?"

Vanessa had forgotten about flamingos. She drove like a maniac to the station.

Ian dragged Kigoro out of the car and into the station.

Within minutes people had been dispatched to fetch the car. From the description it was the Indian car from Ol'Kalou.

An hour later they had the whole story.

Waichagga's name came up, and the fact that he had been wounded in the attack on Naseby.

Within another hour they had Grace's name; they found her address without any trouble.

Dr. Chetty had in the meantime finished his surgery. He had been vaguely expecting his sister-in-law. He put a call through to his brother who ran a shop in Ol'Kalou. He was greeted by a very distressed brother.

"They've killed her and our son," a voice wailed down the phone.

"Stop," said Dr. Chetty. "Killed who?"

"My wife and son," wailed his brother.

"Where?"

"On the road going down to Nakuru."

Dr. Chetty started to shake.

He then told his brother about treating "Black Mamba".

"You must go to the police, now," said his brother, "there must be a connection."

Dr. Chetty went straight to the police; he knew he was in deep trouble.

He arrived just as Grace arrived accompanied by two askaris.

Within a short time he had made a statement, saying that Grace and a gang of blacks had forced him blindfolded to an address in the location where he had been made to attend a black man with a bullet wound.

He gave a detailed description of Waithiru. He identified himself as the brother in law of the dead woman.

Grace's story more or less coincided with Dr. Chetty's. She gave them a detailed description of Waichagga and his henchmen. She also identified Kigoro in a line-up. She described the driver of the pick-up and gave the police the licence plate number.

Neither Dr. Chetty nor Grace made any mention of money changing hands.

"Set up road blocks on every exit from Nakuru," instructed Ian Davies. "Every ten miles or so on the main road."

'Black Mamba' was groggy and sore. There was nothing he would rather do than get home to Fort Hall and disappear. His instincts told him otherwise. They drove the twenty-five miles to Gil-gil without incident and then Waichagga told the driver to stop the pick-up.

"By now they will have road blocks," said Waichagga. "We'll go on foot."

They all looked at him blankly.

"The police will set up road-blocks and we will be stopped."

"Nobody knows what you look like," argued Waithiru.

Waichagga just glared at him. He instructed the driver of the pick-up to go on his way.

"We will wait here one hour; if you don't come back we'll take to the bush," said Waichagga.

The driver drove for less than ten minutes and sure enough there was the roadblock in front of him. He wasn't worried; his passengers had gone. His Kipande (pass) was in order.

He stopped.

Unfortunately for him the police manning the road block were alert and they had the description of the vehicle, the driver and the licence plate. The Indian inspector in charge of the road block was also incensed that one of his community had been murdered. He made the driver pull the vehicle off to the side. He spoke in Swahili.

"You had four passengers in this vehicle, where are they?" he asked after the driver had been told to leave the vehicle.

The driver looked blankly at the Inspector Singh.

"We know you had four passengers in this vehicle, and you left Nakuru about 6pm. There was a Waichagga amongst them. Where are they?" Singh was getting impatient.

The driver was amazed at the accuracy of the information, but he was committed to the Mau-Mau; there was no way he was going to admit to anything. Singh stepped aside, as if on some sort of signal. A rifle butt smashed into the driver's face.

"Where are they?"

No answer.

A boot went into his balls. On Singh's instructions the beating went on for nearly an hour. They got no information. He said nothing, not even his name.

Eventually they stopped. The man was dead. "Drive the pick-up into the location at Gil-gil," instructed the inspector. "Leave the body there, say nothing." One of the askaris did as he was asked.

Waichagga and his party did not wait. They made their way into the bush, intending to walk to Fort Hall, which would take more than two weeks. One problem they had was how to get food on the way; this was solved by Wacheera and Waithiru posing as itinerant labourers looking for work. They would approach a Kikuyu village on a white owned farm, get fed themselves and either smuggle food out to Waichagga and Johanna or ask for some food for the journey. Waichagga dared not show his face and in any event a party of four was far too conspicuous.

They travelled by night and hid in the bush during the day.

'Black Mamba' was meticulous about following Dr. Chetty's instructions in washing and dressing his wound.

It took them three weeks to walk through the bush to Fort Hall. When they arrived the fuss over the attack on the Lawrence farm and the murder of Mrs. Chetty and her son had died down. The other members of Waichagga's party had suggested from time to time the use of public roads or another vehicle hi-jacking; Waichagga's will prevailed. When they eventually returned to the safety of Fort Hall Waichagga was greeted almost like a god. The fact that he had avoided the security forces and returned to Fort Hall was miraculous in itself but the other members of his party embellished the details of the 'escape' and Waichagga's part in it.

The follow-up patrols from Naseby had mostly had little luck and apart from one patrol which captured five Kikuyu, the rest had come back empty handed.

Peter Lawrence was released from hospital about one week after his admission. He was picked up by Robert.

"Who is driving?" asked Peter.

Robert showed him his licence and told him the story of how it was acquired.

Peter spent the next six weeks convalescing.

Gert Boschoff and Robert did a reasonable job of repairing the cottage. There were still bullet holes all over the place but the roof had been repaired and all the windows and doors. The carpenter had made more furniture.

One of Bill's sons, Ken, came to work for Peter, at least for a year.

Peter went for treatment at regular intervals to the hospital. Initially he drove with one arm but the exercises he had been given by the physiotherapist and his persistence in doing them regularly meant that he eventually got back about 80% of the use of his arm. Within a year he had all his strength back although movement was restricted. He would never play polo again.

"I am amazed," said the surgeon. "At best I expected you would have some use of the arm. What you have done is unbelievable."

People in the district were still wary of Peter, even after the attack. He was unable to participate in police patrols because of his injury and although after six months he did his routine work by manning the police station at night he was seldom asked to go out on patrol. Actually this suited him. He thought the conflict was stupid and wasteful; it was quite clear to him that in the not too distant future Britain would have to hand over its colonies to the local inhabitants. There was already some talk about Ghana under Kwame Nkrumah becoming independent. There was no reason why this shouldn't apply to Kenya.

Peter also tried to contact Rafiki. He drew a complete blank for some months and had almost given up hope. Then, one evening a year or more after the attack, one of the servants said there was a person at the back door who wanted to see him.

It was Stanley, who was now a strapping young man of nearly eighteen. They greeted each other in Kikuyu.

Stanley said, "If you want to see Rafiki and Kamau, be outside V. Patel's store in Thika at 9 o'clock three weeks today."

Peter was stunned. "How are they?" he asked.

"Fine," was the only response.

Then Stanley was gone.

Peter had hundreds of questions. He wondered if it was a trap. They'd tried to kill him once. Maybe this was attempt number two.

The police in Nakuru decided not to prosecute Dr. Chetty and Grace Wamboi.

"We'll keep a good eye on them," said Inspector Ian Davies. "My guess is that they will be used again," he rationalised.

Kigoro was tried and hanged for the murder of Mrs. Chetty and her son.

Chapter 21

The farm workers from Naseby had all been deposited in the Kikuyu reserve in their home villages, mainly in the Kiambu, Thika, and Fort Hall districts.

The idea was that the men under the leadership of Kahinga would attack white farms and property and the women would stay at home and organise food for the gangs. Rafiki's job, chosen for her all those years before, was to organise food drops for the gangs in the forests of the Aberdares (Nyandarua) and Mount Kenya (Kirinyaga).

The Mau-Mau had virtually no organisation now that their leaders had all been locked-up in Lodwar: weapons and transport were either non-existent or in very short supply. Kahinga had decided that maybe he should do something about collecting weapons; he had an assortment of rifles and shotguns taken from Halway's place, but in the longer term providing ammunition for his men would be a problem. He knew the police had plenty of weapons, mainly British Army .303 Mark 4 service rifles; he also knew that ammunition for these weapons would be plentiful. The question was, where was there a good supply of firearms that weren't well protected? Luck came his way.

Kariuki had been employed as a junior constable in the Naivasha police station for two years. He had been dismissed on some pretext or another. He thought the main reason was that he was Kikuyu; all the other African policemen were from other tribes. The police station of Naivasha had a large armoury consisting mainly of service rifles and boxes of ammunition. Kariuki knew his way around the station, but he did not know how well protected it was.

Kahinga did his homework well. He and Dibu and Mwangi stayed with some other Kikuyu at the African location in Naivasha. They paid a few visits to the station on various pretexts over a period of a few weeks. What they found out was that in general the station was well manned but on Saturday nights there were occasions when the station was left in charge of an African sergeant and two askaris. Kariuki told Kahinga that in the past, this had happened when the Naivasha rugby team was playing away. Kahinga found out when the rugby team was due to play away next and laid his plans accordingly.

Kinua had been told to steal a lorry in Nairobi and drive it to Thika, where he met Kahinga and twenty of the men from the farm. They armed themselves with the firearms they had taken from Halway; the rest of the people had pangas. They attracted very little attention, as it was quite usual to see lorries with large numbers of labour driving about. Kahinga told Kinua to drive the back way to Naivasha and to go to the African location. He and Kinua then took his people in groups of two or three on foot to show them the police station. They all met in a hut in the location at about 8pm and were given a meal. At about 10pm they all piled into the lorry; Kinua drove it to about two hundred yards from the police station, everyone got out and they went off in groups of four to predetermined places in the shadows a short distance from the station. Kinua stayed in the lorry with the engine running. Kahinga, Dibu and Kariuki walked into the front of the police station; they just walked past the askari on guard duty. The African sergeant and another askari were in the charge office. Kahinga pulled his rifle from the underneath of his greatcoat and shot them both. This was the signal for one of the groups outside to quickly dispatch the unwary Askari guard. Kinua reversed the truck up to a side entrance.

Kahinga and Kariuki looked around the station. There were no other people around. They heard a few yells from the cells.

Kariuki quickly found the armoury keys and he and Kahinga went into the armoury. For Kahinga this was like Aladdin's cave. The walls of the armoury had about three hundred service rifles all neatly kept in gun-racks; they were all beautifully clean and oiled. There was a Bren-gun and numerous boxes of ammunition. There were also about a dozen .38 Smith and Wesson service revolvers.

Kariuki unlocked the chain that was threaded through the trigger guards of all the rifles. Three of the group kept watch and within thirty minutes the armoury had been cleaned out. Apart from the weapons they had taken about ten thousand rounds of ammunition for the rifles (the service rifles and the Bren used the same .303 ammunition) and about one thousand for the pistols. Before they left they quietly unlocked all the cells and told the prisoners to wait for five minutes when they would be free to leave; hopefully they would wait for long enough for the raiding party to get away without raising the alarm. They locked the armoury and all jumped into the lorry and took off. It looked as if they would get away scot-free, but just as they were driving away a European drove up to the front of the station and went inside. He came rushing out waving a pistol when he found the two dead askaris. He put two and two together and followed the lorry. Kahinga was in the back of the lorry; he just raised his rifle and from about fifty yards aimed a shot into the car windscreen.

The car veered off the road and crashed into a ditch. The horn started blaring.

Kahinga made everyone lie down in the back of the truck, on top of their now precious load.

He'd already instructed Kinua to drive back via the Kinangop and all the back roads; they eventually arrived at the village in the Fort Hall district by about 4am. Kahinga had already prepared several hiding places for his valuable haul, mainly in large holes in the floors of the huts of his trusted followers. The holes were covered over with poles and the floor treated with cow dung as normal. Unless someone knew what they were looking for, these hiding places were almost impossible to detect.

Kahinga was amazed at how easy it had been. He was sure that this would not continue. He was also certain that the raid on the police station at Naivasha would wake the authorities up to what they were up against. He was right.

The settler community was up in arms; they couldn't believe that a bunch of untrained savages could just walk into a major police station and take hundreds of rifles and thousands of rounds of ammunition.

The British press and police sat up and started to take notice.

The Governor was replaced.

More British troops arrived.

Kahinga did not waste time. He had no military training at all, but had remembered all Peter's lessons from the days when Peter had trained him how to shoot.

He issued each man with a rifle and, doing exactly what Peter had shown him to do, he personally rigorously trained about one thousand fighters in the space of a few weeks.

There was still very little leadership. Most of the original leadership had been interned at Lodwar. Waichagga was still recuperating. Kahinga decided to carry on himself. His idea was simple: to come out of the bush at night and destroy as much white owned property as possible and then disappear back into the bush; maybe kill a few whites; keep clear of the police and the army. Kahinga needed bases to work from, and he needed food. He decided to make his base the Nyandarua (Aberdares), from where he would be able to attack white owned farms all the way from Thomsons Falls through to the Kinangop.

One day Kahinga collected Dibu, Mwangi, Kinua and seven others to go with him on a reconnaissance. He also took Rafiki with him. She would have to organise the food supply and it was important for her to know where the bases were.

Her heart beat quickened when Kahinga told her what he was doing.

"So this is where it all begins," she thought. "I wonder where it will end."

Little Kamau was being looked after by the wider family; he was now three years old and although he had a pale brown skin and frizzy brown hair, the other children took no notice of physical differences and he was treated the same as any of them in the little games they played. Occasionally one of the older women was a bit harsh with him but generally he was treated like any other Kikuyu child. He was much bigger and stronger than most of his peers. Rafiki thought he was likely to have Peter's build, which would mean he would be huge for a Kikuyu.

Kahinga had also found a WaNderobo whom he thought he could trust. The Nderobo lived in the Aberdares and the forests of Mount Kenya. Witu claimed that he knew the Aberdares well and could guide them to some possible base sites.

Kinua stole another small lorry outside an Indian shop in River Road in Nairobi. The group climbed into it and they drove to a farm on the Kinangop. Kahinga knew the Kikuyu on the farm there. He knocked on the door of one of the huts at about midnight.

Eventually it was opened. The occupants were terrified when the thirteen of them squeezed into the hut. Kahinga told them who they were. Rafiki then left with the women and went to another hut.

Kahinga explained what he was doing and the support he would require. Most of the men had taken an oath of loyalty to the Mau-Mau; nevertheless they were absolutely terrified of this group of heavily armed men. Kahinga had made it very clear what would happen to them if they failed to co-operate. The village agreed to supply food into the base that Kahinga hoped to set up.

This was not likely to be a problem; they could steal posho (ground maize) from their employer and the occasional sheep. Vegetables were plentiful. Kinua drove the lorry into the bush and camouflaged it with branches. He was told that the white farmer seldom came to this part of the farm so it was unlikely to be discovered.

The party made their way into the forest the next day, accompanied by one of the younger women from the farm. She would need to know where the base camp was so she could deliver food there.

The forest was unspoiled by any kind of human development. There were no roads. The only way through the forest was on the numerous little game trails and some larger trails. They came across some elephant droppings. Kahinga put his finger into a dropping: old - it was dry and cold. Witu gradually led them into denser and denser forest; the paths he followed climbed gradually into the mountains. As he went along he showed the Kikuyu the landmarks he used to find his way around. A tree stump here, a particular clump of bamboos there, an old cedar tree there. As they got higher the forest became thicker; it also became very wet. Kahinga remembered from his days on Naseby the inevitable blanket of cloud that covered the whole Nyandarua range most mornings. This meant that they would need shelter up in the mountains, since, even if it didn't rain, it would always be wet. They would also need thick coats, blankets and better footwear. He also wondered about medical supplies. On Naseby Rafiki had taken over the duties of nurse to the farm workers; he would have to consult with her. By mid-morning the cloud had lifted and although it was still slippery underfoot it had warmed up considerably.

As they progressed up the mountain they had seen the occasional antelope and many Colobus monkeys. Witu suddenly put up his hand and halted the group. They listened. Kahinga could hear a curious rumbling sound.

"Tembo (elephant)," whispered Witu. "Resting, about twenty of them."

Kahinga told the rest of the group to wait and he and Witu crept forward.

Sure enough, in a little glade just ahead there was a herd of about twenty elephant, their stomachs rumbling contentedly.

"Shit," thought Kahinga. "This is going to be hard enough as it is without bumping into elephants."

They withdrew.

Witu led them on another game path round the elephant.

Kahinga asked him how he knew they were there. Witu tapped his nose.

By four o'clock in the afternoon they had slipped and slid their way about seven or eight miles into the forest. Witu indicated they should stop for the night. Kahinga looked puzzled.

Witu smiled and then took Kahinga round the base of a very old cedar. There were a few bushes and behind the bushes a large overhanging rock with a great dry area.

Witu explained, "Maybe this is a good place for a food drop; there is a better place for a base two or three hours away. Maybe the women should not see the base camp."

They spent the night there. Kahinga was impressed.

Kahinga made mental notes:

- Boots
- Warm clothing
- Medical supplies
- Food

This trip had given him time to think. Nobody knew he was here and the security forces had no operations up here.

Rafiki had managed well. She didn't particularly enjoy the slipping and sliding but she liked the natural beauty of the place. She also took pleasure in the wildlife, some of which she was familiar with due to her excursions on Naseby with Peter. Although it would be hard work, she could see that the women could keep a constant supply of food delivered to this place without too much difficulty.

Needing to be on her own for a while with her own thoughts, Rafiki had wandered a hundred yards or so away from the group. She thought about Peter; she had heard about the attack on Naseby and wondered if he was all right; she did not know he had been wounded. They were clearly on different sides now. She loved him more than ever but she was committed to having an equal say in how the country was run, and to ensuring that her child had a decent education like Peter's other children. The country would have to change and this was the only way she knew to achieve that change. She wondered about Naseby; for her Peter's dream meant little. Kenya would be better off if he helped run the country, she mused. He knew so much about the place and was sympathetic to the black Africans.

Her reverie was interrupted; suddenly she felt she was not alone. She felt for the Beretta; it was still there. No one else knew about it. She looked about her, and then Mwangi sauntered nonchalantly out from behind a bush.

"Still thinking about that bloody M'zungu and his small prick," he said nastily.

"Fuck off Mwangi, you keep your own small prick to yourself," she answered.

He came closer.

"Come on, he's out of your life; now let me in there," he cajoled.

Rafiki was dead calm. "You come one foot closer and it's the last step you will ever take," she said. Rafiki was aware of Mwangi's reputation for being unscrupulous as far as women were concerned; she had no intention of becoming his next victim. Mwangi laughed.

Mwangi turned as if to go away. Rafiki half relaxed, then he rushed at her and knocked her down. He had his trousers down and was pulling at Rafiki's dress. Rafiki also pulled up her dress but with a very different intention from Mwangi's.

While he was fumbling with her dress she calmly pulled the Beretta out of its holster, released the safety catch, stuck the barrel of the pistol against Mwangi's chest and pulled the trigger.

There was a muffled shot. A look of pure surprise came over Mwangi's face; then he flopped down on top of her, dead.

Rafiki scrambled to push Mwangi's heavy body off her and had just stood up when Kahinga and the others came rushing into the clearing. Rafiki still had the Beretta in her hand. She was covered in Mwangi's blood.

It was quite clear to Kahinga what had happened. Mwangi had been muttering about Rafiki for weeks now. Kahinga had tried to warn him off.

"What happened?" he asked.

Rafiki explained. She was shaking; she had to sit down.

"O.K, O.K, it's alright now," said Kahinga.

Dibu came rushing over; Mwangi had been his friend for years. He raised his newly acquired rifle and would have shot Rafiki there and then. Kahinga grabbed the rifle and pushed the barrel up, and the shot went harmlessly into the bush.

Kahinga kicked Dibu in the groin, pulled the rifle away from him and smashed the butt into his face. Dibu collapsed.

Kahinga looked about him.

"Get up!" he kicked Dibu.

"She killed him!" yelled Dibu.

"Yes," said Kahinga, "and anyone else who tries the same thing will get the same treatment. I will shoot them."

"She's only a woman," volunteered one of the others.

"Yes; she'll be carrying food for you, so you can fight." Kahinga glared at him.

There was a silence. A dawning realisation seemed to come over the group that the women were performing a real job here and were not around just for the convenience of the men.

More silence.

"If anyone takes a woman without her consent and I get to hear about it, I will personally execute them. Do you all understand? I don't care who the person is," growled Kahinga. "Now you, Dibu, he was your friend - you bury him, good and deep otherwise the hyenas will dig him up."

The incident served to enhance Kahinga's fearsome reputation. The men now realised that Rafiki was not to be trifled with.

"Where did you get the pistol?" asked Kahinga later.

"I stole it from Munyu; I took it when you came to take me away from Naseby. I strapped it on. I have plenty of ammunition."

The story spread far and wide over the years and was embellished by many storytellers. No one ever tried to take advantage of Rafiki again. The women also knew they could count on her to protect them.

The next day the woman from the village was sent back with one of the men. Kahinga told her to put enough food in the shelter to feed twenty men for three months. He showed her how to bury it in the shelter and put stones on top of it so the wild animals would not dig it up. The man was told to rejoin the group as soon as he had returned the woman to the village; he was just to follow their tracks.

The next day after two hours walking Witu took them to what turned out to be a most magnificent hideout. Unless one knew it was there the probability was that one would walk straight past. There was a thick screen of bamboo and the tiniest little game path through the screen; behind that was a huge rock and the path continued round the side of the rock; in the cliff face behind was a cave that went fifty yards back. Kahinga could house one thousand men in there. Some bats flew out squawking; there seemed to be no other sign of habitation, either human or animal.

"Why no signs of animals in here?" he asked Witu.

Witu shrugged. There were a dozen Nderobo legends dealing with the place; he certainly was not going to share any of them with a Wakikuyu.

Kahinga looked at him shrewdly. "How many Nderobo know about this place?" he asked casually. If the Nderobo knew, then the security forces would find out in time.

"Maybe a few," was the answer.

"O.K, so that's no problem," he thought. "We'll just have to make sure that there is an escape route that even the Nderobo don't know about."

It was too good an opportunity to pass up. He named the base Tembo (elephant). It was to play a major part in his life over the next few years.

They spent the night there. Kinua had shot a buck, which they grilled on the fire. In the firelight the place was beyond anything Kahinga had ever experienced. He had never been inside a church, let alone a cathedral. It was almost a mystical experience. The others felt it too; they were quite silent. The bats flew in and out of the massive cave. Kahinga listened to all the night noises of the bush. The inevitable hyrax, a yelp here, a crash there. He felt at peace, certainly safe. He looked at the little Nderobo and wondered why he had brought them here. The Nderobo beckoned; he showed him a chimney round the side of the rock and within a few minutes they had scrambled their way on to the top of the rock. It was for once a clear night with a moon; all the stars were sparkling. Down in the valley below he thought he could see car lights on one of the small dirt roads. From the other side of the great rock they could also see right into the hideout. What a great lookout. They had everything here. Later they went down and Kahinga had a word with Kinua; he would stay behind with one other tomorrow and make sure that there was a good water supply and he would also explore the escape route.

The party left the next morning. They scrambled through the little game trails for three more tiring days before coming to another place which the Nderobo thought suitable for a camp. This one Kahinga named Nyati (buffalo). The question was, how were they going to supply it? The Nderobo took them down a game path and a day later they came to a white owned farm on the edge of the forest. This time Rafiki went into the village on her own. They were certain it was a Kikuyu village; few other tribes would be comfortable living right on the edge of the forest like that. She made contact with one of the women of the village at the stream where they collected water. She just came out of the bush and called a greeting; the woman was about to drop everything and run but something stopped her, and she turned around.

"Rafiki said, "Don't be afraid. I will not harm you."

Rafiki was then able to explain who she was and what she was doing, first to that woman and then to a whole group of women in the village. The women responded very positively and promised support. One of them came back into the forest with Rafiki and then returned to the village.

The women were always much more eager to help than the men. Rafiki understood this; instinctively they realised that any change in the society might improve the status of women, traditionally regarded as possessions of men.

The group spent another week setting up two more camps: Faru (rhino), which was opposite the Wanjohe, and a very small camp named Dik-Dik from which they could attack farms nearer to Thomsons Falls. Rafiki arranged for food for all these camps.

The group had now been away almost a month and were anxious to return back home. Kahinga had other ideas; it was time to start destroying white owned property.

He led them from Dik-Dik and out of the forest. After a while he found what he was looking for: a herd of about three hundred contented looking cows. Kahinga showed them what to do - just sever with a panga one or both of the Achilles tendons on the cows' back legs. The white farmer would have to do the rest. Within an hour all three hundred of the cattle had been disabled. Dibu wanted to attack the house.

"No," said Kahinga. "They won't find this until dawn, and by that time we will be back at Dik-Dik."

They slipped back into the forest.

The next morning John Frazer was woken by one of his herdsmen banging on the door.

"Bwana, come quick, they have killed all the cows!"

He took his old service rifle and went with the herdsman to the paddock where his prize Jersey cows always spent the night. They were all moaning pitifully. Every one of them had had their Achilles tendons cut. He was more or less ruined. He would have to shoot them all.

He called the police; he called the press. Eventually he got all the butchers in the district to come and buy and slaughter the cattle. He got very little for them.

Two nights later Kahinga struck again, this time out of Faru base. He and the gang slipped back into the forest.

Four nights later he struck again out of Nyati base. Again he was content to do the damage and slip away. All the bases had been supplied with food. As far as he, Kahinga, was concerned he was now operational; he could go on doing this for months, he thought.

They eventually returned to Tembo base. Kinua was waiting for them.

He'd found a water supply and only the day before he had found a way out of the back of the cave. They now had an escape route.

They decided to go back to Fort Hall. They made their way to the food drop where they had spent their first night in the forest. Kahinga was very cautious; he approached the area and kept it under observation for an hour. Eventually a group of women appeared, each carrying a huge load on their backs, supported by a long leather strap round their foreheads. Most of them were traditionally dressed with multiple bead bangles on their legs, arms and through the lobes of their ears, which over the years had been elongated by putting larger and larger blocks of wood into a hole made in the lobe. Despite the loads and the very slippery conditions they were all chattering gaily.

Kahinga stepped out into the path; the women shrieked, dropped their bundles and fled into the bush.

"Stop, stop," called Kahinga.

Eventually order was restored and they helped the women store the food.

They made their way back down the mountain. All they wanted now was to get home. Kahinga again was cautious; the women went back to their village, and Kahinga, Rafiki and the others went back to the carefully hidden truck. They had been in the bush for some weeks and their sense of smell had become much stronger. Kahinga left most of the group in the bush and he and Kinua crept forward to a vantage point overlooking the lorry. Kahinga caught the faint whiff of soap, then the smell of cigarette smoke. Then he saw them - two white soldiers on an adjoining hill overlooking the lorry that they had so carefully hidden. They kept very still. Kahinga wondered how many more were there, after half an hour he had picked out four African askaris, all under bushes, waiting.

Kahinga waited and thought, "Getting into a fire fight with these people would be a disaster. We would lose."

He wondered how long they would wait.

As dusk approached he had his answer. A Land Rover with a white soldier driving came along the road. "Any sign?" yelled the driver.

"Not a dicky-bird," responded one of the white soldiers as he came out from his hiding place.

All the soldiers emerged from their hiding places. Kahinga was glad he had used caution; there were at least two he hadn't seen.

The soldiers all crowded round the Land Rover.

"Look, we've been watching this lorry for two weeks now; I think we should call it a day. We'll come back tomorrow and take the thing away, let's go," said one of the soldiers, who appeared to be in charge.

"Hey Jimmy," said his companion to one of the black askaris.

"I've been sitting around here in this bush for too long. I need a good piece of black fanny."

He made a crude sign.

The askari couldn't understand the words but he understood the meaning.

They all laughed.

If Kahinga had been able to understand English the soldiers had the unmistakable accent of the Glasgow slums. He wouldn't have cared; to him they were just Wazungu and they all looked much the same to him. The Land Rover drove off. Kahinga told Kinua to get the others.

They removed the branches and piled into the truck. Ten miles down the road there was a herd of cows in a field. An hour later they had maimed another two hundred head. They drove back to Fort Hall.

During the weeks and months that followed Kahinga organised raids on army surplus stores for boots, coats, raingear and other clothing. He raided pharmacies for basic medical products. They had no resources and no money of their own; everything, including transport, had to be stolen. Once they had used a vehicle they abandoned it and set fire to it, usually in a remote location. They tried to leave no traces, no fingerprints.

Kahinga also managed to get several hundred fighters into the bases he had set up in the Aberdares. Some of them had firearms, mainly those stolen from the Naivasha police station; others had "homemade" guns constructed from piping and bits of wood, often with a sharpened doorbolt which acted as a firing pin, and all had pangas. It was Rafiki's job to get all the supplies into the bases as fast as she could. She stole trucks and drove them to the various farms where she had set up supply operations. All the supplies were sent in through the "passive wing" set up by Rafiki; all the people going into the forests were also loaded up with equipment. Rafiki took huge risks, but she tried to use back roads at night, so she was seldom stopped.

She was at home one day, having come back from a particularly gruelling trip, during which she had had to outrun a police vehicle by driving through an African location in Kiambu and doubling back on her tracks. She had taken little Kamau down to the nearby stream to wash both him and her. This was one of the things she missed from Naseby - regular baths. Stanley came rushing up; he completely ignored her nakedness.

"Come quick," he said. "Munyu is here."

She quickly dressed, not that that was difficult, as she wore only a cotton print dress. She dressed Kamau in his little shorts. They were both barefoot. She went back to her hut and crept inside.

There was Peter, looking much the same, sitting on a stool in the middle of the hut. He had been at the appointed place outside the store in Thika and a few minutes later Stanley had climbed into the cab of the pick-up and directed him here. Stanley didn't speak much; he just told him that Rafiki and little Kamau were fine and that when Rafiki was away he, Stanley, made sure that Kamau was looked after.

"Away, where?" asked Peter.

Stanley changed the subject. He had to remember this M'zungu was on the other side now.

Peter and Rafiki embraced; God how he missed her. He stooped down to hug Kamau.

Kamau rushed behind Rafiki for protection and pointed his finger.

"M'zungu, M'zungu," was all he would say, jabbing his finger at Peter, just like all the other little Kikuyu children, who hid when they saw a white person.

"This is your daddy," Rafiki spoke to him in Kikuyu.

"M'zungu, M'zungu," was the response.

He wouldn't come near Peter.

He embraced Rafiki again; he loved her smell, and the feel of her strong, young body.

Suddenly the door of the hut burst open. Peter felt the metal of a gun barrel on his neck.

"Shit," he thought. "So it was a trap."

He looked at Rafiki. Her eyes were wide open.

"Munyu." It was Kahinga's voice. "You will go now; these people are Kikuyu, they belong to us. You have saved my life so I will not kill you but if you come back again I will have to kill you. Go now."

Peter searched Rafiki's eyes - he could see she still loved him. She said nothing.

"You can see we are fine; go now, you have no choice," she said.

Peter held on to her hand for a brief second and then let go.

"M'zungu, M'zungu," was all little Kamau would say.

Kahinga wordlessly ushered him back to his pick-up. He watched him drive off.

Peter was devastated that the visit was cut short, but he was also elated. His relationship with Rafiki was obviously still intact and he could see that both Rafiki and Kamau were at least physically O.K. He wondered how long this conflict would go on and whether there was anything he could do to shorten it. The important thing now was Rafiki; there must be a place for her and for himself in a multiracial Kenya. He tried to think ten years ahead.

Kahinga went back into the village; he was furious. He found Stanley, threw him on the ground and gave him a really good thrashing with a stick.

"We're fighting a war, you stupid young fool," he yelled. "You will go into the forest soon to keep you out of mischief."

※ ※ ※

Chapter 22

Waichagga had recovered from his ordeal and now wanted to return to what he considered to be his rightful place at the head of the Mau-Mau. All the rest of the leadership had been arrested and were interned at Lodwar. He was the next in line in the hierarchy.

He was angry to discover that the upstart Kahinga had taken it upon himself to establish bases in Nyandarua and to raid the Naivasha police station without consulting him. And that bloody little bitch on heat Rafiki - she was running about uncontrolled as far as he could see. The only thing that she was good for was lying on her back. He wondered about the child. Waichagga felt he was a possible bargaining chip. He certainly felt that any progeny of Lawrence's should die, but he might be useful in the meantime.

Waichagga knew he would have to re-establish himself; in any event he had a bone to pick with Dibu and Kahinga. He hadn't seen Mwangi in a while; there was some rumour floating around that he'd been shot by Rafiki. Waichagga didn't really care one way or another; if Mwangi was alive he'd kill him, if Mwangi was dead so much the better.

Waichagga's only interest was personal power. He was not committed to the independence struggle for its own sake; he just saw it as a means to an end. The fact that the other leaders were locked up actually suited him very well as it meant that the coast was clear as far as he, 'Black Mamba', was concerned. He would leave Kahinga to set up the bases in the mountains and establish the supply chains; he would then be ready to kill Kahinga and smoothly take over. He had no intention of spending much time in the mountains himself; he thought he could manage the whole thing from the relative comfort of his base in Fort Hall.

Waichagga had several problems. In the first place he had no knowledge of the mountains or where the bases were or how they were supplied. Secondly, he was poorly armed compared to Kahinga's followers and he had fewer than sixty people he could count on. The rumour was that Kahinga had several hundred well-armed followers.

Waichagga had some advantages however: he was totally ruthless and no one suspected what he was plotting.

Waichagga first started to spread rumours that Kahinga was a coward, that all he was good for was cutting up domestic livestock and that it required real men like Waichagga to attack well-fortified farm houses. The attack on Halway's place and the daring raid on the Naivasha police station were conveniently forgotten.

Kinua and Dibu heard these rumours and came to Kahinga one night to tell him what Waichagga was doing.

"Kill him now and you will have no trouble; his people will fall into line. If you leave him there will be big trouble," Dibu spoke for them both.

Kahinga looked at them. "We are all Kikuyu, all committed to the struggle; none of us have time for these petty squabbles," he said high-mindedly.

"Waichagga is only interested in one thing, power for himself. He will kill you and us; you must not forget James," Kinua added.

Kahinga dismissed them. He now had several hundred men in the forest; he was planning an all-out attack on white farms in the Kinangop, Kipipiri and the Wanjohe. He needed to strike now; the security forces were still in the process of organising themselves and he thought that a major strike now would really give the settler community a jolt. He hadn't thought through what came after that but he did know that if he caused a lot of destruction it would weaken the settlers considerably. Waichagga could wait; he had few followers, no weapons and he didn't know where the bases were. Kahinga felt secure.

Rafiki in the meantime had decided that it was very laborious to contact her supply chain through the mountains; it was much more efficient to access the current members of the passive wing and to continue to build the network by road. She persuaded Kahinga to legitimately acquire a small second hand motorbike and she got Kinua to make sure that it was in good running order. Again with Kinua's help she taught herself to ride it; her driving licence was valid for the motorbike as well as a car. She cut her hair and bought a helmet and she took to wearing trousers. A black woman riding a motorbike might have caused a stir. When she was riding around most people thought she was a man and took little notice. In general she used the back roads and tracks. On the few occasions when she was stopped at roadblocks, all her papers were found to be in order, so although the police were slightly surprised that she was a woman she was allowed to go on her way. She always carried the Beretta but it was hidden under her clothing.

Although from time to time she came within twenty or so miles of Naseby, she went nowhere near Peter. When she had been given the motorbike Kahinga had warned her that if she went anywhere near him both her life and that of the child would be forfeited. She decided it was not worth taking the risk.

Waichagga had done his homework. He had befriended the little Nderobo, Witu. Kahinga needed him less and less and Witu was feeling neglected. Also he arranged for several of his followers to join Kahinga's people in the forest. From them he heard what Kahinga's plans were and made his own plans accordingly. He would get all of his people into the forest and when Kahinga's men were out attacking the farms he would take over the main base.

Waichagga also correctly assumed that most of Kahinga's followers had limited loyalty to Kahinga, simply because he had had limited time to establish strong bonds with them. They could probably be persuaded to follow any credible leader, such as Waichagga himself.

He had heard them call their main base Tembo. He planned to wait there for Kahinga and kill him when he returned from his attack on the farms. He thought that would be easy as surprise would be on his side.

Waichagga had one further plan, and that was to subjugate that little bitch Rafiki. He was offended that a woman had such a big role, and what was worse, she was Lawrence's woman. He planned to use her child to get her into his power.

Kahinga, Kinua, Dibu and all the others had gone back into the forest to organise the major offensive they had planned. Rafiki was busy buzzing about on her motorbike organising supplies.

Waichagga watched and waited. He sent his people into the forest, a few at a time. He made sure he knew all the child's movements.

One night he struck; he and Waithiru smashed down the door of Rafiki's hut. They bound and gagged the woman looking after little Kamau and grabbed Kamau. They dug up the floor of the hut and found thirty rifles and a box of ammunition.

Waichagga had seen how Kinua stole small lorries from various traders, used them and then dumped them. Wacheera had been told to steal a lorry in the same way.

They loaded everything into the lorry including Kamau and they drove to the Kinangop along with Witu, the Nderobo.

Kamau was quiet most of the way, except for the occasional whimper. Wacheera was driving with Waithiru holding Kamau and Waichagga also sitting in the cab. The Nderobo Witu was sitting in the back with the rifles. Kamau suddenly, without warning, bit Waithiru as hard as he could on the arm; Waithiru yelped, as much in surprise as in pain and Wacheera nearly drove off the road, he was given such a fright. They were all tense and anxious, knowing that if they were stopped by the police the game would be up. The Kikuyu generally are reluctant to hit small children, so Waithiru tried scolding Kamau. He was bitten again.

Witu directed them to an area on the edge of the forest where they were met by some thirty of Waichagga's followers. They unloaded the rifles and ammunition and moved off into the forest. Carelessly they forgot to hide and camouflage the lorry.

Rafiki always looked forward to coming back to the home village and to the welcome she always received from little Kamau. She parked the bike in its hiding place and joyfully ran around to her hut. She sensed something was amiss when she saw the door of the hut dropping off its hinges. She rushed inside to find the woman who looked after Kamau bound and gagged. She was in a state of collapse since she had been tied up for nearly a day.

Rafiki quickly cut her bonds and released her and while the woman told her story rubbed her ankles and wrists to help get the circulation going.

When Rafiki heard the story a cold, hard rage crept right through her. Much stronger than any emotion she had ever felt before, much stronger than any hate she felt for the whites. Her enemy was now Waichagga; she would get him, this monster who had dared even think about harming her child. She swore the woman to secrecy and then went and sought out Stanley, who had still not joined the men in the forest. Over the months she had taught Stanley how to ride the motorbike.

She and Stanley then sat down for a while to try to understand what Waichagga was likely to do. It seemed clear that this was some kind of coup attempt. The woman looking after Kamau had heard his captors mention Tembo. She didn't know what it meant but had tried to remember everything she had heard.

Eventually they decided that they would ride the bike to the now much used entrance to the forest on the Kinangop. Stanley would leave Rafiki there and would then try to find Kahinga and warn him of Waichagga's activities before he returned to Tembo after the planned raid on the farms. It would be dangerous and difficult for Rafiki alone in the forest, but time was important; she had to get to that child before he was harmed and it was critical that Kahinga was warned before he walked straight into the trap that 'Black Mamba' was certain to be setting for him.

Waichagga and his men slipped and slid their way into the forest. They had brought almost no food with them. Witu had told them of the food store that had been established near to the Tembo base. Waithiru had been detailed to carry the child, a job for which he was singularly unsuited. Children were always carried by the women on their backs, securely wrapped in blankets tied round the women's waists, leaving both arms free. Waithiru held Kamau first on one hip then the other, and then he held him with both hands in front of him. Once or twice he stumbled and Kamau slipped out of his grasp on to the ground. He didn't know when Kamau wanted to attend to his bodily functions, so he was peed on and was lucky not to have the contents of Kamau's bowels all over him as well. In the seven or eight hours it took to get to the food drop, Kamau was given only a few sips of water. He'd had no sleep and was covered in mud. Not surprisingly, he started to cry persistently. When they arrived at the food drop, there wasn't a grain of food to be had; unknown to them it had all been moved to Tembo base during the previous week. They settled down for a very uncomfortable night. Kamau was fed with a small amount of ogalie and some water that one of the men had with him.

Kahinga in the meanwhile had left Tembo base with one hundred of his followers. Others had been sent to the other bases and would all attack designated farms on the same night. They had decided that Saturday was the best night since many of the Wazungu would be away from their farms, the next day being a rest day. Tembo had been left in the care of Dibu and five or six others who were unwell or unable to join Kahinga's force for one reason or another. There was no need for a well-guarded camp; the security forces were still ill-prepared and the Mau-Mau had the forests to themselves.

Waichagga ill-temperedly woke everyone with the dawn and made the Nderobo Witu take them on to Tembo base. As they approached they stayed hidden in the bush and made Witu go into the base to see the lie of the land. He would still be regarded as a friend.

And so it was.

Witu explained that he had on Kahinga's instructions brought some reinforcements from Fort Hall together with more rifles. Dibu had no reason to disbelieve the story; there were many comings and goings in the base that he had no prior knowledge of.

Waichagga sent his men ahead of him; they were greeted as friends by the inhabitants of the base. Waichagga himself brought up the rear and he had decided to carry the child.

When Dibu saw Waichagga and the child he felt his gut tighten into a cold hard knot. He was just about to flee but on a signal the six men in the camp were set upon by the intruders and tied up.

Waichagga took control of the camp and his followers soon prepared a meal. They didn't really know how to feed the child so he was given an indigestible mixture of what the men ate. Waithiru tried to clean him up but he was still covered in mud. Kamau had tried to empty his bowels properly but most of it ended up on his shorts. The end result was a very dirty, smelly, hungry, thirsty child who cried and whimpered as any three year old in that state would

After Waichagga had set the lookouts he went over to the captives. He said nothing but he gave Dibu a vicious kick in the stomach as he was lying on his side. Dibu was sick.

"We'll see about you later." Black Mamba's evil eyes glinted.

The security forces had from time to time revisited the site where they had found Kahinga's carefully hidden lorry. Some months had now passed and there had been no evidence that there had been any further visits. The patrol was therefore pleasantly surprised when they passed the site and found the lorry abandoned by Waichagga. When they had a look around the area they soon found the footprints and a few rounds of ammunition that had been dropped by Waichagga and his men.

"Looks like about twenty and maybe more," they reported back to base. "Some of them at least will be armed."

Two men were then left there to keep watch: one white, one black.

Luckily for Rafiki she remembered that the security forces were aware of the site. She made Stanley park the bike in a bush and they crept through the trees to a vantage point overlooking the site. They were unpleasantly surprised to see the two men sitting there in the open, smoking. They backed off.

Rafiki told Stanley to go back to the motorbike and find Kahinga and warn him. She gave him very rough instructions on how to find Kahinga. She then crept back to see if she could find a way into the forest without alerting the two watchers. They were still in much the same spot as she had left them; she drew the Beretta and put off the safety catch. It would be easy from here, she thought; just a couple of shots and then she would be on her way. She hesitated, then put the safety catch back on. She found a largish stone and hurled it with all her might down the bank away from the soldiers. They leapt up.

"What the hell was that?" said the white one.

They both ran down the bank to investigate; this was likely to be the biggest excitement they were going to get all day.

As the soldiers ran down the bank into the bush, Rafiki nipped out from her cover and sprinted the twenty yards or so across the clearing and into the forest. She was five hundred yards or so down the game trail into the forest by the time the two men came panting back to their post.

Rafiki made good time; she now knew the trail well. She stopped every hundred yards to see if anyone was following her. Occasionally an animal would crash through the bush, being scared off by her movement. She saw nothing large. All along the track were dozens of footprints and every now and then a boot mark. "Waichagga," she thought.

She made it in very good time to the food drop and was disturbed to find, as did Waichagga's party, that there was no food there.

"How did they feed my poor little child?" she thought.

Her anxiety might have made her careless, for instead of spending the night in the safe shelter of the food drop area she decided to press on to Tembo base, where she arrived just as the short African dusk was transforming itself to darkness. This was where she made her mistake; instead of waiting until dawn the next day when she could see, she decided to try to creep into the base during the darkness and rescue her child.

Rafiki waited by the game trail leading to the entrance to the base. Eventually she caught the whiff of cigarette smoke; she crept closer and eventually made out the bright red of the cigarette against the black of the African night as the guard took another drag. She waited. The man stubbed out his cigarette, then moved a few feet off the path, belched loudly and started to urinate. She crept past him on her hands and knees and when he was out of sight in the thick bamboo, waited again. She could see and hear little; she crept forward foot by foot. After about forty minutes she caught sight of the camp. Her heart leapt into her mouth; there was little Kamau looking absolutely filthy, sucking his little thumb disconsolately and making finger marks in the sand.

She was just about to get up and move towards him when two men jumped out of the bushes just behind her and thumped her to the ground.

"Got you," one grunted.

She kicked and fought like a demon. She had deliberately kept the Beretta in its holster, hidden out of sight, believing that she would need both hands to rescue Kamau. The men eventually subdued her.

"Ah, my little friend Rafiki," grunted one of the men. "Black Mamba will be very glad to see you," he leered.

They dragged her into the firelight and called Waichagga, who swaggered up. He just looked at her with his mean little eyes and slapped her face hard. She winced.

Kamau had seen her and came rushing up.

"Mummy, mummy," he wailed.

Waichagga toed him none too gently away with his boot. One of the men picked Kamau up and got bitten on the arm for his trouble.

Waichagga slapped her again.

"What are you doing here?" he yelled.

"I've come to protect my child."

"Liar!" he yelled. "Who knows you are here?"

Rafiki looked blank.

The beating went on for about twenty minutes. They got nothing out of Rafiki. Then one of the men came up and whispered to Waichagga.

He nodded. She was released and Kamau was tossed in her direction, again none too gently.

"You look after him now, and keep him quiet," growled Waichagga.

One of the men was detailed to keep an eye on Rafiki.

She cuddled her son and he clung to her. She eventually managed to persuade some of the men to bring her water to clean him up and she fed him properly for the first time for three days. Kamau fell into an exhausted sleep. The men tied Rafiki up, and flung her and the child down next to a very sore and sorry looking Dibu.

"They beat me up," he grimaced. "Tomorrow they will kill me."

Stanley in the meantime had raced round on the motorbike to the farm that Rafiki had described. He eventually found one of Rafiki's 'passive wing' accomplices, who, although suspicious to start with became convinced that Stanley was genuine.

She sent all her passive wing members out after dark to the various neighbouring farms to put out an alert for Kahinga. Under normal circumstances the women of the passive wing would know nothing about any potential raids; their job was to provide food into the bases and that was all, so actually finding Kahinga was a job in itself. Too many people moving about during the night could also alert the local white farmers that something was amiss. The farmers on the Kinangop were nervous of the security situation.

One of the local farmers did notice an extraordinary amount of activity in the area. He then found Stanley's motorbike hidden in a bush. The farmer alerted the police reserve; they had a standard procedure where all the women and children were accommodated together in one or two of the larger houses under the guard of the women themselves, all of whom were armed and capable of using their weapons, plus some of the older men who were not fit enough to go out on patrol. This freed up all the able bodied white farmers for patrols.

On the way to the rendezvous another of the farmers saw a Kikuyu woman running along a track; when she saw him she tried to escape but he caught her and took her to the rendezvous. The woman spoke perfectly good Swahili but played dumb and answered all the questions in Kikuyu, which none of her interrogators understood sufficiently well to make much of what she was saying.

"Can't make head or tail of what she is saying - some sort of an internal fight in the Aberdares among different factions of the Mau-Mau, is about the best I can make of it," said one of them.

"There's more to it though – we ought to find out what's going on. We really need someone who speaks Kikuyu."

There was silence; enough time had already been wasted.

"We should get hold of Peter Lawrence," said someone.

"That bloody wog-lover! Even if he did get the truth out of her would he tell us?" said another.

"He was attacked himself, so I shouldn't think he's too fond of the Mau-Mau," a more conciliatory voice offered.

It was well after midnight by the time a rather surprised and tired Peter arrived.

They explained the situation. Peter cleared the room and spoke to the woman in Kikuyu for at least an hour. Once he got her confidence she told him everything. Peter was absolutely devastated when he heard about Rafiki and Kamau. He thought quickly.

"These people need to know about the internal conflict in the Aberdare bases of the Mau-Mau, and they certainly need to know about the planned raids all along the Kinangop, Kipipiri and the Wanjohe. The business of Rafiki and the child is mine alone to worry about."

He went out to meet the group.

"You've gone as white as a sheet," observed one. "What's the issue?"

He told them, leaving out the details relating to Rafiki and Kamau.

"Christ, how many farms are they planning to attack?" asked one.

"At least forty, from here in the Kinangop right through to the Wanjohe and beyond," replied Peter.

"Holy shit!" said another. "They can murder each other as much as they like in the mountains; my only concern is our people and property."

By dawn the security forces and every police reservist in the area had been alerted. This was the Saturday that Kahinga had planned for his attack. Little did he know that, far from attacking lightly guarded farms, he was about to walk into a hornets nest, and all the careful planning that had gone into the offensive would be nullified.

Peter was ignored by the farmers once he had told them what was happening. He was not asked to go out on patrol so he left, taking the woman he had interrogated back to her home. He wondered what he could do about Rafiki and Kamau. He had his Rigby with him and he was equipped for a couple of days in the mountains. He said to the woman, "Do you know this Tembo base where Rafiki and Kamau are?"

She nodded; she had been part of a group that had on several occasions taken food into the mountains.

"Will you show me the way?"

She nodded again. She trusted Peter and felt that he had rescued her from a very unpleasant situation. She had been afraid of what the other farmers might do to her.

They went to her hut and Stanley suddenly appeared out of nowhere.

Peter greeted him. "What are you doing here?" he asked.

Stanley explained his role. "My motorbike has gone," he also said.

"Forget about that, you'll never see it again," said Peter. "The farmers found it; that was one of the reasons they knew that something was going on. Come with me."

So Peter and the woman and Stanley drove to a point on the edge of the forest and then made their way along the game trails towards the Tembo base.

In the meantime another of the passive wing women had eventually found Kahinga and told him what had happened. A brief argument between Kahinga and Kinua ensued. Kahinga was still keen to attack the farms. Kinua said they had to sort Waichagga out first. Eventually they compromised; Kinua would take thirty men back to Tembo base and go in through the back entrance, which they were sure that Waichagga knew nothing about, and Kahinga would complete his attacks and come back to the base by some time on Sunday evening.

On Saturday morning Waichagga woke up at his leisure. When he woke he had a happy anticipatory feeling that something good was going to happen that day.

"Ah, yes," he remembered. "I'm going to sort out Dibu and that bitch Rafiki and her bastard son."

He smiled in anticipation.

He had a leisurely breakfast and wondered who he would deal with first.

"Dibu," he thought. "I can fuck that bitch Rafiki at any time."

Rafiki had been hobbled but her hands were free so she could deal with Kamau. She had moved a little way from the rest of the group to give her some privacy.

Waichagga stood up.

"Bring Dibu," he ordered.

Dibu was brought along with his hands tied behind his back; they had untied his feet.

Waichagga smashed a rifle butt into his face. Dibu would have collapsed except for the people holding him up.

"You killed my brother!" he yelled.

"He wouldn't take the oath," croaked Dibu.

"He didn't need to take the oath from a stupid baboon like you, he had already taken it," yelled 'Black Mamba'.

"He should have told us," Dibu tried to argue.

"He did not have to discuss anything with a stupid, uneducated monkey like you." Another rifle butt in the face. "Take all his clothes off," instructed Waichagga. "Tie him to that tree." Dibu was stripped and tied to a small tree in a crucifix position with his feet off the ground.

Waichagga put a panga in the fire.

Dibu said nothing.

The panga, now red-hot, was put against Dibu's stomach. He shrieked.

The panga was put back in the fire.

Waichagga put his face right up against Dibu's. Dibu was barely conscious. He crapped himself and the contents of his bowels went all over Waichagga's boots.

Waichagga kicked Dibu in the genitals. He grabbed the panga again and stuck the red-hot end into one of Dibu's eyes.

He shrieked a very loud death-like wail. Rafiki hid her head; Waichagga's followers were intrigued and crowded round.

Peter, Stanley and the woman had made good progress. They heard Dibu's shriek carried to them faintly on the wind.

"Jesus Christ," muttered Peter. He'd never heard anything like it – it sounded like an animal in extreme and hopeless pain. They hurried on.

Waichagga decided to leave Dibu for a while, to prolong the agony.

Dibu mercifully lost consciousness.

Kinua had also made very quick progress and he and his thirty armed men entered the cave at the back of Tembo. They had heard the shrieks. Kinua knew it would take almost an hour to get through the cave and get his men into place.

Rafiki was getting increasingly nervous. She had seen the absolutely callous and ruthless way that Dibu had been treated. For some reason they had not searched her; she fingered the Beretta; thinking that she could shoot Waichagga if he came near her. What would happen after that, she couldn't guess.

All the guards had come into the base to watch the fun and games with Dibu. Peter, Stanley and the woman had been able to creep unseen round the edge of the camp under cover. The woman showed Peter where he could climb the chimney up to the rock overlooking the camp. She and Stanley stayed under cover at the entrance to the chimney.

Kinua had more or less got his men into place; he just needed to make sure that no-one escaped.

The scene that greeted Peter when he got to a vantage point on the top of the rock was beyond belief.

Waichagga's men had resuscitated Dibu by throwing a bucket of cold water over him. Waichagga had then cut off Dibu's genitals with a knife and stuffed them into his mouth. Dibu lost consciousness again.

Waichagga then gave another instruction, this time directed at Rafiki. He started to remove his trousers; his ghastly, huge penis was fully erect.

"Dear God," thought Peter, "he's going to rape her. No he damn well isn't," he muttered.

Peter looked through the sights of the Rigby. He was only about seventy-five yards away but he was well above the ground so he would have to aim low. He took careful aim at the base of Black Mamba's neck and squeezed the trigger. The heavy slug hit Waichagga in the left ear and blew away half his head, as the bullet emerged on the other side.

There was a stunned silence for a few seconds from all the people surrounding Waichagga.

Rafiki, still lying down, then pulled out the Beretta and shot the two men nearest her who had been going to hold her down for Waichagga; and just at that moment Kinua's people, who had crept to within thirty yards of the proceedings, opened up and fired volley after volley into Waichagga's troops.

Rafiki clutched Kamau to her bosom and hid behind a boulder whilst the mayhem continued.

"No one is to escape," Kinua told his troops.

And no one did, except one.

Little Witu the Nderobo disappeared as soon as the firing started.

Peter briefly took in the scene from the top of the rock. He could see that Rafiki and Kamau were all right. His instincts were to go straight to them but when he climbed down the access chimney Stanley quietly led him off into the bush.

"We will go now; if they find you they will kill you, even Kinua cannot stop them," Stanley told him.

They slipped off into the bush and by midnight had found Peter's car.

Kinua in the meantime had taken control of Tembo base. He cut Dibu down from the tree, briefly examined his injuries and put a bullet in his head; he was not going to survive anyway, and there was no point in prolonging his agony.

"Farewell my friend," he said.

All Waichagga's followers who had not been killed in the initial onslaught were summarily executed.

"Who shot Waichagga?" asked Kinua after about an hour. Nobody knew. Eventually the woman who had guided Peter to Tembo told him.

"Munyu shot Waichagga," she said.

"Munyu? Where is Munyu?" asked Kinua uncomprehendingly.

"Gone," was the only answer he got.

From that day the rumours spread and Peter acquired a ghostlike mystique amongst the Kikuyu as the story grew. One version was that a large eagle had carried him into the mountains to save Rafiki and his son and then taken him away again.

Another was that he had tamed an elephant to do the same job.

Because of all this no Kikuyu would ever again touch a hair of Peter's head; they knew that if he had such powers, anyone who killed him would in turn suffer a terrible fate.

Kahinga in the meantime had taken his considerable force into the white farming area and before they had touched one cow or torched a hay barn they ran into a patrol of white farmers who had waited in ambush. Twenty of his men were either killed or captured and he rapidly withdrew to Tembo to lick his wounds. Much the same happened to all his forces.

Peter wondered what he should do about the knowledge he had gained on his fleeting visit to Tembo. In the end he decided to write a report, which he handed in at the Ol'Kalou police station; he made the officer in charge sign a duplicate that he had received the report. The police thought he was off his head and ignored the report.

Rafiki and Kamau went back to her father's village.

Kahinga and Kinua regrouped. They joined together the whole chain of events and realised what a disaster the conflict with Waichagga had been. The organisation had been severely crippled as a result of the farmers being unexpectedly informed of the raids. They knew that the Nderobo, Witu, would be likely to tell the security forces where all their bases were and that surprise attacks would be more difficult now that the security forces were taking the Mau-Mau seriously. The 'passive wing' had also been exposed.

Kahinga knew that his organisation was only one of several very loosely connected Mau-Mau operations in the forest. There was no central command and they had no radio or any other contact with the other Mau-Mau organisations. This quite often led to confusion and made their lives even more difficult and dangerous.

Chapter 23

Despite the attack on the farm Peter was almost isolated from the conflict. The white farmers in the district did not want a "wog lover" on any of their patrols and although he knew nothing about it, his god-like status amongst the Kikuyu was as effective a protection as having a battalion of British troops surrounding Naseby. The people in the district recognised that his interrogation of the Kikuyu woman had helped save their farms from attack, yet he was still shunned by almost everyone.

Peter spent his energies in running the farm as well as he could; he also spent time thinking about the future. He felt sure the conflict was futile, for in the end the black African majority of about nine million would prevail over the comparatively tiny white population of sixty thousand, only five thousand of whom were farmers and therefore committed to the country. Many of the whites in the cities were on contract from England and would find it much easier to leave than the farmers would.

He thought the only way to cut short the conflict was for a dialogue to be opened up between the white population, the Government and the Mau-Mau leadership interned at Lodwar. Whilst Jomo Kenyatta represented only the Kikuyu tribe, he had also headed the major black African political organisation in Kenya at the time.

Peter had no one with whom to discuss the subject. He tried talking to Robert but got very little from that source. Robert was embarrassed that Peter was still ostracised by the white community and was playing such a small part in fighting the Mau-Mau. There had been a brief period of reconciliation between them after the attack on the farm, but in recent months the relationship had reverted to what it had been when Rafiki had been mistress of Naseby.

Peter decided to go and see the Governor and offer his services as a go-between in any negotiations. He knew he was uniquely qualified for that role. He went to Nairobi and tried to make an appointment. The authorities kept him waiting a week.

"Who is this fellow Lawrence," asked the Governor of Dick Preston, the Superintendent of Police. "What's he like?"

"Basically a decent, sound fellow," responded Preston. "Pity about the black woman though."

"Black woman?" queried the Governor.

Preston explained about Rafiki and Kamau.

The Governor nodded.

"Speaks Kikuyu fluently, you say?" asked the Governor.

"The best I've ever heard," said Preston. "If you can't see him when he's talking Kikuyu, you assume it's one of them."

"Hm," pondered the Governor.

The Governor eventually agreed to see Peter.

Peter explained his mission: that he believed the only possible solution was dialogue and that in the end the majority black population would prevail.

"So I think one way of really finding out what they think is to talk to the people incarcerated at Lodwar," he added. "I also think that I am uniquely..."

"Yes, yes," said the Governor impatiently. "You speak Kikuyu, you had a liaison with a Kikuyu woman, and you have no official status, so you aren't a threat to any party."

Peter was impressed; he kept silent. He supposed it was worth being kept waiting a week after all.

The Governor sat for a minute or two looking at Peter, trying to size him up. All he could see was strength, both physical and mental. The Governor had spent time in the army during the war and thought, "If I were in some sort of trouble and this fellow was around I'd feel a lot safer than if he wasn't around."

Peter felt uncomfortable under his scrutiny; the suit that he was unaccustomed to wearing became even more uncomfortable.

"Maybe - just maybe - you are what this country needs right now," he finally said. "Look, I'll have to bounce the idea off Whitehall - there's no point in proceeding if they are dead against it - but I think the idea has merit. It would also be sensible to try to nip this violence in the bud before the other tribes join in. We'll be in touch."

He got up, shook Peter by the hand and ushered him out.

Peter was impressed. The man had clearly grasped what was at stake here. He was especially impressed with the point about the other tribes; the Mau-Mau was confined to the Kikuyu and cousin tribes the Embu and the Meru.

Peter knew that nothing would happen in a hurry. He went back to Naseby. Before he left Nairobi he managed to watch Robert playing rugby a couple of times. Peter was amazed at Robert's athleticism and his flair in the field; he could see that before very long Robert would be playing in the first fifteen although he was three years younger than most of the team. Robert was pleased to see his father at the matches, but it seemed to make no difference to their relationship. Sadly, his presence caused Robert embarrassment, since it drew attention to the fact that Peter was reviled by many of the white population of Kenya because of his relationship with Rafiki.

Peter waited almost two months. Eventually he received a telegram inviting him to the Governor's office the following week. The telegram was non-committal but he felt it must indicate some interest in his idea.

This time there was no waiting. The Governor seemed pleased to see him.

"It's all on," said the Governor after the initial pleasantries were over.

Before Peter was able to say anything he said, "You are of course aware of the rumours that Kenyatta is drinking himself to death in Lodwar and that he may not live for more than another year."

Peter nodded. The Governor was obviously looking for a response.

"Of course. My view is that the rumours are almost certainly untrue. Why, for example, would the prison authorities be providing Kenyatta with a bottle of brandy a day (for such was the rumour) when only a few years ago so-called 'white liquor' was banned as far as blacks were concerned? Also, if they are providing him with all this liquor, why do they still have jobs? Thirdly, if indeed Jomo is being provided with a bottle a day, then I suspect much of it is being emptied into the desert sand in the camp; Jomo may think it is in his interests to make the whites think he is an alcoholic. Personally sir, I've chosen to ignore the rumours."

The Governor nodded, "My views exactly. How are you going to handle this assignment?"

Peter had obviously thought about this quite deeply.

"Well, India is now independent, and it looks as though Britain will grant Ghana independence shortly. I assume, therefore, that independence will have to be on the agenda here."

The Governor nodded without saying anything.

"I think the issues from Britain's viewpoint would be what the constitution might look like, what safeguards would be in place for a democratic outcome, and safeguards for the white settlers. Then there would be the status of the newly independent country in the U.N and what aid money might be needed. I assume that Britain will not just hand the country over to the Kikuyu. From the African point of view, the possible release of political detainees must be an issue and the conditions attached to that; the land question is a major issue and of course the constitutional and financial issues will be critical. I think that when I talk to Kenyatta I will just try to get him to talk to see if they have really thought through all the issues and know what they want. They may also not know how much leverage the Mau-Mau campaign of violence gives them. It has barely started; they may want to see how it develops and what the response is from Britain."

"You can make no commitments; you know that don't you?" This was more of a statement than a question.

Peter nodded, "Of course; I'm sure this process will take months, if not years. I am sure that it is not going to be an easy process."

"I want my A.D.C. (Aide de Camp) to go with you," suggested the Governor.

Peter shrugged. The last thing he needed was some pompous fool like an A.D.C interfering.

"It's up to you," said Peter. "He won't understand much of what is being said, since the whole conversation will be in Kikuyu, and, at least to start with, I will have to meet Kenyatta on his own in order to build up a relationship and confidence. How do you think he will react to being in Lodwar for two or three weeks?"

"I need regular reports," said the Governor.

"O.K, well maybe we should meet."

"Now, about payment," started the Governor.

"No, no payment. I assume that transport by plane to Lodwar will be provided and I suppose I can stay in the local guesthouse; otherwise I require nothing," said Peter.

The Governor looked surprised and relieved. He came from the old school and believed that services for Queen and country should be done for the greater good. But then he had a substantial private income; he wasn't sure of Peter's situation.

"Fine; when do you want to go?"

"Perhaps I should arrange it with the A.D.C. What have you told Kenyatta? I think he should have some idea that the visit is going to happen," said Peter.

"He's been told you are going to see him. He doesn't know the agenda; he can probably guess though," was the reply.

A week later the four-seater police air wing Piper touched down on the dusty road near the Ol'Kalou railway station, picked Peter up and took off again. They had alerted the local police, who placed an askari at each end of the piece of road used as a runway to stop any cars but there were none during the ten minute stopover. Two and a half hours later they landed at the dusty little airstrip at Lodwar and taxied to the small corrugated iron hut that served as the control tower.

The A.D.C had greeted Peter warmly when he clambered into the plane. They had had a meeting over a cup of tea at Government house on Peter's previous visit one week earlier; Peter had found the A.D.C. informed and interested in the issues surrounding the political situation in Kenya. He thought he would be an asset in what were certain to become very difficult days ahead.

They weren't sure how long they would be in Lodwar so the aircraft was sent back to Nairobi.

A police vehicle had come to pick them up and they were checked into the small but comfortable Government guesthouse.

Lodwar was a small administrative centre to the west of Lake Rudolf (now Lake Turkana) in Northern Kenya. It was one of the main centres for the Turkana. The Turkana are a warlike, nomadic tribe who thinly populated the semi-desert area mainly to the west of Lake Rudolf. They guarded their territory and cattle with ruthless determination. The prison had been placed there by the authorities deliberately since escape from there would be difficult due to the desert conditions and the fact that the Turkana would never have dreamt of helping a Kikuyu. If they found any Kikuyu hiding out in the area, the probability is that they would have killed them or possibly turned them over to the authorities. Lake Rudolf was about one hundred and fifty miles long and about thirty miles wide at its widest point; it formed part of the Rift Valley depression.

The Lodwar area was comparatively low lying, being only about seventeen hundred feet above sea level. Rainfall was sparse and the temperature hovered above eighty five degrees Fahrenheit on a daily basis with the thermometer often going well above one hundred degrees Fahrenheit. The town itself was a dry, dusty little place with a few Indian owned shops, a police station and the prison. There was also a small administrative centre which housed a courthouse and the District Commissioner, who also acted as magistrate.

The A.D.C., whose name was Brian Johns, had been told to contact the prison authorities directly, who would arrange for them to see Jomo Kenyatta. They were told to come to the prison the next day at ten in the morning which Peter and Brian duly did; they were shown into a dirty, dusty little room containing a small table with aluminium legs and a cracked formica table top. There were three wooden chairs in the room.

"Not a very prepossessing place in which to receive a future head of state," said Brian, "I wonder if we can't do better than this."

They waited about an hour and were eventually told that Kenyatta was sick and was unable to see them. Peter went back to the guesthouse and Brian went to see the prison authorities.

Brian came back an hour or so later.

"Well, I think we've sorted that little problem out," he said. "They've agreed to let Kenyatta come here for our discussions; I told them there was nowhere he could escape to even if he wanted to. Anyway, a warden has to come with him. It's far better than that horrid little room at the prison; I really couldn't see us having any kind of constructive discussion in that atmosphere."

They were told that Kenyatta was sick the next two days as well.

"Maybe we should go back to Nairobi; he clearly does not want to see us," said Brian.

"Give it another day or two; he may be consulting with his colleagues now that we are here. Africans have never understood the European obsession with time; if we left now they would assume we were playing games and were not serious about this issue," said Peter.

The next morning at about eleven, Kenyatta came to the guesthouse with a prison warden. Peter greeted him with the traditional Kikuyu greeting for a chief or a man of importance.

Kenyatta was clearly apprehensive; he didn't really know what all this was about. He was pleasantly surprised at the fluency with which Peter spoke his language. The prison authorities had allowed Kenyatta to wear civilian clothes for the outing and Peter offered him a comfortable chair in the living room of the guesthouse. Tea was brought.

After the preliminary introductions were over, Brian made himself scarce. Peter saw opposite him a slightly overweight man of medium height with a wispy goatee beard going a little grey. He had a white fez on his head, decorated with some intricate beadwork. His eyes were clear, his handshake firm. He appeared calm and confident.

"So much for all these rumours about a drinking habit," thought Peter.

Kenyatta was patient; he looked at Peter and waited for him to speak.

Peter told him he was in Lodwar on behalf of the Governor.

Kenyatta nodded; he knew that.

They talked in Kikuyu about many things: family, the weather, the prospects for the next harvest. Kenyatta asked Peter about Rafiki. Peter tried to remain non-committal but Kenyatta shrewdly assessed that this was Peter's Achilles heel.

"She went back to Thika with the child; because of the conflict I am unable to see her," said Peter.

He needed to turn this conversation around so he asked, "It would be helpful to understand what your views are on the long term future of Kenya."

Kenyatta shrugged. So they wanted him to lay it all out on the table. He knew it was not going to be that easy; he had to keep them guessing.

"Uhuru (freedom)," he said.

Peter looked at him quizzically. "Uhuru for whom?"

"My people," was the reply.

"Which people, just the Kikuyu?" asked Peter.

"It would have to be all the people," Kenyatta replied.

"Have you talked to the leaders of the other tribes?"

"How can I talk to people when I am locked up here? The leadership will have to come from the Kikuyu anyway." This M'zungu was smarter than he thought; he had already said too much.

"So the British want peace," Kenyatta started again.

"The British have thousands of troops in Kenya plus the police and police reserve; they will eventually kill or capture most of your active Mau-Mau fighters," Peter replied.

"Waichagga only needs a few hundred people in the forest to make life very difficult for the Sirkali," Kenyatta countered.

"Waichagga is dead," answered Peter.

He saw Kenyatta start. "Dead? Did the security forces kill him?"

"No, there was a fight in the forest between the different factions and he was killed," answered Peter.

"How do you know this? The security forces have not said anything; it has been in no newspaper," Kenyatta was agitated.

"The security forces probably don't know and will never know. They may not have heard about Waichagga. As far as I know, they think Kahinga leads the Mau-Mau in the forest."

"Kahinga?" Kenyatta was nonplussed; as far as he was concerned, Kahinga was small fry, a non-entity.

"Did Kahinga kill Waichagga?" he asked aggressively.

"No, he was not there."

"Who did then?"

Peter remained silent. Enough had already been said.

Kenyatta asked to be taken back to the prison; he was clearly distressed by the turn of events. It looked as though his organisation in the field was now completely out of his control.

Peter said questioningly, "We will meet tomorrow?"

Kenyatta nodded.

After their visitor had left Brian Johns came bustling into the room.

"Well?" he asked enquiringly.

"I didn't get much out of him; he told me they wanted 'Uhuru', something we already know," answered Peter.

"Is he coming again? He looked rather agitated when he left," observed Brian.

"Yes, he'll come back."

"I've one piece of news - there's a bloody reporter sniffing around; he's wondering what I'm doing here," Brian volunteered.

"You may have to return to Nairobi to put him off the scent and then come back," suggested Peter.

"Well, we'll have to keep a low profile."

"Why is he here? Surely this is a restricted area," Peter went on, "Can't you just pack him off out of here?"

"I could, but it will just make the press think we have something to hide. If he's still here tomorrow I'll do as you suggest - go back to Nairobi for a few days and then come back."

Brian returned to Nairobi the next day and although the reporter stayed on a few days, he picked up no further information and eventually went back to Nairobi himself. There were a few speculative articles in the papers about a possible peace deal, but with little to go on and no response from the Government the story soon fizzled out.

During the time he was in Lodwar Peter took the opportunity to take his camera out and take pictures of the Turkana, who remained virtually untouched by the advent of the colonial government.

Twice during his stay in Lodwar, Peter was allowed to take one of the police Land Rovers and drive on the rough, dusty little track to Ferguson's Gulf on the lake. The lake had a plentiful supply of hippos and crocodiles and there were many birds on the lake shore, which kept his camera busy.

On one occasion Brian came with him and they went out on the lake in a little runabout that the D.C had stored there. They caught a good-sized Nile Perch. Peter explained to Brian that in the dim, distant past Lake Rudolf had had much more water in it than currently and it was one of the sources of the Nile; hence the presence of the fish. Just after they had landed the fish, a squall came up out of nowhere and almost blew them away to the eastern side of the lake. Peter had to use all his skill and ingenuity to get them back to the gulf. When he was alone at the lake, Peter often took a sleeping bag and rolled himself up next to the vehicle for the night. The solitude was a great source of renewal. He loved Kenya; he loved every inch of it. He was convinced he could help with the political solution; he just had to keep working on it.

Peter met with Kenyatta on a daily basis for the next week. He managed to develop a reasonable rapport with him, although Jomo kept his distance. At one time, to try to put Peter off balance Kenyatta said to him:

"They tried to kill you."

Peter grimaced; the memories of that night were all too vivid. "Yes." He showed Jomo the scars on his shoulder.

"Maybe it's better that they failed," he observed.

Eventually they came up with a list of the basic demands that Kenyatta and his leadership group would accept as a basis for peace. These were:

- One person over eighteen, one vote
- Total withdrawal of British forces
- Release of all detainees
- Talks on the future constitution
- Purchase of white owned farms for re-settlement of blacks
- Financial aid
- Membership of the British Commonwealth

"This means virtual immediate independence," observed Brian.

"Yes," said Peter.

"They won't accept a more gradual process where they gain control over a twenty year period?"

"I doubt it," said Peter. "They know that time and history is on their side.

They're certainly prepared to sit it out for a few more years."

Brian and Peter went back to Nairobi and reported to the Governor.

"Well Mr. Lawrence, what do you think?" asked the Governor.

"If the British Government is prepared to garrison the country permanently with large numbers of troops then you can hold on. Otherwise some sort of a constitutional settlement along the lines suggested is imperative," he said. "And the settlers need to know where they stand. The security forces will win the war. What about the peace?"

"We'll see," said the Governor tiredly. "I don't get the feeling that the present lot are prepared to budge, although the bloody nose that we've just had over Suez[15] may help them change their minds."

"Are you going to continue to settle people on the land here?" asked Peter. He knew perfectly well what the answer was. His brother Bill was in charge of settling a huge area of crown land at Mau Narok about fifty miles to the west of Nakuru.

"As you know that is still policy," the Governor responded.

Peter took a deep breath. "You're dealing with people's lives here," he said. "They're putting all their savings into these bloody farms and in a few years they're going to have to leave again. Can't you do anything to stop this stupidity?"

"I understand exactly what you mean, but policy is still to settle the place. It's one way of winning the war against the Mau-Mau," was the response.

"Nine million Africans against sixty thousand whites; you've got a very long way to go," responded Peter.

The ball was now very much in the Governor's court. Peter went home.

"You've been very helpful, thank you," said the Governor as he ushered Peter out of Government house. "I'll be in touch when I have any news."

Some months passed. The raids continued on stock in the areas bordering the Aberdares. The security forces gathered strength and mounted constant patrols into the mountains. An occasional grisly murder of a white farmer and his family made headlines throughout the world.

The intelligence service of the police had been interrogating the Mau-Mau that they captured; they had also intercepted a number of women of the passive wing carrying food into the mountains. They managed to obtain a garbled version of the confrontation with Waichagga but increasingly Kahinga's name came up as one of the leaders of the gangs in the forest

15 1956 Suez crisis where Britain and France invaded Egypt who had nationalized the Suez canal. They had to withdraw mainly due to American opposition to the move.

and members of the passive wing under pressure disclosed that they had been recruited by Rafiki. This information was released to the press along with descriptions.

George Athill read the article with interest. Now was his opportunity to really get his revenge on Peter Lawrence. He found the picture that he had of Kahinga, Kinua, Stanley and the buffalo and he went to the press.

Peter was devastated when he picked up the paper. The headlines on page one of the paper read: "Lawrence responsible for training notorious gang leader Kahinga".

The picture of Kahinga and the buffalo was given prominence. The article went on to describe in detail the fact that Peter had trained him as his gun bearer and had schooled him extensively in the use of firearms.

The article discussed Peter's relationship with Rafiki; the fact that he had fathered her child and the fact she was now in charge of the passive wing of the Mau-Mau.

The article concluded: "Whose side is this Peter Lawrence on? Maybe he should be sent to Lodwar with the rest of the Mau-Mau."

Peter sat and wondered what to do. He realised that the story was substantial enough to get into the British Press and would therefore severely embarrass his family there.

He therefore wrote a long letter to Giles and Louise in England, explaining everything, in particular the fact that the police had known about Kahinga long before he had trained him as a gun-bearer. He also told them about the time when he had listened outside the hut and heard Waichagga conducting the oathing ceremony on Stanley. They knew about his relationship with Rafiki and that she had left the farm with the rest of his Kikuyu farm workers. He stressed the fact that his relationship with Rafiki had never dealt with her membership of the Mau-Mau.

He then went to see Dave Gibb. Margaret was at the door.

"See you've got your just desserts at last," she said to him in her broad Scots burr. "The Lord have mercy on you now."

Dave came to the door. He had little time for his wife's increasingly strong religious views.

"I need your help," said Peter.

Dave nodded.

"Come in," he said.

"It's worse than you think," explained Peter. He then went on to explain his trip to Lodwar and the discussions he had had with Kenyatta.

"Those discussions must continue," said Peter. "It's the only hope we settlers have of getting a say in the final settlement; otherwise we'll be tipped out of here with nothing. We'll be expendable when the chips are down."

Dave was really surprised how far the political developments had progressed.

Eventually they decided the only thing to do was to discuss the whole thing with the Governor. As an afterthought they decided to take Zacharia, who came just as he was: shirt, trousers, army greatcoat, KAR hat and his best shoes, no socks. He always drove his goats into his hut at night so he smelt of goat.

The Governor was horrified when he saw the headlines.

"Get that bloody Lawrence here!" he said to Brian Johns, his A.D.C. "I want an explanation of this. Dear God - the credibility of the discussions we've started with Kenyatta will be shot to pieces when the people in Whitehall see this." He held his head in his hands. As if the situation wasn't difficult enough already.

Brian came back later in the day. "He's on his way; he says he wants Preston here."

"Hm." The Governor looked speculative; he wondered what Peter had up his sleeve. "Get Preston then."

"He says you may also need a Kikuyu interpreter," added Brian.

"What the hell for? He speaks perfectly good Kikuyu."

"He says you may want an independent interpreter."

"I see. All right, find someone."

Peter, Dave and Zacharia appeared at Government house the next day. They were rapidly shown into the Governor's office.

The Governor waved the offending newspaper in Peter's face.

"Have you the slightest idea of what this will do when the powers that be in Britain see it?" he shouted.

"Of course; that's why I'm here."

"All right; my guess is that we have four or five days before the story breaks in the UK. I'm certain the papers there only see our local papers when they arrive by post. I hope that no smart alec will phone this stuff through," said the Governor more calmly.

Dick Preston and a Kikuyu interpreter were ushered into the room, joining Peter, Dave and Zacharia, the Governor and Brian Johns.

"This had better be good," muttered the Governor.

It took about an hour for the story to emerge. They started with Zacharia, who explained how Kahinga and Kinua had stayed the night on their way to Ol'Kalou all those years before, how he had told his employer and had been told that the police had the situation under control. He explained that Kinua was his son-in-law now, much to his regret. He also said he was continuously surprised that the police hadn't arrested the two troublemakers. The Kikuyu interpreter, with a little help from Peter, got Zacharia's story across.

"What a fine old man," thought the Governor. He had noticed the smell of goats, but was more taken with Zacharia's dignity. "It can't be every day that a man like that sits in the Governor's office."

Dave then told of his visit to Dick Preston. Peter did the same.

Preston had said nothing.

"Why didn't you pick them up, Dick, you had enough evidence?" asked the Governor calmly. He knew the answer.

"You know what the policy was, sir. We were told to turn a blind eye. That's the only reason I have. Looks stupid now, but it seemed to make sense at the time," he answered.

"So what do we do?" asked the Governor.

There was a hush.

Then Peter spoke about his brother-in-law in England and that he had already written a long letter to Giles explaining the situation.

"Giles who?" asked Brian.

"Giles Dingley-Ferris," replied Peter.

"Giles Dingley-Ferris is your brother-in-law?" Brian and the Governor chorused.

Peter nodded.

"Jenny's sister Louise married him a few years back," explained Peter.

"Who is Jenny?" asked Brian.

"She was my wife; she was killed in a horse riding accident," Peter responded.

"I'm sorry."

"You say Giles has all the facts, just as you have told me?" the Governor queried.

"He will have shortly; I posted the letter this morning," said Peter.

"Too late," muttered the Governor. "Can we phone him from here?" he asked. "Just give me a minute. Dick and Brian, stay here please," he continued.

The others filed out.

"Dick, do you dispute any of the facts?" he asked.

"No; I acted in good faith though, strictly in line with policy as laid down," Dick replied.

"I know, but it won't stand up in the press; you know that. They'll want blood."

"Of course." Dick pulled an envelope out of his coat pocket. "My resignation," he said dejectedly.

"I'm sorry but I'll have to accept it; you've done the honourable thing. I know it's not all your fault; you were put in an impossible position."

"I did my best," answered Preston.

Peter and the others were called back into the room. A call was eventually put through to Giles.

"Hello, old boy, what's up? Must be something serious if you need to phone me," said Giles down the phone.

Peter explained where he was and that the Governor and his ADC were in the room with him.

"Oh, do give them my regards, I know them both," said Giles.

Peter then explained his predicament.

"Whew, what do you want me to do?" Giles asked.

"Well, in view of the fact that I am the front man in the discussion with Kenyatta, the last thing we need is for my credibility to be destroyed by a sensational article like this. Firstly it misses the point and secondly it is not going to help anyone," responded Peter.

"Can you send me all that stuff in a telegram please? I'm not sure that your letter will get here in time. My sense is that we'll have to nip this thing in the bud today or it will be too late," Giles was now committed.

"Fine, I'll do it right away," said Peter.

They spent a minute or two talking of family matters, and then Brian took over.

"Giles, how are you? I really had no idea you even knew Peter, let alone were related to him. I think we are very lucky; it's important that Peter's name be kept out of the press as much as possible. Too much depends on it."

"We can send a wire from here," said Brian, after the phone was put down.

"O.K.," said Peter.

"All's well that ends well," the Governor was clearly relieved. "Pity about Preston, but he was due to retire anyway," he continued.

"They went out. Dave was talking to Dick Preston.

"I'm sorry," said Peter.

Dick looked at him.

"Not your fault; you did what you had to do. I'm looking forward to my little cottage in Devon," he said.

"The next few days may not be that easy; some explaining will have to be done in the press. You really should have locked that little bastard Athill up. He generated all this heat."

"Too late now," answered Preston. He left.

Peter went over to Dave Gibb. "Thanks; I know this has been difficult for you," he said.

"Well, at last justice may be done. I could never understand why the police didn't lock those two up in the first place. I now understand a little more but, it still seems crazy to me," he said in his broad Scots. Dave left with Zacharia.

Brian and Peter sent the telegram to Giles.

"Now we'll have to deal with the local press," said Brian.

He called the editor and explained the situation. The editor was amazed at the turn of events.

"Why are you going out of your way to protect that weasel Lawrence? He's had this coming to him for years," the editor asked.

"You come over here and not only will you get the story of your life but you'll get some background as well," responded Brian.

The editor and the reporter were shown into Brian John's office. A tall, sunburnt, athletically strong looking person was also there. Brian introduced them.

"Peter Lawrence," he held out his hand.

The editor nearly jumped out of his skin and the reporter backed off.

"Hey, what's this?" said the editor "Some sort of trap?"

"No," said Brian. "Just want to get the facts straight."

"We already have the facts," they started to leave.

Brian blocked the way.

"Just listen for a few minutes," he said.

The two of them listened for an hour while Brian told them the story. They sat in a fascinated silence. Eventually the reporter wrote down what he had heard.

"You can confirm all that with Preston; he has now resigned," Brian concluded.

The reporter left.

"I know this is a free country with a free press," said Brian to the editor, "but just tone it down a bit, if you can."

"You promised me some background," said the editor. His newshound instinct told him there was a much bigger story in the offing.

"Yes, but this is off the record and you can print none of it," said Brian.

He and Peter then told him of the talks with Kenyatta and Peter's role and the likely political developments resulting from them. The editor sat there with his mouth open. Eventually he pulled himself together.

"How do you feel about all that?" he asked Peter. "You have a farm; are you happy to lose it?"

"I will either own my farm legitimately in a political sense, or not at all," was the response. "I am committed to this country and will see it right if I can; I hope you understand," he continued.

The editor nodded.

"Publish any of this and frankly your life won't be worth living," said Brian. "I hope it will give you a lead on to some of the developments likely to occur over the next few years."

Giles in the meanwhile had been busy. He phoned the editor of The Times and went to see him in the late afternoon. He explained what was on his mind.

"Ah, yes, we have a copy of that article in the East African Daily News. We are going to run with it tomorrow morning."

"I don't think so," said Giles.

The man from The Times looked at him expectantly. He knew that Giles would not have come to see him unless it was really important.

Giles showed him the telegram and explained the call he had had from the Governor's office in Nairobi.

"What do you want from me?"

"Well you can't publish the original story knowing all this, can you?" Giles told him. "Can't you make something out of what I have given you? Preston's resignation and all that."

"What about the rest of the papers here?"

"They've been looked after, don't worry; if your story is published this story will die." Giles looked confident.

Eventually on the main news page of The Times a thoughtful article appeared dealing with British Government policy in Kenya and the failure of the police to act on information given to them years previously about the Mau-Mau. It dealt with Preston's resignation and Kahinga's name cropped up again as one of the main leaders of the gangs in the forest. The fact was mentioned that if the police had acted in time Kahinga would certainly have been in jail. Neither Peter nor Rafiki were mentioned.

The editor got a few curious calls from other editors.

"This article of yours has more or less pre-empted a much more interesting story that we were going to run," was the general complaint.

When the situation was explained the story fizzled out.

The East African Daily News dealt with the story in its own way. They didn't quite apologise to Peter but did explain that if the police had acted in time, Kahinga would have been apprehended before Peter had a chance to train him.

Most of the white population remembered only the first article. Peter contemplated taking the matter to court but decided nothing would be gained by doing that. He had lived with the prejudices surrounding his relationship with Rafiki for many years and would continue to do so.

※ ※ ※

Chapter 24

In the meanwhile, life in Nyandarua had in the four years or so that they had been in the mountains become much tougher for Kahinga and his followers. The security forces had been reinforced by large numbers of troops from Britain and the Mau-Mau were really dependant on their own resources. They had no substantial outside source of help. The security forces had found most of their bases and either bombed them out of existence or had taken them over for their own use. Contact with their people in the reserves had been made very difficult indeed; the security forces had dug a huge "security ditch" around much of the forest areas, using mainly Kikuyu labour from the some eighty thousand detainees who had been arrested since the start of the emergency. Also the Kikuyu 'Home Guard' were now better armed and trained and they kept the dwindling Mau-Mau forces still in the forests at bay.

Kinua had been a great source of strength and support and despite the setbacks, he and Kahinga had consolidated their position as leaders among the gangs in the forest. They had virtually no contact with the leadership at Lodwar. Kahinga spent most of his time surviving, so he had very little time to think about the future. He knew he was the most hunted man in Kenya, so he never emerged from the forest.

They concentrated on small gangs of five or six coming out of the forest at night and attacking cattle and other livestock. Occasionally a gang defied orders and attacked white farm houses. Most of those were known to be poorly defended and often the whites were savagely murdered, which gave the Mau-Mau a very unsavoury reputation in Kenya and in the outside world. It was probably one of the reasons that the other tribes in Kenya refused to join up and also why they could not get any help from outside the country. They also spent a great deal of energy in setting ambushes for the security forces and trying to fight them off.

One day, Kinua had set up an ambush with six of his colleagues. It seemed to be the perfect spot. He was lying on top of a flat rock with the Bren gun that Waichagga had once owned; he had a view almost one hundred and fifty yards down a well-used game trail. His other colleagues were in various firing position just ahead of him and to the left of the path, on the upper slope of the path. Their job was to try to protect Tembo base, which had been attacked many times by the security forces but they still held on to it. They waited; they had been there hours now and although they had seen a few antelope skipping through the forest, there had been no sign of any other people.

Then he smelt it - the very faint smell of soap coming in on the light breeze. Kinua and his men had been in the forest so long now and they did not have soap of any kind. Their instincts and senses were fine tuned to such an extent that they were almost as good as the wild animals with whom they shared the forest. He hoped his colleagues had also smelt the soap. He couldn't signal; he had no intention of alerting the patrol that he was sure would come into view shortly.

Ten men did come into view; Kinua was puzzled for a short moment. They were all black and they actually looked like his gang looked; they were dressed in rags and skins. He thought it must be a gang from another leadership group in the forests. Then the smell of soap became stronger.

"Damn," he thought, "it is one of those pseudo gangs." The security forces, when they captured Mau-Mau gang members, tried to convert them to their side and then sent them back into the forest to meet up with real gangs, whom they took by surprise and often shot to pieces.

As usual the pseudo-gang was led by an Nderobo tracker who stopped every few yards and looked about him.

Kinua carefully cocked the Bren; he had all the members of the gang in his sights. He could now see that there were three Wazungu in the group, just by the fact that they were taller than the blacks and they also wore boots. The Africans in the gang all went barefoot. Most of the Mau-Mau by this stage of the conflict had no access to shoes and had long ago decided to go barefoot.

Kinua waited; the group approached - one hundred yards, eighty yards, seventy yards; he'd let them have it at sixty yards. His colleagues were told to hold their fire until he had fired the first burst. He took careful aim; he would try to hit the whites in the group first. They were always the most dangerous because they were well trained and handled themselves well in the bush, especially the Kenya born ones who knew the bush and were fighting for their own survival. He squeezed the trigger; he saw bullets flick at the clothing of the Nderobo and one of the whites. The others in his gang opened up as well. Very soon there were six bodies lying in the path and shots were coming in his direction from the side of the path.

They had a clear plan of action: shoot and then get out as fast as they could before the security force patrol could call for reinforcements, which were certain to be close behind.

He fired a last burst into the bushes to the right of the track and called his men to withdraw. They met at a point about one hundred yards back up the track, all except one.

Kinua was pretty sure that none of his party had been hit but they couldn't go back without putting all of them at risk. There had been a number of desertions; he wondered if his missing man was another one. Life had been very tough in recent months; it was really hard to keep his men happy in the forest.

They ran and ran through the now very familiar game trails back towards Tembo base.

His years in the forest had made Kinua naturally cautious. He decided to access the base from his secret way in rather than from the front. There was some grumbling from his men, since that would take them another two hours.

The pseudo gang that Kinua had ambushed had been part of a much larger operation. There were considerable reinforcements following up half an hour behind; they spent the next hour or two evacuating the dead and wounded from the ambush.

Another group had gone a roundabout way to Tembo base under the guidance of Witu the little Nderobo tracker who had first shown Kahinga the base, then Waichagga. Now, after much persuasion, he had worked for two years for the security forces. They had decided on one last final push to take over Tembo. There were about thirty men in the group that went on the roundabout route to Tembo.

Kahinga was at Tembo with about ten of his followers. Security was lax and in any event they felt secure; Kinua was down the track and would certainly alert them to an approach from hostile forces. Also they were exhausted; they had been on a three day raid through white owned farms on the Kinangop, destroying stock and property.

Witu crept into the base and found Kahinga and his crew all asleep on the ground. He crept back and called the patrol, which consisted of twenty five British soldiers and five Kenyan whites from "O" (Operational) Company of the Kenya Regiment. The Kenya Regiment was exclusively for whites, the idea being that they would provide leadership for African troops in times of crisis. The Kenya Regiment was a conscript battalion and its members had been dispersed throughout the British Regiments based in Kenya to provide local knowledge, language and general liaison. Generally this worked very well.

The patrol moved in quietly and when Kahinga and his men woke up it was with security force rifles stuck in their ribs. The local whites started to interrogate their captives and eventually identified Kahinga.

"We've hit the jackpot here, boys," was the announcement. "This is the notorious Kahinga."

The equatorial dusk had fallen and soon it was completely dark. They tied their captives up and decided to spend the night there. They had rations, plus warm clothing. They would get Kahinga and his friends out to prison the following day.

Kinua had crept into the back of the cave and was horrified to see it overrun by white soldiers. He could see that Kahinga and the rest of them were tied up but otherwise seemed unharmed. He caught a glimpse of Witu.

"Well, he's the first one I'm going to get," he thought.

They waited until the camp had settled down. Guards had been posted, but they were all outside the perimeter of the base. One soldier had been posted to make sure the prisoners did not make a nuisance of themselves.

Kinua set one of his men up with the Bren-gun about forty metres from the sleeping soldiers. The rest of them crept up behind the soldier on guard; they stunned him with a knobkerrie and caught him so he made no noise when he fell. They then cut the ropes binding Kahinga and the others. They all quietly moved to the back of the cave. Kinua in the meantime had identified where Witu lay and went back.

He hit him over the head with the knobkerrie and then cut his throat. He then left. They all scrambled silently out of the cave and were well away by the time the alarm was given back at the base.

When the guard was due to change, the relief guard couldn't find any prisoners. Instead he found his unconscious colleague and raised the alarm. The soldiers then found the Nderobo tracker with his throat cut.

They just could not piece together what had happened. No one had entered or left the base from the front. The five guards stationed there were certain of that. The best they came up with was that one of the prisoners had got free, overpowered the guard, killed Witu and left, probably by a back entrance.

By the time all this had been determined Kahinga, Kinua and their small gang of fifteen were miles away. They had decided the only safe place was Dik-Dik base, which was a good two days' hike away through the mountains. None of the other bases were safe anymore.

The settlers in the Kinangop, Kipipiri and Ol'Kalou areas were becoming increasingly restless and unhappy with the security situation. There had been a huge increase in the security presence. If one believed the papers, at least half the Mau-Mau in the Aberdare forests had been killed or captured; their own patrols as part of the police reserve had been increased. They had been persuaded against their better judgement to keep their cattle in one acre bomas (paddocks) at night under the guard of a watchman whom the police armed with a single-barrelled twelve bore shotgun. The major benefit of this latter move was that if one's cattle were attacked in these one acre bomas the Government paid some compensation.

The attacks still continued. Cattle were being maimed and then had to be shot and farmhouses were still being raided and the inmates brutally murdered.

Peter had been first on the scene of one particularly brutal murder.

He had been going to Tim Williams to discuss the purchase of a breeding mare. Williams was particularly well known for his love and care of horses and he had very fine breeding stock.

Peter had arrived at the Williams farm on the Kinangop early; it was before seven am.

As he got out of the pick-up he could feel that something was wrong; everything was deathly quiet and there was nobody about.

Peter walked round the corner of the house and almost tripped over Williams' mutilated body. He had been brutally hacked to pieces on the path to the stables, together with his Syce (groom).

Peter went to the front door of the house, which was open. He called: no answer. He noticed the telephone on the stand in the hall. He tried it, but it was dead; the wires had obviously been cut. Peter called again but there was still no answer. He hesitated, and then he decided to call the police before he further examined the house. He was very apprehensive about what he might find.

Peter drove to a neighbour, called the police on their phone and went back to the house.

He went upstairs. What he found there was beyond belief. He found Rachel Williams on the bed in a pool of blood. The expression on her face was one of sheer terror. She was naked and her belly had been split open from her vagina to her rib cage; she had been heavily pregnant and Peter found the almost completely formed foetus on the floor next to the bed with its head bashed in. There was a blood mark on the doorframe.

Peter was almost sick on the spot. It was clear that Tim Williams had been encouraged to go outside during the night some time, probably on the pretext that one of his precious horses was sick. He had been butchered. The gang had then entered the house, probably raped Rachel Williams, but while she was still alive had torn her unborn baby from her womb and bashed its little head against the doorframe. Rachel had died in the most horrible circumstances from her injuries and from loss of blood.

Peter then went through the rest of the house. He found the Williams' nine-year-old son very dead, crouched in a corner of his room in his pyjamas with dozens of panga cuts all over his body. From the appearance of the door of his room the gang had had to break it down. The last fifteen or twenty minutes of his young life must have been sheer terror. He would have heard his mother's screams and when they eventually came for him there was no mercy, no escape. He died in the most brutal way in a pool of blood.

The police arrived. Peter took them into the house.

The young inspector, recently out from Britain, almost immediately rushed outside and was violently sick.

Once the police had taken control Peter confined himself to phoning Tim Williams' brother who lived twenty miles away.

Peter had left by the time the press came. He really wondered about the future of Kenya.

The murder made headlines in the local press and then overseas. The brutal nature of the attack was sensationalised and did irreparable damage to any positive image the Mau-Mau might have had. They were now clearly established as a bunch of brutal savages. No one could possibly consider them as an alternative government, and no responsible foreign government would have anything to do with them. The merits of their cause were no longer worthy of consideration.

Meetings were held throughout the district looking for a solution to the security problem. At one particularly emotional and noisy meeting at the Ol'Kalou Country Club, the meeting was just about to break up when a voice at the back yelled: "We've got to get rid of the Kikuyu."

There was a moment of silence. Everyone sat down again.

"Explain yourself," demanded the chairman.

"Collect them all up, put them in lorries and send them back to the reserve."

"What will we do for labour?" asked someone.

"Find men from other tribes; plenty of people have done it, including that wog-lover Lawrence," said the voice.

The arguments went on. Eventually the meeting was called to order and the chairman tried to summarise the situation.

"The proposal is to send all the Kikuyu resident within twenty miles of the mountains back to their homes in the reserve."

Shouts and calls of encouragement.

"The major benefit of this is that the support that the gangs in the forest get from those people will dry up."

Further shouts of approbation.

"So the gangs will no longer have a food supply, and they will have nowhere to hide out. Any questions?"

No one raised a hand.

"All those in favour?"

Everyone raised their hands.

"Anyone against?"

Not a murmur.

Peter was not at the meeting. When he heard about it he wondered what he should do.

Eventually he went to the chairman of the meeting, who, suppressing his hostility towards Peter said, "Well, what do you want?"

The chairman was well aware of the fact that Peter had been first at the Williams house after their murder. Peter's behaviour on this occasion had been beyond criticism.

"My Kikuyu labour force left me, as you may know, a few years back."

"So?"

"There were a number of issues which I found I had to deal with, which you may not have had time to think of," Peter continued.

"Such as?"

"Most of the Kikuyu have livestock on the farms where they work. We need to make sure these are rounded up, sold and the proceeds given to the people who own the livestock."

"O.K.; who is going to do that?"

"I will if you think it appropriate."

"Of course it's appropriate; we don't want to steal anything that doesn't belong to us. But organising all that - you're welcome to it," said the chairman.

Within weeks every Kikuyu family living closer than twenty miles from the Aberdares had been identified; their possessions were packed up and they were shipped back to their supposed homes in the Kikuyu reserve. Something like thirty thousand people were sent back to the reserve in this way.

Peter knew he could do nothing to change the decision, although he knew the real hardship it would cause. He thought the best thing he could do was to make sure that at least some humanity prevailed and he spent much of his own resources in making sure that individual families' livestock was accounted for and recorded. He then had all the cattle, sheep and goats penned into a large boma on a piece of ground near the church. He had made contact with all the butcheries in the region and managed to sell the livestock at reasonable prices over a period of two months. Robert and John helped out while they were back on the farm on holiday.

"How are you going to make sure each family gets what is due to them?" asked Robert.

"I have all the addresses; I will just have to go there and dole out the money," answered Peter.

"How do you identify which animals belong to which family?" asked John.

"That would be too complicated. We know that, for example, a particular family had three cows and two goats; there will be a standard payment per cow or per goat," answered Peter.

Peter eventually sold over one thousand head of cattle, two thousand sheep and two thousand goats. He then made his way through Kiambu, Thika and Fort Hall and managed to find the three thousand families involved.

He did the job out of what he saw as a need to alleviate the hardship that moving all these people had involved. It took him months and many journeys to find everyone but during this time he became very well-known indeed throughout Kikuyuland.

The mystique that surrounded him as a result of the shoot-out with Waichagga's people was enhanced as he was seen around the villages doling out money. It was an act of kindness and consideration greatly appreciated by the Kikuyu.

He tried to see Rafiki a few times during these trips. She avoided him and her father blocked his way more than once. Peter did sense a softening in her father's attitude but he still wouldn't let Peter near her or the child.

The authorities were absolutely furious when they found out what the settlers had done. The last thing they needed was a huge influx of people into an already crowded reserve.

"Who the hell do these people think they are?" fumed the Governor to no one in particular. "Taking the law into their own hands."

Brian Johns, the ADC, was eventually sent into the district to find out what was really going on. He came to see Peter. They greeted each other warmly.

"You're involved in this bloody mess, Peter; what's the background?" asked Brian.

"I wasn't at the meeting that took the decision," said Peter. "I only got involved afterwards and then only on the periphery."

Peter explained what he was doing with the cattle.

"Why this action?" asked Brian.

"It has a long history," said Peter. Peter then went on to explain the feeling in the district that the Government had known about the Mau-Mau for years beforehand and had done nothing about it. He told Brian about the George Athill case, where a person with connections had got off scot-free when he should be in jail.

"The security situation in the district is appalling. The feeling among the locals is that the farmers in this area have borne the brunt of the Government's incompetence and fraudulent dealings and farms are still being raided and people attacked almost on a daily basis. As I said, I have had nothing to do with the decision to move all these people, but it was done out of frustration. The farmers around here are not bad people, but they have seen the value of their farms drop to virtually nothing just because of what they see as Government bungling. We live here, Brian; when you lot have returned to jolly old Blighty on fat pensions, we'll still be here facing the music." Peter became quite heated.

Brian was quite taken aback by the vehemence in Peter's voice.

"The Governor is talking about sending troops in to sort you lot out," said Brian.

Peter went white with anger. "If you are unable to sort out a few thousand untrained Kikuyu running about in the bush, what earthly chance to do you think you'll have against the farmers here, most of whom have some military training, all of whom are well armed and all of whom are really fed up. Think of what the press in Britain would say. For Christ's sake man, talk sense."

They were both silent for a minute.

"Tell you what," said Peter. "Let's go and see Dave Gibb; my guess is that he will agree with much of what I have said."

They drove the twenty miles to Dave's farm. Margaret glowered at Peter but she kept her peace.

On the way there they stopped once or twice to admire the view of Mount Kenya and the Aberdares and the Wanjohe. Peter pointed out the developments that had occurred over the years. Brian was able to admire and appreciate the well-kept, productive farms and the effort that had gone into developing and maintaining them.

"I wonder how long this can last," he thought. "It's as close to paradise as anything I've ever seen."

Dave told Brian much the same as Peter had.

"What do the farmers here want?" asked Brian.

"Control over their own security, and some assurance regarding the future," answered Dave. "Is there any chance the Governor could be persuaded to come up here and see the situation for himself?"

"Maybe," said Brian.

Months later the Governor did pay a three day visit to the district. The security situation had improved dramatically as far as the farmers were concerned. Everyone in the district attributed that to the removal of the Kikuyu and the resultant destruction of the support base for the gangs in the mountains. The action that the settlers had taken still rankled with the authorities but the liaison between the security forces and the farmers had been strengthened and any minor incursion into the district was dealt with quickly.

Brian had persuaded the Governor that to send British troops into the district to "sort out" the farmers was not a good idea and would make an already bad situation worse.

"There are women and children up there," he said. "Can you imagine the sort of press you would get in England if so much as a hair on the head of one child was harmed?"

He shuddered.

The Governor went to several well attended meetings in the district. To make it less formal, the meetings were held in some of the larger houses.

The settlers were now much happier with the security arrangements and were slowly gaining confidence. Land prices had improved slightly.

In all his discussions there was a sense of the need to allay people's fears about the future. Occasionally a farmer sold up and moved to England, Australia or South Africa, but most wanted to stay on the basis that they could live peacefully and properly educate their children.

After the visit the Governor, Peter, Dave Gibb and Brian had a discussion.

"Kenyatta and his successors are not going away," said Peter. "The security situation may be under control now but there needs to be a political settlement."

Dave said, "Independence is really an impractical dream. If you do give the Africans one man one vote I can only see chaos. They have no hope of running this country properly; it will be fifty or one hundred years before that can happen."

"Will the British Government be prepared to garrison this country forever just to protect a few white farmers?" asked Peter. "The world is changing. If there is to be a settlement, then we, the farmers, will have to be part of it and you," Peter pointed a finger at the Governor," will have to foot the bill. I suppose that's the stark choice - either try to keep the lid on the political aspirations of the Africans for a few more years, at heaven knows what price in terms of lives and money, - or to come to some sort of a political settlement, which will have to include the farmers. Clearly the people at Lodwar need to be part of it also; they represent the only coherent leadership group from the African side in the country."

The Governor and his group went back to Nairobi with much to think about.

Rafiki had found it more and more difficult to arrange food supplies into the mountains. Almost all of the Kikuyu in the Kinangop, Kipipiri and Wanjohe areas had been removed and sent back to the reserves. The motorbike that had been confiscated by the police had been replaced and she had spent her time trying to persuade the very few Kikuyu in the area to cooperate with her.

The situation had, however, altogether changed. The families that had been left behind were now thoroughly intimidated and were under threat that if they did not behave they would be sent back to the reserve. Most had come to some sort of compromise arrangement with their employers that they would keep a low profile and behave themselves. Some employers did not want it known in the district that for purely selfish reasons they had kept some key Kikuyu families in their employ. Any breach of security, such as supplying food to the now rather few gangs in the forest, would be severely embarrassing to all concerned. Rafiki's visits were, therefore, less and less welcome. Eventually one of the families deep in the Wanjohe went to their employer. Unusually both the husband and his wife went to see the employer. Rafiki had always dealt with the women directly, so if anything the wife was more involved than the husband was.

"Yes, what is it?" asked Richard Johnson impatiently.

He had wondered many times why he had protected this family from removal. They and their forefathers had been on the farm that he had inherited from his father for as long as he could remember. He'd kept them out of a sense of loyalty as much as anything else.

"Shauri (trouble) bwana," was Abraham's response.

"What bloody shauri, come on, speak up man."

"Mau-Mau," was the response.

"Yes," Richard was more cautious now.

"They want us to send food," Wanjiku, Abraham's wife piped up unexpectedly.

Her husband looked at her sideways.

"The women these days," he thought, "are getting above themselves; they need to show more respect." He didn't say anything though.

"This Rafiki, she came to us to ask us to supply food," Wanjiku went on.

"Yes, which Rafiki? Do you mean Peter Lawrence's Rafiki?" asked Richard.

"Ndio (yes) bwana, the same one."

"When?" asked Richard.

"A few days ago; she says she will come back," Wanjiku had now taken over the whole conversation.

"Why didn't you come here and tell me before?" asked Richard.

Abraham and Wanjiku looked at each other. Clearly she had wanted to come but he wanted no trouble.

"We were frightened," was the eventual answer from Wanjiku.

Richard had some sympathy; the security forces had been unable to protect the whites, let alone the thousands of Africans caught up in this thing. If they didn't cooperate they were often hacked to death on the spot.

"Will she come back?" Richard now asked quietly. The whole conversation was conducted in Swahili because he spoke no Kikuyu.

"Yes," was the almost whispered answer from Wanjiku. She was now terrified. She actually liked Rafiki but the situation she was in was impossible. Her priority now was her family.

"When?"

"Tomorrow night."

"Tomorrow night?" asked Richard.

Wanjiku nodded.

"Where?"

"She will come to the hut at about eight o'clock on a motorbike; she will stay until just before dawn, then leave," Wanjiku answered.

"Are you sure about this?" asked Richard.

Both Wanjiku and Abraham nodded.

He'd heard the sound of a motorbike once in the past few weeks and wondered about it; now he knew.

Most of the farmers nearby were members of the police reserve. Richard went to see his local patrol commander.

"Rafiki, you say?" asked Piet Van Vuuren, the local police reserve commander. "Are you sure?"

"Yes, absolutely," was Richard's response.

"They've been looking for her for years and have not been able to pick her up; it would be quite a coup for our little group to arrest her," Van Vuuren mused.

"Don't you think we should get the police involved?" Richard was becoming uncomfortable.

"No, no, it's only one woman, who hopefully will be asleep; should be easy," responded Piet.

They arranged for a patrol of six including Richard, Piet, George Athill, who lived nearby, and three others.

They all came to Richard's home just before dusk. They would have supper there and when they heard the motorbike would close in over the next two hours.

Rafiki was desperate. Food supplies to the mountains had almost dried up and she had had word from Kahinga that unless she could organise more supplies within the next month, the gangs would either have to eat berries in the forest or come out. She was relying on Wanjiku, who had been a great asset in the early years of the conflict but now seemed a little reluctant; Rafiki was hoping that with a little persuasion she could be prevailed upon.

She rode into Richard Johnson's yard at about eight and was a little surprised to see four or five cars there. Maybe he was having a party. She hoped that meant that the Wazungu would be less alert than normal. Life had been very difficult in recent months and she had had some narrow escapes. She was now well known and if she were stopped at all by any security force people, it would mean certain arrest and imprisonment.

They heard the motorbike from inside the house.

"Dead on time," observed Richard.

"We'll wait fifteen or twenty minutes, then take up our positions," said Piet.

They all checked their weapons and waited nervously, George in particular. He was determined to get Rafiki and he'd armed himself with a police sten-gun with that in mind. Fifteen minutes elapsed and Piet signalled for the patrol to take up their positions. It looked more difficult now that it was dark, and all of them wished there were more than just the six of them.

Rafiki had confidently ridden up to Abraham and Wanjiku's hut, killed the engine of her motorbike and knocked on the door of the hut. She was quickly ushered in. She took off her helmet and sat down. Almost immediately she could feel that the atmosphere had changed from her previous visit. The warmth was no longer there; neither Wanjiku nor Abraham would look her in the eyes. She quietly ate the meal of ogalie, vegetables, gravy and a small amount of meat and chatted about inconsequential things like the weather and the children's health. Rafiki wondered what was up; then it hit her. "The cars," she thought. "I'll bet Wanjiku and Abraham have told Richard Johnson about their visit and the cars are part of the reception committee."

She wondered what to do. Her only hope was immediate flight; if they were relying on her to spend the night here so they could catch her asleep, then they might not yet be in position. She said to Wanjiku as she started putting on her helmet again, "I've forgotten something at the last place I visited; I will be back soon."

She looked at the anxious faces of Wanjiku and her husband. There was no doubt they had guilt and sorrow written all over their faces. They had obviously spilt the beans to Johnson and he had organised a patrol to arrest her.

She went outside into the now cool night. Her best bet was to race the motorbike as fast as she could down the track, through the farmyard and out onto the road. She was pretty sure she could give them the slip after that. Her knowledge of all the little tracks and side roads was now second to none and she would be back in Thika by morning. She had thought of escaping on foot but if they knew she was there they would probably be able to pick her up before she reached the safety of the forest. No, the best bet was the motorbike. She hoped that Johnson and the others were not yet in place.

She kick started the bike; it started first time and she held the engine on low revs for a few seconds.

Piet and the rest of the patrol all heard what they thought was a bike starting up. Two of the patrol had been sent to positions to prevent Rafiki escaping on foot; the other four had taken up positions near the track leading to the solitary hut.

Suddenly the engine on the motorbike was gunned and Piet and his men could see the faint shadow of a motorbike racing down the track in the moonlight. Piet jumped out onto the track and tried to get her to stop. Rafiki swerved slightly to avoid him and accelerated hard down the track. The other two members of the patrol held their fire for fear of hitting Piet. George was the last line of defence; he was going to get Rafiki if it was the last thing he did. He could see the bike racing down the uneven track; he couldn't see her but he took careful aim with his sten-gun at the shape, now not more than forty yards away, and fired. George was unused to using the sten-gun and was not prepared for the barrel to jump up. Most of the shots went high; otherwise Rafiki would have been cut to pieces.

Rafiki thought she had got away; then there was a burst of fire from just in front of her and to the right. She felt herself being picked up and hurled off the bike by the two heavy slugs as they went into her gut. The bike went hurtling off and crashed about thirty yards away. Rafiki lay where she had fallen; she was stunned.

"Got the little bitch," yelled George and he ran over to where she was. He was rapidly joined by the others. Richard Johnson shone a torch into her eyes. Rafiki blinked uncertainly in the bright light.

"She's bleeding from the stomach, I think," said Richard. "I think we should get her to a doctor."

"I think we should finish her off here and now," said George aggressively. "Save us all a lot of trouble in the future." He cocked his sten-gun. Piet van Vuuren pushed the barrel up so that the shots went harmlessly up in the air. He kicked George in the groin and disarmed him.

"No one shoots prisoners on my watch," he growled. George stumbled away.

Richard Johnson brought his car. They had taken off Rafiki's helmet and exposed the wounds in her stomach, which were bleeding profusely.

"We'll have to bandage this up and get her to the doctor in Ol'Kalou as soon as we can," said Piet.

They put her in the car and took her to the house. They laid her down on the veranda and tightly wrapped her up in a multitude of bandages, which partially stopped the blood flow. Richard didn't think of bringing her into the house. He'd never had a black woman in the house in his life - all his servants were male - and he wasn't going to start now. Richard's wife tried to give Rafiki some water.

Richard and Piet wrapped Rafiki up in blankets, and bundled her into the back of his car.

"Try to phone the doctor and alert him," yelled Piet.

Richard was one of the few fortunate farmers to have a phone.

Rafiki had said nothing during this ordeal. She was in shock from the bullets and falling off the bike. Apart from the bullet wounds she had a few cuts and bruises from the fall. She was feeling faint but remained conscious all the way during the thirty minute ride to Ol'Kalou.

The doctor was waiting for them. Piet and Richard carried her into the surgery. The doctor removed most of the rest of her now very bloody clothing and the bandages. There were two bullet holes in the right side of her stomach. They found the Beretta.

"No exit wounds; Jesus, this is really serious. She will die unless she has an immediate operation. There will be massive internal bleeding. She will be dead within hours unless she is operated on," he said anxiously.

Rafiki slipped in and out of consciousness. During the next few hours she was conscious of being put in an aeroplane and being flown for what seemed like hours.

The police had managed to locate an air ambulance and lit a few flares alongside the straight piece of road near the Ol'Kalou railway station.

Within five hours of being shot Rafiki was being operated on in the main black hospital, the Queen Elizabeth, in Nairobi. She was in the operating theatre for several hours and had lost a great deal of blood.

"You'd better not let her die," said the new superintendent of police, John Fawkes, to the surgeon. "We really need her for a major show trial."

"My job is to worry about lives, not show trials," was the response.

The doctor from Ol'Kalou had accompanied Rafiki to the hospital in Nairobi. He wondered if anyone had had the decency to tell Peter what had happened. He decided to phone the Marks, Peter's neighbours.

"Please can you get a message to Peter Lawrence to phone me urgently in Nairobi. It's very urgent," he said.

Peter phoned back from the Marks about an hour later.

"Look Peter, I have very bad news for you. Rafiki was shot and captured last night in the Wanjohe. She's now in hospital in Nairobi. I'm afraid she may not pull through; she lost a lot of blood," the doctor reported.

As the doctor was speaking, an ice cold fear crept into Peter's stomach. Although they had been separated for some years now, his feelings for Rafiki had intensified. He could almost see the end of the conflict, which he hoped would mean that he and Rafiki could be together again. He couldn't bear to think about her dying; and what about their child? He listened to the doctor. "I will come right away," he said. "Will you be there?"

"Yes, I will stay here until you arrive," said the doctor. "The newspapers have now got on to the story, so you will be besieged if you aren't careful," he warned.

Peter drove as fast as he could and a couple of hours later he arrived at the Queen Elizabeth Hospital. He spoke in Kikuyu to one of the gardeners, who gladly showed him into the hospital through the back way.

He found an orderly, who, again because of the language, actually took him to Rafiki's bedside. The whole hospital knew about Rafiki and the place was buzzing with excitement. There was a Wakamba askari outside the door. Even he knew about Peter and, after a few words, let him in without a murmur.

Peter approached the bed. Rafiki was lying peacefully, with all sorts of tubes and drips hanging out of her. She was still beautiful, he thought; he went and held her hand. Her eyelids flickered open and she tried to focus.

"Hello, it's you," she said weakly.

He squeezed her hand.

"I came when I heard," he said.

The doctor from Ol'Kalou came in, closely followed by the surgeon.

"Who the hell are you?" asked the surgeon.

"Peter Lawrence," was the reply.

The surgeon looked blankly at Peter; he'd only been in the country a few weeks and the name meant nothing.

The doctor from Ol'Kalou took him aside and explained the situation. He kept looking at Peter.

"My concern is only for the patient," said the surgeon, "If I think you are hindering her progress I will banish you, otherwise you can come and go as you please."

Peter smiled and promised to behave. "How is she?" he asked.

"Well it will be touch and go for a few days. We've now stabilised her.

I've removed the bullets and I hope that no infection will set in. We'll know in a week."

Peter spent the best part of the day there and then decided to try to make peace with Rafiki's father.

He found the village near Thika and eventually found her father.

"I thought I told you not to come here again," said Wainaina but in a semi-friendly tone.

"Yes, but I have some bad news for you; I thought I would come here myself and tell you," replied Peter.

"Is it about Rafiki?" the old man looked sharply at Peter.

"She was shot and wounded last night; she is in hospital in Nairobi," Peter explained.

"Will she be all right?"

"Maybe; we will know in a few days," replied Peter.

"I knew those baboon Mau-Mau would get her into trouble." He held his head in his hands.

"I'll take you to see her tomorrow," offered Peter.

The old man looked up. "Thank you."

Peter shared the evening meal with Wainaina and the rest of the family. They all spoke of Rafiki and what she meant to them.

Wainaina began to get an inkling of how Peter felt about Rafiki. Little Kamau, now nearly seven, was growing up and was part of the group. He was curious about this white stranger who joined them for the evening meal.

Peter spoke to him a few times in the normal course of the meal. Kamau only spoke Kikuyu. Peter was proud to see what a big strong boy he was. He was confident and held his own in the group.

Peter was certain that if Rafiki recovered - and he couldn't think about her not recovering - she would go to jail, probably for a long time. He would have to talk both Rafiki and the old man into letting him, Peter, bring the child up. Whilst he respected the Kikuyu tradition, he felt that Kamau would lead a much fuller life if he were educated in the European tradition and perhaps went to university outside Kenya, probably Britain. He, Peter, could certainly deliver all that and he didn't think that Wainaina could, especially bearing in mind the rather desultory education that Rafiki herself had received. He wondered what had been done about Kamau's education to date; there was a mission school run by the Roman Catholics nearby; maybe he was going to that.

Peter spent the night in a nearby hotel and picked Wainaina up the next morning. They went to the hospital. Peter had seen the headlines in the East African Daily News: "LAWRENCE'S WHORE, WOUNDED, IN CUSTODY"

He knew it was something he would have to deal with. They tried going in the back entrance to the hospital again. This time the press was ready for them; they had been tipped off.

About twenty reporters from all over the world were waiting for him. There was a mad scramble and questions were yelled at him from all sides.

"Why are you here?"

"I've come to see Rafiki," Peter answered.

"Will she live?"

"I think so, yes," replied Peter.

"Have you no shame? She is a criminal; she deserves to hang."

"She is the mother of my child; whatever she has done I still love her," said Peter.

"You're a traitor to your kind."

"I've suffered more than most of you in this conflict;" he showed them the wounds from the attack on the farms. "My only interest is the long term prosperity of Kenya."

The hectoring went on for about thirty minutes. Wainaina was completely bamboozled by the whole affair. Peter had tried unsuccessfully to push him through the throng.

"Who is that old geezer with you?"

"Rafiki's father, my future father in-law," Peter replied

There was derisive laughter.

Eventually one of the American reporters became more sympathetic, realising that Peter was doing what any decent son-in-law would do under the circumstances. The reporter tried to explain that to his colleagues.

"Where's the child?"

"With his grandmother," replied Peter.

"Who will look after him now?"

"He's being looked after," Peter started to become impatient.

After a few more ribald and insensitive jibes, Peter and Wainaina were eventually let through the throng.

Their picture was on the front page of the local press the next day. This did Peter's reputation with the local Africans no harm at all, though it naturally added to the revulsion felt for him by the whites.

Most Africans who saw the picture admired his courage.

When they arrived at the ward, Rafiki was awake and was looking better. She was pleased to see Peter and Wainaina there together.

Peter took Wainaina to see Rafiki every day. After the first few days, the reporters stopped coming to the hospital and they were allowed in unhindered.

After about a week, when Rafiki was sitting up, the surgeon said to Peter, "I think she is completely out of danger now. There is no sign of infection; I'm sure she'll be O.K."

Peter translated that for Wainaina.

"I expect we can release her within two or three weeks," he added.

Peter knew what that meant. Prison and then a trial.

He saw about getting a decent lawyer for her defence.

After about ten days, Peter raised the question of how their son was to be raised.

"Look, you are going to be in jail for a while, even if there is a settlement," Peter said. "I really would like him to come back to Naseby with me. He can do the correspondence course that you did." Peter smiled at the memory.

"There is a woman in the district who can supervise that and maybe Kinua's wife, Sarah, can come back and look after him. She is now back with Zacharia and he's finding her and her two children rather a handful."

There was a long discussion between the three of them. Wainaina was concerned that Kamau would become 'another little M'zungu' and forget his Kikuyu origins.

Eventually it was agreed that Kamau could go and live with Peter, but that he would return to Wainaina's village for a few days every month and that he would have to participate in the initiation ceremonies that all Kikuyu youth took part in at the age of puberty.

Rafiki was eventually taken off to prison, to await her trial. Peter had seen her every day in the three weeks since she had been wounded. He was more committed than ever to her. He was very anxious about the trial; she could face the death penalty on two counts, firstly, belonging to a terrorist organisation and secondly, carrying an unlicensed weapon. The trial, however, would take months to prepare and then weeks to conduct.

Peter's priority now was to attend to his children. Both Robert and John were at school in Nairobi: 'The Duke of York School for European Boys', as the signboard at the entrance to the school proudly announced. Kamau, as things presently stood, would be ineligible to go to that school since his mother was black.

Peter went to the school to watch Robert play rugby. Robert was now, at seventeen, the star of the first fifteen. John joined Peter on the touchline. This was the week that they played the other large Government school for white boys in Nairobi, the Prince of Wales school. Every age group played matches. Over the years the 'Prinso' had done much better than the 'Duko' in these matches. This year, for the first time ever, it was thought that the 'Duko' had a chance of winning the first fifteen game. The game was hard-fought and very even; with two minutes to go to full time the score was drawn at eight points all. The 'Duko' had the put-in on a scrum about ten yards out. The ball came out to the scrum half, then to the fly half; Robert was playing inside centre. He took the ball on an angled run and without having a hand laid on him went in to score under the posts. The conversion was easy and the 'Duko' won the game by thirteen points to eight. The crowd erupted; Robert was everyone's hero. He came over to Peter and John. Peter wanted to hug him but knew that would cause him embarrassment with his peers; they shook hands.

Peter had arranged with the headmaster to take the boys out for Saturday night. The school was a boarding school so they would have to be back there by 6pm the next day. Peter needed some privacy and had taken rooms at the Norfolk hotel.

During dinner the talk had mainly been about rugby and Robert's great triumph. Peter did not want to spoil the evening, but at the end, over coffee, he turned the conversation round to Rafiki.

"Oh, how is she?" said John. "I want to see her again; it seems years since we last saw her."

"Well, you know she was shot, and she will probably spend a very long time in jail. I'm going to do my best for her but it's a very bad situation," said Peter.

Robert knew what was coming.

"So what's going to happen to Nusu-Nusu?" he asked innocently.

Peter hated that name but didn't react. "I've agreed with her and her family that Kamau will come home and live with us," Peter responded.

"Education?" asked Robert.

"Well he's been at the local Catholic Mission School, but I'm going to use the correspondence course I used with Rafiki," said Peter.

John was delighted. Robert wasn't sure how he felt. He would be taking his Higher School Certificate next year and would then escape to Britain and university, where his father's reputation in Kenya would cease to be an issue.

Peter said, "I understand this is difficult for you both, but we've been through a lot together," he looked meaningfully at Robert, "and this is important to me. Kamau is as much my son as you are and I really owe it to him to do the best I can under the circumstances."

Peter then went on to explain how he thought Kenya would have to change and that in the not too distant future it would be granted independence from Britain. He told the boys that the education in Kenya would have to become non-discriminatory, which would mean that the 'Duko' would have to admit children of other races. He told them in strict secrecy of his visit to Lodwar and his discussions with Jomo Kenyatta and how he thought that Kenyatta would probably be the first African Head of State of the newly independent Kenya.

"If this is all going to happen, what happens to Naseby?" asked Robert.

"Don't know yet," said Peter. "Land is a big political issue. They may want to buy it all back and settle Kikuyu there."

"Will they be able to run it like you do?" asked Robert.

"Not without education and training," said Peter. "Although I expect the land will be split up into forty or fifty acre lots more in keeping with what the African is used to. Maybe we have to find African solutions to African problems. I'm really not sure that imposing European norms on everything here is altogether helpful."

The discussion went on into the night. Robert and John learned what Peter thought about the future; things would certainly change and this would affect them all. Peter also made it clear that becoming a farmer and inheriting Naseby was something they couldn't depend on. He told both boys that education was the key, and if they had a good education, the world could be at their feet.

"Tomorrow," said Peter, "we are going to Thika to see Kamau and his grandfather and their family."

"Fine," said Robert. That didn't bother him at all. He'd spent half his young life playing with the African children on the farm. He would be perfectly at home.

The next day they went to Wainaina's village. Peter had arranged for Stanley to be there; he was now aged about twenty and was also attending the mission school. He hoped to go to Nairobi University within the next two years.

The day went better than Peter could possibly have expected. As soon as they arrived and after the greeting, the boys and Stanley went away and played soccer with all the other village kids plus Kamau. Some of the kids were a little shy of Robert and John but when they found that they both spoke fluent Kikuyu, the barriers came down.

They spent almost all the day there and when the time came for them to leave it seemed almost natural for Kamau to take his few belongings and climb into Peter's car with the other two boys.

Robert started to talk English on the way home but Kamau couldn't understand and kept asking what was being said. They all reverted to Kikuyu.

When they got to the school John insisted that he show Kamau his dormitory. Kamau was completely unconcerned and wandered about as if he owned the place, despite the curious looks he got from the other boys.

Eventually they said goodbye and Peter started on the journey back to Naseby. They picked Kinua's wife, Sarah, and her two children up at Dave Gibb's farm and arrived home by almost nine o'clock. Zacharia had been happy to see the back of Sarah. As far as he was concerned, his son-in-law was a disaster, having spent all of the last few years in the mountains with Kahinga.

"He still owes me three cows as part of the bride price," he confided to Peter.

Peter was elated. He had Kamau back and he could start to educate him. Rafiki was alive when she could very easily have been dead. He knew he had a great battle to face on her behalf but he was ready to face it. He had high hopes that Rafiki would be released as part of a general amnesty when a political settlement was reached.

He tucked Kamau into his bed. It was the first time for years that he had slept in a bed with sheets on. He was used to sleeping on the ground.

Chapter 25

Kamau was soon enrolled with the Rift Valley Correspondence school. He needed daily supervision, so Peter engaged the services of a near neighbour, Maureen Smith, who was a qualified teacher. Maureen came over every day to help Kamau with his lessons.

Peter had built a thatched banda, a wattle and daub house, near the side of the house for the schoolroom and Kamau soon became king of the roost there.

After the first week or so Peter asked Maureen about Kamau's English.

"It's not great, but it's not too bad," she said. "He told me they taught in English at the mission school, so he understands most things."

"The little so and so," said Peter. "He was trying to let on that he understands no English at all. He made me and Robert and John speak to him in Kikuyu."

"He's a devil all right," said Maureen.

Peter could see that she was already becoming fond of him.

Kamau was keen on his lessons and progressed rapidly. He also loved being on the farm with Peter and going round with him in the pick-up truck. He was into absolutely everything; on one occasion Peter found him pouring water from a watering can into the petrol tank of the pick-up truck. He had to explain to Kamau that the water went into the radiator, and he let Kamau help him with emptying the fuel tank and cleaning out all the fuel lines.

Apart from his lessons and travelling around with Peter, Kamau found himself without many friends of his own age. None of the whites in the area would have dreamt of inviting Kamau, a half caste, to their home to play with their children, who in any event even from the age of seven were away at boarding school.

Kamau therefore gravitated to the village where the Wakamba farm workers now resided. He was surprised to find that none of them spoke Kikuyu, but after a few days picked up a few words of Kamba and within a short time he had the soccer game going that Robert and John had had in their younger days with Stanley and his Kikuyu friends.

When John and Robert came back for the school holidays they found Kamau very much at home. Robert was rather disdainful of his younger half-brother and spent very little time with him. Much to Peter's annoyance, Robert insisted on referring to him as Nusu-Nusu.

John's response was quite different, probably because of his fondness for Rafiki, and he really took Kamau under his wing. He got him on Flicker, the little Somali pony, who was now quite old but quiet and entirely suitable for a young beginner. He also taught him how to shoot, using the airgun.

Once a month Peter visited Rafiki in prison in Nairobi and dropped Kamau with Wainaina at his village near Thika. Peter tried to impress on Kamau the importance of maintaining his links with his grandparents and generally Kamau cooperated and enjoyed the place where he had spent five years of his life. The visits helped him maintain his friendship with his Kikuyu friends and his fluency in the language. More and more he spoke to Peter in English.

Peter had engaged an eminent Indian lawyer, Vijaya Singh, to conduct Rafiki's defence.

The charges against Rafiki were very serious: belonging to a terrorist organisation, aiding and abetting a terrorist organisation, and carrying an unlicensed firearm were among the most serious. She was also charged with stealing food, stealing the motorbike, and entering a prohibited area.

Peter, Rafiki and Singh spent many hours preparing the defence. Their defence would centre around three main points:

- That whilst Rafiki admitted to being a member of the Mau-Mau, she claimed she should be treated as a prisoner-of-war since she belonged to a military organisation.
- That all the evidence relating to her supporting a terrorist organisation was totally anecdotal, without a shred of evidence, and should be thrown out.
- The question of carrying a firearm was more difficult. There was no evidence linking the firearm to Peter. The gun had been left by the Italian prisoners-of-war and had never been licensed. In the end they decided to claim that it had been given to her by one of Kahinga's men and had only been used in self-defence.

The latter point at least was true. They waited and waited for a trial date.

In the meanwhile, the situation of Kahinga in the mountains was desperate. The security forces had dozens of patrols in the mountains all the time. Most of the other gangs in the mountains had been killed, captured or persuaded to give up and join the security forces via the pseudo-gang operation. Food supplies from the farms had dried up completely now that Rafiki was in jail; they had been severely curtailed before that, due to most of the Kikuyu being removed by the white settlers from the areas near the forest.

Kahinga and Kinua still had fifteen well-armed men in their gang and no-one except them knew about Dik-Dik base. All the other bases had been discovered and overrun by the security forces, so Kahinga never went near them. They were forced to live on antelope when they had the time to go out and hunt, but they had to be cautious doing that in case it drew attention from the security forces. So their diet consisted mainly of roots and grubs. Every month or so they would go down into the Wanjohe or Ol'Joro Orok areas, attack the livestock on a farm, and burn whatever they could.

The security forces had on their terms almost won the war, but were constantly frustrated by these pin-prick attacks, which demonstrated that the Mau-Mau was still operating and that the armed resistance to colonial rule still continued.

Kahinga decided to take his whole gang to attack a major dairy farm just west of the road between Ol'Kalou and Ol'Joro Orok. This was a departure from the practice of the past two years, where only a few members of the gang at a time had ventured out of the forest and then mainly to attack farms close to the foothills of the mountains and the safety of the forest. It took them two nights to get there; they only moved at night, holing up in dense patches of bush during the day. They did manage to break into a store-room on one of the farms and steal some posho (maize meal), which made an enormous difference to their morale.

They found the farm; the cattle were totally unprotected, since the farmers had sensed that the danger of their being attacked so far from the mountains was very low.

Within a few minutes they had hacked the Achilles tendons of fifty head of purebred Friesian cows in milk and they went on to destroy a further one hundred head. The farmer would be virtually ruined. They withdrew and were six or seven miles away when the farmer discovered his mutilated herd just before dawn. The security forces were now ready for this type of attack and within thirty minutes of being alerted, they had descended on the farm with more than thirty men and some tracker dogs; when it became fully light the police air wing would be brought in by radio.

Kahinga had anticipated this and they threw caution to the winds and made their way back towards the mountains as fast as they could. Part of the tactic when the security forces came too close would be to leave one of their number behind with a rifle and as much ammunition as could be spared, to delay any patrols from following them.

They heard the dogs at about eight in the morning. One of the gang had a large bamboo splinter in his foot and was slowing the rest of them down. They found an outcrop of rocks which had a clear view of the approaches for about five hundred yards. Kahinga and the rest of them escaped into the dense bush behind and ran on; the sooner they could reach the mountains the better.

Corporal Smith was leading his patrol of ten British soldiers. The dogs and the Nderobo tracker were having no trouble following the trail. They came to an open patch of ground with a cluster of grey rocks at the far end. A shot rang out.

"Shit," he thought. "They've decided to stay and fight it out."

He knew there were fifteen of them at least in the gang. His primary concern was the safety of his men. He quickly organised a counter attack with a Bren-gun and two other soldiers shooting at the position from the front, whilst the rest of them went in a circling movement through some bush to the left of the Mau-Mau position. He also called in reinforcements. The Bren was moved closer with the two soldiers providing covering fire; when the Bren was in place, the soldier with that weapon kept firing whilst the two soldiers caught up with him. The firing from the position in the rocks intensified. During one of these manoeuvres one of the riflemen was slightly wounded in the arm. The other soldier decided to take him back to the road for medical attention. The soldier manning the Bren kept up the covering fire and eventually Corporal Smith and the rest of his patrol attacked the position in the rocks from the cover they had crept through. They rushed through the bush, firing as they went, and were surprised there was no return of fire. When they arrived at the position, they found one very ragged Kikuyu, dead with five wounds. He had long hair and Corporal Smith and his men were almost sick when they smelt him. He probably hadn't had a proper wash for two years. There was an army service rifle and about fifty empty shell cases next to the body.

"Only one of the buggers," he said. "We'd better get after the others."

They had been delayed almost two hours, by which time Kahinga and the rest of the gang were two miles further away and within close reach of the forest.

Corporal Smith radioed his position and the situation. By this time more than one hundred men had joined in the hunt. By just after midday, when Kahinga was only about one mile from the refuge of the forest, a plane from the police air wing spotted the gang and called in the reinforcements, who were rushed by road to the appointed position.

Although the gang almost made it to the forest they were forced to turn around and defend themselves. They all found positions and fired volley after volley at the approaching military. Kinua was on the Bren. He said to Kahinga, "Get out now, while there is a lull; leave me two men; we can keep them away for a couple of hours."

Kahinga went with ten of his men. Kinua and the other two kept up a furious firing rate, shooting at everything that moved.

The Bren started to jam and fire slowly. Kinua knew what the problem was. When the gun gets very hot, one needs a larger gas port to let the gases from firing the gun escape more readily. There are four ports on the Bren; he loosened the now very hot barrel, turned to a larger hole on the port with a round of ammunition, and then reassembled the gun. This had taken thirty seconds. He had taken aim and was just about to fire again when there was a large explosion from a mortar bomb behind him; he saw his two colleagues being blown up by the blast and a few seconds later a very large man fell on him with a bayonet to his throat.

"Got you, yer bastard," said the voice. Kinua just heard a lot of voices, since he understood no English, but he knew the game was up. He'd given Kahinga an hour. These people didn't have a hope of catching Kahinga in the forest.

Kinua was pulled roughly to his feet. The Bren was made safe.

Kinua was then violently sick. He couldn't stand the smell of soap from his captors.

He was in rags; barefoot and quite thin from his poor diet and long sojourn in the mountains. His hair was long and matted and had lice in it.

He was handcuffed and taken to a Land Rover.

"Got one here," said the soldier. "Unharmed." "There are two dead in there."

Kinua was eventually taken to Nairobi for interrogation.

Kahinga and his gang ran into the forest with the time that Kinua's action had bought them. A few hundred yards after they had reached what they considered to be safety, they stopped for a breather.

"Safe at last," said Kahinga.

He could not have been more wrong. As far as the security forces were concerned, this was the last major operational gang of the Mau-Mau. The best known leader, Kahinga, was probably leading it. They had put their noses out of the forest and the security forces were determined to make the most of it, so troops and police were poured into the area and the Aberdare forest was flooded with patrols.

Kahinga of course had no radio and had had no contact with the outside world for almost two years. He couldn't possibly understand the changes to the security environment and the fact that the Kenya Government of the day was absolutely determined to capture him as soon as possible.

So the group continued at a much more leisurely pace through the forest towards the Dik-Dik base.

Kahinga had always been cautious when approaching any of his bases. He and one other went to within one hundred yards of the base and then watched for ten minutes. He was just about to give the all clear when he caught a slight movement out of the corner of his eye; it was a soldier lying in wait. Suddenly the whole picture became clear; he could see another ten or twelve soldiers spread out at intervals in front of the base, all lying quietly in wait for him. They withdrew rapidly, joined the others and via a game trail that only they used, started to run straight up the mountain. In order to minimise their tracks they ran on the side of the trail. The objective was to go over the top of Nyandarua, down the other side to Nyeri and then if possible make for the forests of Kirinyaga (Mount Kenya) near Nanyuki.

They stopped every hour for five minutes for a rest and drank from the streams in the mountains whenever they could. They had small amounts of ogalie cooked from the posho they had stolen two nights earlier, and some strips of dried meat.

Once when they were resting in a bush, a platoon of soldiers clattered past noisily, going in the direction opposite to the one they were taking.

"Good," thought Kahinga. "Maybe they will cover all our footprints."

They went up over the top of Nyandarua and then made their laborious and slippery way down the other side. They travelled at night, which was more difficult because of the dark and more dangerous because of the wild animals.

Unbeknown to Kahinga the security forces now had more than two thousand armed troops and police pursuing his now much depleted gang of poorly equipped men.

The anxiety in the security force headquarters grew when they had had no contact with the gang for two days, then three days, then four. They were being made to look ridiculous. The news of this pursuit had been the subject of numerous press briefings, in the expectation that Kahinga's capture was imminent.

Kahinga and his men had covered forty to fifty miles of really rough country per day since Kinua had made his stand. They were now in more open country between the forests of Nyandarua and Kirinyaga and they saw and presumably were seen by a number of people.

Gradually a picture began to emerge at police headquarters, since because of the publicity many of the sightings were reported.

A further one thousand troops and police were sent to the Kirinyaga area.

Kahinga and his gang had had the majesty of Kirinyaga in full view all day and although it was now dusk they confidently ran on in the expectation that they would reach the safety of the forests there during the night.

Kahinga then asked guidance from Ngai the God that all Kikuyu believed was resident on the peaks of Kirinyaga. Comforted, the group ran on. They came round a corner on the path they were following; the whole group was dimly visible in the waning daylight.

Two Brens opened up on the group from about two hundred yards away and then there was a volley of rifle shots.

Everyone in the group was either hit or dived for cover. Kahinga was shot in the left arm, the right thigh and the stomach. Before they could collect their thoughts, about fifty soldiers and police charged across the open ground. One or two of Kahinga's men managed to shoot back. Then it was all over; they were completely overwhelmed.

"Three dead, five slightly wounded and one severely wounded, two unharmed," was the verdict.

"Do you have Kahinga?" yelled the commanding officer.

"I think so sir, severely wounded, sir, needs immediate attention, sir," was the response.

Kahinga was put on a stretcher as far as the road, then taken to Nanyuki hospital and then transferred to Nairobi.

A few days later, when it was clear that Kahinga would survive, he was paraded in front of the world's media. What they saw was a rather thin black man with very long, unkempt hair; he was naked to the waist and below it was covered by a white sheet, which contrasted with the blackness of his skin. What struck people most was his eyes; some saw the frightened eyes of a captured, wounded animal; some people saw contempt; most others saw defiance – continuing, on-going defiance. This may have been a captured man, but it was certainly not a broken man, not in any sense of the word.

Chapter 26

Robert had now taken his Higher School Certificate and his results were such that he had gained easy entry into Oxford University in Britain. Although he had a deep understanding of the Kikuyu, he felt that much had been stolen from him as a result of his mother's death and his father's relationship with Rafiki. He felt that he had been confined to the fringes of society through no action or fault of his own. Whilst he had enjoyed and really treasured his relationship with Stanley and the other Kikuyu boys and girls on Naseby, he would have liked to have similar close relationships with boys and girls of his own kind. Although friendships had existed, they had not developed because of parental interference. Most parents wanted their children to have nothing to do with Peter Lawrence or his children.

Robert was certainly the leading boy of his year at school both in terms of academic and athletic ability. He felt that in his last year at school he should have been head boy, but even before it was announced he knew in his heart of hearts he would not be given the post; the parents and the board of Governors of the school just would not have stood for Peter Lawrence's son to have been made head boy. For the same reason he was never appointed captain of the school rugby fifteen, a post he richly deserved both in terms of playing ability and leadership. His attitude towards Kamau was strongly coloured by these experiences, which had to a greater or lesser extent gone on since primary school.

Towards the end of his school career he had been selected to play for an East African fifteen against the British Lions, who were on their way from one of their regular trips to South Africa. The Lions won the match easily but they were very impressed with Robert's performance, he being the only schoolboy selected to play for East Africa, and the British players showered him with invitations to join their respective clubs back home.

Once Robert had his university acceptance, he couldn't wait to get out of Kenya. He was beginning to realise the deficiencies of Kenya's political system, but he did not feel responsible for the society and had been deprived of many of the benefits enjoyed by other 'European' boys. He was not bitter, but was keen to make a fresh start in a country where no stigma was attached to him.

Despite the fact that he had fought side by side with his father in the attack on the farm, his relationship with his father was still distant and the return of Kamau to Naseby was an added aggravation.

Peter and John took Robert to the boat train in Nairobi and after an entertaining but uneventful voyage from Mombasa to Tilbury in the London docks on a Union Castle boat, Robert found himself in Giles and Louise's mansion in Belgravia in London.

Kamau was very happy on the farm. He missed his mother and didn't really understand the concept of prison but John had taught him to ride and shoot and he was going from strength to strength in his lessons. He still spoke English with a bit of an accent but his skills in the language were improving all the time.

Kamau was puzzled by a few things in his new, exciting life, however. He could not understand his brother Robert's attitude towards him. Kamau could see that he and Robert were very much alike; apart from his own brown skin, they really looked like brothers and it was clear that although he was ten years younger than Robert they were very similar in character and ability. Robert left to go to Ulaya (overseas), so the mystery remained. He was also mighty troubled by the fact that he could not go to the schools that John had attended. As far as he Kamau, could see, he could now ride, shoot and play soccer almost as well as John, and they had the same father; so why could he not go to Nakuru School and then to the Duke of York? He asked his father.

"Those schools are only for white children," explained Peter.

"Am I not white?" asked Kamau.

"No, you are a lovely brown colour."

"Do they have schools for children who are a lovely brown colour?" asked Kamau.

"No, not yet." Peter was embarrassed.

"So where will I go to school then?" asked Kamau

"You will stay here with Mrs. Smith, but maybe things will change one day and you will be able to go to the schools that John and Robert went to with other black and brown boys," replied Peter.

Peter was really troubled by this exchange; how could he possibly explain to Kamau the privileged position whites had in Kenya and that this privilege did not extend to him. He could see that Kamau had all the outstanding characteristics that had developed in Robert; in fact he could see Kamau turning out to be very similar in character to Robert. Peter felt that, despite many efforts on his part to change the situation, Robert had grown away from him. He understood the reasons but was powerless to do anything about it. He felt he had almost lost his eldest son because of the way that society was run in Kenya; he was determined to do his utmost not to lose Kamau, to whom he was really close, for the same reasons. He hugged the handsome little boy. Another thought crossed his mind: "What would happen if the white government sent Rafiki to the gallows?" He couldn't bear thinking about that and how Kamau would feel about him, Peter, a white man, in the years ahead, when he grew up and was able to understand what had happened.

Peter wrote a long letter to Giles in London explaining what he, Peter, saw as the essential need for there to be a political settlement in Kenya. He also wrote of the per sonal consequences that the current impasse was having. He asked Giles to see if he could talk to Robert and get him to understand why things were as they were, and convince Robert that he should not blame everything on his father.

He finished the letter off: "Giles, I know you have some influence at the top levels of Government; please try to persuade them that they need a settlement here and that within a short while there will have to be elections and a black government. We have no other choice. They must also release Kenyatta as soon as possible."

When Giles received the letter, he had a very long, sympathetic chat with Robert, who was staying with them.

"A very fine man, your father," Giles said to him.

Robert was amazed; few whites in Kenya had done anything but vilify Peter. He just stared at Giles.

"I've never seen such courage," Giles went on. "After your mother died and Louise and I got married, he then became involved with Rafiki."

Robert nodded.

"Having made the commitment, he really stuck by her under the most difficult possible circumstances."

Robert had never considered the situation from this point of view before.

"When she left Naseby, he had every possible reason to abandon her and

Kamau; from what he has written in his letters, both the white community and the Kikuyu wanted this as an outcome at the time."

Robert thought this was true.

"After a while he would have been welcomed back into the white community and his association with Rafiki would have been forgotten."

Robert started to understand the point.

"It seems to me that Rafiki gave him something, some understanding that he would not have had otherwise.

I truly, truly admire him; he's stood by her through thick and thin and now he's got this trial to face. I know of no other man that would not have backed off long before this."

Robert wondered why he hadn't seen it this way before.

"Now tell me your feelings," said Giles.

Robert explained his own situation and how he felt he had really lost out as a result of the situation in Kenya and his father's actions. He felt somewhat foolish explaining all this after what Giles had just said.

"I understand exactly how you feel," said Giles. "But there are many other people who have suffered far more than you have from various types of discrimination. You will see this in time."

Giles went on," You are an extremely able and talented young man; you will have every opportunity to make something of yourself here in England and even back in Kenya. Your brother, Kamau, I understand from Peter has similar abilities to you; think about how he is being discriminated against. He can't even go to the schools you went to, let alone worry about being rugby captain or whatever." Giles put his arm around Robert. "Come and talk if you need to; I know this is difficult."

Robert had many, many chats with both Louise and Giles and eventually his letters home became more understanding and conciliatory, and more frequent.

"I wonder what Giles has done or said to Robert," thought Peter. He kept his own counsel and just welcomed the change.

Peter also wrote to the new Governor about his ideas for a settlement. Brian Johns had moved on as well; Peter was ignored. The Governor saw his job as beating the Mau-Mau and then turning Kenya into the productive colony it had been before the war. He certainly wasn't going to listen to Peter Lawrence, who he understood had some sort of liaison with the Kikuyu woman who was about to stand trial for her life.

Peter also made one or two attempts to see the new Governor but was turned away quite brusquely.

The Governor described Jomo Kenyatta as "the leader who will take this country to darkness and death; he will never be released." This was in response to numerous questions about the Kikuyu leader's possible release.

The Governor was out of touch with the issues of the time. His attitude was no help to Peter, either personally or in his desire for reform in the country.

Chapter 27

Rafiki was eventually brought to trial. The Crown thought that it had a watertight case and the prosecution was going to demand the death penalty. The political atmosphere in Kenya had hardened considerably since the defeat of the Mau-Mau, the capture of Kahinga and the advent of the new Governor. Many of the white settlers thought that they could return to the pre-war situation where the whites were in control and the blacks knew their place. The British Government was still encouraging farmers from Britain to move to Kenya and to settle the large tracts of Crown land that had recently been made available for settlement; Bill was still furiously settling newcomers in at Mau Narok.

As far as the Government were concerned this was a show trial. They had won the war and they wanted to show the Kikuyu, the black population at large and the world who was in charge. The date of the trial was therefore telegraphed well ahead.

Simon Ndegwa was a bit of a showman. He had made an outfit from the colours of the Mau-Mau flag: black for the people, green for the country and red for the blood they had spilt. He had a red baseball cap on and a huge pair of ex-army boots. He went to the first day of the trial, since it was his day off, and he waited patiently outside the courthouse along with about two thousand other Africans of all tribes and ethnic groups for the trial to start. Simon had a very shrill tin whistle with him. There was also a group of drummers waiting.

The police van appeared with its escort. The crowd waited expectantly. Simon had gone along for a bit of fun. Suddenly he found himself in front of the waiting masses. He blew his whistle long and shrilly.

"K-A-R-I-B-U, welcome" he yelled.

The crowd responded, "K-A-R-I-B-U."

The whistle shrilled. The drummers started. Then Simon was suddenly in his element. He had the crowd in his hands. The whistle shrilled three times. Simon was doubled over with his hands pointing outwards; he was like a conductor.

The drums throbbed.

The whistle shrilled.

The people started to stamp their feet in unison. This was repeated a couple of times. The crowd had now warmed up.

"RA-RA-RA-RAFIKI," yelled Ndegwa.

"RA-RA-RA-RAFIKI," the crowd thundered back.

The whistle shrilled.

The drums throbbed.

The people stamped their feet.

"RA-RA-RA-RAFIKI," yelled Ndegwa.

"RA-RA-RA-RAFIKI," the crowd responded.

The police contingent looked around nervously and fingered their weapons.

"Take it easy men," said the inspector in charge. "Nothing to worry about."

Rafiki had not been outside the prison in two years and looked forward to seeing Nairobi again and identifying her favourite landmarks. She had little time for that; she could see Ndegwa and the crowd outside the courthouse.

"RA-RA-RA-RAFIKI," went the call.

The hairs on the back of her neck stood up. She had no idea the trial would attract so much attention.

She was eventually bustled into the courtroom.

Rafiki looked around. The courtroom was a large dusty room with high ceilings and fans moving slowly in the ceiling; flies buzzed around. The public gallery was full, as it would be during the whole trial. The jury, already sworn in, consisted of eleven white men and one Indian man (a sort of token, thought Rafiki). They all stood up when the judge came in; he had a funny looking wig on and was wearing flowing robes. Rafiki nearly burst out laughing but no one else took any notice, so she managed to control herself. Peter was there, as he had said he would be every day of the trial. Rafiki was prettily dressed in a floral cotton dress and western style shoes, and her hair was neatly frizzed out. She looked anything but a terrorist killer. The judge, of course, was white.

The noise from outside was clearly audible and unsettled the judge and the prosecution.

"RA-RA-RA-RAFIKI," the call could be heard continuing.

Rafiki didn't fully understand court procedure but after some initial statements and her pleas of "not guilty", which she had agreed with Singh, her defence lawyer, the trial started in earnest.

The first charge was that of belonging to a terrorist organisation. The prosecutor's case centred round the fact that she had seven cuts on her upper right arm.

Singh tried to prove that the seven cuts were not necessarily proof of her belonging to the organisation. He produced a white and an Indian witness, both of whom had seven cuts on their upper right arms. Both had claimed it was the result of a teenage game that they had played when reports emerged in the press about the seven cuts being the insignia of the Mau-Mau. He also proved that Rafiki had the cuts on her arm when she was fifteen. The prosecution were unable to find a single witness that could testify to the fact that Rafiki had attended Mau-Mau meetings; in fact, being a woman, she had not. Singh had decided that Rafiki should not take the stand so that she could not be asked directly whether she considered herself to be a member of the Mau-Mau or not. The defence thought that the prosecution had not really proven its case.

On the charge of aiding and abetting a terrorist organisation, the prosecution produced twenty Kikuyu women who testified to the fact that Rafiki had forced them to steal food and carry it into the mountains. Rafiki knew all of them. All of them had willingly co-operated with her. She wondered why they were speaking out against her now; there seemed to be no reason for it.

Then Rafiki realised that all of them had husbands or sons in jail. When one of the witnesses was asked how Rafiki forced them to carry food into the mountains, she responded hesitantly, through the Kikuyu interpreter, "with a gun."

"Please describe the gun," said Singh.

He knew that none of the passive wing members had ever seen the Beretta that Rafiki carried and was found with.

The woman stretched out her arms; clearly she was describing a rifle. Several others said the same thing and described the only gun they had ever seen, which was a rifle. Singh called Piet Van Vuuren to the stand.

"Please describe to the court the weapon you claim you found on the defendant the night she was captured," Singh asked.

Piet van Vuuren described the Beretta. Singh then recalled the women to the stand in turn and asked them where their husbands were, and in some cases, their sons. The first woman came up.

"Where is your husband?" Singh asked.

"Hola camp."

There was a hushed silence through the courtroom. Hola was the notorious prison camp that was reserved for "hard line" Mau-Mau captives. Recent reports in the press indicated that the prison authorities beat prisoners on a daily basis. There were ugly rumours of prisoners actually being beaten to death.

"Why is he there?"

The woman shrugged. "Mau-Mau," she whispered.

"Why are you telling these lies about the accused? She did not force you to do anything; you carried food to your husband, didn't you?" asked Singh.

The woman looked confused.

"Answer the question," said the judge.

"Did you carry the food to your husband in the forest?"

The woman nodded. "Yes."

Singh went on, "Who told you to tell these lies about Rafiki forcing you at gun point to carry food to the people in the mountains? She rode a motorbike; how could she carry such a gun?"

The woman was now terrified. "The police tell me to say these things then maybe our husbands will leave Hola camp and not be killed," she responded.

Singh had all the women return to the stand; most of them told a similar story.

Singh was triumphant; the prosecution's case was falling apart. His triumph came too soon.

One woman stood her ground. "My husband is at home," she responded when asked. "Rafiki," and she pointed, "came to our village on the farm in the Wanjohe once every month. She made us take food to the bases in the mountains: Nyati and Dik-Dik and Faru bases. She had no gun."

"So why did you do it?" asked Singh.

"We were frightened; we thought some of the Mau-Mau would come and kill us if we didn't take food."

"Where was your husband?" asked Singh.

"Working on the farm, he was a tractor driver there," she said proudly.

"What did your husband say about all this?"

"He was frightened also."

"So what did he tell you to do?" asked Singh.

"He told me nothing, he just wanted to do his job and have no trouble."

Rafiki got bored. As far as she was concerned, everyone was lying or being forced to say things they did not want to. Everyone in the courtroom was frightened. She wanted to scream that she had helped the Mau-Mau by supplying food because of the injustice caused by the system. She wanted to tell them that her son couldn't go to a white school even though his father was white. She really missed Kamau. She was not allowed to see him in prison but Peter brought her photographs from time to time; she could see he was growing up and she was missing his childhood.

The barracking from the crowd, led by Simon Ndegwa, continued for several days. During the lunch recess on the first day, Peter went out and joined the crowd. He joined in with Ndegwa and together they shouted, "RA-RA-RA-RAFIKI."

"RA-RA-RA-RAFIKI," the crowd responded.

The police inspector was contemptuous.

"Look at that wog-loving bastard; he should hang with her." He had no doubt that Rafiki would 'get her just dues' as he saw it.

The police did nothing. The world's press was there and there was no need to spoil the show. The crowd was rowdy but posed no threat.

The next day followed much the same pattern as the first, except that the crowd was bigger and there were two others dressed like Ndegwa leading the crowd on.

After the first few days the police inspector said to a colleague, "Take a look through these binoculars; there are now six 'leaders' all representing different tribal groups. This is no longer just a Kikuyu thing. This is big; this is national. The trial has unified the blacks." He went on, "See the first fellow, he was here from the beginning, he's a Kuik (Kikuyu), but the next one is a Kamba, then we have a Luo and then a Kipsigis and so on. We're going to have to break this up."

The inspector had been born locally; he knew what he was saying.

The next day he decided to call in the riot squad.

Simon Ndegwa had a brother in the riot police. He managed to get word to Simon that they had been called out for the next day.

Word spread round the townships: "Do not go to Rafiki's trial tomorrow."

Bearing in mind there were no telephones in the townships the communication and discipline were excellent. There was almost no one outside the courthouse the following day. The three hundred riot police with their helmets and batons looked and felt ridiculous.

The press laughed at the police. The inspector was furious.

The following day a few hundred women gathered. They were completely silent the whole day.

The police were baffled. The riot police stood down.

The six 'Ndegwas' and a large crowd were back in full force the following day.

Peter came out at lunchtime and danced and chanted with all the 'Ndegwas'.

"The police will not touch them now," was the general word. "They have Munyu's protection."

This pattern went on for a week. If the riot police were called there was either no crowd or a crowd of silent women. The inspector was becoming frustrated. The police were being made to look ridiculous in the press, who had now also picked up on the fact that the crowd was multi-ethnic. He was getting orders from his superiors to "sort the bloody thing out."

The press and the newsreels were now reporting the trial on a worldwide basis. They were putting the British Government on trial by questioning the colonial ethic, talking up the multi-ethnic nature of the crowd outside the courthouse, questioning the make-up of the jury. From the Government point of view the 'show' trial had become a public relations nightmare.

Inside the courtroom the presence or otherwise of the crowd had a big effect on the mood. When the crowd was at its noisiest the "RA-RA-RA-RAFIKI" clearly unnerved the witnesses. When the crowd was absent there was an almost unnatural hush over the proceedings.

The arguments went on for days; Singh would not let Rafiki take the stand. In the end he felt he had put enough doubt in the minds of the jury about the Crown case. It was clear that the police had tampered with witnesses and he would try to get the evidence they had submitted thrown out.

He had a consultation with the judge on the matter. "The police have clearly tampered with the witnesses; the evidence of those witnesses should be dismissed and deleted from the record," Singh made his point.

The prosecution demurred.

The judge refused. The evidence stood. The Indian member of the jury, a Mr. Masood, was a nervous little man who owned a draper's shop in one of the mainly Indian areas of Nairobi. He had very reluctantly been pressed into service on this jury; he had no real interest in the proceedings. All he wanted was to feed and educate his three children and make a reasonable living from his shop. His neighbour was thinking of going to England to live; maybe he would do the same someday.

One day when he got home his wife came out anxiously.

"Jamal (their eldest son of six) has not come home from school today. Maybe we should go to the police," she said.

"How late is he?" asked Masood.

"About an hour."

They never went to the police except as a last resort. Most Indians distrusted them, knowing that even if an Indian was put on their case he would inevitably be of a different religion or caste. The Masoods were devout Muslims and had no time for their Hindu brethren.

"We will wait, maybe phone a few of his friends," said Masood.

"I have already done that," said his wife, "there is no sign."

An hour later, just before dark, the phone rang.

"Yes," answered Masood.

"Do you want your son back?" a European voice said down the phone.

"Who is this, what do you want?" asked Masood.

"Do you want your son back?"

"Yes, yes, what have you done to him?"

"Just listen then: that black woman is to hang; we want no nonsense from you. You vote against and you will never see your son again. You have seen what we can do," said the voice.

"Where is my son?" whispered Masood.

"He will walk through the front door in five minutes," the voice responded.

The phone went click.

Masood sat there sweating. Sure enough, five minutes later Jamal walked in, eating an ice cream.

His parents fussed over him. "Are you all right?" "Did they hurt you?"

Jamal was fine. He had been picked up from school in a car and had then been blindfolded and driven round in the car until he had been dropped outside his home. The people were kind to him but he didn't really see them.

The Masoods were terrified.

"Get off that Jury, call in sick," pleaded Mrs. Masood.

"No, no, I know what to do; no harm will come to us," he replied.

Eventually the settler community became really fed up with the proceedings. They had won the war but were clearly losing the peace. They decided to do something about the crowd outside the courthouse.

The six 'Ndegwas' were in full voice. There were now almost five thousand in the crowd. A group of about two dozen white settlers came around the corner, all armed to the teeth. Luckily the inspector and a posse of fifty askaris were on the spot. The inspector took immediate action.

"Halt," he said to the settlers.

They halted.

"Disperse," he ordered them.

They demurred.

"Arm," he instructed his police.

George Athill came to the front of the settler group.

"Take no notice," he yelled.

The inspector acted quickly. Two shots rang out. George dropped down dead. The group of settlers were shocked. Nothing had prepared them for this.

Press cameras clicked, newsreel cameras whirred. The black crowd was now silent.

"Disperse now, or face the consequences."

There was no response.

"Ready!" he yelled. The police raised their weapons.

There was a moment's hesitation, and then one brave settler soul gave the order. "Unload," he yelled. "Disperse!"

The tension disappeared and so did the white settlers.

The police breathed a sigh of relief.

The crowd continued, "RA-RA-RA-RAFIKI."

Inside the courtroom, there was consternation on the faces of the judge, the jury and all the court personnel. A few people from the gallery ran out when they heard the shots.

The press had a field day. George was vilified as a right wing extremist. His previous misdemeanours were all remembered in the articles that followed.

Rafiki felt no satisfaction, only mild sadness when Peter relayed the events to her the next day.

The political initiative was now clearly in the hands of the black Kenyans.

The trial dragged on. When the charge came up relating to the possession of an unlicensed firearm the prosecution brought Piet Van Vuuren to the stand again. He testified that he had found the weapon on Rafiki when she was captured. Singh's defence was that she had been given the gun by another member of the Mau-Mau for self-defence and she had never used it against the security forces. All this was true but the charge stood; the evidence was incontrovertible.

The other charges, mainly of theft, were unproven as far as Singh was concerned. The motorbike was registered in Kahinga's name and he, in a written affidavit prepared by Singh, said he had given permission to Rafiki to use it.

In summing up, the prosecution relied on the evidence of the woman who had told the court that Rafiki had organised the food drops into the mountains and on that of Piet Van Vuuren, who had found the gun on Rafiki.

"It is up to you, the jury, to find this woman guilty as she undoubtedly is," he concluded.

He asked that the maximum penalty be imposed.

Vijaya Singh in his final summing up relied on the fact that there was no hard evidence to prove that Rafiki had belonged to the Mau-Mau, that the police had tampered with witnesses and that the evidence of the woman who claimed they were forced to go into the mountains should be dismissed. As far as the firearms offences were concerned, he relied on the fact that Rafiki had never used the Beretta against the security forces.

Rafiki was dressed in her best dress and looked really glamorous to the people waiting in the gallery.

"Does this woman look like a threat to society?" thundered Singh. "The prosecution case has no credibility; this woman should be found not guilty and returned to society, to look after her son."

The jury were out for two days. As they filed back in, both Singh and Rafiki looked at them to see if there was any hint as to what the verdict was.

One by one the judge read out the charges:

"Belonging to a terrorist organisation."

"Guilty, M'Lud."

The gallery gasped.

The judge banged his gavel. "Silence."

"Aiding and abetting a terrorist organisation."

"Guilty, M'Lud."

"Possession of an unlicensed firearm."

"Guilty, M'Lud."

The cases against her on the minor charges were dismissed.

Rafiki examined the expressions on the faces of the jury. The whites to a man looked triumphant; the Indian looked disconsolate.

Rafiki maintained her dignified posture although her stomach had contracted into a hard knot. This courtroom looked so mundane, so non-threatening, yet its business was deadly serious as far as she was concerned.

The judge was addressing her. "You, Rafiki Wainaina, have been found guilty of the most serious charges; do you have anything to say before sentence is passed?"

"Yes your honour," she said in a clear voice in English. She had not given evidence so most of the public gallery were surprised at the very good English she now spoke.

"Please proceed."

"Your honour," she had been coached by Singh how to address the court. "I am here because of the fundamental injustice that my people, the Kikuyu, and indeed all Africans under the British yoke, have had to suffer. You have come here and taken the country from us; we are now slaves in our own country. 'Hewers of wood and drawers of water', to use your own biblical terms. My own son, who even has a white father, is also treated the same; he is unable to get a proper education in this country. You call this justice?" She waved her hand round the court. "No sir, this is persecution. Whatever you do to us, your honour, I am certain that the armed resistance to your rule will continue and that within a few short years you and your colonial brothers will be sent back from where you came and we will again run our own affairs as Africans. As a Kikuyu and as an African, I do not recognise the authority of this court and these white men in the jury; I will not ask for your mercy. You will do what you will do." She sat down.

There was a momentary silence; then the Africans in the gallery erupted: they shouted and stamped their feet.

"Clear the court!" The judge banged his gavel. "Clear the court!" He was furious that he had provided a platform for a political statement that would reverberate around the world. "The court will recess until Monday morning," he concluded.

Peter went to see Rafiki the next day. She wept in his arms, in the little visitors' room where they had met so many times in the prison.

"They want to hang me, I know," she said.

"Look, it's not the end of the road," said Peter.

"There is an appeal process; we'll appeal the verdict immediately."

"Yes of course, but it will be no use, I can tell," said Rafiki miserably.

When the court reconvened on the Monday morning, the judge had had a long weekend to think about the verdict and the sentence he would pass. He knew his duty; he would do that duty and uphold British justice.

"Rafiki Wainaina, please stand while sentence is passed," the judge said sharply. "Rafiki Wainaina you have been convicted of the most heinous crimes and I have no alternative but to impose the maximum sentence."

She looked at him steadily across the court. The fact that this foreigner in her country had the right to sentence her at all angered her.

The people in the gallery moved uneasily.

"Rafiki Wainaina, you have been found guilty of belonging to a terrorist organisation. You will be taken to a place of incarceration and hanged by the neck until you are dead and may the lord have mercy upon your soul."

The court gasped.

"Rafiki Wainaina, you have been found guilty ...."

She stopped listening. She just thought of her childhood, of the carefree days running over the green hills of Kikuyuland; a small smile broke out across her face. The judge looked disconcerted.

"What is she smiling about?" he thought. He continued. "Two death sentences and twenty years for the possession of firearms. Sentences to be served concurrently," Rafiki heard the judge add.

"How can you serve two death sentences?" thought Rafiki. Rafiki looked up at Peter in the gallery. He waved, but he was looking at the judge.

Something made the judge look up; all he could see even from that distance was a set of clear, blue, cold, hard eyes and Peter's hand waving at Rafiki.

The court was immediately silent, aware of this byplay.

The judge stood up and immediately something that felt like a steel fist tore into his chest. He dropped all his papers, clutched his chest and fell down the steps from his podium onto the courtroom floor, his head twisted grotesquely backwards and his legs still on the steps. He was dead.

The court was hushed. The orderlies quickly ran to the judge's aid.

Rafiki was hurried into the cells beneath the courtroom.

"Munyu's curse," went the whisper round the gallery. And so Peter's reputation and mystique further increased among the Africans.

Firstly, none of the 'Ndegwas' or any of the black crowd had had a hair of their heads touched and secondly, the minute the death sentence had been passed the judge had died. The story of course grew as it was passed from mouth to mouth. Some of the newsreels featured it in their reports.

The news of Rafiki's conviction and sentence and then the sensational nature of the judge's death filtered its way into the crowd.

"RA-RA-RA-RAFIKI," they chanted as she was driven away.

'LAWRENCE WHORE TO DIE' yelled the papers.

They had not understood the sea change that had occurred in the sentiments surrounding the political future of Kenya.

The application for an appeal was dismissed. Rafiki was to hang. A date was set three months hence.

The Government wanted closure on this issue as soon as possible. The whole thing had been a disaster from the beginning.

Peter appealed to the Governor for clemency. He received no response.

The prison authorities made preparations for Rafiki's execution.

The white hangman came in and made a surreptitious appraisal of Rafiki. He had been very busy over the past few years plying his ghoulish trade.

"About 150 pounds," he said to the wardress. "Too much rope and we pull her head off when the trap drops; very messy. Too little and she might take ten minutes to die; again very messy. One drop, one clean break, that's it."

"Why don't you just weigh her?"

"No, no, we never do that," was the answer.

Peter's last visit was absolute torture. He had tried everything he could think of to get the sentence changed. He had talked to the press; the local English language press was hostile as they thought Rafiki was getting her just desserts. The vernacular press supported him wholeheartedly but they had no power or influence where it mattered.

Peter had phoned Giles to see if he could do something. Giles had promised to do what he could, but nothing had transpired.

He just could not believe that it had come to this. His precious, precious Rafiki was going to be hanged, and he was helpless to prevent it.

Peter spent his last visit talking about his love for her and about the really good times they had had together.

They talked about Kamau. They remembered everything about him, how he had been as a little boy, his naughty side and how, despite all the setbacks and the disadvantages he had to cope with, he was developing into a really fine young person.

"What have you told Kamau?" she asked.

"Nothing yet, I haven't told him anything; he knows about the sentence though," said Peter.

"What about his education?"

"If he can't go to the Duke of York, I will send him to England. Giles and Louise will look after him."

Rafiki nodded. "You think there is a chance he will go to the Duke of York."

"Yes, things have to change here and soon," replied Peter.

When it was time to go they embraced. Wainaina and Rafiki's mother had also been in earlier and said their farewells. Rafiki tried bravely not to cry but in the end the flood came. Peter comforted her and in the end the wardress came and led Rafiki sadly back to the cells.

It looked as if it was all over. In the prison Rafiki was given her last meal.

"Ogalie, meat, vegetables, gravy," was what she told the fat Wakamba wardress. She ate her meal and tried to sleep which was impossible.

She went through every step of her life and she shed many tears at the thought of her son who she now knew she would not see grow up.

They came for her just after 5am. She was handcuffed and taken down to a room near the gallows.

A priest appeared. She didn't ignore him; she just didn't see him. The prison Governor appeared, another white man; he read out the sentence. She barely heard it. They were going to kill her; all this ritual she supposed made them feel better. This was the white man's way. A simple spear through the heart was what she would have preferred.

She was taken to the gallows room. Faintly she could hear from outside the prison the same call as she had heard in the courtroom: thousands of voices raised, "RA-RA-RA-RAFIKI," and the call of the women trilling.

The execution team heard it too. It clearly unnerved them. They wanted this business finished. Still one minute to wait. The prison Governor was a stickler for protocol.

"Six am was the time set; six am it shall be," he said.

A hood was put over her head. She was lead up to the gallows trap.

The rope was put round her neck and tightened. Everything was silent.

Rafiki's life flashed before her. She hoped that the trap would soon fall and it would all be over.

"RA-RA-RA-RAFIKI," came the call of the crowd.

Peter had fetched Wainaina; they went to the prison gates in his pick-up at about 5am. He had been told the body would be delivered to him at about 6:15.

A sizeable crowd had already gathered. All the 'Ndegwas' were there. The drummers were there. At about 5:30am they started slowly.

"RA-RA-RA-RAFIKI," yelled the 'Ndegwas'.

"RA-RA-RA-RAFIKI," the crowd responded.

The women trilled. By now the crowd was approaching ten thousand strong. Peter and Wainaina joined in. The police stood by watchfully.

The clock ticked by. 5:45; 5:50.

Peter had been shivering in fear and trepidation whilst sitting in the car.

This was far better he thought, as they continued the call.

"RA-RA-RA-RAFIKI."

At 5:59 they stopped. They all faced the prison. There was complete silence. No one moved. One could have heard a pin drop. Almost everyone was crying silently, big wet tears down all their black glossy cheeks. Everyone felt a huge sense of loss, as if one of their nearest and dearest had been prematurely taken from them.

At ten past six Peter went to the prison gates.

The women started their mournful wailing.

At 6:15 a few people started moving in and out of the prison on their daily business.

At 6:30, no word, nothing. At 6:45 the same.

Just before seven a prison guard beckoned to Peter. He and Wainaina went forward and into the prison.

The Prison Governor greeted them frostily. "Come this way," he instructed. They were taken to the horrid little visitor's room where Peter and Rafiki had met so many times. Nothing was said. They were left alone for fifteen minutes. They were shocked. What was going on, how much more torture did they have to endure?

Then the door of the room was pushed open and a very dazed looking Rafiki pushed through it.

Peter couldn't believe his eyes. She was alive; she had not been hanged. He hugged and kissed her. He pinched himself. Was this a dream?

"What happened?" he eventually asked.

"They stopped it, one minute before six," she answered breathlessly.

The Prison Governor came in with a black look on his face. "Orders from London," he growled and then went out.

So it was true. She was not to hang. He and Rafiki and Wainaina hugged and hugged and danced.

At about eight o'clock Peter and Wainaina were ushered out of the prison. They would see Rafiki later.

The crowd were now getting restless. Peter stood in the back of his truck with Wainaina and addressed the crowd.

"They stopped the hanging," he said simply. "Orders from London."

He was having trouble taking it all in. Then many hands grabbed him and hoisted him and Wainaina shoulder high.

"MU-NYU," yelled the 'Ndegwas'.

"MU-NYU," the crowd chanted.

They were carried off through the streets of Nairobi blocking the early morning traffic. After a while Peter asked them to change the chant. He was now certain that Jomo Kenyatta's release was imminent.

"KE-NYA-TTA," came the chant.

"KE-NYA-TTA," roared the crowd.

An exhausted Peter and Wainaina found their way back to the truck by about midday. The crowd dispersed.

The city was abuzz. Clearly something big was about to happen.

After Peter's call, Giles had been very busy in London. The British Government under Prime Minister Harold Macmillan had concluded that the British colonial empire was doomed; the only question was how and when was independence to be granted to the various dependencies and under what constitutional arrangements? So when Giles went to see the Colonial Secretary he had a ready audience.

"Oh, yes, Lawrence," said the Colonial secretary. "I'd almost forgotten about him; didn't he act as a go-between a few years back?"

"Yes, he's still there; he could do the same again," said Giles.

"What's your relationship with him?"

"Brother-in-law," answered Giles.

After some discussion in the British Cabinet it was decided in principle to release Kenyatta and the other detainees and then arrange a major constitutional conference. Having Peter as a go-between seemed superfluous at this stage. A decision had to be made when to arrange the release and when to advise the Governor.

At 2a.m. in London the final cabinet meeting had determined that an announcement regarding the release of Jomo Kenyatta, together with the release of the other detainees, would be made the next day.

As the meeting came to a close, the Permanent Secretary to the Cabinet said, "Gentlemen, there is one other item."

They all looked tiredly at him.

"This woman, Rafiki Wainaina, is due to be executed at 6a.m. local time. Under the circumstances this may be inappropriate; if she were in jail she would probably be released in a few months."

"Dear God!" said the Colonial Secretary, "We can't let this happen; it will just cause more uncertainty and probably riots if it comes along with the announcement."

They phoned the Governor there and then; it was 4a.m. in Nairobi.

"The Prime Minister wants to speak to you," explained the telephonist when she put the call through.

"Governor here."

"Prime Minister here," he went on to explain the decision to release Kenyatta and hold constitutional talks.

"There is one other rather pressing matter," said the Prime Minister.

"Yes."

"It concerns the death sentence to be carried out on Rafiki Wainaina."

"Yes, I signed the death warrant this morning" said the Governor.

"Then unsign it," said the Prime Minister. Under the circumstances the execution cannot go ahead, do you understand? It will not go ahead. Kindly phone me back when it has been stopped. I understand it is due to take place shortly."

"Yes, at 6a.m.," said the Governor.

The Governor had phoned the prison and was told the Prison Governor was busy. The phone was put down. He got dressed and rushed down to the prison; he was eventually admitted to the gallows area at five minutes to six and stopped the execution personally.

"What do you mean, orders from London?" asked the Prison Governor.

"The Prime Minister himself phoned," said the Governor.

"How do you know it wasn't a hoax?"

"I know the Prime Minister's voice; now give me the death warrant." He tore it up. "I will send you an official communiqué today," said the Governor. He was very agitated. This was not the way to go about these things.

"What do I tell the prisoner?" asked the Prison Governor.

"Anything you like," was the response. "She is likely to be freed along with the rest of them within weeks."

Rafiki had been taken back to her cell. She was transferred that day to a cell in the block for long-term prisoners. She was relieved to be away from the ghoulish horror of death row.

She was still mesmerised by the events of the morning. Instead of being dead and cold in a box she was warm and alive and shortly to be released.

She had waited for the trap to fall. Waited and waited.

Then she had heard the sound of several muffled voices. The rope had been roughly pulled off her head, the hood removed. She had been led back to her cell. No one had said anything. She had then been reunited with Peter.

The Governor phoned London back at 5a.m. London time.

"I commuted the death sentence," he reported. "I had a few minutes to spare.

There was palpable relief in London. The announcement regarding Kenyatta's release was to be made simultaneously in London and Nairobi the next day.

Peter phoned Giles in London. "What's the background?"

"Just the usual muddle," was the answer. "They will announce a constitutional conference and general elections shortly. I expect there will be an African Government heading an independent Kenya within two years."

Peter described Rafiki's and his own ordeal. Giles listened in horrified silence. They then went on to other issues.

"Land, of course, will be one of the big political issues to solve," said Giles.

"Yes," said Peter. "The British Government will have to provide funds to buy the farmers out, otherwise you will not have a settlement that anyone can live with."

"I'll warn them," said Giles.

"They've already been told; I told them all that when I dealt with Jomo in Lodwar."

"Maybe they need reminding, "said Giles. "By the way, are you going to be part of the new set up?"

"If Jomo wants me, yes. I hope I'm invited to the conference in any case; I have a few bones to pick," replied Peter.

Jomo Kenyatta and his fellow detainees in Lodwar were released to a tumultuous welcome through the streets of Nairobi.

He immediately went to work and set up KANU (Kenya African National Union) as part of the new dispensation. The party was dominated by the Kikuyu but did try to attract the support of other tribes.

Another party, KADU (Kenya African Democratic Union), was set up to represent many of the smaller tribes in Kenya. They were less cohesive than KANU since they represented many disparate interests; really the only thing they had in common was to try to counterbalance the Kikuyu influence.

The British delayed the release of the other detainees, including Rafiki, arguing that they were criminals, not political prisoners. The argument took six months. Eventually both Rafiki and Kahinga were released from prison, along with most of the other prisoners. Hola camp and its inmates were left alone. The British had much to clean up there.

Peter took Wainaina to fetch Rafiki and they first went back to Thika where Rafiki's family were. Peter had taken Kamau there and left him with his grandmother. He didn't think a ten year old should be exposed to the horrors of a prison. Rafiki was quite thin and had aged a bit but was otherwise in good health. She couldn't believe her little baby had grown into this tough little ten year old. She cuddled him but he was clearly uncomfortable with that, so she let him go and play. He was really pleased to see his mother again. Peter had told him that she had been sentenced to death, which he didn't really understand. He didn't want to be cuddled but wouldn't let her out of his sight, until they got back to Naseby.

When they got home to Naseby, Rafiki saw that it had hardly changed. She asked Peter about the bullet holes in the front of the house and Peter described the attack. She had such fond and happy memories of the place.

They made love for the first time in eight years that night. Rafiki could not believe how her fortunes had changed. Six months previously she had almost been executed; now she was free and back home and watching her son grow up. She and Peter had much catching up to do, she could see that; they both expected to be part of the negotiating process in London, this time on the same side.

The farm was looking great and going well. Bill's son Ken had now fully taken over the day-to-day management. Peter would be free to go to London if he was needed.

Chapter 28

During the weeks after Rafiki's release from jail, she and Peter had much catching up to do. They both had scars from the conflict, both physical and mental. Rafiki had on-going nightmares about her near execution, which gradually diminished as she always woke from those nightmares in the warmth and security of Peter's arms.

The war had been won and lost by both sides; the Mau-Mau had lost the war in the bush but appeared to have won the peace. The British had conclusively won the war in the bush but had decided that a major on-going military commitment to maintaining Kenya as a dependency was too high a price to pay. The only issue for the British government was how to extricate themselves at the minimum cost both financially and in electoral terms in Britain.

Rafiki and Peter expected to be involved in the constitutional settlement; they realised that Jomo Kenyatta had many things to do and catch up with since his release; he would contact them when he was good and ready.

Rafiki loved Naseby and re-explored every inch of it with Peter. They both knew that they would spend extended periods away from the farm, so most of the day to day running was left to Ken. Kamau was, of course, thrilled to have his mother back home. John was very pleased too; he'd always liked Rafiki and they got on well. Robert was in England at university but his letters to Peter were more understanding and conciliatory than before.

One Sunday morning, when Peter and Rafiki were still in bed, he said to her, "I was wondering what you think of the idea of us now getting married."

There was a short silence.

"Get married, are you serious?" asked Rafiki. "After all this time?"

"Yes, I'm dead serious."

Rafiki was non-plussed. "You will have to speak to my father."

"I have already done so," said Peter.

"What did he say?"

"He wants twenty head of cattle as a bride price," said Peter jokingly.

Rafiki hit him with a pillow. "Twenty head?" she responded, "I'm worth far more than twenty, maybe one hundred or two hundred."

"The normal number is six," said Peter.

"Six?"

"Yes, plus a sheep for the feast and five hundred shillings," Peter laughed.

"You will not get me for twenty head," she pretended to get out of bed.

This started a wrestling match and they eventually made the most passionate love.

"Twenty head," muttered Rafiki.

"No, no, that is really a joke," said Peter. "What I have been doing over the past three years, though, is to give Wainaina most of the bull calves born here; you remember we used to slaughter them for our own use?"

She nodded.

"I have also given him a few heifers and have started an artificial insemination programme with his own herd. He'll have the best herd in Kikuyuland within five years."

Rafiki was fascinated.

"But I'm serious about the wedding," said Peter.

"Oh, yes, where will the wedding be?" said Rafiki.

"So you agree to get married?" asked Peter.

"Agree, disagree, who I am to argue; I am a good Kikuyu girl, if my father and my future husband have spoken then what else is there to discuss."

She hid her smile behind her hand.

"Are you happy about it?" Peter persisted.

She belted him with a pillow. She was absolutely thrilled.

Peter then explained that they would get married in the Kikuyu tradition in her father's village and then in the Christian tradition in London.

"London, you mean Ulaya; why there?"

"Well, two reasons really; one is that your father says he wants to visit Ulaya once before he dies to see where all these strange Wazungu come from and the other..."

"Ulaya, my father wants to go to Ulaya?" Rafiki was curious.

"Yes, he's really keen," said Peter

"And the other reason?" asked Rafiki.

"Well I spoke to Giles about this..."

Rafiki interrupted, "Giles - is there anyone except me that you haven't spoken to?" she asked.

Peter smiled and went on.

"Giles wondered whether he could arrange the wedding in London, perhaps just before the constitutional conference."

"We haven't been invited to the constitutional conference," said Rafiki.

"We will be; I spoke to Mzee..."

She hit him with the pillow again. "You really have spoken to everyone about this," she pretended to be upset.

Peter knew her well enough not to be fooled.

"Well, I had to get everything organised," he said lamely.

So it was settled.

More than one thousand people eventually attended the wedding ceremony at Wainaina's village in the Thika area. Peter managed to persuade Dave and Margaret Gibb to come and the Nicklins, the Marks, and even Gert Boschoff. The rest of the guests were Kikuyu and included Jomo Kenyatta and most of the new leadership of KANU.

Kenyatta greeted Peter warmly.

"You will come to the constitutional conference in London," he said. "We will need you there, especially on the land question."

"And Rafiki" asked Peter.

"We need her also, women's interests," was the response.

The ceremony lasted three days. First Peter and Rafiki went through the Kikuyu marriage ceremony, conducted by the local witchdoctor. Then various groups of maidens were on parade, conducting their traditional dances, followed by the young men.

Wainaina had arranged for several oxen to be slaughtered and slowly roasted over coals. There were copious quantities of the very best Njahe traditional beer.

Peter and Rafiki joined in the dancing from time to time, much to the delight of the guests.

Peter managed to renew acquaintance with many people. Eventually he found Kahinga. Kahinga was quite shy to start with; Peter supposed the many years in the forest had made him shy of human contact. Eventually they managed to spend an hour renewing their old friendship. Kahinga asked about Peter's role in the death of Waichagga.

"There have always been rumours that you shot him," said Kahinga, "but we could find no trace of you; there was just a woman who said you did it."

Peter explained to Kahinga what had happened.

"Ask Stanley," said Peter, "he probably saved my life by whisking me away from the scene when he did. If I had gone into that cauldron, I think Kinua would not have been able to save me. Which reminds me - where is Kinua?"

"Hola camp." Kahinga's face went grave. "They must close that place; terrible things are happening there," he said.

They did not really touch on Kahinga's role in the Mau-Mau or the murders; this would have to wait until another day.

The ceremony went on. All the white guests left after the first day. Peter and Rafiki managed to snatch a few hours' sleep here and there.

The press had somehow found out about the wedding. Their attitude towards Peter and Rafiki had changed dramatically since the political landscape had altered. They were now wondering how they were going to survive in the years ahead under an African government.

Glamorous pictures of the happy couple appeared on the front pages of the daily papers and there were features elsewhere in the newspapers dealing sympathetically with other parts of the three days of feasting.

Rumours had been circulating ever since Rafiki's release about her miraculous escape from the gallows. She refused to say anything about it but the press had eventually found the fat Wakamba wardress, who told them everything she knew. Ghoulish stories started to appear in the press. Eventually Rafiki managed an interview with a couple of reporters and with her glamour and obvious charm, she persuaded them to write about her hopes for the Kenya of the future, independent and free from discrimination.

John and Kamau were absorbed into their age groups in Wainaina's compound. John, of course, spoke the language well and once he had been dressed up as a young Kikuyu warrior he participated in all the dances, some of which he knew already. Peter saw nothing of the boys for the three days. He secretly wondered what John had got up to; there were some very pretty young girls, dressed just in their traditional little leather aprons. Enough to get the red blood cells of any young male racing round his body. Kamau had always been part of his group and had been accepted completely by them over the years; he came back to Rafiki's side from time to time during the ceremony, for reassurance and to make sure everything was real. Robert had not been able to come; he would, of course, be part of the ceremony in London.

Wainaina was beside himself with pride and joy. A few short months ago his daughter was about to be executed and now she was the toast of the community. His son-in-law, although a crazy M'zungu, seemed to understand Kikuyu tradition and certainly the language. He had also helped him improve the quality of his herd; his cattle were now rapidly becoming the best in Kikuyuland and this added hugely to his reputation and prestige. Also adding to his prestige was Kenyatta's presence at the wedding.

"Munyu says you are going to Ulaya with him," Kenyatta said.

"Yes."

"Ulaya; why do you want to go there?" asked Kenyatta.

"I want to see the chief's house; I hear it is very big."

Kenyatta laughed.

"Buckingham Palace," said Kenyatta. "Yes, it is very big."

"You've been there?" asked Wainaina.

"I've seen it from outside, but maybe we will be invited inside at the constitutional conference," he responded.

"I also want to see these cattle breeders that Munyu talks about," added Wainaina.

"Where will you stay?" asked Kenyatta

"Munyu's brother-in-law," was the response.

Kenyatta had heard of Giles.

"Don't think all Wazungu live like he does," advised Kenyatta. "You must see some poor people as well."

"They have poor people in Ulaya?" Wainaina was astonished.

"Yes, many," responded Kenyatta.

Wainaina nodded. He was going to learn much, he could see.

"Make sure that Munyu takes you to a few pubs," added Kenyatta.

"Pubs, for what?"

"They are neighbourhood drinking houses," said Kenyatta. "People go there to drink and talk."

Wainaina nodded.

"Just men?" he queried.

Kenyatta laughed.

"No, women as well."

"Ah, that's why the Wazungu are getting weaker; the women have too much strength in that country," said Wainaina.

Wainaina was really looking forward to his visit.

Peter took hundreds of photographs at the ceremony. He had a steady business with Jay Firmin. Whilst the farm was now doing well, it seemed that his land and that of many others would be bought by the Government for the resettlement of the African population. He expected to be a member of the new parliament of an independent Kenya but he thought he would need a supplementary source of income. He wasn't sure, but he assumed that parliamentary salaries would be quite modest, as befitted a developing country like Kenya.

Eventually the date for the constitutional conference was set. It was to be held at Lancaster House, a large but unprepossessing looking building set back from The Mall in London. Peter and Rafiki were part of the team representing KANU and the new Kenya.

Peter, Rafiki, Wainaina, John and Kamau all went to England about three weeks before the conference. Rafiki's mother, despite entreaties from all concerned, absolutely refused to go. The idea of flying terrified her, so she stayed at home. First they had the wedding ceremony to enjoy and then Peter was determined to show Rafiki, Wainaina and his children something of the country. He'd only been there once himself, but he was sure that Giles and Louise would point him in the right direction.

They went by BOAC Super Constellation, which had cut the old three day journey down to about twenty four hours. From Nairobi they flew to Entebbe in Uganda, which was at a lower altitude than Nairobi, so the plane could take on more fuel for the long haul to Rome, and then on to London.

Wainaina and Rafiki were both terrified when the plane took off; they did not see how it could possibly get off the ground. Once they were airborne, Peter was able to show Wainaina some of the landmarks. They could see Mount Kilimanjaro when they took off, then they flew past Mount Kenya and saw Mount Elgon and then Lake Victoria on their way to Entebbe.

Wainaina somehow coped with the food and Rafiki showed him how to use the utensils on the plane. The food was totally alien but he managed to force some of it down.

When they eventually flew into Heathrow airport in London, all of them marvelled at the beautiful green of the English countryside and the neat, well laid out and orderly fields. Peter remembered that from his last visit; it compared starkly with the dry dusty landscape of Africa.

"They can keep many cows on these green fields," observed Wainaina.

Louise met them at the airport and whisked them away to the large mansion that she and Giles occupied in Belgravia. They had a daughter of six and a son of four: Belinda and Angus. These children simply adored Robert and were really looking forward to having the visitors from Africa.

They took John and Kamau and even Rafiki in their stride but were quite unprepared for Wainaina.

Wainaina was a short (about five foot six), very black man with a shaved head and he had long, stretched ear lobes which had been made bigger and bigger over the years by putting larger and larger blocks of wood in them.

Peter had, prior to their departure in Nairobi, managed to outfit Wainaina with western style clothing, which he found uncomfortable although it fitted quite well. When they got to the house Wainaina was given his own room with an ensuite bath and toilet. He had never seen a flush toilet in his life before this trip and he had made a few clumsy attempts in the plane and the various airports on the way to England. He was relieved when Peter explained to him how to sit, what the paper was for and how to flush the thing. He was pleased with the bath; Peter showed him how to run it and control the temperature of the water. Wainaina's biggest problem was that he had never, in his seventy years on earth, slept alone in a room; he had spent nights at Naseby but had shared one of the children's rooms. He was quite happy with the bed - he even had one at home in Thika - but his hut at night was normally full of people: his wives, children, goats, dogs, guests. The idea of sleeping alone in this sort of antiseptic atmosphere frightened him.

"Where are you sleeping?" he asked Peter.

Peter showed him.

"I think I will sleep on the floor here," he said.

It took all Peter's persuasive powers to get him to accept the arrangements. When Peter showed him where he could store his clothes, he calmed down and accepted the situation.

He had eaten at Naseby on many occasions, so he knew the rudiments of how to use a knife and fork. The first evening they were having fish. He had never in his life seen such an array of utensils. He kept a close watch on Peter so that he would know what to do. Then he saw what was on the plate.

"Samaki (fish)," explained Rafiki. "Try it, it's very good."

"Looks like Nyoka (snake)," said Wainaina.

He tried it and somehow ate it.

Belinda in the meanwhile was intrigued with his ears.

"What happened to your ears?" she asked.

"Shush, Belinda, don't be so rude," said Louise.

Wainaina spoke to Louise in Swahili, having been told she had spent time in Kenya.

"Don't worry; does she want to know about my ears?" he asked.

He eventually got her to come to him and play with his ears, and by the end of the meal she was sitting on his lap.

Peter had had visions of having to take everyone round the sights together. Louise, however, took Rafiki in hand and they spent days worrying about what Rafiki would wear on her London wedding day. Robert took charge of John and Kamau and, when he was able to tear them away from the television, took them to Madame Tussaud's and the Tower.

Peter thus had Wainaina to himself. They first went to Buckingham Palace. He was impressed with the guards in their tall bearskin hats, but he was more impressed with the size of the place.

"Truly this is a very important chief," he observed.

"Where does she keep all her cattle?"

It was inconceivable that such an important chief didn't have any cattle.

"Maybe in the country," replied Peter.

They then went to Westminster Abbey. He just could not believe the size. Wainaina had, of course, seen many churches in Kenya but was truly impressed with the fact that Kings and Queens of England had been buried in this place for hundreds of years.

"Jomo told me that we must visit pubs and see how the poor people lived," said Wainaina.

He marched confidently into a pub near where they were staying in Belgravia.

"What are all these bottles?" he asked Peter. "I thought people came here to drink beer and talk; perhaps this is just for the women; the men drink beer."

Peter tried to explain the variety of drinks. They both had a pint of the best British bitter.

"Truly you Wazungu have many things," he said. "If all the people in the world had this much, would there be anything left?"

Peter couldn't answer.

They then went to Brixton, which Giles had said was a poor area. Wainaina could see that the people here were less well off than those in Belgravia. He also noticed that many of the people in the streets were black; they were new immigrants, mainly from the West Indies.

Wainaina said, "Are all the poor people in the world black? Are the black people always going to be poor?"

Peter then hurriedly arranged to take him to some of the poorer streets in the London dock area.

Peter had planned a very small, personal ceremony with Rafiki in a church Giles had found in Chelsea. It was just to be family, and he was anxious to try to bring Robert back into the bosom of the family.

Unfortunately the media had picked up from the papers in Kenya the fact that Rafiki had almost been executed and then they had found out about the wedding ceremony. When the little party arrived at the church, there were photographers and reporters and a couple of T.V cameras. Somehow they managed to keep the press out of the church. After the ceremony, Peter and Rafiki agreed to pose for photographs. Rafiki looked young, strong and beautiful and the white dress she wore contrasted starkly with her brown skin. The media were really only interested in her; she was gracious and charming and although she answered most of the questions directly, would not discuss her experience with the gallows. She was asked what she hoped for Kenya and answered, "I hope that we can control our own destiny in Kenya like you do here in your own country, and that we Africans are no longer treated like slaves or second class citizens in our country but have full political rights."

She didn't want to draw attention to Kamau, so she didn't mention the education system, and she didn't want to upstage the rest of the Kenya delegation, which was due to arrive in London shortly. She, after all, would only play a minor role in the discussions. In the end the media treated her kindly and published articles querying the justice of a system which nearly sent such a person to the gallows, when it was obvious that she posed no threat to society but would be a great asset to the new Kenya.

Before the conference began, Wainaina and the children, Kamau and John, went home to Kenya.

Wainaina was looking forward to being with his wives and cattle again, eating ogalie and drinking his traditional beer. He could certainly see that the British were a large and powerful race but he thought that his country would be better off on their own, under the leadership of people who understood the country.

John and Kamau had had a great deal of fun. John had to return to school and Kamau to his lessons at Naseby with Mrs. Smith. Rafiki hoped that as a result of the conference, Kamau would be able to go to the same school as Peter's other sons.

The conference lasted much longer than anyone wanted. The British had only one objective and that was to extricate Britain from the situation with as much dignity and as little cost as possible.

On the opening day of the conference, Kenyatta laid down much the same terms as he had discussed with Peter in Lodwar:

- One person over eighteen, one vote
- Total withdrawal of British forces
- Release of all detainees
- No special privileges for any racial group
- Purchase of white owned farms for re-settlement of blacks
- Financial aid
- Membership of the Commonwealth and United Nations

The British wanted:

- Westminster style government with some constitutional guarantees ensuring a two party democracy
- Some guarantees for the white settlers
- They offered to keep some British troops there for a number of years
- Some financial aid

Nothing was said about the farmers.

On the first few days the whole group met together. Peter happened to be seated opposite the incumbent Governor, who had persistently refused to see him on any issue, not least of which was the sentence passed on Rafiki.

From time to time the Governor glanced up into Peter's cold, blue eyes. He glanced down the table at Rafiki and saw a beautiful, charming, accomplished woman. He could not believe the situation he was in. A few months before, he had been the all-powerful Governor of one of the jewels in the British Empire and now he was having to face the personal hostility of Peter Lawrence and almost daily articles in the press about the ordeal that Rafiki had gone through; the tone of the articles was that a great injustice had been done. He was confused; at the time he had thought he was doing his duty and that the objective was to maintain Kenya as a colony. He could now see that Britain wanted to unload the burden as quickly as possible. He could also see for himself Rafiki's appeal; she had completely charmed the whole British delegation. And he had to face on a daily basis those cold, hostile eyes of Lawrence. The whole process started to unnerve him.

The KANU delegation started to notice.

"Munyu, the Governor is scared of you," one said.

"He is looking sick, have you put the Munyu curse on his head?"

Peter was barely aware of the Governor's presence. Certainly he had glanced in his direction once or twice and wondered how such an innocuous looking man could have had such a devastating effect on his family.

After a week the Governor was taken ill. He did not reappear at the conference. The Kikuyu all said it was because of Munyu's curse.

The conference dragged on, partly as a result of the KADU faction thinking that KANU had been given too much.

At one point early in the conference, there was a discussion about the remaining detainees, most of whom were held at Hola camp.

"These people are common criminals," a member of the British delegation said.

"Anyway, why are you so interested?" he asked Peter pointedly.

"I know people who have been sent there," said Peter. "There is a fear that whatever they might have been convicted of, there is a good chance of their not coming out alive." He was thinking of Kinua.

The British delegation was all too aware of Peter's and Rafiki's history. They did not need any further publicity of that nature. Hola was closed and the detainees released. Some years later a report was released, indicating that an uncounted number of people incarcerated there did not survive. No one was ever prosecuted.

The other major issue as far as far as Peter was concerned was land reform. The problem was that since British occupation, as a result of Pax Britannica enforced on the warring factions, there had been an enormous population explosion among the Kikuyu and other tribes. Much of the land that the whites occupied was entirely suitable for occupation by African peasant farmers. The British for their own reasons had encouraged settlement over the years; indeed even in the year the conference was held, the Settlement Board of Kenya had a stand at the Royal Agricultural Show in Cambridge advertising the fact.

Peter made it clear that he owned a farm in the area concerned but that he had been charged by the delegation to deal with the issue and intended to do so.

"Could you please instruct the Settlement Board to stop advertising here," he started off.

"How do you know they are still advertising?" one of the British team asked belligerently.

"A distant cousin of mine phoned me last week; he was all for selling up here in Britain and moving to Kenya," replied Peter. "It took all my powers of persuasion to convince him that as far as settlement was concerned, the game was over," he continued.

Most of the delegates were speechless. They couldn't believe this sort of muddle existed.

"We'll look into the matter and have it stopped," was the final answer.

Peter's position on behalf of the settlers was quite simple: the farmers would stay unless they were bought out on reasonable terms, which would enable them to move to another country and start again. There was only one party that could provide the funds for a buyout: The British Government.

The British delegation eventually agreed to provide a significant sum of money for the buyout, provided their agents controlled the valuations and the money. This was agreed by all parties concerned.

The KANU and KADU delegations went home to arrange and fight the first democratic election in Kenya.

Peter had to find a constituency; Kenyatta had asked him to be Minister of Agriculture in the first independent Kenya Government on the assumption that KANU won the election, which he was confident it would.

Peter and Rafiki went home to Naseby, knowing that their time was limited there and that they would have to start afresh on another of life's adventures.

Chapter 29

Naseby had never been more productive. There had been some recovery in the economy resulting from the euphoria created by Jomo Kenyatta's release and the final constitutional settlement. Produce prices had risen and Naseby was sending more milk, wool, and lambs to market and selling more quality livestock than ever.

The valuers representing the British Government had inspected and made offers on all the white owned farms from the Kinangop right through to Thomsons Falls. The valuations were not generous and the pay-outs were all less than the valuations, on the grounds, in many cases including Naseby, that the farm was 'overdeveloped'. Theoretically at least, any farmer could refuse the offer and continue as he was. Virtually all the farmers, to whom an offer was made, accepted, including Peter.

The offer was for the land only; Peter had managed to sell his now very high quality herd of Ayrshire cattle at an auction on the farm a few days earlier. His reputation was such that the sale attracted wide attention, despite at least a hundred other similar sales, so he managed reasonable prices. He sold all the other livestock to whoever would take them. The pigs went to Uplands bacon factory; the sheep were given a final shearing and then sold to various butcheries in the district. All the remaining crops had been taken in. During the previous week he had had an auction of his farm machinery and equipment, which realised very little since all the others farmers in the district were doing the same thing. He paid off all the farm workers and gave them generous bonuses, dependant on length of service. The farm was to be resettled by Kikuyu, so all his Wakamba and Luo people who had replaced the Kikuyu would have to go back home.

The farm was to be divided up into fifty acre plots, one per family.

According to his calculations it would accommodate thirty families. He had employed thirty-five families. It also seemed clear to Peter that the people settling the farm would need training in farming methods if they were to produce even a fraction of what he had been producing. He understood the political need for the purchase of the farms but he wondered if there was a better way of resettling the Kikuyu than converting these highly productive farms to subsistence agriculture.

The day before they left he got up early and rode round the whole farm. It was as empty as the day seventeen years earlier when he had taken it over, but what a difference he had made in those seventeen years. The place was completely fenced; there were contours to prevent washaways; mature pastures continued to grow. He had drilled boreholes for water and piped that water all over the farm. His dream had been fulfilled almost completely; he had converted this piece of African bush into a beautiful farm, much of it with his own hands, most of it with his own drive and ability. Was it all for nothing? Tomorrow his dream would be gone; it would be nothing more than the dream it always was.

Peter was almost at the same place as he had stood seventeen years earlier when he first saw the farm. The view of the Aberdares and Mount Kenya was unchanged; it was just as enchanting as it had ever been. He wiped a tear away. He would probably never enjoy this view again; there would be no real need for him to come back here. He continued his ride. He remembered the idiosyncrasies of every field; he had helped to plant every fence post on the whole farm. He took it all in - every tree, every bush. He wondered what would become of it all, but in his heart of hearts he knew that none of what he had created would survive; in another seventeen years it would be back to what it was when he bought it, and seventeen years after that, "Who knows?" he thought, "But whatever happens, you can't turn the clock back. This place has given me seventeen years of the most exciting and tumultuous time I could have imagined; I should be grateful for that."

The next day Peter, Rafiki and Kamau went into the village of Ol'Kalou to say some final farewells; John was at school. Many farmers in the district were grateful to him for his part in the settlement. What they had retrieved from the buyout of their farms was the dignity of being able to pay off their loans and having some money to start again somewhere else. Others blamed him for what they considered to be a fiasco at the constitutional conference, where the whites had lost everything. They felt that in his role there he had 'sold out' the white farmers. Peter felt that, besides some compensation, at least finality had been achieved, and they would not have to go on for years wondering what was to happen next.

He went to see Mr. Shah and shook him warmly by the hand to bid him farewell.

"Will you be staying on then?" asked Peter.

"For a while, yes, then we will be going home," was the response.

"Home, where, Ahmadabad?" asked Peter. He was aware that they were Gujaratis.

Shah frowned. "No, no, no," he said. "We will go to Bristol; we already have a small shop there."

"Bristol, in the west of England?" asked Peter.

"The very same."

Peter looked at him admiringly. These people had had it all worked out years before and had taken action to preserve their families. They kept out of trouble, serviced the community admirably and when it was all over went on their way.

They shook hands again.

"I'll look you up if I'm ever in Bristol," he said.

Peter then went to the little churchyard alone. Rafiki and Kamau had a few chores still to complete in the village.

He went to Jenny's grave and for one final time tidied it up. He pulled the few weeds that had grown since his last visit. He read the stone:

JENNY LAWRENCE

1921 – 1950

BELOVED OF

PETER

ROBERT

JOHN

Very simple but it spoke volumes to him. He looked around. There were five other headstones in the churchyard; he had known all the people and had been to all the funerals.

He thought, "Did we really belong here? Our time here was so short. In one hundred years' time, will anyone even remember the white aliens who settled here for those few short years and then disappeared?"

He was woken out of his reverie by Rafiki's warm hand being slipped into his. She smiled at him.

"Do you miss her?" she asked.

He thought, and then said, "We had such a simple dream, Jenny and I. We came here to build something for ourselves. If she had lived we would have somehow come to this point of time and maybe our only option would have been to return from where we came. She died and the despair that I was left with has been transformed into a richness that I can't describe. I now know that despite the colour of my skin I am of Africa; I have a black wife and a brown son; I am truly blessed."

She hugged him tightly.

He went on, "When I rode round Naseby yesterday, I knew that all the work, all the effort of my seventeen years there would come to naught. Maybe that is the only salvation that Africa has, to destroy or at least neglect what the unwanted colonials brought and to build it up in our own way."

She looked at him and said nothing. He took one last look at the now tidied grave site. They both said a prayer and went on their way.

"If she is watching you, she would understand and be proud of you," said Rafiki.

"I hope so."

They got into the pick-up. Peter had to do a few chores to do in Nakuru before they drove on to Nairobi and their new home in the suburb of Karen.

For the last time they drove back up the dusty road to the farm, past the stone water tank, over the little bridge, past the entrance to Naseby. The place was somehow different; it was no longer his, it was just another farm. That part of his life was past, but he had much to look forward to.

※ ※ ※

Chapter 30

Kahinga Kinyore was angry and bewildered. He was living in his father's village; the same village he had left seventeen years earlier to join the Mau-Mau and then to go to work for Peter Lawrence.

As was the case seventeen years before, all he owned was the clothes he stood up in: KAR hat, army greatcoat, shirt, trousers, and car tyre sandals on his feet. He did have his wife, Wanjiru and two fine sons, but he had no cattle, no money, and no possessions.

He felt he had been by-passed deliberately by the leadership in KANU. Certainly they had included him in the political process that followed Kenyatta's release from prison, but he did not attend the London conference and had been sidelined ever since.

"Maybe it's because I cannot read and write," he reasoned. Then he became angry. "I spent years in the forest risking my life every day, while those who are now in power drank brandy and played cards in Lodwar - and now they ignore me."

His companion and fellow warrior Kinua was in much the same position, if not worse. Kinua had been released from Hola camp at death's door. He had suffered endless beatings and a poor diet and received virtually no medical attention during the years he had been in prison. He was now gradually returning to health under the care of his wife Sarah; it would still be months before he was fully fit.

Kinua's father-in-law, Zacharia, had refused to have anything to do with him, so he and Sarah were staying in Kinyore's village.

Kahinga called Wanjiru.

"Tell Kinua to come and enjoy some of your beer tonight," he said. He could easily have run the errand himself, since the hut that Kinua and Sarah occupied was only fifty or sixty yards away. He liked to keep Wanjiru under his thumb though. She dutifully did his bidding.

Kinua limped over at the appointed hour.

"You seem to be much better today," offered Kahinga.

Kinua nodded.

He too was angry. Like Kahinga, he had risked his life, only to be ignored.

"The leadership of KANU have had their use of us; now we are left like the testicles of a castrated calf to be eaten by the jackals and the ants," said Kinua.

Kahinga nodded. "What shall we do?" he asked.

"Steal some guns and go back to the bush until they listen to us," replied Kinua. "The British will go soon; we could easily beat the other Kikuyu fighters."

Kahinga shuddered. The thought of returning to the hell of that life had no appeal.

"Munyu has now been elected to the Government; he will be Minister of Agriculture," Kahinga probed.

He saw Kinua's eyes light up.

"Maybe we should go and see him," suggested Kahinga.

Three days later, Peter and Rafiki were enjoying a cup of tea on the veranda of their new home in Karen, Nairobi.

The servant approached.

"Two men have come; they say they want to see you," the servant said to Peter.

"What do you think they want?"

The servant shrugged. "They say they know you," was the response.

Peter went out and found Kahinga and Kinua sitting on their haunches under a tree. Peter had seen Kahinga at the wedding but he barely recognised Kinua.

He greeted them enthusiastically and invited them to have tea. The conversation went round and round: the weather; crops; the health of the family.

Peter knew that they hadn't come for nothing; they would tell him their woes in good time.

Kahinga eventually said, "You are now minister in the Government?"

Peter nodded.

"We," he indicated Kinua and himself. "We spent all that time in the forest and now we have nothing."

Peter nodded.

"Those baboons in Government spent ten years in Lodwar drinking brandy and playing cards; they now have everything," Kahinga went on.

Peter looked at him.

"We need your help; we can't read so we must learn, but we also need a job," said Kahinga.

Peter had started to understand their predicament almost as soon as he had set eyes on them. Despite the Mau-Mau years, they were almost like extended family to him.

The next week the Minister of Agriculture had two new drivers and Peter had found a tutor to teach them how to read and write. Kahinga and Kinua and their families moved into two spare huts on Peter's property in Karen.

Kahinga became Peter's personal driver. They both knew that a man of Kahinga's leadership qualities was capable of better, but it was a start.

There were many issues to be dealt with from both Peter's viewpoint and Kahinga's.

Peter still had no idea why he had been suddenly left in the lurch on Naseby, and the abduction of Rafiki had caused him much anguish. He wondered about Kahinga's role in the forest gangs and whether he had had anything to do with any of the grisly murders which had taken place, particularly that of Halway.

Kahinga wondered about Peter's role in the conflict; he knew of Waichagga's attack on Naseby and he thought that Peter had been a member of the police reserve.

They had much to talk about and much to work out in the ensuing months.

※ ※ ※

Lightning Source UK Ltd.
Milton Keynes UK
UKHW020640291021
393035UK00010B/715